## Also by Susan Choi

*Trust Exercise*

*My Education*

*A Person of Interest*

*American Woman*

*The Foreign Student*

# Flashlight

# Flashlight

a novel

## SUSAN CHOI

FARRAR, STRAUS AND GIROUX
NEW YORK

Farrar, Straus and Giroux
120 Broadway, New York 10271

EU Representative: Macmillan Publishers Ireland Ltd,
1st Floor, The Liffey Trust Centre, 117–126 Sheriff Street Upper,
Dublin 1, DO1 YC43

Library of Congress Cataloging-in-Publication Data
Names: Choi, Susan, 1969– author.
Title: Flashlight : a novel / Susan Choi.
Description: First edition. | New York : Farrar, Straus and Giroux, 2025.
Identifiers: LCCN 2024053346 | ISBN 9780374616373 (hardcover)
Subjects: LCGFT: Novels.
Classification: LCC PS3553.H584 F54 2025 | DDC 813/.54—dc23/
    eng/20241118
LC record available at https://lccn.loc.gov/2024053346

*Designed by Gretchen Achilles*

Our books may be purchased in bulk for promotional,
educational, or business use. Please contact your local bookseller or
the Macmillan Corporate and Premium Sales Department at 1-800-221-7945,
extension 5442, or by email at MacmillanSpecialMarkets@macmillan.com.

www.fsgbooks.com
Follow us on social media at @fsgbooks

1  3  5  7  9  10  8  6  4  2

*For Dexter and Elliot*

# Flashlight

**Louisa and her father** *are making their way down the breakwater, each careful step on the heaved granite blocks one step farther from shore. Her mother is not even on the shore, for example seated smiling on the sand. Her mother is shut inside the small almost-waterfront house they are renting, most likely in bed. All summer Louisa has played in the waves by herself because her mother isn't well and her father is unvaryingly dressed in a jacket and slacks. But tonight he has finally agreed to walk the breakwater with her. She has asked every day since they first arrived. Spray from the waves sometimes lands on the rocks and so he has carefully rolled up the cuffs of his slacks. He still wears his hard polished shoes. In one hand he holds a flashlight which is not necessary, in the other hand he holds Louisa's hand which is also not necessary. She tolerates this out of kindness.*

*"One thing I will always owe your mother is she taught you to swim. Because swimming is important to know how to do, for your safety. But when she gave you lessons, I thought it was too dangerous. I was very unfair."*

*"I hate swimming."*

*They both know the opposite is true. Perhaps her father recognizes her comment for what it partly is, a declaration of loyalty to him, as well as for what it mostly is, a declaration by a ten-year-old child who is contentious by reflex. Far over the water, far beyond where the breakwater joins with a thin spit of sand, the sunset has lost all its warmth and is only a paleness against the horizon. They'll turn back soon.*

*"I never learned to swim," her father reveals.*

*"I don't believe you," she scoffs. Everybody can swim.* Though it's true he always makes a big deal when she wants to get in or even get near the water.

*"It's true. I grew up a poor boy. I had no YMCA."*

*"The YMCA is disgusting. I hate going there."*

*"Someday, you'll feel thankful to your mother. But I want you to act thankful now."*

These are the last words he ever says to her.

(Or are they the last words that she can remember? Did he say something more? There is no one to ask.)

\* \* \*

Louisa lay awake staring into the dark. The ceiling showed itself in a narrow stripe of light, first sharp like a blade and then more and more soft, that crossed the ceiling from the doorframe. The door was very slightly cracked open because Louisa was afraid of the dark. This didn't use to be the case. Every night with maddening slowness her mother would retreat from the room, clumsily bumping her wheels, to a point that Louisa would want to scream at her. When her mother was finally out in the hall, she hesitated, one hand on the doorknob, the door almost but not fully shut.

"Close it all the way, please," Louisa would say in a sharp, grown-up tone.

The first time she'd said this, it was because she couldn't stand another second of her mother being there, peering in through the crack. Then she said it every subsequent night the same way, having realized that it was, without being a wrong thing to say, satisfyingly hurtful. There would be another brief hesitation, which Louisa didn't mind, because it showed that her mother was indeed satisfyingly hurt. Apparently her mother would have liked for Louisa to ask for a story, or a kiss, as if Louisa were still five years old. Her mother never expressed this desire but it was nakedly clear. Such naked wanting to be wanted made Louisa's mother even more repellent. The door would click into its frame heavily; it was that kind of American door that

Louisa had almost forgotten existed in the year she had lived some-place else. A door meant for closing. Louisa would lie in the dark, her unsparing mind tracking her mother's wheelchair down the hall and imagining hidden trapdoors hinging open beneath it. Meanwhile the dark slid itself onto her chest like a snake, organizing its weight into neatly stacked coils that might go on forever and bury her, crush her, if she didn't leap out of bed just in time and, with deft skill, reopen the door. Louisa was a master at handling the knob. She wasn't clumsy, like her mother, or thoughtless, like her aunt. No sound escaped as the light was let back in, the darkness destroyed. Back to bed, to gaze up at the stripe.

Tonight sound was coming in also. She couldn't make out the words but she knew they were talking about her. This morning, in-stead of going to school on time, she'd been taken by her aunt to a building downtown to be examined by a child psychologist. No one had used these words, "child psychologist." They had called it an ap-pointment about her grade level, which at least at the start she be-lieved. She had been halfway through the fourth grade when she and her parents had left the US for Japan, and during their year in Japan she had finished the fourth grade, all the workbooks and readings and tests they had brought, and she'd finished the Japanese fourth grade as well—she had done fourth grade *twice*, in *two countries*, but was being made to do it over again, had been put back as if she had failed.

The appointment had been in a brick office building with a half flight of stairs at the entrance, and as they climbed her aunt had said, "This is why your mom couldn't come with us, because of these stairs. I called ahead to ask if there were stairs at the entrance and sure enough they told me there were. Your poor mama."

"She's not sick," Louisa said.

"What's that, honey?"

Louisa was silent.

"I didn't hear you, honey."

Now Louisa could pretend *she* hadn't heard. This was effective. No one was ever listening closely—even the people who especially claimed to be listening were not really listening.

It was this way with the man at the appointment. "My name is Dr. Brickner," he said, making a show of bending down to shake her hand. He had already made a show of leaving her aunt in the waiting room, and another show of reassuring Louisa that her aunt would be right there waiting for her, as if Louisa were in any fear her aunt might disappear. Louisa's aunt was like a bright light Louisa couldn't turn off. On the nights Louisa's mother wasn't up to it, it was her aunt who tucked Louisa into bed and then lingered too long in the doorway. Louisa's aunt broadcast her kind disposition by constantly tilting her head to one side, crinkling her eyes, and compressing her mouth, as if to savor all the good-tasting mirth trapped inside. Sometimes, performing this face for Louisa, Louisa's aunt added reminiscent comments about her two grown-up sons, and how precious it was to be reminded of them by Louisa's presence in her home. Louisa doubted her aunt felt this way. Until she and her mother had moved here, Louisa had never heard of this aunt, or this uncle—her mother's actual brother, apparently, whom Louisa was now supposed to pretend she'd known about her whole life. Her whole ten years of life when she had never heard their names, or seen their photos, or received a card or gift from them on her birthday, or answered the telephone and heard either one of them ask for her mother or father. Now she lived in their house and drank orange juice with them staring at her. They behaved toward her the way all adults did since her father had died, with a combination of hearty attention and squeamish discomfort.

"*Brick*ner, like this ugly brick building we're in," the man had gone on heartily. "That's how you can remember! But my first name is Jerry, and I'd like you to just call me that. Can I call you Louisa?"

"So I don't need to remember," she said.

"What's that?" He pointed his grin at her. "What did you say?"

"I said I don't need to remember 'Brickner,' like this ugly brick building, because you said I should just call you 'Jerry.'"

The man reared back and raised his eyebrows. "Let me guess: you're a very smart girl."

"At least enough to be in fifth grade."

"Oh, I'll *bet*. Oh, I'm sure there's no doubt about *that*," "Jerry" blathered, not listening, which was when she knew the appointment was not about grade level.

The room was full of admittedly interesting things: art supplies and those faceless wooden figures meant for posing, as well as actual dolls of different sorts, ranging from the sloppy-floppy Raggedy Ann style to the "realistic infant" style with a hard plastic head, hands, and feet and queasily soft trunk, arms, and legs meant to be hidden beneath frilly clothes; wild-haired Barbies and those soldier-Barbies for boys, the G.I. Joes. There was an off-kilter dollhouse, the kind meant to be played with and not just admired, with cluttered furnishings in slightly different sizes, as if there had been disagreement about which scale to use. Louisa knew about scale, about one foot = one inch. Her father had made her a dollhouse the year she turned eight. That had been the year of her passion for a store at the mall called It's a Small World, which sold shrunken elaborate gingerbread homes into which she would gaze, mesmerized, with the peculiar sensation of leaving her body and slipping amid those wee wonderful things, things she lacked words for and so had to learn one by one, fireplace irons and grandfather clocks and hat racks and claw-footed armoires. The young heroines of the books she most liked lived in houses like these, full of little wooden knobs and dust ruffles and embroidery, each stitch of which was as small as those tiny black seeds that are lofted by dandelion fluff. Their every visit to the mall, her mother gave her twenty minutes to browse in the store as a matter of policy, placidly ignoring her pleas that they actually buy something. Her father, by contrast, only needed to hear her plead once. Off they had stormed to the mall, her father lambasting her mother's cheapness the entire drive there. Into the store and then immediately out he had stormed, once he'd seen the first dollhouse price tag.

"I can make *that*," he'd said.

The tiny nails tacking the thin walls of hobby plywood together made the walls split and splinter, their front edges exposed and unsanded. The roof had been "shingled" with strips of a rough rubber matting found in the basement. Wallpaper scraps were cut down to size for the walls and the floor. He'd even built much of the furniture, sitting at the kitchen table night after night in his undershirt, with a glass of beer near at hand and his pipe clamped between his rear teeth, cutting and gluing strips of balsa to form the crude shape of a canopy bed.

Her father's labor awed and grieved her. Louisa had been horrified by the clumsy, indelicate house, though her horror was silent. He was toiling to make something ugly she didn't desire. Yet, over time, she'd realized that this, too, held the charm of the small. Her mother sewed tiny pillows and bedspreads and the bed canopy, showed Louisa that postage stamps could be put into brown cardboard frames to make art for the walls, that a length of embroidery yarn could be wound in a tight ball the size of a pea, and pierced through with two straight pins in an X, to look just like someone's miniature knitting.

Then she'd spent hours on the floor, gazing into her strange hand-made house. The very few items within it that were consolatory gifts her parents bought her from It's a Small World—the grand piano with its blue velvet cushion, the four spindly chairs—looked out of place. Wrong.

"Louisa?"

She was startled to find Dr. Brickner just over one shoulder. She turned away from the dollhouse, stepping neatly around him, and dropped into a chair. Moments before, the thing to do had been to shirk his eye contact and look at the things in the room that weren't him. Now he'd caught her interested in something, and the thing to do was shirk that something. They were alone together, and no one had told her how long it would last. But let it last forever: she wouldn't give him anything.

"You can play with the dollhouse," he said, and she was pleased to hear a tinge of supplication. "That's what it's there for."

"That's okay."

"Would you like to draw? I have terrific drawing stuff."

"That's okay. I don't really enjoy drawing." Right away she regretted this offering. Sure enough, he caught on. Perhaps he was actually listening.

"What kinds of things *do* you enjoy?"

Certain adults could do this, Louisa had noticed. Instead of *oooh-*

ing or saying *You sound so grown-up when you talk*, these adults deftly plucked your own words from the air and then flicked them back at you, with a straight face, as if they thought you might somehow not notice and become hypnotized. It was a game, and not a playful type of game but a competitive, scorekeeping game, the quick-witted adult snatching one bit of you after another.

"What's that flashlight for?" Louisa asked him, and his mind had to spring to "flashlight" and pretend the question was one he'd expected.

The flashlight stood on the windowsill, bulb end pointing down. The windows in the room were very large and high with very deep sills, and the deep sills were very cluttered, as every surface in the room was cluttered. There were potted plants set close together and in the bits of space between them ugly "artworks" made from balls and tubes of clay incompetently stuck together, and other knickknacky arts-and-crafts garbage Louisa supposed other children had made during appointments. The flashlight hardly stood out. Dr. Brickner had to crane his neck around in awkward almost-panic to find what she was talking about.

"It's to see in the dark!" he said clownishly.

"You have lights."

He abandoned the clowning. "It's in case of a power outage. Which doesn't happen often, but it could happen. Especially if there's an earthquake."

"Where I lived before I moved here, I felt earthquakes all the time."

"In Japan."

She was disappointed somehow that he already knew this, but of course he already knew everything. "Can we turn out the lights?"

"It won't be dark."

"You could pull the blinds down."

"It still won't be dark—it will be *dim*," Dr. Brickner predicted, but he was already doing it. The blinds were an ancient unreliable mess and they clearly were never let down—as Dr. Brickner struggled with them they fought back, their long metal strips rattling and seesawing slantwise and releasing a dust plume before they seemed to surrender

and fall all at once. The dust, dissipating, glinted erratically, as if flashing a code, where it crossed the slim rays of afternoon light streaming
in through the gap that remained where the blinds did not quite meet
the wall. Dr. Brickner, reaching over his desk toward the chair where
she sat, held the flashlight out to her. It was satisfyingly heavy. Louisa
slid the plastic switch with her thumb and a pale cloud of light appeared on the ceiling.

"Oh good," he said. "I thought the batteries might have gone dead."

"If they were, and this was an earthquake, then you'd be in trouble."

"Very true."

She played the light over the ceiling, almost forgetting about him.
The ceiling was far above her, twice as far as the extinguished overhead light—the hideous kind that looked like a huge upside-down ice
tray suspended from wires. Beyond the enormous ice tray, the faint
pool of light rippled over the ceiling and slid down the wall. It seemed
alive, a being both at her command and mysterious to her. "Doo-doo-
doo-doo-*dooooooo*," she sang out, inexplicably goofy herself. She was
singing the notes everyone nowadays recognized, the UFO's greeting
from *Close Encounters of the Third Kind*.

Dr. Brickner laughed. They gazed up at the ceiling as if something
were actually there. "Did you like that movie?" asked his voice, which
she found was more tolerable than when she had to look into his face.

"It scared me." She was surprised and annoyed by her honesty.

"Why?"

She shrugged, waving the beam over the ceiling as if in erasure.
"Just in a fun way. Like Halloween stuff."

"Is that really all you meant?"

She'd let the door open a crack, but he was too large and slow to
slip through; she had already closed it. She almost felt sorry for him.
The hidden side of her contempt for adults was pity: that they proudly
imagined they understood her and then blundered, while she had to
pretend to be caught. She sang the alien greeting again, conducting
with the flashlight to make a five-pointed star in the air.

"Did you like *Star Wars*?" Dr. Brickner wondered.

"Sure."

"So you like sci-fi."

This she couldn't allow. "*Close Encounters* isn't *sci-fi*. Everything in that movie is normal. That's what makes the aliens feel really real."

"And that's scary."

"No. Those aliens aren't scary at all. They're nice."

"Then why would their being real scare you?"

"It *doesn't*. And besides, when they land, they look fake."

"But you just said they felt really real." He was onto something, his triumphant tone told her, as if he won a point for every little crack where her words didn't fit themselves smoothly together. She swung the light into his face and he squinted but didn't scold her, so she swung it away again as a reward.

"I didn't. They don't."

"But the signs that they're coming—the weird radio sounds, the lights in the sky, the dad who builds the tower out of mud and his family thinks he's gone crazy—maybe *that* felt really real?"

She said nothing.

"Normal life turning strange—did *that* feel really real? Are there things in your own life that feel that way?"

The flashlight dropped out of her hand, its butt end striking down on the cold tile floor with a noise like a gunshot. It clattered onto its side, rolled a few inches, stopped. Louisa wiped her palm hard on the front of her jeans. After they'd arrived in Los Angeles, her aunt had taken her shopping. All her life she'd worn skirts, kilts, jumpers, pinafore dresses, sandals, oxfords. When she looked at her body in blue jeans and red sneakers, it didn't feel or look like her body, which she had never before thought of as feeling or looking like hers, which she had never before had to think of at all. She stretched her arm toward the flashlight without otherwise moving. Its light had been trapped, like the sun through the blinds, and spread over the floor in a wedge.

"When I was getting ready to meet you, I talked on the phone to your mother," Dr. Brickner resumed. "We talked a long time. I had lots of questions about you. She wanted to help me as much as she could." Louisa's arm dangled over the hard wooden arm of the chair,

fingers slack, nowhere close to the bleeding flashlight she was no longer attempting to reach. Its light spilled and spilled from its little round
porthole. "She told me that when you were found on the beach in
Japan, where your father had drowned, you told people your father
was kidnapped."

"No I didn't," Louisa said quickly, without looking up. She stared
at the wasted light painting the cold tile floor. Whenever the next
earthquake came, the batteries in this flashlight would surely be dead.
Maybe, because of not having a working flashlight, Dr. Brickner
would also be dead. Louisa might take the blame for this, for wasting
the batteries now. She wondered how much of the fault for his death
would be hers.

"Your mother wasn't there when they found you, but the person
who found you reported that you said this."

"I never said that," Louisa said again. "I don't know what she's
talking about."

"Louisa," Dr. Brickner said, coming around his desk toward her
and propping his rear on the edge, so that his suit jacket, which was
already rumpled, bagged out at his shoulders and looked even worse,
"do you know what 'shock' is?"

"If you rub a balloon on a wall and you touch someone else you
can give them a shock," she recited. Perhaps she had read this in *High-
lights* or *Cricket*. She couldn't remember.

"True, that's electrical shock. But that's not the shock that I'm
talking about, though the feeling can be similar. Like a sudden, sharp,
frightening feeling. Does that make sense to you?"

"An electrical shock isn't frightening," she countered blandly, fixing
her eyes on his tie pin. It looked like a paper clip holding his tie to his
shirt.

"Maybe I'm not explaining well. Sometimes I'm better at listening
than talking. Maybe you talk some more and I'll listen."

"That's what you've been trying to do since I got here."

"And this room is full of tricks to get children to talk, but you're
too smart for them."

"I'm too smart for compliments. I don't like them."

"I've noticed that children who deserve them don't like them."

"I don't deserve them."

"Don't you? I said you were smart, and you agreed with me. You said you were too smart for compliments."

"Being smart shouldn't get compliments. Being smart isn't something I did. It's just something I am. And I don't like it," she added after a moment.

"Why not?"

"Other kids are obnoxious to me. I don't have any friends."

"Your mother told me you've always had friends. In Michigan you had friends. In Japan you had friends. It's only since you've moved here that you haven't had friends."

"I don't want friends."

"Why not?"

"I don't like people asking me questions."

"Like me?"

She shrugged. "No offense."

"It's my job to ask you questions." He pushed off the edge of his desk and went behind it again. "Hand me my flashlight, please."

She obeyed him before it occurred to her that she might not. Too late, though he didn't seem to have marked it as a point in his favor. He was simply shining the flashlight down onto his desk, where white, yellow, and pink sheets of paper appeared in its pool of light. "You see, one of my bosses is called the Los Angeles Consolidated School District, and when they send me a pink sheet of paper with a child's name on it, that means I have to ask that child questions or they won't send my paycheck. You might think our meeting has to do with you, but it really has to do with Mrs. Brickner, my wife, and Kelly Brickner, my son, who's a sophomore at USC, and Cheryl Brickner, my daughter, who's a junior at Westinghouse High School. It's really because of them that I'm asking you questions—and because of the Los Angeles Consolidated School District. And the reasons *they* want me to ask you the questions—well, let's see what they wrote on your form. 'Defiance, disruptive behavior, deception, peer-to-peer conflict, tardiness, truancy, larceny—'"

"What's that?" she interrupted.

"Which?"

"The last one. Larson-something."

"Larceny. A fancy word for stealing."

"I've never heard that."

"Do you mean you didn't know that you're accused of stealing?"

"No, I've never heard that word. Larson—"

"L-A-R-C-E-N-Y. We've found the limits of your vocabulary. Would you like to talk about larceny? You don't look very sorry about it."

"I'm not."

"I'm sure your parents taught you not to steal."

But this was just the point. Stealing was a thing you were *told* not to do, you were *told* was wrong, but why was it? Why did calling it wrong make it wrong? What bad result came when you stole, apart from people just making a fuss? Sitting in the supposedly nice restaurant her aunt and uncle had taken her to while her mother was getting more hospital tests, she'd put the saltshaker from the table in her pocket and taken it home. What bad thing had happened? Only that the saltshaker had moved from the center of the soiled tablecloth at the supposedly nice restaurant to a box in her closet. Sitting in the office of the school principal, Mr. Wamsley, she'd stolen a pen set off his desk. It had consisted of a pen made to look like a twig, a sort of trough for the pen to lie in made to look like a hollowed-out log, and a small cup for thumbtacks or paper clips concealed in what was intended to look like the miniature stump of a tree. It was the sort of thing Louisa might have begged her mother to buy her father for his desk as a Father's Day gift when Louisa was seven or eight, before she realized, as she now realized about so many things, that it was not charming and pretty but ugly and cheap. While Mr. Wamsley consulted with her teacher just outside the door, Louisa removed her windbreaker and rolled all three of the desk items into it and sat with the roll on her lap the whole time Mr. Wamsley was lecturing her, and then walked out with the roll in her hands. In what way had Mr. Wamsley then suffered, for no longer having those things on his desk? A stupid girl named Dawn Delavan brought little plastic blue elf figurines, each with a different absurd attribute like a wizard's hat, a paintbrush, or a harp to the classroom, and though these disappeared one at a time, Dawn Delavan never learned to stop bringing them, she just fussed and cried to their teacher, Miss Prince, while Miss Prince trained her cold steady gaze on Louisa.

"You don't think that stealing is wrong?" Dr. Brickner said now.

"I know that it's *wrong*. I don't see why. I don't see what difference it makes."

"Kidnapping is stealing, isn't it?"

He lowered the flashlight onto the surface of his desk so that its light shrank beneath it and vanished along with all the white, yellow, and pink sheets of paper describing Louisa's problems and her crimes. Then with a click he turned the flashlight off. Twilight settled around them, taking on the dim shapes of the room. Dr. Brickner set to work raising the blinds, which required much more effort and time than the lowering had. He had to haul on the dangling cords hand over hand as if they were a part of something really serious, like a boat or flagpole. The blinds screamed in protest as they rose, but finally sunlight broke into the room. It was orange, like the light from a fire. Ever since they had arrived in California, Louisa had noticed the light. Even Dr. Brickner, who presumably wasn't new here, seemed surprised by the light and gazed out the window for a moment before sitting back down in his desk chair to face her.

"When you told people your father was kidnapped, I think you meant he'd been taken away from you. Stolen. Death steals the people we love."

"But I never said he was kidnapped," Louisa repeated. "My mother made that up. She makes everything up."

Dr. Brickner answered with a contemplative expression. *I believe you*, he seemed to want his expression to say. Louisa gazed back at him unflinchingly, first clothing him with pity, then contempt, and then pity again, trying to decide which was best, as if he were a paper doll. There was nothing on his desk anymore to obstruct their calm view of each other, and Louisa wondered if he would notice, and thought that if he did, she would find a new outfit for him. She wasn't sure if she wanted to have to do this. She wasn't sure if her suspense, as she

waited, was eager or fearful. These two possibilities would seem to
have opposite meanings but they felt the same way. Now Dr. Brickner
took a pen from his jacket breast pocket and dropped his gaze from
her face to a notepad. As he filled the pad with illegible writing his face
was serene. He seemed to have found what he needed. "Why don't
you play with the toys while I finish my notes," he suggested as he
wrote, but of course she did not move. He didn't repeat the suggestion. When he was finished writing, he came around the desk again
and said something about what a pleasure it had been meeting her.
He put out his hand and she shook it without standing up. If he found
this rude he didn't let on. Then she followed him to his office door
with her arms crossed at her back, and after more pleasantries with
her aunt he disappeared behind his door again and Louisa's aunt drove
them home in the car.

She dug the flashlight out from where she'd concealed it in the
crack between mattress and headboard. Aimed at the ceiling, it made
a frail jellyfish of light, pierced by the stripe from the door. Walking the beach at sunset, her father always brought their flashlight, its
weight and shape awkwardly housed in his slacks pocket. If she let
go of his hand and ran ahead a bit before turning back, she'd see the
flashlight tugging his waist on one side. He'd been particularly cautious, her father. At restaurants he would poke through her food with
a fork before letting her eat it. In crosswalks and even on sidewalks
he was afraid she'd be hit by a car, and although she had turned ten
years old still held her tightly by the hand any time they walked out
in public. He feared the ancient wildness of domesticated animals
and would not let Louisa have a pet. And he must have feared darkness, always bringing that flashlight despite how long the sunset lived
in the sky, despite how easy it was to see their way down the beach
even on nights when they looked at the stars. Except for that very last
night, when they finally walked on the breakwater, and went so far
it was totally dark before they got back to shore. They'd needed the
flashlight to be sure of their footing on the slippery rocks, her father's
grip almost crushing her fingers. When the flashlight fell, it landed
almost noiselessly in sand.

This fact—that the flashlight, in falling, landed almost noiselessly in sand—rippled over her like the pale cloud of light on the ceiling. It was not a memory, as Louisa understood memory: a fragmented, juddering filmstrip of image and sound. This wasn't something but nothing, an absence where a presence was expected. There had been no clattering onto the rocks. There had been no splash in the water. The flashlight had landed almost noiselessly in sand.

Her father, it was understood, had slipped and fallen off the breakwater, and drowned. Louisa had been found unconscious on the shore. Her father, his body, had not been found at all. Currents explained Louisa's father's body's disappearance. Shock explained Louisa's ending up, without remembering how, on the sand. All of it was sad. None of it was surprising. The flashlight had landed almost noiselessly in sand but Louisa must have dropped it there herself, she must have obtained the flashlight from her slipping, falling, drowning father, walked the rest of the causeway of slippery rocks to the shore, and dropped the flashlight almost noiselessly herself.

What had happened to that flashlight? She had only remembered it now, holding this flashlight, gripping its warm metallic heft, and aiming its porthole of faltering light. She loved this flashlight, and not just because she had stolen it from Dr. Brickner. It was a faithful object. It had been lost, without purpose, before she had snatched it away. She would have to get fresh batteries for it; she would steal them from the rack at the checkout the next time she went with her aunt to the store.

Her door swung open and the spill of light from the hallway washed over the ceiling and drowned her jellyfish. "Louisa?" came her mother's cracked voice. The whole chair bumbled through the doorframe, banging and scraping in haste, and then her mother was on her, having somehow launched herself across the space between wheelchair and bed. Just as Louisa had told Dr. Brickner: Her mother didn't need that chair. She was faking.

"Oh, Louisa, Louisa, oh, sweetie," her mother was keening, drowning Louisa in touch as Louisa thrashed her away. Her aunt was also busying into the scrum.

"What a sound, like she's being murdered!" her aunt cried. "It's making my hair stand on end!"

Why wouldn't they leave her alone? She kicked with everything she had and the flashlight fell out of her covers and crashed to the floor. It made such a bang that her mother and aunt gasped and froze. Then her aunt saw the cause of the noise and picked it up from the floor.

"When the doctor called this evening and told me you'd taken his flashlight, I gave him a piece of my mind. You've made a liar out of me!" her aunt said.

Then they did leave her alone, though she didn't see which of them yanked the door shut, plunging her in darkness.

# Part I

# Seok

**At last he goes** to school.

He's been waiting. He can't remember a time he wasn't waiting, the same way he can't remember a time he couldn't read. The ones that make simple sounds and the ones that are entire pictures, ideas. The first time he ever saw a book was when he entered the schoolroom, a place he views as *his* but heretofore unreasonably withheld from him. The orderliness, the discipline, the ever-changing chalked strings of words instead of just the same street signs that never say anything new. The glorious singing and shouting, the fierce battling in the dusty school-yard against dummies of scrap wood or sacking and husks, the inordinate amount of time spent tending vegetables in the garden, learning to use different tools including the almost-as-tall-as-you shovel, helping out the old men at the docks to coil their ropes by running the rope dizzyingly in a tiny circle because your arms are too short to do it any other way, in other words every kind of activity besides school-work (but there is a bit of this, too, and that feels like a lot, to one who's never held a pencil or brush or a bottle of ink of his own). He loves all of it; he assumes his ordained place. In the pecking orders, those of the other children no less than those their woman teacher recognizes (no men in classrooms anymore, a disappointment he soon forgets), he's at the top.

All of this he associates with his new name, another transformative improvement. He loves the way it sounds in the mouths of his new friends, his school friends, only some of whom are friends from before, from the dirty passageway ever narrowed by handcarts and scrap heaps and laundry cascading from every possible anchorage that he will not understand for some years is not even a street, just as he will not understand for some years that the crooked concavity decorated by his own family's laundry is not even a house so much as a clever improvisation of his father's. Everything within the concavity is an improvisation of his mother's, including the stiff, colorless cloth of his trousers; they're too poor even for dye. But with school this had to change, as did so many other things; he does not know or think to wonder what his mother did to get the dyed cloth for his school pants. The things he does see her do, her eternal kneeling to a little handful of vegetables or a little water in a pot or a lapful of fabric, are so permanent a part of his experience he does not recognize his mother as productive, he does not recognize that everything that comes in contact with his body, or that makes its way inside, has been somehow created from just short of nothing by her.

His friends from before also have new names and he does not think to wonder if they wonder about them, because he does not wonder about his own new name, only appreciates how well it fits him, especially when hallooed after him with admiration and ill-disguised longing by the other children, all of whom want him for coconspirator: *Hiroshiiiiiiiii*, they holler as he knifes past. The name his mother and father still call him does not unfurl this way, it is unexpandable, truncated, blunt, and though it was once so intimate to him he did not notice it or anything about it—it was included in his body, part of the way things always were—that name has been lopped off and seems like an always-lopped thing, this muffled stub of a sound like someone gulping down a sob or indigestion.

*"Hiroshiiiii!"* comes the holler and he never turns, never seems to slow down, but imperceptibly he allows a creaking handcart to interfere with his path, he rotates like a top to eye the meager market stands, he knocks away a small rock that has bedded itself in his foot sole. By these slight concessions which his peers never grasp he makes

it possible for himself to be reached. Other children strike him as a little slow, unaware of his ways of accommodating them. His ability to hide this difference between himself and other children is pure instinct. As his self-consciousness develops this knack will recede, but for now he can still camouflage and his nascent distinction takes only desirable forms: he's the number-one boy, his qualities bedazzle generally and especially the old and slow-moving who never suspect that this boy is the thief who accounts for the shortfall at the end of an already bad market day.

The other boys catch up and off they go on their rounds, roughhousing between the vendors, who sit like solemn stones beside their little piles of mountain ferns or frail carrots drawn slightly too soon from the dirt because the leisure to wait for a vegetable doesn't exist anymore. Despite the decline of rations, these boys are still round-cheeked from their parents' sacrifices, some of them even show dimples. Their reckless play cracks smiles across a few vendors' faces; a few sets of hunched shoulders hitch with amusement. "Be careful, you boys," a few warn, as sure enough the puppylike tangle of limbs sends a couple of boys sprawling and wailing. Now the old vendors rouse themselves from their spots, circle the fallen to check for split skin or snapped bones, nod with eventual satisfaction as the hurt boys, tear- and dust- and snot-streaked, slowly regain their footing and reassemble their pride. "Go on now, you're all right," the old people confirm before resuming their vigilance over heaps of foodstuffs that are not quite perceptibly smaller. The uninjured boys have long since melted away down the cluttered streetscape.

Around a corner the boys, those who did the pushing and those who were pushed, divide the spoils with practiced efficiency. Hiroshi by unspoken agreement adjudicates. When he later deposits the edible contents of his pockets in front of his mother, she regards them without comment. They are the only fresh vegetables she'll cook with all week. His father, who comes home every day in clothing so stiffened with dirt that his mother uses the hand broom to beat him all over like a rug before he undresses and joins them inside, is unaware of this system by which the evening soup bowl is enhanced. Hiroshi has a little sister, Soonja, just learning to walk, and a little brother, Seung, who doesn't yet crawl. Obviously neither of them has a school name yet.

These silent transactions between himself and his mother are perhaps a reason his mother is restrained when he brings home the school note that he and his classmates have spent the morning transcribing. His note is particularly excellent, his teacher had praised it, gazing on him as she often does with a mixture of frank affection and distracted contemplation. The note is part of the continuous, exciting life of school that in just a few short months has displaced the world of home—school is where he lives, home is where he briefly eats and sleeps, his school friends and his teachers are his people, his parents and toddler sister and squalling blanket-bundle brother often seem to him like strangers, so total is their separation from, their ignorance of, the world in which he vibrantly exists. At school, a sense of purpose and progress infuses every moment. That same week they had harvested the peas from their garden—Sensei with her pale slender fingers had shown them how to press down on the seams of the pods so the seam zippered open, disclosing the fat peas so snug in their line. She had shown them how to gently spring them free, and then each pod's peas were spilled on a cloth around which they knelt, struggling to free yet control their bouncing, exuberant peas. When all the peas had been spilled on the cloth like green stars, their sensei showed them how to group the peas in tens, then how to count the groups of ten, then how to know, from the number of themselves and the number of peas, how many peas each of them should receive in their palm. Then they had each taken up their allotment of peas and—been allowed to eat them! And the peas had been sharp with the brightness of life, Hiroshi had thoroughly chewed up and spread out the taste of each pea on his tongue, and no food had ever been so delicious. They made their eating of their handfuls of peas—he could have tossed his down all at once, they all could have, they were all always hungry, yet they weren't even tempted to do this—take as long as it possibly could, which was helped by all the laughing and talking they did. They had grown these peas entirely themselves; it was the first thing they had ever done together as a class, remember? Remember sprouting the dried peas so that each grew a tail? Remember carefully bedding each sprout in the ground? Remember giving the frilly pea plants bamboo poles to climb so that each plant could reach for the sun? These were the same bamboo poles they had used in their bayonet training, when they stood in the dust of the schoolyard in only their shorts, and, gripping their poles very tight with two hands, stabbed, and stabbed again at the battered dummies they'd inherited from the upper-grades students, who had made them of gunnysacks stuffed with husks, while their teacher shouted through her cupped hands, "You must be fast but also take aim! Do not stab your classmates! Do not stab your foot!" Now that the peas had been harvested, they would reclaim the poles and have bayonet practice again.

"So, read it," his mother finally said of the note he held open before her. She made no comment at all about the beauty of his characters or the near-total absence of ink spots, and he felt sharpen into a point the sadness and disappointment that always stole into him once he was home, as if he'd stabbed the bamboo pole into himself. But once he was reading the note, the excitement of its contents renewed in his mind and the pain in his gut was forgotten.

The children continued to glorify their Emperor and their nation, explained the note, by glorifying their classroom, the shared site of their learning, which efforts made the room ever more safe, comfortable, and instructive to themselves and anyone who might visit. The children had accomplished great things on their own!—among other decorative activities, painting banners bearing patriotic slogans as well as images of uniforms and armaments—but some help was needed from the mothers. Each child would be making a padded cushion for his or her desk chair, each cushion to consist of two quilted layers. The two layers would be joined on two sides that met at a corner, and left open at the other two sides. This way, the comfortable seat cushion also doubled as a head cover—Sensei had made hers already, and had shown her students how it opened to fit on her head like a hood. In the beam of his mother's expressionless stare Hiroshi mimed the same actions: snatching up the invisible cushion, pulling apart the two sides and ducking his head in, then hunkering swiftly for safety, the hood anchored by his palms flattened over his ears. Hiroshi ran swiftly in place, there being no space in their home for him to actually run.

"Why?" his mother finally said. "Why wear the cushion on your head?"

Already he had the sense, though he could not have named it, that the glory and the urgency of war were somehow absent from his home. That the manner in which things mattered everywhere else— even that they mattered at all—left off at their threshold. He only vaguely knew—because its ingloriousness did not hold his interest— that his father variously dug holes and trenches, moved rocks and dirt, and otherwise contributed his steadily diminishing force to the inexhaustible demands of new roads. This, in ways both direct and indirect, also was part of the glory and the urgency of war. But even if he had connected his father's lengthy absences and brief, hollow-eyed presences with the war, he would not have further connected the war with that sifting of dirt from which his father stepped, leaving footprints behind, when his mother and the hand broom were done. The war stayed outside. The war failed to include his home, or his home failed to be worthy of the war. But this was what school was for.

As this complex understanding moved through him, his exasperation with his mother gave way to an entirely different feeling of kindliness for her. For the first time he felt consciously how helpless she was without him.

"For the bombing raids," he patiently explained. And then he left her for his after-school life of the streets, at the same time giving no thought to the impossible injunction he had placed on her. Somehow, the squares of quilting appeared on the morning he needed to bring them to school. He was six years old in the spring of 1945. Though worldly for a child of his age, there still were things he didn't know.

He'd had less practice with a needle than with a brush, and the stitches assembling his cushion were correspondingly rudimentary. His effort, however, was as exceptional as always, and Sensei had praised his cushion and shown it around to his classmates: see how she could yank the two sides open, see how she could pull the cover tight around her head, and Hiroshi's stitches held strong without threatening to tear. He would have the use of this cushion/head cover for a good long time, Sensei told them all, inviting his appropriate pride, and indeed his cushion long outlasted the war. It long outlasted his adored, gentle sensei, who after the war's end got married and left the classroom, to be replaced by a male sensei who, though he'd spent the war doing the sort of important brain work that did not involve combat, refused to speak of it because, as he angrily informed them, they were far behind their grade level and would never make their contributions to society if they did not hurl themselves into the effort. But this new effort was not tangible, comprehensible, or enthralling, as the war effort had been. One afternoon a fresh disturbance rearranged the afternoon street, which recently had happened so often that Hiroshi was less aware of the difference between uneventful and agitated than he was aware of varieties of agitation. There had been that summer day of the war's abrupt end, when running shouts had streaked past like comets until one threw open the door to the classroom and their principal, shocking in his loss of composure, cried out that the Emperor was on the radio and they all must run home to their parents immediately. There had been a different tone of clamor the day American troops first arrived in their small seaside town. Today's disturbance was somehow furtive. It zigzagged like a mouse rather than sweeping all persons with it like a tide. It found Hiroshi in the form of a friend of his mother's, one of their slum's sisterhood who treated all the children with equal rough authority. She yanked him close and barked, "Get your mom out here fast," in his ear.

In the distance he heard shrill whistles, lively cracks like artillery fire, and beneath them at slow intervals a more menacing, thunderlike boom. Such phenomena would generally empty the crowded street in the direction of the sound, and yet he sensed a hesitancy around him, and observing eyes followed him as he ran. "Auntie Kim says come fast," he conveyed, and somehow his mother, with his sister by the hand and his brother on her hip, unquestioningly followed him.

"I told you!" Auntie Kim said to his mother. "I told you!" Whatever it was she had said to his mother couldn't be guessed by Hiroshi as he darted his glance back and forth between his mother and the source of warlike noise that had come into view: a ragtag parade, perhaps three-times-ten women and men, messily anticipated and flanked by running children and a few wobbly cyclists. The formation of persons was loose but their repeated shouts were loud, and several poles bobbed from their midst, from which snapped a standard-size United States flag such as he had already seen flying from the back of military vehicles on the coast road; a white flag so many times larger than the US one, of so much seething, undulating fabric that three men were struggling to control it on its pole; and a skinny white banner. The symbols on both the enormous white flag and the skinny white banner were illegible to him. He could see a colored medallion at the center of the flag, red and blue swirled together like the crests of two waves; and at the corners of the flag, short and longer black dashes making different designs. On the banner were markings that, unlike those on the flag, he knew for certain were words, but unnervingly, they were not words he recognized.

"What does it say?" he asked his mother urgently. "What are they yelling?"

Auntie Kim snarled in disgust. "The smartest boy in his school, and he can't even read his own language."

"I can read!" he said furiously. "If they write it correctly!"

But the women were ignoring him now.

"Aren't they afraid?" his mother implored, sounding frightened herself.

"I told you," Auntie Kim repeated.

"But what if they're arrested?"

"They won't be. The Americans say we're liberated now."

"The Americans were our enemy," Hiroshi scolded the mothers. Was it possible this was the first time he'd ever seen his mother outside their home? She certainly acted as though she had never been outside before. "They inflicted unthinkable cruelty on us. Our job now is to take them in hand and show them how to make peace."

"Korea is free," Auntie Kim concluded, and then, to him: "Are you paying attention? That's what the banner says! That's what they are shouting! That's our own Taegukgi!"

The fishmonger on the main shopping street owned a radio and sometimes Hiroshi loitered nearby and watched him tune it, the man's calloused fingers touching the dial so slightly Hiroshi could not even see the dial change position, but something would shift, out of spraying static would resolve spoken language, like a melting in reverse, the puddle lifting into a lace of snowflakes. Something like that happened after Auntie Kim spoke. Hiroshi understood that the incoherent noise that had meant nothing to him was in fact two languages, overlapping and dismantling each other until his realization helped him tease them apart: the language he spoke and wrote at school every day and spoke at play and in the streets of his town; and the language his parents used with each other, mostly late at night when they thought he was asleep. He knew this language also, he understood it when he heard it directed at him, but it rarely left his mouth and he had never learned to write it down. The parade had moved past and the crowd closed in its wake as if trying to decide whether to join. The enormous flag heaved and snapped in the distance like a sail pulling free from its mast. *Korea is free!* and *Long live Korea!* and *Out of darkness, into light!* were all three being uttered in his school language and in his parents' late-night language, both at the same time, so that as his intense concentration on the cacophony flagged, and as it drew farther away, the filigree of clarity collapsed, and all he heard again was meaningless noise.

"But what's Korea?" he asked as they turned to walk home.

"Let me die," Auntie Kim said.

"Korea is the homeland of Koreans," his mother told him.

"But what are Koreans?"

"We are," said his mother. "You are. That's why your name isn't really Hiroshi, it's 석."

"What do you *mean* my name isn't Hiroshi?" he cried.

"I told you," Auntie Kim said to his mother again.

His mother replied, "But what choice did we have?"


His parents' homeland was an island called Jeju, where mer-women raised glittering heaps of succulent bivalves from the deep, where

oranges the size of melons and sweeter than candy so weighed down
the boughs of the trees that a person didn't even have to stretch to pick
the fruit, and where the soil was so rich, being the gift of an ancient
volcano, that it was almost good enough to eat on its own. Why his
parents would ever leave such a paradise was a question it would not
occur to him to ask until he was older, by which time he would know
that it's possible to be poor anywhere. He no longer remembered that
his knowledge of his parents' island's wonders came from the ancient
bedtime stories told him by his mother, which, like the island they
concerned, belonged to a bygone halcyon period, his toddlerhood, before his younger sister had arrived.

Even if he had remembered his process of learning, he would not
have known that Jeju Island was not one of Japan's many thousands
of islands, because this had never been mentioned. For his mother it
went without saying, just as for Hiroshi it went without saying that
this island, like all the other islands that made up his known world, was
Japanese. To learn it was not Japanese but Korean was so profoundly
disorienting that the greater discovery, that he himself was Korean, was
for the moment secondary. He pined for some tangible proof, but the
map of the Japanese Empire had disappeared from his classroom along
with all his and his classmates' decorative efforts, all their colorful drawings, all their painstakingly calligraphed slogans and songs, everything
except their seat-covers/bomb-raid-head-protectors, spared perhaps by
their deceptively domestic appearance. Even the Imperial Rescript, basic as the blackboard, had been replaced by a pale rectangular ghost on
the wall. Almost every textbook but those pertaining to math had also
vanished, to undergo some process called revision, which made their
intemperate sensei angrier than ever, and more disinclined than ever to
notice Hiroshi's particular gifts, which hadn't gone away just because
the war and the empire had. Yet the day Hiroshi arrived at the door
to the school building so early even the custodian wasn't yet there,
and once his sensei finally arrived made a deep bow and scuttled, eyes
on his own toes, in that man's wake all the way to the administrative
offices in which no student was allowed, his sensei did finally turn to
him, to ask with bitten-back impatience what he was doing there.

"I'd like a map to study, Teacher," he told his teacher, still studying his toes.

"Straighten up. For what reason do you want to study a map?"

"To learn where different things are, Teacher."

"What things? There are many things and many maps."

"To learn what are the islands that are Japan and—what aren't."

His sensei's lips compressed with what could have equally been distaste or contemplation. "You've chosen an unpropitious time for such an interest," he said, and sent Hiroshi to their stripped-bare classroom, even more discouraging a place when entered all by oneself. But at the end of the next day his sensei, while dismissing his classmates, called him forward to his desk. Once they were alone he removed a bright-colored pamphlet from his briefcase. "One Nation, One System! The People's Transport Network: Comfortable, Modern, Far-Reaching." Stylized pagodas peeked out from behind stylized hills; a pen-and-ink locomotive and steamship stood shoulder to shoulder, ready to span land and sea. Dwarfing them was the familiar blood-red sunburst logo for Sunrise Toothpaste.

"This is my personal property," Hiroshi's sensei said, unfolding the map so it covered the desk. The map was breathtaking, so beautiful Hiroshi felt a strange pain in his chest. He'd never seen anything so bright, clean, and beguiling. The land was yellow, with green mountain peaks surging across it like arrows, the sea was bright blue, and the rail lines—for that was what this was, Hiroshi understood, a map of all the trains and where they went—were dark red ribbons twisting over the landscape, with the countless circles of their stations strung densely along them like beads.

The map could not accommodate the size of the rail network without breaking it into pieces. While the greatest part of the map was a skinny rectangle almost as long as Hiroshi's wingspan that pressed the four big islands into its borders, obliging them to lie flatter than they did naturally, there were three more panels of yellow land, green mountain, red rail line, and blue sea that Hiroshi struggled to connect to the map of the empire that had once been so familiar a part of his classroom. But his sensei touched a fingertip to each of those panels in turn. "Formosa, Chōsen, and Manchukuo you must now disregard. And I'm afraid this map does not show all the thousands of our smaller islands, because they are not reached by train. I think that was your main interest? But this is the only map that I own."

"I don't need to see all of the islands. I'm just looking for the one called Jeju."

"Jeju?" His sensei paused a moment. "Ah. Kang-san, I believe you mean the island that we call Saishū. It's a big island. It may appear here." His sensei leaned toward the map and adjusted his glasses to sit a little closer to the tip of his nose, and Hiroshi imagined him during the war, doing the sort of brain work that is even more important than combat, and riding the modern and far-reaching trains with the aid of this map. "Here it is," his sensei then said, laying his finger near the base of Chōsen's dangling paw, where it disintegrated, just where the paw's claws would be, into many tiny islets that might not even be fully detached, and one larger and farther-off oblong like a fallen-off toenail. So it was true. The island was a part of Chōsen. It held no green arrow-shape mountain, no red ribbon of track. It was itself held, by wispy black threads, to the paw, as if in danger of floating away. "Our ferry system linked Saishū to the peninsula," his sensei said, explaining the threads, "though I can't say whether any ferries still operate. That would be up to the Americans in their infinite wisdom." Hiroshi's riveted gaze no longer took the map in, his desire to take it home with him had become so overwhelming. He only wanted to be alone with it, to pore over it as long as he liked, to trace the routes of the tracks with his fingers. He was still so stunned that Jeju had an outline and location and alternate name it hadn't even occurred to him to find the town in which he himself lived, the bright white bead indicating the station with its single set of tracks and peaked-roof station house, the front façade of which held his town's most reliable clock. He was still struggling to choose the right words to ask his sensei, whose show of favor to him today was so unprecedented, how he might stay with the map just a little bit longer, when, like a reverse magic trick, in a few quick folds his sensei made the map disappear behind the Sunrise Toothpaste logo—and then that too was gone, into the briefcase. Hiroshi was so stunned by the dispossession it took him a moment to realize his sensei was still speaking to him.

"Then your parents are from Saishū, Kang-san? Though with your surname I suppose you could be a Formosan." Hiroshi could not follow the thread of this at all; his gaze kept straying to the briefcase, as if enough silent imploring might cause the map to creep out again on its own power.

"My parents are from Jeju, from Saishū," he managed to confirm.

"And will they return there, as so many Koreans are doing?"

Return there? Why would his parents return to a place they had left? But this wasn't Hiroshi's own wise comment, it was the argument he heard day and night, whether between his parents, or between his mother and Auntie Kim or another such woman friend, or between his parents and some other agitated pair with whom his parents both agreed and disagreed often at the same time. "Will you go back?" "Why go back to a place that we left?" "Because it's different now—" "Yes! Worse!" There had been the story of Auntie Kim's brother, who had been cheated ten different ways just getting as far as the port of Senzaki, a long expensive journey as it was; who had then been made by the American military authorities to give up all the money and goods he had brought with him, so that he boarded the "liberty ship" with barely enough yen in his pocket to eat for a week; who had found on his arrival in Busan late at night that he couldn't even change his yen into won, so that he had to beg a meal and sleep on the street; and whose prospects had steadily diminished from there, because southern Korea was a place of sheer chaos, presided over by Americans who could not even coordinate the two ends of a single boat journey, but greeted with dismissive bewilderment the very same people who'd been herded to Korea by the Americans running Japan! Auntie Kim's brother had finally stowed away on a boat coming *back* to Japan, minus his life savings, minus working papers. He now smuggled Koreans like himself as well as contraband into Japan. This was what happened! And in the next breath the very same Auntie Kim was imploring, often with tears splashing off her chin onto the floor, "How can we *not* go to Korea, our own country? That is finally free?" While someone else demanded, "One thousand yen per family? Or for each person? Could the baby be counted?" And another cried, "How can you ask this? What does it matter if you'll starve there in three weeks, or six?"

"I don't think they want to return there," Hiroshi said now, though in having the question posed to him, and by his sensei, the prospect became suddenly real, a real thing that might really take place.

"I hope not. It would be a shame, for a boy like you, who clearly has prospects. Prospects that could have gone far, when all of us were one people, one nation. Now a boy like you is meant to go back to the peninsula, where the very universities that our Emperor built are being stripped of their scholars and books. But the Americans, in their wisdom, would not like to hear me talk this way. They would call this a glorification of our imperial past. They would find me, possibly, an impediment to democratization. I would certainly not want to be that. I am, however, glad to hear that your parents have not dropped everything and gone running for 'liberty ships.'"

"Yes, Sensei."

"And your name?"

"My name?"

"Your given name. Perhaps you have heard that the Americans, in the interests of democratization, are concerned that we teachers should not discourage our students from using their given names, even if these are not Japanese. You don't feel discouraged from using such a name, do you?"

"I don't have another name besides Hiroshi," he said honestly, and then realized this wasn't correct. "Oh, I do!" he said, feeling the surprise of discovery. "But I never use it. I don't know how to write it."

His sensei did not say, *What a shame*, or, *In that case, you must learn*. Instead he said, "I hope you enjoyed the map."

"I did enjoy it very much, and appreciate it very very much. Thank you very much, Sensei, for the opportunity to see it." He wondered what additional expressions of gratitude and appreciation he could add that might inspire his sensei to give him the map forever or even just for one night, but his sensei had already stood, cueing Hiroshi to bow as his sensei took leave.

Now Sensei's word "democratization" seemed to find Hiroshi's ears all the time. In the interests of democratization, the Americans were letting Koreans start up their own schools, where for the first time their children could learn the Korean language—or at least the Americans had so far done nothing to stop the schools from being set up. It took time for this news to make its way to Hiroshi's small town with its small—yet larger than Hiroshi had known—number of Koreans. By the time the news arrived, it had already been invalidated by further developments the news of which would also take time to arrive. But still, the news seized his mother's imagination. It was as if the shock of that day when Hiroshi had brought her to see the parade had finally ceased its reverberations and left her strangely alert, different than she'd been in the past. The nearest Korean school was said to be setting up in Kanazawa, an hour away by train, but Hiroshi was nine, more than old enough, all the adults agreed, to manage a simple train ride while safeguarding his six-year-old sister. "Change schools?" Hiroshi cried, horrified by the seriousness of the conversation, the number of adults involved—lately it seemed that every person who'd turned out to be Korean in their town was squeezing through their door at all hours of the night, while Hiroshi and his now three younger siblings were trying to sleep. They'd formed a Committee of Koreans Who Live in Japan, and seemed to consider his home that could barely fit its occupants' bedrolls their emergency headquarters. "I won't change schools, I'm top boy! My sensei says I have prospects, he's been loaning me books!" This stinging rebuttal only made the committee trade glances. The discussions of a new school continued, somehow not despite but because of his protests.

The whole debate was soon nullified, at least so far as it touched on Hiroshi; the culprit was democratization again. This time, the word was invoked bitterly: no sooner had the Korean schools opened than the Americans were ordering them closed, on the grounds that the Koreans who had opened the schools were too much allied with

the Japanese Communist Party. "And so what if we are?" Hiroshi's father exclaimed, to the murmured assents of the room. Hiroshi's father
also was changing—or perhaps he was reverting to a person he'd been
in the past, a person who had scraped together the cost of passage and
permits, who had led his young wife, their first child in her belly, onto
the ship that carried them and the single box that held all their possessions from Jeju Island to the port of Busan, from the port of Busan
across the lurching East Sea into the Kanmon Strait, from that eye of
a needle into Japan's inland sea and across its whole length to the port
of Osaka, never knowing if, at the end of that journey, work, food, and
shelter would surrender themselves to his quest to obtain them. How
could Hiroshi, the son of a man who was beaten like a rug by his wife
every night, have suspected the existence of such a daring person? "The
JCP are the only Japanese who ever gave a damn if we Koreans on road
crew got paid the same wage as the Japanese men. They're the only
ones who ever gave a damn if we got our arm broke by some fool and
got fired when it wasn't our fault. That's why our committee stands
with them, because they stand with us! But the Americans are saying,
Those Koreans—they're an enemy people. They're *anti*-democratic.
That's why they're killing us on Jeju. All the while saying, Why won't
you go back to Jeju? Last year you could starve there, now you'll also
get shot!"

If the Emperor had never spoken over the radio, announcing it was
time to stop fighting and create a grand peace; if all the people who
turned out to be Koreans had not begun shouting *Freedom* and waving
new flags in the street; if there had been no "liberty ships" transporting floods of them to that paw-shaped peninsula, and leaky, sneaking
fishing boats smuggling scores of them back, even poorer from the effort of returning to the homeland than they'd been the first time they
had left; then Hiroshi might have kept on being lonely in his family in
the way he'd never noticed let alone minded, instead of being lonely in
this new way, in which his family seemed to contain scores of strangers, and his realm of happiness—in the classroom, with Sensei—was
somehow a source of outrage, another of so many outrages to be
debated deep into the night. When his parents had sailed away from

Jeju they'd been part of a great emptying of their impoverished island, until for every family still living on Jeju, it was said at least one of their members had left. And when Hiroshi's father made his way north and east from Osaka, always chasing the new chance of a job, other Jeju islanders were always alongside, so that the handful who finally set roots in this far-flung small town on Japan's western coast still were links in a chain, down which modest sums flowed to the people back home, and, in the opposite direction, news and gossip flowed to the people who'd left.

In March of 1948, when Hiroshi was nine, Jeju islanders protesting the division of liberated Korea into US- and Soviet-occupied zones were fired on by the soldiers of the US-backed provisional government in the south, and in April the back-and-forth between the two sides mushroomed into all-out war; for every family who'd sent one member to Japan in the previous decade, there was one member at least who'd been murdered by the government forces, often an old man or a child. The same month in Kobe, riots broke out when the Japanese police tried to enforce the US order to close the new Korean schools. In May, despite the ongoing protests, elections were held in the US-backed half of Korea, leaving no way to rejoin south and north. The Americans wanted only to cement the regime they'd installed, led by the same man who had ordered the bloodshed on Jeju, Hiroshi's parents and fellow committee members agreed. Even here in Japan, to which more Jeju islanders than ever were now trying to flee, it was clear the Americans scorned the Koreans as ignorant rabble or worse. The committee members who had fought for the schools, and for other measures for Koreans that were simply fair and right, were threatened with deportation to the new US-backed southern Korea, where the US-handpicked president vowed to throw them in jail, incorrigible Communists that they obviously were.

One afternoon Hiroshi came home to find his mother and her friends awaiting him with a square of paper that they seemed both to fear, and fear for; he must wash his hands immediately before he touched it, how did a smart boy like him get so filthy? The square of paper, when he had finally been permitted—though it felt like compelled—to examine it, held three sentences in English, including several words he'd never seen before. This was a blow, as his most recent triumph in school was in the subject of English, in which he'd swiftly caught up to his sensei (who said to him, in that unsettling tone that mingled reprimand and praise, "Soon you'll be teaching me"). Yet here, alongside newly familiar terms like *US Forces* and *Korean* and *army* were mysteries like *inasmuch* and *oppression*:

> *Honored Commanding General of the Great US Forces!*
> *I am a Korean schoolchild who lives in Japan. I beg your*
> *permission for my revered teachers to freely teach me Korean subjects*
> *in my own language, inasmuch as it was your Great Army that*
> *liberated me from ruthless Japanese oppression!*

"I don't understand some of the words," he admitted at last, but his mother made a sound of impatience.

"It's not for you, it's for American soldiers. You only need to copy it in your best English writing. And don't make mistakes."

"I couldn't make mistakes if I tried!" he said, deeply offended. "And why should I copy it if you already have it?"

"Because it's a letter from a schoolchild, isn't that what it says? That's what we were told that it says!"

"But I don't want to send this letter! I don't want Korean school!"

"It isn't from you, it's from Soonja. You're to sign it, *Kang Soonja aged 6.*"

"Have her do it herself!"

"You know she's too little to write anything! Can't you do this one thing for your dongsaeng?" And so he set himself to copying the letter, not so easy with his mother and the aunties all crowding and following hawkeyed each stroke, as if to catch him subverting the message.

No local Korean school with the required, impossible permit materialized in their town as a result of the letter, and Soonja followed him to ordinary school that spring. If his mother blamed Hiroshi, or his penmanship, for this latest defeat at the hands of the American imperialists, who were apparently no better than the Japanese imperialists, at least no one said so to his face. Nor did he receive any credit when, the following year, such a school did open its doors. In the interval, his parents' noisy committee had changed, in his view for the better, if only because it withdrew from the foot of his bedroll to some other accommodation. It called itself a branch office of an Organization that had knitted itself out of countless committees all over Japan. The Organization achieved what the riots in Kobe had not: not just Korean schools but other good things, like mutual-aid groups for small-business loans, and pressure on the government to make Koreans into citizens, not just leftover subjects who'd lost even the scant rights they'd had when Japan had been an empire. The Organization didn't limit itself to the welfare of Koreans who lived in Japan but campaigned tirelessly for reunification of the now-two Koreas. The Organization's many small offices, which sometimes doubled as the small businesses of its officer-members, flew the flag of the Democratic People's Republic of Korea, the new name for the north, for it was the DPRK that called for reunification, and that championed the rights of poor working Koreans. Its southern counterpart, the American-backed Republic of Korea, called any Koreans who objected to its policies Reds, and with seeming relish reiterated its threats to jail and execute them.

In 1952, at the same time that Hiroshi started regular high school, the Organization's long-promised Korean high school in Kanazawa finally opened. His younger siblings (except the new baby, Jeong, who was still too young for school at all) were already attending the Korean primary school that Hiroshi's parents' branch office had done so much to launch, his own father building the shoe cubbies, his own mother sewing the blue and red flags. The Americans had finally left Japan, satisfied with the state of democratization, but there was a war now between the two Koreas; it was imperative the North win, so that the two sides were reunified into just one Korea again. At eleven, Soonja had been in charge for years of Seung and the youngest girl, Yeonja, but after his dismissal Hiroshi still sometimes walked to their school, so much smaller and shabbier than his own, to watch them at play in the dust of the yard, to walk them home, holding the two younger ones' hands while Soonja shouldered their backpacks. His three siblings loved to sing their school songs, the tunes of which had settled in Hiroshi, but the words of which he barely understood; and often the three of them laughed and teased in the language Hiroshi could less and less bring to his tongue, even as his English had become so advanced it was hard to believe *inasmuch* had ever caused him trouble.

He knew his parents longed for him to change to the Korean high school in Kanazawa, less for his sake than the school's. He was a prize pupil, the pride of their town. His attendance would transfer that pride to the school. But "these private ethnic schools are not in full conformance with our education laws," his old sensei said, when Hiroshi asked him for advice. "They're permitted to operate, yes—but their graduates can't sit for our top university entrance exams. If you go to such a school, you throw away all your chances."

Hearing this he felt both heartbreak and relief at a cleavage that had formed through no fault of his own. "And so I can't consider it," he explained to his parents, realizing a distance had opened already, for they hadn't even asked, although he knew it was the thing they most wanted.

After a time his father said, "We understand and respect your decision. But there is something else. You're fourteen, a grown man. We know you will do what you want, but please consider this most firm request."

"Anything," he said, from so wanting the distance to close, and from feeling so alarmed at being called a grown man.

"We would like you to go by the name that we gave you, at home. It's confusing for your brothers and sisters. And now that they're schooled in Korean, we don't like the sound of 'Hiroshi' coming out of their mouths."

He no longer remembered becoming Hiroshi; he no longer recalled the bright banner it seemed to have trailed behind him as he ran. It was merely the way he'd long answered to roll call. It felt like a painfully undersized thing to give up, given the somberness of the request. "Of course," he told them. "I'm sorry I didn't think of it first." That night when the family sat down to eat, he reminded his younger siblings he was *Seok*, that "Hiroshi" was only a name he wore outside their house, like a coat.

Despite his stellar entrance exam scores he wasn't admitted to Todai. He was also rejected from Kyoto, Tohoku, and Keio. In the end he received a place at the Tokyo Technical College. Later in his life he would claim that this humiliation came as no surprise, that he expected and even hoped for the destruction of his Japanese prospects because it revealed to him, before he wasted real effort, that his future lay elsewhere. But this was a face-saving lie. He was devastated—an experience he had never so much as intuited despite being the son of his parents, whose entire lives had demonstrated systematic unfairness. He remembered his parents blossoming in their Organization, his siblings singing their Korean school songs, and was reminded for the first time in a very long while of his own happy zeal the last year of the war, a little boy whose belief in his Japaneseness hadn't yet been corrected. The correction having finally arrived, he had no outlet, such as his parents and siblings had found, for his disappointment and shame. He had never been a political student, to the contrary had carefully avoided political clubs, meetings, casual conversations, and even people—he'd felt he couldn't afford it. Sometimes, the unjustly downtrodden took up arms and fierce miens, but equally often they turned the other cheek, studied harder, camouflaged themselves ever more behind obedience and merit and bided their time, believing against all evidence that the future would bring something better, for them if for nobody else. He tried to be the second kind of ruined person. Despite his unfriendly appearance, despite his bone-deep competitiveness, he was still a poor boy, climbing the one ladder offered to him. He moved to Tokyo to begin his new life, and vowed to demolish his classmates in the race for what second-rate prizes there were.

Yet, disillusioned as he was, when his parents decided to abandon Japan he was dumbfounded.

He'd been living away from his parents for three years when they appeared at his door unannounced and insisted on sweeping his little desk clean to lay out a flyer. "WELCOME TO YOUR HOMELAND!" it proclaimed. The Democratic People's Republic of Korea, having celebrated its tenth year of existence, invited its wandering brothers and sisters to return to their homeland. The economy was booming—the flyer pictured factories and farms, and new high-rise apartments. Ocean passage, furnished apartment with garden, job training and placement, even the cost of higher education for children, all were part of the resettlement offer for the first ten thousand Japan-residing Koreans to sign up, which his parents had already done, with numerous friends and neighbors from the Organization, which was acting as liaison between the DPRK and the Japanese government. They—and he, they assumed—would sail at the end of the month.

At first he thought they were joking, though his parents were not prone to humor. His parents' loyalty to the DPRK was the loyalty idealists offer the most potent symbol of their most distant hopes: like most of their friends, they viewed the DPRK as the standard-bearer for eventual reunification, and the eventual uplift of the poor and downtrodden worldwide, not just within its own borders. But their expressions of allegiance to the DPRK were those of people whose lives have eased enough to allow them to do things like plan a "DPRK Friendship Celebration Day" of picnicking and songs. In other words, his parents, unceasingly hardworking, had finally made stable lives for themselves. They would always be poor, but all five of their children were in school. No one went hungry. Seok thought it must be some scam—there could not be a boat, let alone cooperation from the Japanese government, which still refused to recognize the DPRK. It was only when his parents received their government transit papers, via the Organization, and were begging him to hurry up and see about his own, that he realized the actual grinding of actual gears in a single direction was well under way.

There was indeed a ship, provided by no less than the International Committee of the Red Cross. There were government-sponsored, completely free "repatriation trains" that would funnel "repatriates" from all over Japan to the port of Niigata. In a panic, he spent his week's budget on train fare—notably not government-sponsored—to his hometown, his first visit since leaving for school, to reason with them. Yes, he reasoned with himself as he rode, theirs was the constricted, the already foreclosed, life of the underclass; of the Permanent Resident Alien whose ten fingerprints are all kept on record at each prefectural office but who would never hold a job in such an office, nor any proper job with a pension, because of not having Japanese blood. He himself was not yet able to fully grasp the repercussions of his inability to see his future in Japan, but he knew to a certainty there was also no future in either Korea. Reminding his parents of this should have only been a matter of stating the facts, but his parents' years of lionizing the DPRK made them utterly credulous of the words in the flyer, utterly dazzled by its color photographs. Did he not see the beautiful high-rise apartments? "I see a building," he tried to say kindly, "and all that tells me is one single building exists. They probably built it for taking the picture." But no, his parents resisted him passionately, he was a brilliant student, everyone knew this, but he wasn't so worldly—in fact, he lacked the range of experience his old parents, and their many friends, together possessed. It was clear to see—just look at the flyer—that in the DPRK the promise of jobs and social welfare for all was finally being fulfilled. If you got sick, they sent you to a doctor. If you got disabled, they gave you a pension. The Organization had hosted an actual party official from the DPRK who'd shown floor plans of the apartments, all with plumbing and an *indoor gas cooker.* "Every modern convenience" was the phrase the official had used. If Seok had only been at that presentation: *Everyone* had signed up! There had even been some anxious elbowing and pushing, until the DPRK man assured them there was room for them all. And Seok could see that it wasn't a handout. They would work as they had all their lives—but this time for fair wages, and an orderly modern society. Most of all, for their homeland.

"Your homeland is Jeju! No one you know's ever been to the North, no one you know's buried there! And flawed as it is, Japan is your *home.*"

"A home that will never be a homeland," they countered.

He couldn't claim, later, to have had the prescience to know it was vastly too good to be true. He only felt sure things could not be exactly as advertised. Barely five years separated both Koreas from a devastating and still-unresolved war. They had no famous schools there, no internationally recognized society and culture. That his parents were in raptures about indoor plumbing to him said it all. Yes, Japan denied its resident Koreans access to every kind of privilege that existed—but the privileges *existed*, was the difference. Would they not rather keep fighting for access to them than venture someplace where those privileges might not exist at all? Did this bald appeal for new citizens not make them suspicious, that a nation so desperate for them might be desperate in other ways, too?

Soonja also put up a fierce fight, though her reasons were different. She was dating a Japanese boy. She was only seventeen, but as the date of embarkation approached she eloped, dropped out of high school, and moved in with her new husband's family. If anything, the catastrophe destroyed all chance of second thoughts. "Why would we stay where our daughter has made herself dead to us?" his mother demanded through effusions of tears. Seung was fourteen, Yeonja was twelve, and Jeong, the baby, was nine. They were all so changed from the last time he'd lived under the same roof with them Seok felt he hardly knew who they were, but he also felt their fates were in his hands and he argued with his parents right up to their day of departure and then right down the length of the train platform. A brass band was playing. Colored bunting had been attached to the sides of the train, over which "repatriates" who had already boarded hung out opened windows, weeping and laughing, grasping at the hands of well-wishers. A group of local schoolchildren, in blue hats and red sashes, were handing out carnation corsages and boxes of fruit tied with ribbon. A banner hung from the station house read, in both Japanese and Korean, WE WISH JOY TO KOREANS REPATRIATING TO THEIR HOMELAND!

"They were *born* in Japan, they can't *repatriate* someplace they've never been!" Seok raged while his siblings stood by silently. His father was unmoved. "They're Koreans," was all he replied.

His mother wept, clinging to him and pleading with him to change his mind, as if it were he who was turning his back on the parents who'd given him life, and the land where that life had been led—and indeed it felt that way, as the train filled and filled, and more and more waving arms and flushed faces squeezed together at the train windows. There was everyone; here was Seok. "You're the one who decided to go," Seok reminded his mother, as their tears splashed and mingled on their clasped hands. He could not scold her. "I hope you find the life of your dreams."

"You're my son! Come home with us!" his mother moaned, toppling heavily against him as if she had fainted, so that their last moments were a clumsy grappling, as he helped his father half carry her to the train steps.

"I'll see you again, Mother," Seok promised her.

To his three younger siblings he said, "Take good care of our parents. They're old, and they never had school. They can't even write in Korean."

"I wish you'd come," said Jeong.

"I'll stay here and keep a place for us, in case you change your mind. I'll always be here. And your big sister, too. This will always be your home."

"I don't want to change schools," Yeonja whispered.

"It'll be okay. Your brothers are your friends no matter what."

To all of them, he said, "You need to write me a letter each week. You can take turns, as long as I get one every week. You'll have to buy stamps when you get there. It's a different country from here, and they'll use different stamps."

"We know that," said Seung.

"I got you these to start." He'd bought them a package of airmail paper and envelopes. Into one of the envelopes he'd placed a thick stack of yen bills, nearly all the money he had. He handed the package to Seung, making sure he saw the money. "You're the first son, while you're there and I'm here. You're in charge. Don't lose the money."

"Won't they have their own money?"

"I'm sure you'll be able to trade this for their currency. Be smart with it."

Then abruptly they were no longer with him. Nor did he see them, like their fellow passengers, hanging out the train windows and waving—but he turned away, afraid that he would.

The first letter arrived within days—from Niigata. "Dear Brother," wrote Yeonja,

> We're still in Niigata in a place like a school dorm with cots. Korean people are here from all over Japan. They're all waiting to get on the ship. Before anybody can get on the ship everyone has to sit in a Special Room for Confirmation of Free Will and be asked the same questions. There are only a few Special Rooms so it's taking a very long time. The questions are, Are you departing Japan of your own free will? Is your desired destination the Democratic People's Republic of Korea? I copied them down from a big poster hung on the wall. They asked our family yesterday but we still have to wait until everyone else has been asked. There's an outdoor play yard with a good jungle gym where Jeong plays and a big cafeteria where we have meals.

No mention of anyone answering no to either one of the questions, but Seok still had the peculiar sensation of time standing still: The irreversible moment had not yet occurred. They were still in Japan.

Or, they'd been in Japan when she'd written the letter. Unreasonably, he thought of traveling to Niigata. But why? They had said their goodbyes.

The second letter took more than two months to arrive. It was dated three weeks after the first. After this, the lags would only grow longer—between the letters, and between each letter's date and its arrival in Seok's mailbox.

> Dear Brother,
>     We were very happy to get off the ship and step foot in our homeland.
>     Our homeland is even more beautiful than we expected.

*Many people were standing onshore when we got here, to give us a welcome. We were so happy to see them, our Korean people.*

*Mother feels much better now we are here than she did on the ship.*

*It will be nice to have a garden. Maybe you can send us cucumber, pepper, radish, and pumpkin seeds. Spinach and squash. And any other kinds, if you can please label them.*

*Dear Brother,*

*Thank you for the seeds. How great to have such a beautiful land to plant seeds.*

*You asked about our apartment. It is beautiful just like we hoped. Mother says she is surprised that she misses her house shoes. She says if you happen to go in the market and see the house shoes that she always liked best, that have thick felt inside, you can send them. You might see warm socks at the market. If you do you can also send those. If there is a warm blanket you can send it since you're already sending the socks.*

*Dear Brother,*

*I am sorry I caused you such worry. Of course our home here is well heated.*

Seung never took up a pen, and he and Jeong both went almost unmentioned.

*Our brothers are both very well, I am sorry I caused you such worry not mentioning them. Yes, I am studying hard. I am learning many things I did not know before.*

The letters were vague in their news: Everybody was "happy" and "well." They were contrastingly precise in their requests: for aspirin, underwear, soap powder, tea. Seok wondered if their jobs were not paying enough? Oh no, not at all, they were sorry to put him to trouble, if he wanted to send them some packets of nori it was only because they were missing the brand that they ate in Japan. In his last year at the technical college Seok took a night job to pay for these care packages, sending each off to the only address he had ever been given, a postal delivery depot. He got occasional looks from the clerk, and began alternating among several different post offices to avoid being noticed as someone sending quantities of parcels to the DPRK. Not a single sentence in Yeonja's rare laconic letters revealed a single detail about where all these boxes were arriving, whether in a town or in the countryside, in the mountains or next to the sea. Despite what he said in his letters he was less worried than increasingly angry, at what he saw as his parents' stubbornness. Clearly it hadn't turned out as they'd hoped. They were in a place so backward it even lacked soap. But they would not let his sister say so; they would hold up their heads to the end, while demanding he send them wool hats. He imagined his mother in the background, dictating a list, Yeonja in the foreground with a pen—where were the men? Where was his father, where was Seung? He could no longer restrain his scolding. "I have not had one word from my brother," he wrote. "I have to wonder if you are really better off over there than you were in Japan." After this, he expected to hear some specifics. Instead, the letters grew even more infrequent, and even less detailed. If not for their dates, and some seasonal fluctuation in the items requested, he couldn't have guessed at their order.

He graduated from the technical college with the highest distinction it offered, accepted a poorly paid teaching-assistant position, applied to do graduate study at Todai, and was turned down again. Again he was also turned down at Kyoto and Keio. A numbness descended on him within which he was not even angry or sad. Yet, one day in his department hallway, he was stopped short by a colorful flyer that spoke to every secret hope he didn't know he still harbored, and the biases so deep within him he did not even know they were there. *Scientists— Engineers—Mathematicians—Study in the US—All encouraged to apply— Funding opportunities available.*

At the informational session, the white American man on the opposite side of the table studied his Foreigner Residence Card. "Your birthplace is Ishikawa Prefecture," he confirmed.

"Yes."

"But you're a Resident Alien because you're Korean. That's kind of a bind, isn't it?"

"I cannot disagree."

"Your English is excellent," the man said, although since introducing himself Seok had hardly spoken. "If you're accepted to our program, our foreign students' division will work to get you approved for a visa, but I can tell you right now you'll need a Right of Return to Japan."

"I don't want to return to Japan," he said, for the first time acknowledging this to himself, though he hadn't forgotten his promise to Jeong. Rather he'd been struggling against the belief that Jeong, and his mother and father and Yeonja and Seung, had moved somehow beyond reclamation. He couldn't stand to be where they'd once been.

"I can see why you'd feel that way, but you'll still need the Right of Return. However, we can help with that. Any difficulties we should be aware of?"

"Difficulties?" he repeated, as if this word had proved a challenge to his English.

"Arrests, political activities. I've heard it said about Koreans in Japan that they're all Communists, but you certainly don't look like one."

"I'm certainly not one," he said over the thundering noise of his heart. His solemnity made the man laugh.

"You're certainly an excellent student. In the US we know how to appreciate people like you."

"Is University of Massachusetts Amherst near Harvard?" Seok asked as he stood from the table. This made the man laugh again.

"We're practically neighbors," he said.

Eight months later, Seok took the train to see Soonja, whose marriage, he sensed, was extremely unhappy. He could barely fill the silence, the rare times she called. They seemed to resent each other for reasons they couldn't have named. He had bought himself a suitcase, and absurdly—he was conscious of how absurd it was but couldn't make himself do otherwise—he took it, empty, all the way to Soonja's, though he wasn't even staying the night. Soonja gasped when she saw it, clapped a palm to her mouth to contain her hungry admiration.

"Can I open it?" she begged.

"There's nothing inside—I bought it right before my train and then I ran out of time to drop it back at my room. That's the only reason I dragged it all the way here."

"I just want to see the lining," she implored, and, pretending reluctance, he let her. She first obsessively swept the only open patch of floor in her tiny apartment before laying the suitcase at its center with a care she might have shown a sleeping child. She zipped the suitcase open and knelt, regarding its empty inside. Then her child toddled into the room and made for the exciting play object. Soonja snarled, "Don't you touch it! Get out!"

When the child had fled, wailing, he attempted to say casually, as if not scoured by self-reproach, "Now that I'm leaving, you have to be the one to keep contact with them, in case they ever decide to come back."

"Do you think that *you'll* ever come back?"

"No," he said.

# Anne

**At first Anne** tried to hide her pregnancy. She had the idea that the more pregnant she was when Adrian noticed, the more likely he'd be delighted. From Cairo to Jerusalem to Damascus they continued, just the adventure to throw away her life for if she hadn't also been throwing up everything that she ate. Pale as death, her sylphlike (his term) body on its way from barely there to nonexistent (he also admired, perhaps too much, that she wore the clothes of a twelve-year-old boy), she nevertheless was determined to keep stumbling along within the muscled half hoop of his arm. She was spurred by her pride, in having gone from zero prospects behind a hardware store counter in Toledo, Ohio, to the bed of a man who spoke half the languages of the Holy Land, and had the prophet's beard and zealot's eyes, too. If only he wasn't so exceptionally brilliant—having after all abandoned his divinity doctorate because its offered wisdoms were superfluous to him—that he turned out to have known from the start. Not only that, but he reprimanded her for dishonesty.

"I can't imagine what he'd see in you," Anne's sister had said several months earlier, after having met Adrian at her philosophy reading group. He had been invited as guest speaker and enthralled everyone, to the point that Anne's sister, who was engaged to another group member, was obliged to act deeply offended when he asked her out in front of her fiancé. His response to her rebuff had been a gallant,

"In that case perhaps you have a sister as attractive as you that I might like to date?"

"Introduce me anyway," Anne had exasperated her sister by saying—Anne from whom her family already expected the worst, when they thought to have expectations at all. She was the youngest, her family's means would have been modest if the children had been less numerous, and when the following spring Anne left these people behind, along with her chance at a high school diploma, it wasn't due to feelings of neglect so much as lifelong habits of solitude, the product of an upbringing in which, despite or because of the house being so crowded, she'd always felt herself alone.

Adrian explained to her that she would be alone again, and flew her back to the US even more secretively than they had departed. There he made every arrangement—her several months' detention in a widow's boardinghouse outside Boston, her "lying-in" at a discreet, dilapidated Georgian structure marooned in an enormous rolling lawn across which withered nuns, in dowdy gray skirts and cardigans and support hose, shuffled on their errands in the service of the fallen. It was just what Anne would have expected of a sanatorium for incurables, except that here the women didn't leave by dying.

The afternoon Anne went into labor she was swiftly removed from the residence to the infirmary, where the vengeance of God tore her entrails out by the roots; where her involuntary animal howls terrorized her own ears; where she was maddened by the vision of a taut balloon of blood, the size and hardness of a basketball, forcing its way out of her and exploding, and painting her thighs with its gore. In her blind agony she forgot she was having a baby. She was apparently very unruly, was later told she'd scrambled off the table and bitten and clawed at the nurses who tried to restrain her. She remembered none of this. She did recall that she'd been promised anesthesia, a spinal injection to manage the pain. "You went into labor so quickly, we didn't have time for the shot," the nurse replied, in a smug, blaming way. It was as if Anne's precipitous labor were of a piece with her precipitous whoring around, so that the missed pain relief was just what she deserved.

She was allowed to spend a few days with the baby while the adoption papers were put in order. Every breath she took, she took with her nose and mouth pressed into his skin. A dewy salt scent as of freshly churned butter. She understood those heretofore alarming Greek myths in which parents devour their children; these were stories of love. Even Adrian, coming upon her this way, almost asleep in the hot little nest of the baby's flesh, was benign and approving. Perhaps one day she would have another baby, when she was ready to assume this most sacred of tasks.

Adrian placed the papers in front of her, watched as she signed them. The agreement was not merely thorough, but thoughtful, he explained. While Tobias was now solely, legally Adrian's, Anne would be informed of his progress through life. When Adrian judged the time right, Tobias would be equally informed of Anne's existence. "I'm an enlightened man," Adrian noted, adding that his wife, who was thrilled to be becoming a mother, was also enlightened, having supported Adrian through many spiritual quests.

Anne walked out of the home the next morning at dawn, before breakfast was served. She refused a nun's offer to call her a cab. Her parting gift from Adrian was a few hundred dollars in cash. She could take the commuter train east, into Cambridge and Boston, but there was the risk she'd run into somebody she knew—some Toledo striver wrapping up freshman year as Anne hadn't and wouldn't. She took a bus west, to Springfield. Some boy asked if she was a "Smithie," so she took another bus north, to Northampton, which was apparently where Smith College was. She was surprised to realize that, on the outside, she did look like a Smithie. She was nineteen years old, dangerously pale and thin yet despite or because of this pretty, acceptably shabby in the leather sandals she'd bought in Israel and her navy-blue canvas culottes, which hid months of dirt as well as might a military uniform. She had two blouses, one cardigan, one shirtdress, one pair of old loafers, and one pair of jeans. She walked gingerly down the main street, everything that she owned wadded up in her purse. Beneath the culottes, she was trickling a thick, rusty stream into a creased sanitary napkin that kept twisting on the thin elastic belt to which its two ends were anchored, so that she'd feel the cold viscosity of her discharges painting themselves on the upper insides of her thighs, and she'd remember the vision of birthing a blood basketball. But no one here could see the filthy sanitary napkin mashed into her crotch, or the slack collapsed folds of her belly, like a fallen soufflé. Her haggard appearance, her air of incipient or recently failed suicide, were not unusual in this environment. She found a message board, a room for rent, a job.

The man who hired her was Dr. Louis Grassi. Upon meeting him she felt a tidal warmth rise from her feet to the crown of her head, leaving in its wake pure release, as if the bloody knottedness she'd recently become was gently dissolving. This man was going to take care of her, but would not ever touch her; he would be afraid of the very idea. He was an "odd duck," a "confirmed bachelor." He peered at her with the mischievous eye of a parrot, and yet like a parrot he also seemed secretive, lonely, likely to abruptly hide his face in his wing. He lived in a disordered Victorian house a few blocks from the campus, and already counted a housekeeper, a gardener, and a handyman who understood the boiler among his occasional staff, but he needed someone who could read his handwriting and type, skills that almost all females at that time possessed but that Dr. Grassi pretended made Anne in some way indispensable. He soon had Anne admitting that she wasn't a student. Perhaps he'd known it the first time they met, the same way she had known he was the kind of man who wouldn't ever marry, but who required a female comrade, someone with whom the sense of understanding existed on a chemical basis, without the perilous prerequisite of actual intimacy.

"Oh, Anne, if you're not enrolled at the college you're going to unleash the pedagogic busybody in me. I'm going to start drawing up reading lists."

"I'm not teachable," Anne said, which of course wasn't true. She had always been a reader in a family of readers. She remembered her poor mother, used down to a bundle of bones, standing for hours at the ironing board with a book propped open on the shelf in front of her. And herself, walking down the street at age seven or eight with her face in a book, tripping on a piece of broken sidewalk and splitting her lip, and when presenting herself bloody-faced, her mother saying with interest, *What's this book? Any good?* What she might have meant, but which she was ashamed for Dr. Grassi to know, was that she hadn't finished high school and was foolishly proud of the fact. Going back to finish somehow never crossed her mind. She thought of high school graduation as a condition she'd forfeited permanently, like being a virgin.

Dr. Grassi, with his intuition, pretended to accept her rebuff, while leaving books piled all over the small extra office, right next to his kitchen, where the typewriter was. She would read on her lunch break, which for her own satisfaction she enforced at thirty minutes with the use of the stove timer. Dr. Grassi never checked on her, and always protested that she must be undercounting her hours. He was a professor of English who was writing a confusing and ponderous book about the poetry of Wordsworth, and geology and communing with nature, the meandering chapters of which made up most of Anne's work at the start—he wrote his chapters in longhand, which Anne would type into a fair copy, which Dr. Grassi would then cover over with longhand corrections, which Anne would then type up again. But he soon let her know he was actually writing a novel. That she wasn't a student made her especially qualified to work on it, because it meant she wouldn't gossip to her friends about how strange it was. "It *is* strange, isn't it?" Dr. Grassi asked her anxiously.

"I don't read it," Anne lied. "If I read while I type, I make too many errors. I only see letters and spaces. They don't really add up into words."

"Well, thank God," said Dr. Grassi with clear disappointment. "I wouldn't want you to tell your girlfriends what a ridiculous novel I'm writing."

"I don't have any girlfriends to tell," Anne said honestly.

In time she did; in time, almost despite herself, she had a life. It seemed that only the demonstrably crazy or criminal could succeed in not establishing a life if they stayed in one place. With Dr. Grassi Anne rang in the sixties and a few months later her own twenties;

so many milestones gave her the sense that the following year would be just as momentous, that she would be someone else somewhere else, but 1961 and twenty-one came and went, then 1962 and twenty-two, and Anne remained roughly where she had landed. Her secretarial abilities got her more work than Dr. Grassi could offer, but she continued as his most trusted typist, and eventually as his very gentle and dishonest editor and protector. She would be indignant that his novel was rejected again, she would take out her red pen and suggest yet a further revision. She took classes in Amherst, almost as much for Dr. Grassi's sake as her own, though never enough to complete a degree. For a while she'd be ferociously determined, the novels of Hardy or Eliot would form heaps on her floor, she would spend nights and weekends typewriting her papers, she'd be praised by professors who admired her for returning to school at twenty-one, twenty-two, twenty-three, who gratified themselves by encouraging her. She never managed to remain their prodigy, although neither did she outright disappoint them. They continued to imagine, and perhaps she equally continued to imagine, that she would muster the energy someday. It was an article of faith that a woman as bright as she was, who read as much as she did, who seemed so independent as she seemed, must be able to transform herself, on the strength of her own brains and effort, regardless of her lacking the support of a husband or parents.

One day she took the bus into Northampton to see Dr. Grassi. She'd been living in Amherst but had just moved to Hadley, to avoid a man in Amherst she'd mistakenly thought that she liked. She'd made this same mistake with every man who'd shown interest for now going on half a decade. "You're going to run out of towns," Dr. Grassi said to her. "Why don't you come with me to see my old friend. I can promise he won't make a pass."

The old friend had once been Richard Martin, or Martin Richards— by the end of the afternoon Anne had forgotten this generic and fraudulent name, as its erstwhile bearer intended. A classmate of Dr. Grassi's from Princeton, Martin or Richards had traveled to East Asia after college and never, in the sense of having residence, returned. He had made a study of many different strains of Buddhism and ended up catching one of them incurably, to use his own jovial words. "Waku," he said, gladly pumping Anne's hand. Waku was the name he'd assumed in his new life, which had now been his life for thirty years.

For a man in gray robes, with a rope for a belt, and wooden sandals like a pair of little tables strapped under his feet, Waku seemed very loud, jolly, and irreducibly American. He was tall and round, an overfed John Bunyan—it was far from the sort of physique Anne imagined in Asia, or in a monastery, let alone an Asian monastery, although she knew nothing at all about Asia. Waku retained the friendly, honking accent he'd acquired in a Midwestern childhood, and the gosh-golly manner as well. It was endearingly difficult to picture him among the mute geishas and frilly pink trees that were Anne's sole associations with Japan. As if Waku realized this, he excused himself from the parlor of the campus guesthouse to fetch down his traveling companion, a Japanese-appearing young man who stopped at the stairs' halfway point, as if he might still retreat undetected, and squinted at them through a private miasma of, possibly, jet lag.

This was a person not drawn with pen and ink but molded with a knife from hard clay. His jaw, his cranium, even his ears seemed to feature so many right angles Anne imagined an impenetrable fortification built from casts of his head. A fierce ridge of bone shaded his eyes, imperfectly softened by eyebrows, so that he seemed to be incredibly affronted, even with his face in repose. He had very dark, very thick, short-cropped hair that stood up off his head like black turf; Anne wanted to shrink to the size of a fairy and walk through it barefoot.

"Louis Grassi, my old friend from bright college days, and Miss—oh, what a dummy! Forgive me, my dear, I've been up in a little tin can for the past thirty hours . . . this is Mr. Kang . . ." Waku clopped around on his loud wooden sandals, clapping them all on their shoulders. "Sit down, please sit down, we'll have tea . . ."

They had tea. Waku explained his work: he was a self-taught translator of Japanese Buddhist devotional poetry and was making this visit in the hopes of securing the interest of a university press. Anne's indispensable skills as a typist were recommended; her "real" work as an autodidact then was anxiously appended; in both cases by Dr. Grassi.

Mr. Kang's situation was revealed: He was embarking on a doctorate in electrical engineering at UMass. He turned out to have met Waku just a day and a half previously, at Haneda Airport. The coincidence of their shared destination had effectively shackled the taciturn, fierce-browed young man to the unavoidably voluble Buddhist; across the sea, across the hemisphere they went, Haneda to Seattle, Seattle to O'Hare, O'Hare to Logan; still no escaping the bond, together they had ridden the bus to Springfield, and then to Northampton, that very bus on which Anne rode, and bled, five years previously. Mr. Kang was entirely alone in the world, he was destined for verminous graduate housing, Waku would not hear of his declining Waku's hospitality.

When she knew Serk better, Anne would more fully appreciate the comedy of his American arrival, involuntarily attached to an oblivious Japanophilic monk. And when Anne had known Serk even longer, if perhaps not correspondingly better, she would recall Waku's deter-mined kindness, which Serk barely repaid with civility, and wonder if Waku had in fact not been oblivious at all. Perhaps Waku had seen in Serk what Anne didn't yet know to look for: the inexhaustible source of grievance that made Serk a permanent traveler, even then, his first time on a plane, his first trip overseas.

When the day had cooled down, they took a walk amid the frilled and fluted campus buildings like so many white wedding cakes, across the verdant quad that made Anne think of the enormous living flag of an ancient, undiminished aristocracy. She always half expected to be arrested for stepping on it. Dr. Grassi and Waku were walking to-gether, Waku unselfconsciously drawing attention with his ungainly footwear. It took an effort to lag behind them, but Anne made it. Mr. Kang—Serk—matched his pace to hers.


At first they were like any pair of lovers. The extent of their physical compatibility awed them, and they were grave and dedicated in its service. Much of the time they felt no need to talk. When they did talk, the somber intensity of their sex carried over, but the fit was less snug. They rarely laughed, bantered, chided. Each disclosed his or her life to the point of their meeting with an air of cool regret that tended to ratify their prior isolation, ratify their meeting. The world had not been fit for either of them; this suggested they were fit for each other.

Anne found herself exaggerating the stinginess of her family, their frail affections, their capacity for censure, which in truth were qualities that barely applied. Anne's siblings had deplored her affair with Adrian, but rightly. When she exiled herself from them they did not hunt her down, they did not drag her back, yet it wasn't from a deficit of caring. They were decent, loyal people, but it was in the family style to leave large spaces, to accept a lack of explanation, to assume that aid not requested was aid not required. Their father had imposed seven successful pregnancies and at least a few miscarriages on their mother; all of them adored and admired her, but only the oldest girls could remember conversation with her, mostly because at some point each had tied on an apron and started to help. The boys went out into the neighborhood at age eight or nine and found work. Anne's brother Mel, at age four or five, had fallen from a chair while trying to make himself lunch in the kitchen and broken his arm; he told no one, and it was only discovered when they saw him at the table that night, his face the color of paste, and unable to lift his own fork. Their father had been a failed inventor, passing most days and nights in a workshop out back full of half-built contraptions; if he appeared, it was to rant about ideas of his that unscrupulous people had stolen. And yet there had always been music, and books, and the concerts they staged, with their mother as their audience of one, standing enthralled at the foot of the stairs, her apron still damp from the dishwater. Anne on the bottommost step, or the topmost, far outside their mother's line of sight. Anne was the last of them all, unlucky seven. Least expected, least needed, last in line for the attention of a well-meaning mother who'd run dry of it around child number five. Anne had been washed and dressed by her sisters, protected and scolded by her brothers, but a little bit neglected by them all, who perhaps eventually saw her as their collective failure. This suspicion was the real reason she sometimes disliked them.

To Serk, though, she presented them as people purely to escape.

How else to justify having escaped them? For, unlike her, Serk had no
family at all.

None? No one?

"I am alone in this world entire and completely!" This was said
more with annoyance than grief.

Serk's English was outstandingly expressive, and he was proud of
it—unlike some foreigners, he was not inhibited by native speakers. If
he wasn't speaking in a situation, Anne learned, it was because he was
bored, scornful, or wary, not because he was shy. His reticence was
often taken as timorousness, which combined with his angry good
looks was found charming by these mistaken observers. If only, Anne
thought, they could afterward hear what he said.

"Stupid woman."

"These goddamn son-bitches."

He hated most of all people who fawned on his origins—they were
so proud of themselves, for showing an interest in faraway places.
Pursuing this theme, Serk once interviewed a monkey at the Springfield zoo:

"So glad to meet you. I've been so wanting to welcome you into
this country.

"Is it true you join us here from *Africa*? Oh! How fascinating.

"You must demonstrate that very special way that you eat the banana. You *peel* with your *toes*? What a beautiful culture you have!"

So it wasn't true he never made her laugh. Sometimes, early on,
she felt she'd split her sides from laughing, when he mocked her countrymen, when she was his ally. It was important, then, not to make
those mistakes, to find the right way of learning about him. Avoiding
fascination, exclamation. Yet also avoiding pretenses of knowledge,
assumptions that turned out to be wrong. If she succeeded she might
be rewarded with a rare story of his Japanese boyhood. Of stealing
a baked sweet potato and burning his fingers. Of hiding under old
boats overturned on the beach. He was barely two years older, yet he
seemed to have come from the faraway past. His stories were devoid
of other people; they contained just one small boy, alone.

Their third summer together they planned a civil service wedding, to be performed by the Smith College chaplain and attended by their few college town friends, a ragtag international group, all of them distant from homelands except Dr. Grassi, though Dr. Grassi was also exiled, from wherever he'd once been a picked-upon boy. It was not a context in which any guest was likely to wonder, let alone ask, why neither the bride nor the groom had invited a blood relation. But the groom had been informed of all the bride's family members she preferred not to see. The bride still knew nothing. Anne didn't view the impending wedding as an event that required greater knowledge, so much as an event that might bring knowledge forth. She had a feeling of time running out. "Is there really no one you should write to? Do you really have no family at all?"

"That's none of your goddamn business!" Serk exploded at her. "Who the hell are *you*, to ask about *my* family?"

After that, even the depopulated memories of boyhood were no longer shared. Something Anne had said or done inhibited Serk, closed the half-open door. Trying to determine what her error had been ran the risk of committing another. Anne bit her tongue and waited. It did not occur to her that the briefly opened door, those slender glimpses of the past, might have been the exception to a rule of pure silence. It did not occur to her that, far from ruining the enchantment she and Serk briefly shared, she might have created it, for one who'd never had anything like it, and whose inability to sustain it was no fault of hers.

Louisa was born the year after their move to Rolling Prairie, where Serk had his first real professorship at the state college. Among other frantic preparations, Serk bought them a Kodak Instamatic. Through all of Louisa's infancy Anne managed to take just one good picture, of Serk in their armchair from Goodwill and impossibly tiny Louisa propped up in his lap, little more than a bundle of bunting with a shock of black hair and a pair of black eyes half eclipsed behind a pair of fat cheeks. Yet she already shared not only Serk's expression, but his force of personality. The two of them appeared identically regal, and grim, as if awaiting a correction of substandard conditions.

Anne and Serk rarely used the camera, because they were always so harried and flustered, as if the baby were a permanent emergency; when Serk blessedly left to teach class Anne was so tired, less from the baby than from his hectoring worries, that she would fall asleep on the floor next to Louisa's playpen while Louisa lay gazing from her solemn black eyes. But she wasn't really an emergency, Anne felt, nor was she generally solemn. She was fat and game, she chortled as if to assure Anne against Serk's conviction that she would promptly die if her diaper change or her bottle were the slightest delayed. Anne was certain Louisa smiled earlier than other babies, that when Louisa started pointing, she was expressing a complex idea for which she'd soon have the words. And indeed it seemed that Louisa had hardly begun to sit up by herself when, as Anne drove her home from a visit to the pediatrician, from the enormous throne of vinyl bumpers and chrome bars and leather straps Serk had installed in the car's back seat as if preparing for his child to be launched in *Sputnik*, Louisa cried distinctly "Aitch! Aitch!" and Anne, swiveling just in time to see her baby pointing with triumph at the H-shaped goalpost of the high school football field, nearly drove off the road in her shock. She almost hadn't told Serk, but of course she'd told Serk; their belief in their child's extraordinariness was the only thing they still shared with each other.

Anne often wished that she could simply be alone with Louisa, that the nightly moment Serk burst through the door apparently convinced that Anne had nearly killed Louisa in his absence could be put off indefinitely. One time after Louisa had started to crawl, Serk came home to find her with the diaper cream tube in her fist, and though she'd only been slobbering on it he shrieked with fury at Anne, and only made himself forgivable by going to pieces, actually weeping at the vision, all in his mind, of Louisa chewing through the diaper-cream tube and swallowing small bits of metal that would tear through her organs. As Louisa grew bigger, Anne had to campaign for each toy—it seemed there was no toy, not even a soft rubber ball, that might not kill a child if the child had such a negligent mother as Anne. And yet, one day after Louisa had started toddling, and toddled outside stark naked, and there finding mere nakedness insufficient also uprooted a pair of Anne's zinnias and gloried with them while Anne, almost crying from laughter, took more pictures with the Kodak Instamatic than she had the whole previous year, their racist old neighbor came outside in his undershirt shouting that Anne should be locked up for letting her (half-breed, Anne would have bet that he wanted to say) child parade naked in public and what was worse taking photos, and Serk had stormed over to the neighbor's that night, and shouted that his daughter was an innocent baby, and her mother had done nothing wrong, and if the man wanted trouble Serk could give it to him with Serk's *fists*!

So there were moments like that, when Anne could feel that Louisa brought Anne and Serk to the same side. But the moments when they were divided were far more numerous.

Long before the public nudity scandal, when Louisa was just one year old, Anne enrolled her in a baby swim class at the Y, new studies having shown that children should learn swimming before they turn four, and Anne having turned out to be the kind of new mother who reads the new studies. Serk had been so incensed he'd shown up at the Y and shouted Anne down in the parking lot, but Anne had not survived their marriage thus far to surrender to this much unreason. The earth was more than half-covered with water, she shouted back at him, how would he like it when his daughter fell into some water and drowned, because in his ignorant fear he had not let her learn how to swim? And though the fight had far from ended there, the following week, when she was squeezing Louisa into the sausage-skin swimsuit with ruffles ringing the tummy that made her picture Louisa as a baby hippo in a ballet tutu, the door to Serk's study remained closed. Anne put Louisa in the car and started the engine, and Serk did not chase them outside. Then Anne drove away toward the Y—who would ever guess, from this road between endless cornfields, that nearby were great lakes like inland oceans, that indeed all of this had been ocean in some ancient time?—and it suddenly occurred to her that perhaps her hypercritical, volatile husband, who had crossed a vast ocean to live in this country, himself didn't know how to swim. Perhaps his rage was concealing his fear.

---

Anne was alone in the kitchen when the astonishing phone call arrived to reverse the conditions of almost seventeen years. Louisa at school. Serk teaching class. Anne washing the breakfast dishes staring sightlessly into the yard. But of course, it occurred to her later, Adrian would have chosen this time. Midmorning, midweek, the housewife's time alone to make her lists. A decade into marriage and Anne had still not improved her housekeeping, still had not made her lists, and even without the call wouldn't have gotten out of the house for at least another hour with her poorly organized single list in hand to make her poorly organized rounds. She still listed by need, not location. She still drove to the hardware store and stared at the word *milk*, then drove to the grocery and stared at *paintbrush*. But perhaps Adrian allowed for her having evolved. He called at nine a.m. as if to catch her before she departed, little knowing she was still in her housedress, her hands covered in suds. Or perhaps he knew exactly how little she'd changed and had called at this hour to catch her this way.

Regardless of Adrian's thought process, she was alone. That was what mattered, that no one had been there to see her face change.

"Norma and I have decided to send Tobias to his grandparents' this summer. We would like you to spend time with him. Perhaps introduce him to your daughter. He will like that. He will miss his sisters."

*His sisters who* aren't *my daughter*, Anne might have said if she hadn't been speechless.

Adrian's tone proceeded from as lofty an altitude as ever. If anything his condescension traveled even further, but the very proposal was evidence of desperation. They were clearly, unprecedentedly desperate, Adrian and Norma, his wife. Only desperation could have brought about such a phone call. For much of the past year, since turning sixteen, Tobias had been exhibiting extraordinary behaviors. Precise examples were withheld, but Anne gleaned an impression of wild gusts of fury, directed equally at self as at others. School had become impossible, as had home life. Adrian and Norma of course could have weathered any storms that Tobias presented, but the safety of his two younger sisters, these sisters it had previously been Tobias's lifelong habit to adore with a selflessness uncharacteristic of regular children, could not be risked.

These sisters must be ten and twelve, Anne calculated. Both ahead of Louisa. There was something the matter with them, Anne had always suspected. It came across in the annual letters Anne received at a post office box per the adoption agreement she'd signed. For example, over the years Anne had learned Tobias was "a great help to his sisters, particularly in the matter of their physical therapy," or that Tobias had "designed clever flash cards, colorfully decorated with his own art" to assist his two sisters, then both at an age where they might have been reading, "to recognize letters and numbers." Yes, something was wrong with them both; Anne's imagination had long ago sketched the rough picture. Birth defects, flattened faces, uncoordinated limbs. And tending to them—therapeutically pumping their legs on the exercise mat, unsqueamishly wiping their drool, illuminating with whimsical drawings their alphabet flash cards—their gold-haired, straight-backed, handsome older half brother. Anne hadn't seen or smelled him, clutched his body, heard his mutters and squawks, since the first forty-eight hours of his life. It had been sixteen years of the annual letter, the annual school photograph from the crown of his head to his collar, without knowing how tall he was or what his voice sounded like—without any right to know beyond what the letter disclosed, by the terms she had signed. And now to be told he was strange and incorrigible, that something was wrong with him, too.

"I'm sure a change of scene will help," she heard herself dumbly agreeing. Yes, she remembered that Adrian's parents lived just an hour outside Rolling Prairie, over the Indiana line. Tobias would join them when the summer began. In the fall he would enter their local high school. Anne was encouraged to pay him a visit, spend time, here was the grandparents' telephone number.

Twelve years ago, she might have sobbed with gratitude. Nine years ago, she might have screamed with outrage. In this moment, there was only stunned, mute compliance. It was almost as an after-thought that she asked, "Does he know who I am?"

"Of course," Adrian said with offense, at her suggestion that he might have violated the thoughtful agreement. Then he added crisply, "He knows you are his mother *biologically speaking.*"

That put her in her place, didn't it. By the end of the call she was wishing Adrian and Norma luck in surmounting the difficulty, express-ing regret it had happened.


The strawberry farm lay along the state highway Anne drove every year in late July or early August when it became so hot the molded-plastic pool filled from the garden hose no longer quenched Louisa's desper-ation to be fully submerged. The worst of the summer heat coincided with the worst summer doldrums; the yarn crafts they happily pursued in the other three seasons made their sweaty skin crawl from the fibers; the garden they'd thrilled to in June was a region of insects and drought; and baking of course was impossible. Even without the contribution of the weather, the mood as they set out was already heated, crackling tinder for the strawberry farm's sign. Up from featureless farmland and yearly amnesia the sign reared with its enormously red, luscious berries that continued to taunt despite the farm being long since picked clean; hot and sweaty Louisa erupted with the yearly complaint. *Every* year they missed out! *Every* year Anne swore they would pick-their-own next year, *every* year Anne forgot once again!

Tobias's arrival that June brought the strawberry farm for the first time unbelatedly into Anne's mind. Once it was there, it took on an ordained appearance. Anne couldn't form a single other idea of what to do with Tobias. Strawberry-picking would be wholesome, menial, far from her home. It would not only make Louisa happy but absorb her full attention. At age almost-eight, Louisa seemed to Anne the lucky prisoner of her own waking dreams. She could spend hours gaping en-raptured at a Mason jar full of trapped bugs. And Tobias was not quite seventeen, as good as a ten-year age difference at a time in their lives

when those ten years would be worth more than ever again. It might be
enough to confer mutual invisibility. If not, at least indifference.

But scarcely has Anne begun driving than Louisa's head snaps up
from her book as if alerted by a loud noise or strong smell. "This isn't
the right direction," she says.

"I'm picking up a friend to bring with us."

"Who? Marguerite?"

Anne isn't ready for this. "Just a young man who's staying nearby
for the summer."

"Why's he coming with *us*?"

"He's the son of some family friends. I told them I'd show him
around."

"*What* family friends?"

"No one you know, Louisa."

"Are you sure I don't know them?"

"Very sure."

"Then how do *you* know them?"

Anne is driving too fast; she stamps the brake and Louisa lurches
and snaps back, the book flying out of her hands. "Hey!" she cries,
fumbling after it.

"That's what happens when you distract me while I'm driving."

After a moment of silent travel, Anne risks a glance in the rearview
mirror. Louisa stares down at her book, almost certainly at the wrong
page. Anne cannot make it up to Louisa without undercutting her
own authority. It crosses her mind that she behaves worst to Louisa
when already worried she's not doing well. Then, Louisa's mere existence seems to throw emphasis on Anne's shortcomings, and Anne in
self-defense throws guilt and blame back, which against justice stick.
Louisa is a high-strung, fastidious child, always quick to believe she
has failed.

But she is equally a powerful, confident child when conditions are
right: the genetic hauteur that is Serk's contribution.

Coming to the end of the elaborate directions, Anne is startled
to find that Adrian's parents live in a mobile home park, of the kind

where the wheels of the trailers are hidden by trellises and boxes of fake or real flowers. *We're not going anywhere*, the trailers insist, but the tidy one belonging to Adrian's parents is still much smaller than the very small house Anne and Serk and Louisa live in; indeed, the person who must be Tobias has to duck as he comes out the door at the sound of the car. Anne's breath leaves her, takes up again slightly off-rhythm, as if this were a filmstrip someone had poorly spliced. By the time Anne manages to get out of the car, two more people have squeezed out of the trailer and attached themselves to either side of Tobias like a pair of ugly old dogs to their princely master. Tobias is taller than Anne, but otherwise her own younger image. Either the annual photo in its fixity and flatness has fallen even wider of Tobias than most cheap portraits do, or this past year has both subsumed his boy's shoulders and chin within those of a man and filled the outlines as closely as those might be filled with an essence of Anne. Even the ugly old people who must be Adrian's parents, whom Anne has never met, whose idea of her, because entirely of Adrian's making, must be as unflattering as proud adherence to the facts will allow, seem awed. They stare back and forth as if at a pair of celebrities.

"Toby, won't you give Anne a kiss," rasps the old woman finally. Jeannette is her name, Anne remembers. Her stooped, barrel-shaped husband: Roland. They are old, slow, and heavy, and they live in a small mobile home. The unfitness of the arrangement unnerves Anne profoundly. For a moment Adrian's judgment, which has so demeaned her and misshapen her life, comes seriously into question—for, despite that judgment's concluding so strongly against her, for the sake of this boy standing before her she's had to believe it was sound.

Louisa has gotten out of the car and come to stand next to Anne, leaning against Anne's hip in her way of not affection but aggression, demanding Anne bear her whole weight. Tobias steps forward and pecks Anne's cheek as if she were an aunt, reaches down and tries to shake Louisa's hand, oblivious to or politely ignoring Louisa's instant effusions of hatred, her refusal to meet his hand with hers, her sideways flinch away from his approach and into Anne's side as if she were a toddler of two. Can Louisa discern the resemblance? Anne prays she cannot. Any adult with eyes could, and Louisa is, as all her teachers say, precocious—but just this year she argued with Anne that their black-and-white Zenith showed pictures in color, refusing to believe Anne's explanation that it was her own rich imagination, filling in what was missing. "I'm not *imagining*," Louisa shrilled, reduced to angry tears. "I can *see* Big Bird's yellow and Oscar's green and his trash can is gray!" Louisa retreats to the car while Anne explains to Jeannette and Roland in excessive and unasked-for detail where the farm is located and what it is called and even, as the awkward moment stretches on, how she and Louisa have driven past so many times but never yet managed to stop.

In the car Tobias stares ahead, remote and self-contained, as if riding a bus. Anne can't stop prattling on about the scanty features of the region, the possibility they will see an Amish buggy on the road (they do not), the presence, not far off, of the state park with the nice lake for swimming. Tobias sometimes barely perceptibly nods. His reserve is ambiguous. Unlike Louisa's, it doesn't broadcast resentment or suspicion, though perhaps if Anne knew him it would. Anne doesn't know him. Their brief association long ago, when he lived in her body and then a few days in her arms, has no bearing. Even his physical resemblance to her doesn't invite intuition. If anything it has the opposite effect. The longer he sits beside her in the car, the stranger he seems. She's reminded of a television show, perhaps it was a *60 Minutes*, about twins separated at birth and raised with no contact and then reunited. Look at the twin boys, men now, both mathematicians; in their separate childhoods both built the same model airplanes, played the same position in baseball, refused the same foods. Twin girls, raised on opposite sides of the country; in the same year both chose the same Butterick pattern for their mothers to make them, even the same color fabric. A mystical bond. There is no such thing here but its opposite, a vacuuming absence of sympathy. Louisa and Tobias's blood bond hadn't even crossed her mind until now, hadn't even accrued the reality required to merit disavowal. It's as if Anne has lost the knack for basic math, can't finish the simplest equation. The tie between Louisa and Tobias must be equal to the tie between Tobias and herself, but the further she pursues this fundamental idea, the more evasive and bewildering it grows. Does Louisa intuit Tobias, on the basis of blood, as Anne somehow cannot?

At the strawberry farm they are given their baskets, pointed to the rows least picked-over, warned that at the far side of the field on the property line is an electrified fence behind which they'll see horses at pasture. "So don't try to pet 'em! There's warning signs but we still like to mention, when folks got young children," the woman tells Anne. Anne feels the woman is making a rather big show of her kindness. Scorching them with the beams of her approbation, likely thinking, *What a handsome blond boy, the very likeness of his mother, and what a scowling and dark little thing, that one must be adopted, perhaps one of them "boat people" you see in the news.*

They have the fields to themselves as they move through the rows. The sky is flawlessly blue and despite the early hour the sun beats down like noon; somehow it had not occurred to her that a vast agricultural field would not have any shade. Enjoyment seems impossible. She hears her voice inexhaustibly nagging. *Oh, here's a good one, look, Louisa, it's shaped like a heart! Have you tried one yet? No? But they're your favorite fruit and these are going to be so much better than the ones that we buy at the grocery store, those have been in the fridge and that ruins their sweetness.* Periodically returning to the edge of the field, trading full buckets for empties, noticing that each time they resume, Louisa strays a little farther away. Now she's a dozen rows over, her curtain of jet-black hair hanging down, hiding her face.

"Louisa!" Anne calls. "Don't go close to that fence."

"I *know*," Louisa says irritably.

"I'll take them," Tobias, appearing out of nowhere at Anne's shoulder, says of the newly full buckets, and it might be the first time he's spoken.

Runnels of sweat sting Anne's eyes. She fills her bucket again, finds an empty one sitting nearby. They are picking too much; they already have far more than they'll eat or than Anne can preserve; the activity has exhausted its usefulness and now they're driven on mechanically as if there might be a hope they could strip the field bare. *Stop,* Anne tells herself. Straightening up, she sees Tobias some distance away, upright also and empty-handed now, no longer picking, just walking along between rows. He has an air of leisure, even pleasure. Anne's chest lifts: Perhaps this is all he needed. A moment of freedom. Perhaps whatever has gone wrong with him won't go wrong anymore. As if in reprimand for such outsize self-congratulation, her heart quickens: Louisa has vanished. But no, she's just gone the opposite way, toward the tent of the farm stand, where the proprietress sits. Louisa looks hot, finished with it. "Sweetie?" Anne calls. Louisa straightens up, gapes back at her. "Sweetie?" Anne calls again, and then obeying the signal of Louisa's face turns to follow the line of her gaze. Past the far side of the field, where the rows end and give way to grass, she sees Tobias standing just at the electrified fence, and behind the fence a horse walking toward him.

"Tobias!" Anne shouts. Though it can't be, this feels like the first time she's spoken his name. Even as she's shouting, he unhesitatingly steps forward, reaching both arms through the fence, as if to clasp the horse around its neck. With quick violence his body flies backward and he comes off his feet, like something meant to be funny, a scene out of one of Louisa's Bugs Bunny cartoons. He lands hard on his back in the grass with an audible thump that Anne feels like a blow to her chest and that steals the air from her lungs so she can't even call as she runs; her voice seems to grunt senselessly in her ears as it does when she's trapped in a nightmare. Tobias lies flung in the grass, his skin ghastly and gray like damp plaster. Dead. Arbitrarily she birthed him, arbitrarily she's killed him. "What in God's name was he doing that for!" cries the farm woman, somehow right behind her. "What on earth! Like he did it on purpose!"

Later on, Anne will hear the explanations: The fence is designed to deter, not to kill. That is, to deter animals, with the shock it delivers. Humans, it is generally expected, are deterred by the yellow and black warning signs.

This only explains his survival. It doesn't explain why he did it. For that explanation, they seem to be looking to her: the farm woman, the paramedics, even Louisa, platter-eyed and motionless and disregarded at the margin of the bustle, all traces of sulk and sass gone, replaced by lonesome fright. She's seen accidents before, saw a young friend with her arm sliced wide open and soaking a towel in blood, but there's something worse here, something sinister in how willful the mishap. Hence the silent demand for an explanation that Anne can't supply. The paramedics frown in concentration, cinch the blood-pressure cuff, shift him onto a stretcher, Tobias's eyes gazing up at the sky. He'll be taken to St. Joseph's. Anne follows behind, one hand cupping Louisa's brown shoulder, the other rooting frantically into her purse for the grandparents' number.

"I've got your berries all put in quart boxes," the farm woman shouts in reminder. Anne turns to her in surprise and glimpses, before it can change its expression, the woman's cold, judging face.

When Jeannette and Roland arrive they are amazingly decent to Anne, almost apologetic. They share a seemingly abashed expression as if they had sold Anne a defective bill of goods and only half hoped to get away with it. Or perhaps this is Anne's own feeling she sees in their faces, perhaps they had not expected catastrophe any more than she had but are only better at absorbing it. They tell her not to wait, to take Louisa home. Incredibly Tobias's vitals are normal, he will be kept under observation a few hours to be sure and then discharged. Anne is halfway back to the car with Louisa when she realizes she did not even ask to see him. Then Louisa says that she needs the bathroom and Anne almost groans aloud, to have her failure to have asked to see Tobias given this chance for reversal she doesn't desire. She takes Louisa in the main, not emergency, entrance and they don't see Jeannette and Roland.

Louisa dawdles in the stall; when she finally comes out she stares into the sink drain as if hypnotized. Anne feels like a talentless actor intoning her lines when she says, "Louisa, I'm so sorry that happened. That must have been scary." No reply. Louisa only plays with the drain stopper. "I know this might seem confusing, but I need you to help me with something. Can you do a big favor for me?" Still no reply.

Louisa is not a child who thrills to doing "favors" for her mother. Anne should know better than to use such a ploy. "I need you to keep our day secret from Daddy. I'll tell him about it. But I need to wait a little. Okay? Can you make sure you don't mention it to him?" She shouldn't be surprised that a request for secrecy immediately breaks her child's silence, by stoking her suspicions.

"Why?"

"I just want to tell him myself."

"But who was he?"

"Who was that boy?" Anne repeats, as if Louisa could possibly mean someone else. "Tobias? I told you. He's a friend."

"He's a kid. Adults aren't friends with kids."

"Of course they are. And Tobias is a big kid. He's sixteen years old."

"Are you not going to tell me because of he's dead?"

"He's not dead!" Anne cries. "What on earth made you think that?" As if she hadn't thought it herself.

"He *should* be! He touched *electricity*," Louisa wails. "On *purpose*." Serk has drilled into Louisa, with his usual hyperbole, the many dangers electricity poses; he has stoked the belief in his daughter that if she so much as touches the plug of a lamp she'll be zapped into a smoldering pile of bones.

"He's *not dead*," Anne repeats angrily, towing Louisa back toward the car as if she's done something wrong and deserves to be punished. At the car Louisa screams. In the passenger seat where Tobias had been, the strawberries, cooking in the trapped heat, have bled a crimson stain around the sodden bottoms of their boxes. "What happened to the strawberries?" Louisa screams, as if the strawberries have been each and every one murdered.

"What are you thinking of, screaming like that!" Anne screams back.

Arriving home, Louisa runs to her room and slams her door. Anne goes into the kitchen for a cookie sheet, and back outside slides the sheet under the disintegrating quart boxes, leaving the lurid stain without trying to clean it. It's pointless, it will never come out. The strawberries, though, are not as far gone as she'd thought. They're all right for preserving. Anne puts them in the fridge, cookie sheet and all, and approaches Louisa's shut door with self-conscious kindliness. "Sweetie?" she calls. Cracking open the door, Anne sees Louisa prone on her bed, face pressed into her pillow. The poignancy of her little tush in polyester shorts. Anne realizes they're too small, Louisa's panty line shows. Toes together, heels splayed, motionless. Anne wonders how Louisa can breathe but knows Louisa will not, for the world, turn over to let Anne see her face.

"Sweetie? I think the strawberries will be all right. I'll make preserves."

Further silence. With further kindliness, as if observed by a jury, Anne goes to Louisa's bed and lays a hand on her still-hot, heat-trapping heap of thick coarse black hair that is of such a foreign quality to Anne, though Anne sleeps beside a similar head of hair every night. At Anne's featherlight touch Louisa thrashes with such force Anne leaps back from the bed.

For the rest of the morning and afternoon Anne waits for the call from Adrian, even hopes for it, for the merciless lashing he'll give her, but the call doesn't come. Then Serk is home and she prays it won't, scorches the minute steak, tells Serk that Louisa has come down with a summer cold and Louisa unknowingly cooperates, doesn't come out of her room. Anne checks and finds her fast asleep and reflexively glances upward in gratitude for this small mercy; she did wake Louisa very early. She pulls Louisa's covers over her, goes out to finish the dishes. The phone rings and she snatches it up.

It's not Adrian but Jeannette, her voice thin and bewildered. Tobias had come home all right, gone to sleep, gotten up, had a late lunch all right, but around six p.m. he collapsed. The paramedics and an ambulance again, St. Joseph's again, yet this seemed not to do with the fence—or, rather, the fence seemed to do with *this*: They'd found a growth in his brain. Enormous, "the size of a plum," so that the doctors said it must have been there, and growing, a very long time, perhaps all the previous year. If it wasn't gotten out he would die.

"They're taking him by helicopter to Detroit," Jeannette says. "His parents are flying, they'll meet him there later tonight." In the moment, Anne doesn't hear the no-doubt-unintended exclusion of herself in Jeannette's phrase "his parents," would not have cared if she did. She's only aware of a last chance.

"When's the helicopter leaving?"

"The doctors say soon as possible."

"I'm coming," she says, and hangs up. In the den Serk looks up from the TV; his stern expression shows he already discerns irregularity. "Marguerite is having an emergency. She's sick and her car's broken down. I'm going to take her to the doctor," Anne declares, the lie unspooling easily, carried along by an emotional logic that itself feels true. Marguerite is Anne's only friend, the only person Serk knows of who might exercise such a claim on her, and the only person in whom Anne could confide that she'd told such a lie, and the reasons. And Serk is afraid of Marguerite and keeps his distance from her.

"When will you be back?"

"I don't know. Don't wait up. Louisa's already asleep."

Tobias has been placed in an induced coma as a precaution against seizure. At his bedside Anne sits ringing with panic like a fire alarm except nobody hears her; perhaps in some other part of the world dogs are whining with pain as their eardrums explode. A ventilator screwed onto his smooth face, wires taped to every visible part of him; she longs to feel his body warmth, his soft baby warmth, which is of course irrecoverable. She finally places her palm on his shin where it's hidden beneath the coarse blanket. She tries to think what she would say to him if he were conscious, tries to say it anyway. I've never forgotten about you. I've always loved you. You have always been my child, nothing changes that. It's no use; these wash-worn phrases make everything worse, she might as well be acting out a scene in *General Hospital*. What use is she to him?

If he lives, she'll change everything. She's full of wild, inchoate vows she doesn't know what to do with; of course, she doesn't know how to pray. Her prayers are like those duds in a fireworks display where the thump of the rocket launch keeps on repeating but no bloom of light fills the sky.

Then the helicopter is ready and Tobias is taken away.

When Anne returns home, Louisa's clothes from the day are lying in a heap on the floor of the bathroom, soaked with ghastly red foam. In the kitchen the cookie tray Anne loaded up with the berries and put in the fridge has moved to the kitchen counter and is heaped not just with the spoiling strawberries but chunky pink vomit. Even before Serk starts yelling, Anne knows all that has happened. It took more effort, Anne thinks, for Serk not to have dumped the smelling tray in the trash, not to have dumped the rancid clothes in the washer. But Louisa has been bathed and is sleeping in clean pajamas between clean sheets. Her bedroom floor, the kitchen floor, the bathroom all have been mopped. When Serk is finished telling Anne what he thinks of her, he takes the car key and drives off. And he takes the stain with him, it occurs to Anne with an emotion she needs a moment to name. Satisfaction. It satisfies Anne to think of Serk driving away with that stain at his side.

In the darkened bedroom, Louisa—damply sweet-smelling, as it turns out not sleeping at all—surges into Anne's arms. Holding her, Anne thinks guiltily of how much she loves when Louisa is ill, and clings to her all pliant and soft, like the baby she no longer is.

But Louisa is also sobbing. It takes Anne several guesses to understand what she's trying to say. "I didn't mean he *should* die. I just thought that he *would*."

"He's not dead," Anne tells her again and again, "and he's not going to die. He's just fine," repeating on faith what in fact she will learn the next morning, in a call from Jeannette: that the surgery has been successful, that the tumor's ripe fruit ("like a plum") has been gently eased out, and Tobias will live.

As yet only believing, not knowing, Anne soothes Louisa, until Louisa is falling asleep.

"And I remembered not to tell," Louisa whispers, when Anne tucks her in.

When judged ready for discharge, Tobias returns home with Adrian and Norma to complete his recovery. What a blessing to see his affliction removed. He is once again the gentle, helpful boy he always was. Are we not truly blessed, to live in this great age of medical miracles? Tobias's sisters are overjoyed to have their "Toby" back. It is judged wise to withdraw him from school for a while, he will catch up when he regains his strength. Humbly do we thank glorious Christ for our numerous blessings, Happy New Year, 1977—all this Anne learns from the annual letter, which though longer and more pious than usual is otherwise of a piece with the rest of the series.

The door which so unexpectedly opened swings shut again, disappears. Anne's letter to Adrian requesting to visit Tobias is politely rebuffed. Recovery, Rest, Avoidance of Excitement, Reassess Condition in Future. She sees Tobias open his arms to the horse, fly back onto the grass. Neither Adrian nor Norma ever calls or writes to reprove her about it, and she wonders if they know. Perhaps Jeannette and Roland, feeling culpable as well, haven't told them. Tobias could tell them. Has he? Has he chosen not to? Or has he forgotten? Perhaps the trauma to his brain has caused memory loss and he remembers nothing, not the strawberries or horse or electrified fence or Louisa or Anne. Not a trace of their brief time together.

At first, she can't bear to believe this. Then she can't bear not to. He could ask Adrian and Norma's permission to call her or write her. Even if denied, he could do it in secret, by contacting her through the grandparents. For months she expects this to happen although at the same time she never expects it to happen. She promised to change everything if he lived and of course she's changed nothing.

# Serk

**Late at night** the meagerness of his campus, the ugly square buildings that all had been built in the previous decade, the absence even of
mature trees let alone a stained-glass window or an ivy-coated brick
wall, bothered him less because less visible. Growing up as he had,
such images of stained glass and ivy had twined themselves irresistibly
into his ambition with the tenacity of ivy fixing its myriad feet to a
wall. He didn't even know where these mental images of his had come
from, though he supposed Japan had not lacked that kind of aspirational architecture, modeled on the British medieval cathedral, some
of which had even survived the war. In his youth he had associated
these careful imitations of centuries-old religious structures of stone
with the modern, the future, and now he associated the ugly square
buildings of his campus not with the modern or the future but with
failure, which perhaps betrayed his total lack of understanding of art,
but he had never had the luxury to study such things. This was why he
needed the help of the woman at the library, Barbara. Had it not been
so late, had the library been open, he would have gone there. That was
a beautiful building, in his opinion the best in the town. It had been
built by the American philanthropist Andrew Carnegie, Barbara had
told him. But it closed at 5:00 p.m., and it was currently 10:00.

He'd been watching PBS in the recliner when his daughter had
appeared at his elbow and climbed onto the armrest. When he'd

switched his beer from one hand to the other to make room for her, he'd felt her clamminess despite the warm night. "Where's Mommy?" she'd asked with her face in his shoulder.

"You have fever? Let me feel your forehead." He'd tried to tuck her hair out of the way.

"No," she'd evaded, springing off his lap. "I want to go back to bed." He hadn't heard her take the tray of fruit out of the fridge, a heavy task, and somehow get it to her bedroom. Just a few minutes later he was sprinting down the hall to her, the *NewsHour* not even having come to an end. She must have devoured a quart of the soggy, spoiled berries in just a few minutes.

That obvious negligence—putting their child to bed without dinner, leaving spoiled fruit in the fridge to tempt her—was connected to his wife's other, ambiguous negligence, of leaving the house at an hour when she never went out. He didn't believe the lie about Marguerite and the doctor, but he also didn't have any other guess where Anne had gone, while at the same time his daughter's violent vomiting had terrified him. His only recourse was to stay out of the house for the same length of time that his wife had stayed out, to make the point to her by action that he couldn't have put into words. It was too late for everything, certainly too late for the beer he badly wanted. He wished he'd thought to bring one or two from the fridge, but this might have betrayed him as having no compelling destination. It might have let his wife guess that he was only coming to sit at his ugly desk, in his ugly office.

He had nevertheless tried to make the office comfortable, because once in a while, when he was teaching night classes, Anne brought Louisa to drop off his dinner, and then Louisa crawled everywhere and pored over everything in a state of inexplicable but charming fascination. She was old enough, even, to help him in his project of transforming his humiliating office. She had begun making him decorative objects, and these he carefully displayed: the cardboard orange-juice can disguised to seem made of wood with glued Popsicle sticks, in which he put his pens; the crumbly plaster bowl, in which he put his spare change; and the lumpy clay paperweight that was meant to resemble a turtle, though its four legs had not stayed attached. Only five and six years old when she'd created these things; her mind was always at work, it amazed him. He was trying to make her a present as well, and nights he didn't feel compelled to leave the house, blown on a gust that he couldn't control, he worked on the gift in their basement, and entered a rare sort of peace from using only his hands, not his mind.

At least, with it being the summer, he had not had to see anyone "burning the midnight oil," as happened during the school year. His building, like the campus in general, was utterly deserted. His office's other domesticating object was a hot plate, and he brewed himself a cup of instant coffee while removing from the locked drawer of his desk the accordion file in which he kept correspondence. He had a letter in progress that he extracted, as well as the series of received letters. It bothered him that their glaringly foreign airmail sheets, outweighed by their numerous conspicuous stamps, arrived so often at his office, despite such exoticism being, as he knew, almost expected of him, as the only foreigner on the permanent teaching staff. That he was using his college letterhead and not an airmail sheet himself was pure vanity for which he'd pay with the stamps.

Running his eyes over his characters, he read, where he'd left off, "I cannot even begin to consider this without having confirmation in hand," and then he had to go back to the most recent letter to refamiliarize himself with Soonja's latest equivocation. Or perhaps it was confusion, or ill-founded conviction, or just a function of her wretched written Japanese, arrested at the level of a child; she'd never had a scientific mind in the first place, her emotionalism often caused her to misrepresent supposition as fact, and being obliged to write him in her poor Japanese because his written Korean was undeniably worse likely added resentment to the other counterfactual tendencies in her personality; they might have last seen each other almost twenty years before, but he was still her elder brother. He still remembered all her shortcomings.

"The permits are certain, the time is not certain, it cannot be made certain until <u>you</u> because for just a short length so <u>you</u> are the problem as I said in my letter before. Should I tell our parents you say <u>NO</u>?"

Serk now further removed his cigarettes from the locked drawer, and the filthy ashtray he did not even empty into his office waste-basket, but carried outside to some distant trash can, for fear Louisa might come by with Anne to surprise him while there were still butts and ash in the wastebasket. He knew better than the health-crazed Americans the damage cigarette smoke could do to a child. He'd had to put an end to one of Louisa's neighborhood friendships because the child's mother smoked, even while driving with the children in her car.

It took him a long time, actually longer than he'd meant to spend in his office as Anne's punishment, to rebut Soonja's latest, despite the fact that her latest contained little information that was new. Ever since the start of this year they'd been conducting the argument, across the sheets of seven letters so far, his current one making eight. Even as he restated his position once again, he felt how it had weakened from conviction to stall tactic. Until this year he and Soonja had exchanged no more than five letters in their lives, the bare number required to notify each other of their address changes and big events. She knew he had a wife and a daughter. He knew she had divorced, that her two sons were grown. It was not that their lives were so uneventful—they were as eventful as most lives, he supposed. But the blinding blank that year after year kept re-effacing their shared family, like an eraser that never stopped rubbing, seemed to rub them out, too. Serk would stare at a blank sheet of paper and his hand couldn't reach for a pen. And if his and Soonja's letters over two decades were insubstantial, the rarer letters that Soonja had received from their family members were even more so. They seemed to regurgitate state news broadcasts her-alding record crop yields while in the next sentence asking for mung beans or any other nonperishable. It was not even clear, often, who'd sent the letter; their siblings were grown, Soonja couldn't discern their handwriting.

But at the start of this year had come a sudden eruption of news and of new urgency, conveyed first to Soonja, then via Soonja to Serk. Their father was unwell. The DPRK government was issuing permits for the Wonsan-Niigata ferry. These details in themselves maddened Serk with their vagueness, whether the vagueness began with their parents, or was added by Soonja, or both: What was their father's illness? What care was he receiving? What was the prognosis? If their father was ill, did this mean their mother was well? What about their siblings? And these permits—what exactly were they permitting, and when? Could their family return to Japan permanently? Letter by letter, Soonja grew more confusing or perhaps more confused, but also more insistent: They were coming, he must come, he was an American with a green card and wealth, he must drop everything and just come. Stop these demands for guarantees!

To be reading and writing such words, no matter if they were in Japanese, then folded and sealed, then presumably traveling in the guts of an airplane with no one slitting them open en route, filled him with inchoate fear so that he sometimes grabbed the one photo he kept in the office, of himself and Louisa when she was an infant, and stared at it as if the image might otherwise disappear. He hadn't forgotten the UMass Amherst recruiter who asked, "Any difficulties?" He hadn't forgotten any part of his visa process, or the interview his first year of grad school, when despite the perfect legality of his visa a pair of government men showed up asking for him in his department, then took him into a conference room for a conversation about why, though he'd come to the US from Japan, he had a Chinese last name. His explanation, true though it was, had rattled implausibly in his own ears—that while the Kang name did occur in China, it occurred more often in Korea; that while Koreans occurred more often in Korea, they also occurred in Japan—while the actual question, not explicitly asked nor explicitly answered, still was clear to them all: Are you or have you ever been a member of, or sympathetic to, or affiliated in any way with a member of or sympathizer with, the Communist Party?

He could only hope Soonja no longer had ties with the Organization, although, apart from her first-grade year, theirs were the only schools she had ever attended; but he could not risk asking her this in these letters he imagined being read by people other than her; and the fact that she never named the Organization could equally mean she'd left them long behind, or that she was so deeply involved that she fully understood the poor appearance such involvement gave. When she wrote phrases like, "I have it on authority they're coming, the permits are for older people in good standing, obviously that is what our parents are," he heard the voice of a central authority, but was she mimicking her parents' letters, or an authority closer at hand?

He covered no new ground in the letter he sealed that night and put in his briefcase to take to the post office, but there was in fact something new he not only had omitted from the letter but wished he could omit from his mind. If he hadn't been a scientific man he would have called it a sign that supernatural vengeance exists, for the person who tries to renounce his birthplace. The college where he earned his living, obscure in every way, as distant reputationally as geographically from Harvard, was nevertheless pursuing "educational exchange" in the form of sister schools in Asia. This meant, of course, "free" Asia, particularly Taiwan and Japan. There were government grants. The idea had predated Serk; he sometimes suspected it was the reason his candidacy for the job had been successful despite his teaching evaluations from grad school, which described him as aloof and impatient.

That fall, Serk's college announced it would send a member of its history department as a visiting professor to Japan, starting the following April. Before the history professor was chosen, Serk was asked if he would like to be considered and said he would not. But the following spring, Serk's department chair approached him about it again. Barely a month into the Japanese school year the history professor had asked for his time to be shortened. His family, Serk's department chair explained, was having a hard time adjusting. The thought was that Serk could replace him. "But I also have a family," Serk said. "My daughter begins the fourth grade in the fall."

"Our thought was, for you there would be no adjustment—"

"It's been very many years since I've been in Japan."

"Just think about it. It would haven't to be September—it could be next January, in time to do their third semester. Lots of time to prepare! Take the summer to think it all over. You'd be doing us all a big favor!" Serk gave the man no reason to hope, any more than he gave Soonja reason to hope. Yet against his every inclination, he was thinking about it. Which did not mean he was considering it—but it would not leave his mind.

That summer, on the way to his office he often stopped at the library. He had come to know Barbara after spending so many hours sitting in the children's section, puzzling over stacks of books he'd gathered off the shelves on the basis of uncertain instinct, that she had probably thought he was some sort of pervert, or so deficient in his English he could not read the books for adults. But once he began to explain, she understood him immediately. "My daughter," he had started off before pausing, not because his English fell short but because his daughter so exceeded description, even her nursery school teachers agreed, "doesn't . . . she isn't . . . this one"—showing the woman the rhyme book called *Green Eggs and Ham*—"she enjoyed when very small—"

"She needs books with more words, and fewer pictures. Where complicated things are going on."

"Yes!" he said gratefully. "She has the books about the bear—"

"She has the Winnie-the-Pooh books? Well, those are wonderful, and just right for most children her age. But it sounds as though she needs books she can stretch toward, as well as books that are comfortable."

So had begun his almost secret life as a library patron, always visiting in the quiet mornings, on his way to his classes, because by the time he left campus each evening the library was closed. Although he knew that the Children's Room must often hold actual children, afternoons and weekends when his own child, and his wife, shared a realm he could not seem to enter, his Children's Room was always empty, with the exception of Barbara, who was long retired, she told him, from a career of teaching children. She had clearly lost none of the qualities— of taking children very seriously, and remembering all of their likes and dislikes—that must have made her an excellent teacher. "And how did *Taran Wanderer* go over?" she asked him as he surrendered that book and its three predecessors.

"She likes this so much we are going to buy our own set."

"Didn't I predict that would happen? Now, my suggestion for this week came out just recently. It's the same author as *Charlie and the Chocolate Factory* but it's very different in style, quite a bit more advanced. This is one that you'll want to read with her."

He would not have admitted to Barbara that when Louisa agreed to be read to at all, it was Anne who did the reading. He was never invited, but nor would he ever have asked. His accented English antagonized his own ears; he feared to think what would happen to Louisa's unaccented, effortless English if she had to listen to him more than strictly necessary.

"How harmful is it, if children are taken away from their country and put into school somewhere else?" he heard himself abruptly ask Barbara, as she checked in the old books and checked out the new ones.

"Do you mean, if the child and her family all go together to a foreign country? That's not necessarily harmful at all. Living abroad can be a wonderful experience for children."

"But what about their native language? Would it cause any problems?"

"To the contrary. The child would not just recall their first language but acquire a second. Children pick up a new language almost without trying. Once they're adults, it's a much bigger effort."

He knew better than most of her patrons how true her words were. But they meant more to him, coming from her. "Thank you," he said, gathering the new books and fitting them carefully into his briefcase.

That August at the college "meet and greet" his department chair, trailed by an unfamiliar Oriental couple, chased Serk down with huge waves and repetitions of his name in a way that could not be avoided. "I'm so glad you're here," the department chair cried. "I was just telling Mr. Lee about you." Mr. Lee, the department chair revealed, was a graduate student from Seoul. He was here on a new fellowship. "So you'll get him settled, show him around! And I'm sure Mrs. Lee will also be happy to have Mrs. Kang's company."

When the department chair had left them, reprising his awkward jog across the parched grass while waving hugely at some new person real or imagined who drew his attention, the young man and his wife launched into bows and honorifics. The young man had a military haircut and wore a black suit in which he must have been very uncomfortable given the heat. The wife was doing only marginally better in an ugly long-sleeved dress that looked like a churchgoing outfit. Serk's own wife, in her narrow green sheath with no sleeves and her frail sandals that in no way concealed her slender white feet, as usual was drawing furtive glances from his colleagues Serk pretended not to notice. Serk and his wife argued about many things—most things—but her knack for dressing herself was not one of them. She seemed not to make any effort, and she was always the best-looking woman. To the couple, cutting short their entirely familiar recitation of the gladness his acquaintance bestowed, Serk said rudely in English, "I don't speak Korean." He'd had to stop himself from mirroring their bows, it was such a deep reflex, but stopping had only required the internal reminder. He'd been an American a long time.

Mr. Lee straightened and his wife followed suit. There was a brief silence.

". . . Good afternoon," Mr. Lee finally said, with confidence in his words, if a struggling accent. "I am pleased to meet you."

"I have never stepped foot in Korea. I was born in Japan."

"Ah," Mr. Lee said.

"Would your wife like to come shopping with me?" Serk's own wife abruptly broke in. "It's a small town, but we have some good stuff. There's a German deli that sells meats and mustard Serk likes. He's says they're the only cold cuts he's ever had in this country that have any flavor."

Serk took his wife's arm and steered her in a smooth arc until they were walking away. "Pleased to meet you," he tossed over one shoulder, as Mr. Lee and his wife made their bows of farewell.

Louisa had begun collecting stamps; Serk bought her an album for them, and a starter pack of world stamps and hinges. Over the summer he'd also built her a desk in the shape of an L, with one of the surfaces for the height she was now, and the other a few inches higher for the height she'd soon be, and he'd painted her a little chair to match. She sat there for remarkable stretches of time like a veritable scholar, lov-

ingly arranging her stamps and, when at last she was satisfied, affixing
them with the hinges. She arranged her stamps by color and picture,
with as it seemed to him no regard for and perhaps no awareness of
nations of origin, and he saw her stamps much the same way, as so
many candies for the eye to enjoy. Even with their cancellations, they
evoked for him no thought of the borders and distances it was their
primary purpose to cross. They were innocent of human transaction.
And even when Louisa, for a game, made a postal route of the inside
of their house, and sent him letters to his armchair and desk, and to
her mother via the kitchen fruit bowl, he drew no connection between
this game of hers—which belonged to the realm of delight of which
she was always the center—and the secret burden of his letters with
Soonja.

One evening as he turned the car into the drive he saw Louisa waiting on the front step for him; she leaped up and rushed for his car window before he'd shut off the engine. "Careful, careful!" he cried, for
you never knew when a running car, even in park, might unexpectedly
move, but she was too overcome with excitement to hear him. She
had an envelope in her hand.

"The postman brought this for you, it has foreign stamps! Please
can I have them? Please *please*?" Of course she could have them, he
perhaps even said, before his eye caught the script on the envelope and
he snatched it from her, to peer at it more closely.

In the house he slammed the door to his study and tore open the
envelope, unaware of where he'd left Louisa stunned in his wake.
Then he stormed out of the house again, still blind and deaf to his
daughter and whatever appeal she made.

By now he had unavoidably come to know Mr. Lee, or rather
"Tom," that being the young man's solution for Tae-Min. He'd been
made more aware than he'd ever desired of Tom's recently concluded
compulsory military service in his homeland, which Tom seemed to
view as having conferred on him a statesman's grasp of geopolitics.
Serk had even endured, thankfully with a beer in his hand, Tom's
sophomoric diatribe on the subject of US imperialism, "and yet here
you are, enjoying US dollars," Serk had pointed out, on one of the

too-many occasions they were thrown together by the college's social machine because they weren't merely the only non-whites, but both Orientals, which surely meant they had all things in common. Yet Serk wasn't aware of a similar fallacy underlying his fury as he banged on Tom's office door and, hardly waiting for an answer, threw it open and the envelope onto Tom's desk. "What goddamn shit is this?" he demanded. "How would you dare it! Giving the place of my *home*— where my own child *lives*—"

Tom studied the envelope. "Do you think I sent you this?" he finally asked.

"I am *saying* you sent it!" Serk cried. "I don't know what the hell you are—some kind of *spy*—"

"A spy who is also so stupid, he travels all the way to New York to mail a shitty propaganda to a person he sees every day?"

"Do you think *I* am stupid? You gave the address of my home to these people! I've never gotten garbage like this in my life! *You* come, and one month later the postman is handing this shit to my child!"

Tom unlocked the lockable desk drawer, the same on his desk as on Serk's, and removed an envelope from it: of the same cheapness, so that it drooped as Tom held it out by one edge; addressed by hand in the same combination of Hangul translated to English for the names, English only for the addresses; and stamped in the same hybrid way, with a domestic US stamp that had the same "New York, NY" cancellation, and the same addition of a second, invalid and superfluous, stamp that was pure decoration. Tom's stamp was different, but clearly from the same series: lavish rectangular oil paintings, in appealing pastels, of a broad-shouldered, tall, smiling man amid other adults. On Serk's stamp, the man knelt at the edge of a field of wheat, touching the stalks with one hand and gesturing with the other, while a group of men and women in traditional Korean peasant dress smiled in apparent appreciation. On Tom's stamp, the same man, but wearing a lab coat, gestured at surrounding shelves of some kind of supplies while white-clad nurses and doctors apparently listened while clapping their hands. "I received mine yesterday," Tom said. "Mrs. Lee and

I are listed in the local White Pages book. I recently confirmed it. I assume you are, too."

Serk felt that the roots of his hair were awash in hot sweat. "Are you telling me that someone in New York is reading the local White Pages for this town in the middle of nowhere?"

"I'm only telling you I have nothing to do with you getting this thing. But if you think that no one is aware of you, the only Korean-named person in your doctoral program all the years you were there, the only one on this whole college faculty, you are more humble than you appear. You told me you don't speak Korean, but you seem to understand it well enough."

"My Korean is a child's."

"But that's enough to read the stamps, isn't it? 'Dear Leader Comrade Kim Il-Sung, Happy 60th Birthday, 1912–1972.' Whoever possessed these stamps has been saving them for a special occasion. Can you read the captions?"

Although it upheld his earlier hyperbole, that he did not know Korean, it still made him feel foolish to admit he could not understand the captions. But without any snide or scornful expression, only squinting at the minuscule characters, Tom read, "'Another Record-Breaking Harvest.' Mine is 'Visiting the Vaccine Factory.' Would you like me to read you the flyer inside?"

"I don't need to hear that to know what it says."

"On that point we are in full agreement."

Before he left, Serk forced himself to do what he knew he must, though it was difficult. "I apologize for the accusation. I was very upset."

"Don't think any further about it. I disliked receiving this also."

He was ashamed to have accused the other man, yet resentful to feel ashamed. The enigma of the episode wouldn't diminish. He considered asking Soonja outright if she still had ties to the Organization— if this entity even still existed—but his hand couldn't put this in writing. She was his sister, she would never hand over his mailing address to a longtime pro-Communist group. But perhaps she'd had it taken from her, without knowing? In his most recent letter, sent not long before, he had admitted to Soonja that, far from preventing his spending a term in Japan, his college was actually trying to send him.

His acquaintance with "Tom" did not become more intimate, nor was it damaged. Serk wanted neither development; he wished he'd never met Tom at all, although he was unaware of the clarity of these feelings until the night the phone rang long after Louisa's bedtime—an hour at which the sound was always as unwanted and shattering as an air-raid siren.

Anne had snatched up the receiver even before he was out of his chair, but after listening a moment bewildered, she held it out to him. "I think it must be Tom's wife."

It was true: he did not speak Korean. Yet it was equally true that there were modes of the language he had never forgotten. A woman's frantic despair; he did not need to catch all the words to feel the unforgotten helplessness, fear, and frustration engulf him. "Quiet, quiet!" he shouted. "Slow down! I can't hear so damn fast!"

It was indeed Mrs. Lee. Tom was gone, she was screaming and crying; he had gone out and never come back. How should she know *where* he'd gone? She only knew he had meant to come back, and that he *hadn't* meant something had happened! She *knew*! No, she didn't know *what*!

The same obscure outrage that impelled Serk to drive to the Lees' boardinghouse that very night—Anne, astonished, insisting on coming with him after getting a neighbor to sit with Louisa—equally impelled Serk to find the woman utterly implausible once he was faced with her. If she knew of no reason whatsoever that Tom might disappear, then what made her think that he had? How did she know he wasn't sitting on the side of the road with a flat tire? Or asleep in the bed of some girl—he was sorry to say such crude things—or sitting on a plane back to Korea? How did Mrs. Lee know *Tom* was the emergency, perhaps he had his own emergency that had called him away? It proved impossible to reason her away from her groundless conviction, and she'd also lost the patience of her landlady, who proved equally determined to have Serk remove Mrs. Lee to his own home. "Goddamn crazy woman," Serk concluded, pulling Anne back to their car before any transfer of Mrs. Lee into their care could be completed. This earned Anne's most scorching glare in response, but it was easy for Anne to feel saintly and sad, not having any comprehension of the irrational, argumentative, and self-canceling things Mrs. Lee had been saying.

In the coming weeks Tom did not reappear, and then Mrs. Lee also was gone. Whether she'd gone to meet Tom, his "disappearance" having been a misunderstanding, Serk didn't learn. He was too consumed by the preparations for his own departure. The decision he'd avoided for so many months had erupted at last. His department chair announced he must make up his mind; Serk told Anne he'd been offered a working sabbatical; and suddenly what had been a most unlikely scenario appeared as a last chance, to be regretted if it wasn't seized. To Soonja he wrote, "I ask that you afford me the time that I need to explain to my wife and my daughter, who know nothing whatsoever about our family, and who will have a very hard time understanding it, being Americans."

# Part II

# Louisa

**Of course there was** something the matter.

Louisa thought it must have to do with the tickets. Perhaps they weren't paid for, or were for the wrong day, or went the wrong place, or went the right place but left from some other airport. Whatever was wrong, her father and mother had been at the counter in a growing argument with the woman who worked there, who called for another woman in the same kind of bright uniform, with a starchy white blouse and striped scarf. Then a man in a blue blazer had come, and person by person it was almost a crowd, with raised voices and jostling. Louisa wasn't even sure which voices belonged to her parents, nor could she see them anymore. But they were at the middle of it, as always.

Louisa's parents were people for whom things went wrong. The car got lost in the lot, or the driving directions were bad, or the check to the gas company never arrived and the stove was turned off. They misplaced things, or forgot facts, or disagreed on the facts, with each other or with other people.

"Japan?" Louisa had said when her parents told her.

"Daddy's been invited," her mother said. "You know he was born and raised there. We can see his homeland. We've never even been out of the country."

Never *even* been "out of the country"—it was a strange thing for her mother to say. Why would they ever go out of the country? Not long ago Louisa's father had driven her across two sets of state lines— from Michigan through Indiana all the way to Chicago, Illinois—to eat his favorite kind of Japanese noodles at a restaurant run by other people from Japan. Louisa didn't know anyone else, on her block or at school, who had done such a thing. She certainly didn't know anyone who went "out of the country." As the raised voices kept overlapping, and the impatient people kept jostling—for the flight was supposed to be boarding, and yet the line of ticket-holders hadn't moved—Louisa, still holding her book very close to her face, crept her backpack up onto her lap, and opened it with her free hand. Item by item, she took inventory. All her carefully chosen equipment embarrassed her now. A travel-size *Code Cracker*, the game to which she was addicted; her little aluminum compass; her foreign-stamps collection in an empty checks box from the bank. Accoutrements of the world traveler, so far as a nine-year-old girl could guess. Her parents had not offered much in the way of suggestion. For a few months before their departure, her mother had taken a Japanese class, sitting down with Louisa each night after dinner to do her own "homework" from an orange and black book. Then her mother started skipping her homework, and said she'd more easily learn when they actually got there. Louisa's father had come home with a set of real-leather suitcases which nested together when empty, and which being real leather were needlessly costly and led to a loud argument. For these reasons and others Louisa could see it was all a bad plan, another instance of her parents not thinking things through. They hadn't made the year of their absence match up with a grade, so that Louisa would miss the second half of the fourth grade and the first half of the fifth. They hadn't tried renting out their house until after the school year started, when most new families would already have someplace to live. They hadn't listed the things they would need to take first, and then bought the luggage to fit, nor saved the price tag from the real-leather luggage, which was not only too costly but it turned out too small, so that they couldn't return or exchange it. They'd done nothing to spare themselves panic, although Louisa had never expected they'd take it so far that the trip wouldn't happen at all.

She hadn't wanted to go anyway, so why wasn't she glad? Perhaps because they had finally rented the house, and couldn't go back, she thought angrily. But was that the real reason? Was it possible that the mystery of urgent preparations, which she hated, was the very thing she felt disappointed to lose?

She should have remembered that crisis, though rarely averted, was often shouted down and elbowed aside. She saw her mother, red-faced, hurrying through the crowd toward her. "Louisa! Why are your things everywhere? Get them packed up, we're boarding."

After they got off the plane at the Tokyo airport, before they found their greeters, or even their luggage, a little boy with black hair like a glossy black bowl pointed and gaped at Louisa. "*Gaijin!*" he cried in thrilled horror. The boy was dragged off by his slim, black-haired Japanese mother, who sternly hushed him, and yet at the same time stared over her shoulder at Louisa.

"Why are they *looking* at me!" said Louisa with fury.

Just like the Japanese mother, her own mother said, "Shhh!"

"But *why*—"

"It's just they're not used to Americans."

"I don't look *American*." All her life she'd been asked what she was, where she came from—in the second-grade Thanksgiving play she'd been cast as the sole Indian. She'd expected the disadvantages of brown hair, brown eyes, and brown skin, all imposed by her father, to be clear advantages here. Wasn't this where he came from? It must be her mother's fault. Her mother who was saying, as if to protest her own blameworthiness:

"Of course you look American. What on earth do you mean, that you don't look American? For one thing you're much taller than children are here. You're even tall for your age back at home . . ."

They were standing with three very similar men in black suits, all slender and short, who were bowing and bowing to Louisa's father, who, to Louisa's and even her mother's shock, bowed in return.

The men took them to a hotel attached to the airport, and that—except for being full of staring Japanese people—could almost have been in Chicago. They ate a horrible meal of raw fish, including a chunk of what Louisa realized must be raw octopus, white like a bone with a bright purple rind and part of a suction cup on it. Louisa turned her face away from the shining wet pieces of things the very smell of which made her gorge rise. "Enough!" her father cut short her complaints, suddenly wheeling away from the three men, with whom he'd been jabbering incomprehensibly. "Eat or be quiet!"

"Eat the rice," her mother whispered, and slid an arm around her. Louisa wanted to cling to her mother and cry. She instead went as stiff as she could, until her mother took her arm away.

Then they slept in their hotel room, for perhaps a whole day. Even after waking Louisa felt she would never wake up, sounds and objects slid around her queasily as if she had a fever, but she was told she was not at all ill, she was made to get up while she wept for a bed. They went on a sightseeing tour, with several dozen old Japanese people, endlessly clomping on and off a huge bus. Pagoda towers surrounded by moats, raked rocks surrounded by walls, dwarf pine trees and giant statues of a cross-legged man who could barely be seen through gray clouds of incense. Louisa was so tired, and so hungry, she barely felt her legs underneath her, or saw where she went, and later on, when her father had their photos developed and showed them to her, she recognized almost nothing.

At the end of the tour all the grim staring Japanese people and she and her parents had been made to line up for a portrait, Louisa in the front row although she was not just the same height as, but taller than many of the shriveled old ladies. By instinct, though she had never felt less happy in her life, when the photographer held up his hand for attention, she stretched out her cheeks in a grin. The photographer stepped out from behind his tripod and called out, "Shutchomouf!"

The old people on either side of Louisa glanced slantwise at her.

Louisa's face hurt from her outsize and fraudulent smile. She wished he would hurry and take it.

"Shutchomouf!" he shouted again.

Her mother was somewhere behind her, and her father in the very last row. She heard him exclaim, as if to a child who's been warned many times, "Louisa! He says not to smile!"

*Shut your mouth!*

She clamped her lips shut, although in her confusion the corners of her mouth remained raised. Later, when they looked at this photo, she would seem to be wincing from indigestion.

Japanese people don't smile for photos, her father later explained. This would be just the first of a great many things she would wish he had told her beforehand.

This was also the start of her Japanese Smile. Even when it was all right to smile, she could no longer smile like she used to. She kept her lips pressed together, concealing her teeth, despite her mother urging her to "smile naturally." "You don't look like Louisa when you smile that weird way," said her mother. But Louisa didn't feel like Louisa, so she didn't see why she should look like her, either. She kept smiling her Japanese Smile. She also started walking with her head bowed, in the hopes she'd seem shorter.

After the miserable sightseeing tour they had packed their bags again, checked out of the American-style hotel, and been taken by one of the three black-clad men to the train station. "We're not staying in Tokyo?" Louisa exclaimed, not that she liked Tokyo. But she expected that anything else would be worse.

"Of course we're not staying in Tokyo," her father said, as if it that were ridiculous.

Even then, after just a few days, Louisa had noticed a change in her mother, or perhaps it made more sense to say she hadn't noticed her mother, and this was the change. Her mother, whether she was happy, or angry, or paying too much attention to Louisa, or not paying enough, had always been vivid. She had always been *there*. Now you could almost forget she was standing right there next to you. At the Japanese restaurant, or on the tour bus, or in the Tokyo train station, as Japanese people talked and talked to Louisa's father and Louisa's father talked and talked back, and as Louisa grew more and more red-faced and angry at all this talking that she couldn't understand, her mother was not only silent but absent. She gazed into the distance. She ignored everything Japanese, and everything Japanese ignored her. Even once they had boarded the train and were alone in their row she had stared into space, while Louisa's father leaned across her to point out the window and tell her the sights.

They were going west, through mounded hills and flat, glittering fields and one little town after another. Where they were going would be a town, too, not as little as these ones that flashed past in the blink of an eye, but nothing like Tokyo, either. It would be a large town or small city, a simple place with factories where people worked, and a college of engineering that was where Louisa's father would teach. "We should have stayed in Tokyo," Louisa said in disappointment as the train pulled into the dingy train station. The station had a pretty pagoda-style roof but its stucco walls were streaked gray with grime. Wires crisscrossed the gray sky everywhere. Dark hills ringed the town like a wall.

More Japanese men met their train, but compared to the three men in Tokyo these were rumpled, and friendlier, and Louisa didn't hate them quite so much. Their hair flopped in their eyes when they bowed, and their mouths showed yellow, crooked teeth when they smiled, and they insisted on taking them all to the town marketplace for some sort of pale gooey dumpling that Louisa found she liked. This excursion had been the first time Louisa grasped parts of the conversation, without knowing how. They were going to get a snack. She was a girl with a good appetite. She was tall for her age. Her age was discussed a great deal—yes, she really was nine. Yes, American children were taller, and she was tall even for an American. The first days in the town had been a little like the first days in Tokyo, with nothing but sightseeing and eating, but somehow less awful.

The town was an ugly, crowded, loud place where you recognized what was a restaurant by the plastic toy food they displayed in the window, and where early in the morning, and then again in the midafternoon, the streets filled with children all wearing white hats with chin ties, and red leather rucksacks, the girls in dark blue pleated skirts and the boys in blue trousers or shorts. If Louisa wasn't spying on the life of the town out the fourth-story windows of their new, smelly, cold, damp apartment, but actually out in the streets with her father, the other children would stare frankly at her. Girls would lean their heads together and whisper. Boys sometimes pointed and shouted and then ran away with their red leather rucksacks bouncing hard against their backs. She would feel herself flush, and would press her lips into a line, and clench her fists until her nails bit half-circle dents in her palms. She longed for a white blouse and a blue pleated skirt and white hat with chin tie and red rucksack, and to get rid of her stupid American clothes.

There was much talk between her father and mother at night when they thought she was sleeping about whether she ought to go to school, and if she did, where. Before they'd left home her teachers had given her mother a whole year of worksheets and workbooks, phonics and division and the Facts about the States and whatever else she would need to keep up with her grade while away for a year. It had filled an entire suitcase. Now that they were in Japan, she didn't want to do any of it. It all seemed ridiculous.

She could see that her father agreed, and that her mother didn't have the will to fight. Louisa was briefly elated, to be excused from that suitcase of homework. She didn't realize this meant she would go to the school here in town.

The next day her father took her to the school uniform store, and badly as she wanted the uniform she'd sooner give it up, and almost anything else, to avoid being sent to a Japanese school. "I'll do my phonics," she pleaded with him, clinging to his hands, pouring tears, as the bent gray woman at the uniform store struggled to pin her in place, to wrap the tapes around her shoulders and her waist, to measure from one shoulder to the opposite hip, from her waist to her heels, all the while clucking in disapproval.

"Stand still!" Louisa's father scolded her.


They had all been equally, unpleasantly surprised by their new home, a cluster of rooms on the top floor of a stained concrete building that reminded Louisa of the concrete parking structure where her parents left the car when they'd driven downtown to apply for their passports. This Japanese apartment building had the same damp feel, the same damp smell. Some turns of the dank and dark stairwell had an even worse smell, as if someone had gone to the bathroom right there on the floor. Who in the world would do this, when anyone using those stairs had to live in that building, and so ought to know where the real toilets were? But the toilets were the worst thing of all: They weren't actually toilets at all, and they weren't even in the apartments. All the toilets were together, in shared rooms at the ends of the halls on each floor, and, at least in the girls', they were no more than troughs in the floor. With toilets like that, maybe it was no wonder that people just peed on the stairs, although Louisa had never seen anyone do this. She hardly saw anyone in the building. There was one old woman downstairs who for hours on end swept the sidewalk, and one old man on the roof who tended an outdoor collection of bonsai, and had shouted at Louisa, and shaken his bony fist at her, although she hadn't laid a finger on his plants. Between these two, top and bottom, all was silent and lifeless. The building was as run-down and bad-smelling as a slum. This was the word Louisa's mother had used. "You said they'd be giving us VIP treatment!"

"It *is* VIP," Louisa's father shouted back. "We have four whole rooms. Do you know how most people here live? Four or six people in *one* little room. It's a goddamn poor country!" But it was clear he was also upset. Louisa didn't know if this was because he'd also expected something nicer, or because Louisa's mother was complaining so much. Louisa's father loved complaining but he hated other people complaining, as if he thought they were saying a thing was his fault.

"What does VIP mean?" she asked. Of course they ignored her and kept arguing.

Still, even with the dinginess and dampness, and the smell, and the cold—for some reason the building was always bone-cold, even when it was sunny outside—Louisa grew used to it. She grew used to descending the stairwell alone. She grew used to walking to school alone. She grew used to buying food on the shopping street on her way home. She grew used to being known to some people, a figure of well-meaning fun.

"Ha ha!" the old tofu vendor called out. "Ha ha! American girl! Any tofu today?"

"No, thank you," she knew how to say. "Maybe some other day." She smiled with her teeth hidden, her lips pressed together, and tried to keep walking while not seeming to hurry. Seeming to hurry looked rude, although seeming to linger looked like she was shopping for tofu.

"When will you buy my tofu, American? Eat tofu and live a long life."

"My mother doesn't like tofu," Louisa explained, as she always did, edging away with her teeth-covered, lips-closed-tight smile.

"American mother!" the woman called after Louisa, half-scolding and half-forgiving.

She made her way several stalls down, to the egg vendor, and paid for the eggs with the usual head-bobbing and bowing and smiling with teeth covered and lips pressed together. She was best-known to the vendor of eggs. Her mother made omelets almost nightly for dinner. It was the only local food she'd figured out. Louisa had come home from school more than once and found her mother at the Western-style table in the dim little kitchen, still wearing her green zip-up housecoat, as if she had sat there all day.

"Are you doing good in school? Studying hard?" the egg vendor demanded.

"Yes, sir."

"Smart girl! When will you bring your good parents to meet me?"

"American!" Other vendors waved to her as she made her way

more purposefully through the crowd, having bought everything on her list. "Ha ha! Robert Redford! McDonald's!"

Coming back to their building, she shifted the grocery bag from one hand to the other to unshoulder her rucksack and get out her key. Up the stairs past the second and third floors, as always encountering no one. Her father claimed it was because the other people in the building worked such long hours, they were gone before Louisa went out in the morning and back after she had come home. Her mother claimed it was because the whole building was derelict and wasn't supposed to be lived in at all. Either way there was no one else on the fourth floor. In between the toilet rooms and their apartment was another strange room that had only a Japanese bathtub, which was shaped like a box and fed by snaking rubber hoses, and so deep that Louisa could stand up in it and still be submerged all the way to her armpits. Louisa's father said regular Japanese people took their baths at bathhouses—they had to take them together, in public, the way back at home you might go to the pool. Their not having to do this was more of the "VIP" treatment. But Louisa's mother never used the bathtub, at least not that Louisa could see, though this might be because Louisa's mother no longer got dressed.

Coming down the fourth-floor hallway, she could hear the radio through the rice-paper panels in the flimsy hall door. She slid the door open and let herself in, and slid the door shut again, knowing that her mother hadn't heard her because her mother had the radio playing so loud. She took off her shoes and lined them up on the shoe rack, continued into the tiny kitchen, put her rucksack on the table, and unpacked the groceries, and her mother still hadn't heard her. Her mother was stretched out in the next room on the Western-style sofa, in her green housecoat and her ragged white slippers, with one arm lying over her eyes. She couldn't tell if her mother was listening or had fallen asleep. Some days the radio played classical music, and some days it played news, but most days it played awful songs with squawking tunes and squawking women who sounded as if they had bad indigestion. She knew enough Japanese now to know that all these songs were about either the four seasons, or heartbreak, or a dead person, or, most commonly, all those things rolled into one. They were awful, sappy songs that gave Louisa a headache, and were nothing like the thunderous music her mother liked to listen to at home, the symphonies by Beethoven and Mozart. But she didn't think her mother even listened here. She just wanted the radio on, making noise. It was as if having the radio on was her mother's way of being in Japan, a way that kept her from having to leave the apartment or meet any Japanese people.

When she knelt at the low table next to the couch to spread out her homework, her mother sat up suddenly and looked at her wild-eyed. Maybe she really had been asleep. "Oh!" her mother said. "I lost track of the time. Look at me, I'm still in my housedress."


After a few months Louisa's Japanese was so good, it was easier to pretend she was a Japanese girl, like her classmates. Of course, being called "American" in the marketplace ruined it. Walking home from school with her friends and catching sight of her reflection in a shop window, her white hat sticking up so much farther than everyone else's, her feet so disgustingly large, also ruined it. She would remember that she wasn't Japanese and she never would be. But those were fleeting moments of disappointment. The rest of the time, from the moment she left her building in the morning to the moment she returned at the end of the day, she *felt* Japanese. It was a complicated feeling because she felt unlike herself. It was as if she'd stepped into a movie and was doing so well in her role that no one else knew she was only pretending. Sometimes she could make the feeling last all day, and even all the way upstairs and through the door, but as soon as she saw her mother, the feeling was ruined.

A few times, her father had said, "Why don't you get home from school earlier, and take Mommy out for a walk. Show her all the places in town that you've learned. Take her shopping with you."

"Okay," Louisa had said, but she still hadn't done it. She knew her mother didn't want to go out. But what was worse was that she didn't want to go out with her mother. She didn't want to be seen with her.

One night as they were sitting at the kitchen table, eating omelets, her father said, "We're taking a trip tomorrow. We'll get on an eight-fifteen train."

"Why?" she said.

"To visit an old friend of mine who lives next to the sea. We can go to the beach."

"But I have school."

"You can miss a day."

She looked in dismay at her mother, but her mother was looking down at her plate, eating her food in slow bites, as if Louisa and her father weren't there. At home only contagious chicken pox had ever been considered a good enough reason to skip school. "But I don't want to miss a day," she said, which she'd never said before about school.

"It's just one day."

She finished her omelet without tasting it, staring down at her plate. Her father had likely come up with this trip as a way to get her mother to leave the apartment. In that case, why couldn't the two of them go by themselves? Every day that Louisa lived in Japan and felt more Japanese and more embarrassed to be seen with her mother, she also more and more felt another bad way—guilty—which in turn made her feel yet a third bad way—angry. She felt it to the point that she wished her mother might in some painless way disappear.

And then the next morning, the first thing her father said on waking her was, "Mommy isn't feeling well. She's not coming with us."

Louisa hardly spoke on their way to the station, for how glad and how awful she felt. The train glided through green and gray countryside, the occasional rice field flashing out like a mirror in the white morning sun. Her father was silent. Usually he would be snapping the newspaper open and closed, sometimes making a disgusted noise in his throat in reaction to something he'd read. Or he would be leaning over her, pointing out the window at this or that, giving a lecture. Her father always made a big fuss out of the things that he taught her, insisting upon her attention, speaking in a slightly raised voice. Now, though, he wasn't reading, or talking, or even looking out the window, but staring straight ahead, as if he saw something far past the seat backs and the dull metal wall of their train car and even far past the nose of the train. Almost no one else was traveling their direction this hour. The train car was practically empty. The strange thought crossed her mind that her father could already see down the tracks to the ocean.

"*Where* are we going?" she asked him, to break the silence.

"I told you. To visit my friend."

"Who's the friend? How do you know him?"

"Her name is Mrs. Ishida." Suddenly her father produced a newspaper from inside his briefcase. "Did you bring homework?" he asked from behind it. "I'm going to read."

It had never occurred to Louisa that her father's friend might be a woman. Back home, her father had no woman friends. In truth, back home her father had no friends at all.

They rode all the way to the end of the line. Stepping onto the platform, she smelled the ocean. Although she'd flown over the ocean, and this was a nation of islands, she had never yet been to the Japanese seaside. "I want to see the beach!" she cried.

"First we're going to Mrs. Ishida's. Then we'll go to the beach." They set off down the uncrowded platform and through the uncrowded station.

No one paid attention to them as they walked, and Louisa's chest swelled with relief and her shoulders straightened up to their actual height. She strode along arrogantly with her arrogant father, his Japanese newspaper shoved under his arm, his Japanese questions business-like and even brusque as he asked for directions. Mrs. Ishida, Louisa imagined, was a twinkle-eyed white-haired old woman in a dark blue kimono who would bow while extending a tray full of sweet buns and candy. Louisa had installed her in an old-fashioned Japanese house with scrolled eaves and a quaint wooden bridge arching over a pond full of koi. But Mrs. Ishida turned out to live in just the same kind of dingy, cluttered, damp-smelling apartment building as everyone else in Japan. Louisa and her father ducked under one clothesline after another, tripping over babies' toys, as they made their way down a second-floor breezeway reading the numbers on the matching wooden doors. When Mrs. Ishida's door opened, no twinkle-eyed white-haired old lady stood there but a slight, youngish woman who stared at them as if they'd made an error, knocking on her door.

"Where is your wife?" the woman finally asked.

"She felt sick. Here is Louisa."

"He-*low*," the woman began awkwardly, in English.

"She understands Japanese," Louisa's father broke in. The woman was clearly relieved.

"Hello, Louisa," she said. And then, as if she'd reminded herself to say this, "I've dreamed of meeting you for so long." Louisa wondered how this could be true, but she knew not to ask. She smiled her Japanese Smile.

They walked down tilting streets to the beach. It was a cold day, still too early for beachgoing, though some old people, bundled in thick quilted coats, sat in chairs on the sand, looking out at the choppy gray surf. Louisa knelt in the sand and dug with a shovel that Mrs. Ishida had given her, until her kneecaps and shins ached with cold. Her father and Mrs. Ishida, sitting on a blanket far back from the surf, talked for what felt like hours, about what Louisa could not hear or guess at. Every time Louisa approached them, her father would wave her away.

"Go play," he would say.

Long after she was cranky with hunger she was finally summoned and handed a bento. Her father and Mrs. Ishida, who had talked so energetically for so long it had sometimes looked to Louisa, from the distance, as though they were having a fight, had fallen silent. They stared out at the ugly gray water, their four eyebrows bunched up and their two foreheads creased by two similar vertical lines. Louisa noticed that neither was eating.


Later on that chilly afternoon Mrs. Ishida insisted on taking a photograph of Louisa and her father as they stood shoulder to shoulder, unsmiling, with the restless gray water behind them. And later still they stood again at the door to Mrs. Ishida's apartment, amid the clotheslines and the laundry clipped with pink and blue and yellow plastic clothespins, and Mrs. Ishida bent and stared at Louisa as if her face were a map of someplace Mrs. Ishida was going, where she wouldn't be able to bring the map with her, so that she had to memorize it on the spot. She stared at Louisa so long Louisa blushed, and then her face turned cold, and then she herself stared at her sneakers, which were stained at the toes from beach water, and coated with grit.

Finally Mrs. Ishida said, "Thank you for coming to see me. I'll see you again very soon."

Louisa hoped not.

"Wait here," her father said, and instead of at last saying goodbye to Mrs. Ishida he unexpectedly followed Mrs. Ishida inside her apartment, closing the door behind them. Louisa thought she would cry from exhaustion and irritation. She laid her head on the rail of the breezeway that ran the whole length of the building and looked out on a grimy courtyard. No one was around. Long as the day already felt, all the children must still be at school, all the adults still out at their jobs. She wanted to walk away, back to the station, and give her father the fright of his life. That would serve him right if she just disappeared. But she was too tired to move, and then her father had come out again, and they were walking together, her father tugging her along, so as to not miss the next train.

"Why did you leave me outside?" she complained.

"I had to speak with Mrs. Ishida a minute."

"You talked with her all day!"

"Don't use that rude tone."

"Who was she, anyway?"

"I told you. She's my old friend. You'll know her well someday."

Hours ago, when they had set out for the beach, Louisa had felt a traitorous pride, walking in between her father and Mrs. Ishida. Pride because both of the adults were narrow and tall and had same-enough faces as everyone else in the street, and identical hair. No one turned at the sight of a different-faced, pale, blue-eyed woman, because that face wasn't along on this trip. The presence of Mrs. Ishida proved Louisa could blend herself into Japan, if only her mother were not there to give her away. She had dared to pretend that her father and Mrs. Ishida were really her parents, for everyone seeing them must have assumed this. But now, far from wishing that Mrs. Ishida could be her real mother, Louisa never wanted to see her again. When her father voiced the opposite thought, she said, "Why? I don't *want* to know her."

Her father yanked her sharply around to face him. "I said, don't use that tone!"

"But why do you want me to know her?" she wailed, although she told herself, in a mind's voice even rougher than her father's, *Don't cry*. Her father's face seemed to flicker with shadow and light the way their little yard would back at home, when a gusting wind lashed at their neighbor's enormous oak tree. Then the wind died and her father looked sorry, and tired.

"You'll understand later," he said.

They bought return tickets and boarded their train. Even before the shabby back sides of the buildings had given way to the humped hills and the glassy rice fields and the lengths of unpaved country road that sometimes slipped alongside the tracks for a short time and then slipped away, all of it looking smoky and dull in the dusk, she was struggling to keep her eyes open. Then she must have slept, so soundly that she didn't wake up until her father was hitching her onto his shoulder.

# Anne

**The trip came into** their lives like the so-called machine of the gods that Anne vaguely recalled from a time she'd let Dr. Grassi badger her into auditing Ancient Greek Drama. The machine, in her mind, not a divine interference but a puppetlike raven the size of a house, cawing an earsplitting caw, churning up a tornado of chaos with its ungainly enormous black wings. A blindness of airborne trash and a deafness of wind: with scarcely any discussion they were renting the house, putting their things into storage, withdrawing Louisa from school halfway through the fourth grade. Anne was aware that her new secret unhappiness played a large part in making this possible, by ensuring her numb compliance. She had begun experiencing what she was determined to believe were freaks of an overactive imagination but more and more seemed like actual symptoms. Losses of normal sensation, and gains of ghost sensations that shouldn't exist. Pushing through the hangers in her closet, her arm would suddenly not do its job. Aiming for a chair, she would miss it. She had prickling where nothing was touching her; she felt her limbs rearranging themselves into comical creatures, the woman with one leg and three arms and a clubfoot coming out of her skull. Not for the first time, she thought, *Divine retribution*, another machine of the gods. Her doctor diagnosed inadequate sleep, a bad case of the blues, and nervousness about the coming Big Change in her life, by which he meant the trip, a cause that would be its own cure: once they got there, and Anne saw there was nothing to fear, she was certain to feel a lot better. But there was another Big Change that her doctor knew nothing about.

On October 4, 1977, Anne had woken knowing what date it was without having to look at the calendar. For once, she had not anxiously expected the date for so many days running as to miss it when it finally arrived, in the way of failing to find some lost object that is out in plain sight. For the first time, she had already mailed a card, one so heavily written over it qualified as a letter. It detailed the forthcoming trip and included their overseas mailing address. October 4, 1977, was Tobias's eighteenth birthday. In the legal documents kept hidden with the annual letters and photos in the accordion file in her closet, this event was anticipated in detail.

On January 1, 1978, she and Serk and Louisa boarded the first of three planes. Chicago, Los Angeles. Los Angeles, Honolulu. Honolulu, Tokyo. At some point, transpacific, they crossed the International Date Line, which meant the trip took either two days, or none. Was that right? That they either jumped forward, or back? Perhaps they arrived in Japan in the old year and rang in the new year again.

They had been there just a month when Anne opened the mailbox assigned to their wretched Japan apartment and found, instead of the usual nothing, an envelope inscrutably Japanese in every usual way except for the bizarre appearance of her name. Her name was inked on the letter's outside in clear, confident capitals, indicating a writer at home in the English language. Yet the Japanese characters looked no less confident, at least to Anne's ignorant eye. She had not been able to comprehend the physical relationship between the confidently bilingual letter; herself, the apparent recipient; and Tobias, the letter's apparent author.

At first she imagined some Japanese stranger who was fluent in English and writing on behalf of Tobias. But the letter was in fact from Tobias, written in a marvelously regular hand very much like Anne's own, which had so often helped her secure employment. And the letter had been mailed by Tobias from a town in Japan a brief train ride from the town in which Anne found herself—because Tobias was in

Japan also, incomprehensibly, as if the force of the shock he'd received from that electrified fence had continued to radiate, its leading edge pushing him west, over the Plains and the Rockies and the coast of California, all those places Anne herself had seen for the first time gazing down from the plane that Tobias was somehow pursuing, across the Pacific, at last to touch down on this string of exotic islands.

It was a fanciful notion, but not entirely without its grain of truth, for that day they'd gone strawberry-picking was all he'd ever had of her, the only island of his lifelong archipelago on which she resided, and yet he'd come seeking her out. Hadn't he? The fact of the letter was astonishing, but its contents were brief; the hand beautifully clear, but the words rather vague.

*Dear Anne,*

*Thank you for your letter of last autumn wishing me a Happy Eighteenth. No need to say Sorry for not having written before. This letter to you is many times more belated than yours was to me. I'm glad you let me know about your coming to Japan. I hope it's not too strange for you that I'm in Japan also. I would have written you sooner but I thought you might want to get settled. I'm not far from you and I would like to come see you. Please let me know if I may visit.*

*With my very best wishes,*
*Tobias.*

That he didn't call her *Mother*, but *Anne*, touched her. It seemed a gesture of friendship and mercy, a sweeping erasure of debt by the one to whom so much was owed. She wrote back immediately with all the unconditional enthusiasm of an unmarried aunt for a favorite nephew; perhaps this was the role she was meant to play. She did not ask why he had come to Japan, or when exactly, or what he was doing, or how long he was planning to stay.

The numbness and the tremors in her legs and her hands, the drifting black clouds in her vision, the fatigue like a version of death, at this time still were intermittent visitations. It was still possible during

their hiatuses for her to pretend that they did not exist. Even with a relatively functioning body, though, her standoff with the language paralyzed her. Immersion in the country had if anything made matters
worse, because nothing sounded remotely like the slow and friendly
promptings of Mr. Ogawa, the teacher whose Japanese night class she
had well-meaningly and briefly attended. The simple mailing of her
answer to Tobias presented a bewildering series of obstacles, the address to be copied with photographic precision lest she inadvertently
add or subtract a stray mark, the postage overpaid because she had
only airmail stamps, and finally the gauntlet to the corner mailbox, ex-
changing bows with staring neighbors every step, the neighbors' bows
unsuccessfully masking their staring, because this might be the first
time they'd seen her outdoors. After mailing the letter she scuttled
back inside and slept the rest of the day. The excursion had been so
exhausting it almost seemed that should be the end of the adventure,
but it hadn't been. Tobias had come.

Remembering the harrowing perfection of his sculpted face and
golden hair and golden skin on the day she'd last seen him—and also
the evacuated eyes and the silence, her own nervous chatter pouring
into the void, her sidelong glances as they drove, like glancing at Mi-
chelangelo's *David* if one happened to have stolen that statue and made
off with it in the front seat of a car—Anne nervously rehearsed her simple questions, her simple and welcoming face, and then found herself
facing a brand-new Tobias, so changed that she failed to conceal her
shock. And so voluble she didn't need to. "Oh, I know," he said with
a laugh, "I'm a vagabond now," but this hardly seemed the adequate
term for a person so thin that his collarbone protruded like the blade
of a plow, whose skin was sallow and pocked, hair greasy and lank. He
was carrying all his worldly possessions in a school backpack—it might
have been the same backpack he had used in his high school career,
which had been suspended by his brain surgery. She couldn't get him
to sit still and eat some fried eggs—"What a wonderful apartment!"
he cried, springing in and out of the cramped little rooms. "How wonderful to sit this high above the street! This avenue of ginkgoes, I've
cycled down it several times, now I find that it's yours! But how have

you been? What have you seen? What are your impressions—and Louisa's?" This Tobias bent his attention on Anne like the beam of light trained through a lens that devours with heat, and also greeted every utterance of hers with an attention that almost vibrated—at last it was possible to ask how he was, her fears of her possible tactlessness proving misplaced. "I had a growth in my brain," he reminisced cheerfully. "You might remember—they found it that summer I stayed with Grandmère and Grandpère. That summer we met. I mean, apart from when I was a baby," he amended, merrily laughing again.

"Of course I remember," Anne managed to say.

"When it got taken out, something wonderful happened to me. I wish there was a way to describe it exactly. I know there must be, but I'm still trying to figure it out."

"Your parents were so relieved to have you back to your old self," Anne said, remembering the anodyne phrase from the holiday letter. She was pleased to have said this, "your parents" implying that she felt no resentment at not possessing that designation, "relieved to have you back" giving the impression Adrian and Norma often communicated with Anne. But if Anne thought Tobias required such demonstrations, she was wrong. He didn't seem to require anything.

"I wasn't back to my old self," he corrected, though without a hint of reprimand. "I *stopped* being my old self that day. That's what's wonderful. Or I wouldn't be here."

In Japan, did he mean? Or, alive? She didn't have the chance to ask, he had so much else he wanted to tell her. He was surviving in Japan on the sufferance of its many different temples; Tobias stayed with the monks in exchange for his labor, which he provided without stint, tending plants, raking gravel, sifting stray bits of gravel out of uncooked legumes, cooking the legumes, laundering robes in great tubs by hand, cleaning toilets, scrubbing burned rice from the bottoms of pots, processing donations and prayer requests from passersby, freshening offerings of flowers and fruit, running errands, creating lanterns out of candles and cups, contending with vermin and cats, slithering around traditional scrollwork roofs on his belly under the blistering sun repairing cracked tiles and cleaning out gutters, and otherwise

serving as uncomplaining jack-of-all-trades and wifely household
drudge. For all this Tobias was granted permission to sleep in whatever temple he found himself serving that day—the actual temple itself, great pillared vault that it was, with its smooth, clean, extremely
hard floor and its permanent dusk clinging to the roof beams, which
was also where all the heat went—and to partake of the same meals
as were offered itinerant beggars: a bit of rice, a dab of miso or on
great days maybe sundry flakes of fish, a jolly yellow confetti of sour
daikon. All delicious, Tobias assured Anne, with his happy smile at the
edges of which she was certain the molars were already gray.

As he told her all this they were sitting in the cramped little
kitchen, with its single window smothered in the crown of a ginkgo,
and its unplaceable smell that evoked for Anne the unclean bowels
of the earth, and that must have something to do with the plumbing.
The breakfast dishes were still in the sink; he'd come just when she'd
said to, like an obedient lover, an hour after Louisa and Serk had both
left for the day. "When I heard about the tumor, I was so scared," she
tried to begin, but he seized on her words in a way that she hadn't
expected.

"Everyone finds them so frightening, as if they're grenades! But
*why*, when they come from ourselves? When my growth was removed,
the surgeons disposed of it—and everyone was surprised when I said
that I wished they had not. I should have had it, don't you see? It was
mine. I would have understood myself sooner, I think, if they'd given
it to me. But," he allowed after a moment of silence, for Anne didn't
know what to say, "I'll understand myself anyway, somehow. It'll just
take me longer."

After that day he came regularly, always late Thursday morning
as she'd specified. Every time, he came with the backpack, which his
worldly possessions barely half filled. It seemed that it was not possible to have a day off from the monks. Rather, each time, Tobias left
them as though he'd never return. Then he'd return the same evening,
as if starting anew. It was always possible to regain his position of pe-
onage, but never to have it kept waiting. "But don't they notice that
you always leave Thursday morning, and always come back Thursday

night?" Anne asked, to which Tobias said, "It doesn't matter if they notice or not. And it really doesn't matter if it happens to be Thursday. There's going to be some Thursday I don't leave, or some day I leave that's not Thursday, or some Thursday that I don't come back." Anne wondered if perhaps he didn't want to leave the backpack unattended, but given its contents this seemed doubtful. It contained nothing but his few clothes, all of which Anne had witnessed in use within just a few visits, and all of which were one unravelment away from being rags. Anne wished she had her Singer with her. At home she made almost all Louisa's clothing excepting her panties and socks and her wool winter coat. Because she couldn't give him clothes, Anne had given Tobias a toothbrush and toothpaste from the apocalypse-minded overstock of American toiletries she had packed for Japan, which had made Serk ask her where she imagined they were going. And she'd given Tobias a bar of Ivory soap and a soap case, a hand towel and washcloth, and a bottle of Flintstones chewable daily vitamins, which he'd regarded with oddly tender delight, as if she were some sort of innocent savage, presenting him with her magical cure of crushed berries and leaves. She several times had the uneasy feeling, withstanding his radiant gaze, that he was the adult and she the child. As for her gifts, she saw no evidence they were used.

Her childish helplessness in Japan with regard to the language led to the subject of Tobias's contrasting knack—first for German and French, and now, it turned out, Japanese. "I'm sure you can speak it a little," he encouraged her. "Just being among people, you're picking it up. Don't be nervous to try."

"But I'm not around people, I don't see anyone, because I can't speak. And so I can't speak—because I don't see anyone."

"Then I'll teach you," he decided with excitement. "We can speak Japanese on my visits."

"No!" Her objection burst from her with too much force—he must wonder what made her so panicked. "I just want to get to know you," she explained. "Without a—new obstacle."

She had somehow flattered him. "That's so kind, Anne," he said.

His gift for languages couldn't have surprised her given who his father was, yet their conversation left her with a sense of surprise that she eventually realized pertained to herself. The surprise was that she—who had never mastered a second language and at this point almost surely never would; who hid indoors in foreign countries with the many types of soap she'd brought from home for fear of having to use something different; who was a hopeless homebody who missed her Singer sewing machine—persistently attached herself to men who spoke many languages and hauled her into unknown territories and seemed to be comfortable nowhere, so that they inflicted on her a discomfort she could have avoided. She had done it with Tobias's father—briefly, but with lasting consequences. She had done it with Serk—at greater length now, over a decade of unease.

Why did she do this? There had been numerous men, it was simply factual, and not vain, to state, who had wanted to give her a home with a room, spacious and sunny, for her sewing machine, and perhaps as important had wanted to love her for being, as they saw it, so exceptionally cultured and bright, an exotic of which they'd be proud. Anne was, at least until recently, beautiful enough to turn heads; she'd known it, and been careful with the framing of her beauty, just enough risk-taking with her clothes, and so among most people she was thought to have extraordinary class. And Anne was musical—she knew a great deal about classical music, from growing up in a household where despite their modest means she and her siblings all had an instrument or two, and music was played constantly if not exceptionally well. Anne had read all of Tolstoy and Dickens, she cooked well and baked better, she eschewed dowdy knitting in favor of complex embroidery—she had been expected, even by herself, to attend college, to teach, and to marry. Even running away from her family to the Holy Land had been the sort of rebellion that would have enhanced her after the fact if it hadn't turned out as it did.

"I suppose your father taught you languages," she'd said that day, thinking of her own bestowal on him of her beauty, which he'd squandered in the space of a year.

"He didn't teach me so much as he just talked to me in different languages, and then I talked back. That's the best kind of learning, when you don't even know that you're learning. What about Louisa? Does she speak Japanese?"

"She's picked up a lot, just by being around people, like you were saying. She's going to school with Japanese children. The first couple weeks she would come home and cry, because she didn't understand anything and had no one to play with. Then she stopped crying. Then she stopped coming home!—I mean, right after school. Because now she has playmates. She even does the shopping for me. She's so brave. She's learned the whole town."

"I'm going to show you the town. Let's go walking. Come on! You've said you never leave your street."

"Not today. Louisa will be home soon. You ought to get back to your monks."

"You just said she doesn't come straight from school. She stays out with her friends."

"Not every day. Not necessarily." But now he had her laughing, her fending-off of him a game, as if he were courting her. His eager smile a Cheshire-ghost of her own lovely, unhindered smile, which looked out at her no longer from the mirror, but from a few photographs that she kept carefully in a box—to pass on to Louisa, she told herself.

She didn't go out with him that day, not just because she embarrassed herself, but because he embarrassed her also. She couldn't imagine what the dwarfish egg-shaped busybody on the ground floor, a Mrs. Hama-something, whose sole purpose in life was to sweep the sidewalk, must make of Tobias in his mendicant's rags with his filthy backpack. By this point in the Thursday arrangement he must have been noticed. Perhaps he was taken for a holy man, but more likely he was taken for a crazy white person, another sorry member of her tribe. She wondered if the sweeper, or the housewife on the second floor with the Prince Valiant haircut and the series of bright-colored polka-dot smocks with side-ties, or the itinerant soup vendor who often set up outside and whose tea-colored broth full of fat white raw-appearing worm-resembling noodles had become Louisa's favorite dinner, could discern the obvious resemblance of Tobias to Anne, if it was clear to them he was her son. Or did their anomalous whiteness blind onlookers to the shared face, the shared eyes, the shared smile, because to them white people all looked the same, no two could ever look *more* like each other?

And so she resisted going out with him that day—but the anxieties caused by his presence were increasingly offset by worse anxieties caused by his absence. She recognized a growing dependency, a fear he would tire of her, that a Thursday would come that he didn't return. Nothing in Tobias's behavior supported this fear. It originated only from Anne but was no less tenacious for having one source.

When he came on the following Thursday she was wearing slacks, clean socks, and a polyester blouse with a pattern of flowers. Her hair, which had not been cut since months before they'd come to Japan, was long enough to pull back at the nape of her neck. She'd gone so far as to powder her face and apply lipstick, which required extreme concentration; her hand kept shaking and she twice had to scour herself clean and start over. Tobias—at least this post-strawberry-picking Tobias—had never seen her thus painted. And so again she felt the unruly energy of seduction when, having heard his arriving footfalls, she made her way into the vestibule and said, "Leave on your shoes."

The town sat in a bowl of dark hills but was not particularly pretty, or quaint. Nor was it large, with a city's anonymity. Anne was reminded of all the aspects of the town she'd disliked when they first arrived here, the cluttered feeling everywhere you turned, nowhere to walk on the street without kicking a dog, or tripping over someone's bucket of tofu, or being honked at from behind by a scooter, or, most shocking, a tiny loud little car forcing its way where it seemed even one or two people were too much to fit. And the storefronts that were really just more heaps of things, crates of stringy dried somethings or glistening spiny somethings that might equally be sea creatures as nuts from a tree, and bundles of socks and hankies and Naugahyde house shoes, all thrown in your path, and leading back to an ambiguous region from which involuntary glances must quickly recoil, for there was some oblivious shrunken grandpa propped on a stool in his jock shorts, watching a tiny TV, with all the unselfconsciousness of a man in utter solitude, or there were children sitting on a square of linoleum, eating white cubes bathed in glossy brown juice while completing their homework, perhaps children who knew Louisa, who seeing a white woman staring at them would realize they were seeing Louisa's near-mythical mother. How did these messes convert into mere mingy homes after dark, how was all that unattractive bounty squeezed back in the box? Did the children sleep atop heaps of dried squid tentacles? Was the old grandpa plopped, in his jock shorts, atop the soft raft of factory-fresh unsold jock shorts? And even when you found your way off the market streets, onto the backstreets, with their promising dampness and hush, you were soon tangled in somebody's laundry, or staring your round blue eyes out of your pale white face into their pungent bewildering kitchen.

But wading back into these streets alongside Tobias, Anne's initial stiff embarrassment, her determination to get through the walk for the sake of having done it, gave way. She went through the looking-glass. Tobias was not just tolerated by the townsfolk, as the wandering shabby eccentric had been tolerated by civilization going back to the time of the ancients. Tobias was known. And he wasn't just known, he was liked. He threaded his way amid the heaps and piles of wares with the quickness of a goat, bowing and smiling all the while, making for this person and that, singing out *Konnichiwa!* and then far more that Anne could not follow, he was reaching back to keep her nearby, from time to time he even took her hand. He seemed to spread light before him, those in receipt of his attention fairly glowed, they came toward Anne bowing and stretching their hands out and radiating their joy at thus being enlightened, and as she blushingly received all this homage Anne received her enlightenment also, she realized what Tobias was saying:

*My mother.*

*How are you today? Please come and meet my mother.*

*Hi there! May I introduce my mother?*

*I agree. She's very beautiful.*

*It will never be the same again,* Anne thought with mingled pleasure and fear, *I'll never be stared at again by these people, now they know me and think I know them.* Making their way to the tiny town park so that

Anne could sit down on a bench—she was so tired she thought she'd
fall down—she asked Tobias, "How can you possibly know all those
people?"

"I come to town every Thursday! Also," he added after a moment,
"I spent some time here when I first came to Japan. It was before you
had arrived. I wanted to see where you'd be."

"How long ago did you first come?" she exclaimed.

"Last October. The first thing I did, before I ran out of money, was
to see all the temples I could, so I could see them surrounded by red
and orange leaves."

Last October!—at the outside, just two weeks after hearing from
her. "Why did you come here?" she made herself finally ask. She didn't
want to know it was all just a strange accident, that he hadn't in fact
changed his life to be closer to her.

"It might sound strange, but I knew I'd be going somewhere, as
soon as I turned eighteen and could make decisions. All the previous
year, after they took out the tumor, I had three different jobs and I
saved every penny I earned. My parents"—he used the term without self-consciousness—"probably thought I was saving to go back
to school, but I wasn't. I was saving for the trip I was going to take,
wherever it turned out to be. I got a passport, in case the trip was
overseas. So when I got your letter, you see, I was ready. I had quite a
lot of money saved up, but the plane ticket to Tokyo took most of it."

"And—this is where you mean to be?" Anne concluded nonsensically. She was defeated. Even though she'd asked him outright, he
hadn't answered her question, while at the same time not seeming
remotely evasive.

"Of course!—until I'm meant to be someplace else."

"And how will you know?"

"I just will."

The last thing he wanted to show her before she went home was the
temple—one of his favorites, Tobias told Anne, with the mingled deep
pleasure and slight self-mockery of the connoisseur of a peculiarly spe-
cialized realm. For all its homely unremarkable appearance, the town
had great religious significance, Tobias told Anne, for its religion was

unique, having been founded here by a female prophet—a wife and mother, just like Anne. The female prophet's spirit was understood to occupy the temple grounds, and there was a beautiful small structure made specifically for her meals: attendants placed a steaming bowl of rice there every day, and prayed for their prophet's enjoyment as the steam from the rice wisped away. The temple complex was by far the nicest part of the town, Tobias said, describing the temple itself, its outbuildings, the gravel courtyards, the stone walls, the clipped pines, and the burbling koi ponds in the manner of an agent for a rambling estate, with much attention to the quantities of gravel, rice, and tree-pruning involved, and much speculation as to how often masonry or prayer mats were replaced. Anne couldn't form the first idea of his religiosity: Was it the harsh exclusionary sort, like his father's, which saw all belief types but a single righteous one as terrible perversions? His father even went so far as to brand all his fellow believers as near-heretics, because they lacked the insights that were exclusively his. Or was Tobias's religious feeling the beneficent and condescending sort, which found something to praise everywhere? He was eighteen years old, prematurely benign, with each one of his ribs on display. Anne had made it her mission to fatten him up, but he ate like a monk even when he was with her. It was a triumph if she sold him on a single boiled egg. It was possible, she thought fearfully, that he was mad— that the growth in his brain had not been fully removed, or that the removal itself had done damage. It was also possible that her own current orgy of mental door-slamming, her strict avoidance of her surroundings, her marriage, her daughter, and the rising mutinies of her body, made him appear to her promiscuously open. He seemed willing to embrace anything. Was this because he was empty, a raven-ous void, or because he was full?

The style of worship at the temple was also unique in Tobias's ex-perience. There was singing, and drumming, and chanting, all very beautiful, but there was also a unique sort of dance: all the worship-pers did synchronized movements with their torsos and arms while they were down on their knees, and then they got to their feet and executed even more complex movements. The hands did the hula, the

feet did the hora—these were Anne's ridiculous and bigoted associations, as she sat on the bench, mouth agape, once Tobias had sprung
up to demonstrate. "I may have some parts of it wrong," he ended
breathlessly, dropping back beside her on the bench. "It's much easier
to do it in a group, you just follow along without thinking."

A pleasing sense of outrage was congealing in Anne. "I think this
must be what Louisa was complaining about. She said that all the children at school were taken out every morning to some enormous pagoda and made to do a dance she wasn't taught, and that she couldn't
pick up, and she was horribly embarrassed." This complaint, very
shrill during Louisa's first weeks of school, had gone quiet a while ago.
Perhaps Louisa had managed to learn. Or perhaps she had realized the
dance was religious, and no longer wanted to solicit Anne's outrage—
because Louisa knew what Anne thought of religion. Anne's outrage
would be about that, not about Louisa's mortification at seeming
clumsy and stupid.

As it was, although Anne did not want to admit it. "They take the
children from *school* to the *temple*? And they take them every day?"

Of course, was Tobias's reply, how else could they attend morning
service? Everyone in the town attended services, and at other hours,
when the bells were broadcast over loudspeakers, those who were not
at the temple, whether out on the street, or at work, or at school in a
classroom, would kneel facing the temple's direction. Had Anne not
noticed this? Had she not heard the bells?

Certainly she'd heard them—along with many other unfamiliar
noises. No, she hadn't noticed the whole town abasing itself toward
the temple, because she was always indoors, and alone.

The town had briefly turned itself inside out for her—she'd grasped
what it was to belong there, to step out her door without feeling the
atmosphere flinch in alarm. For a blessed instant she'd forgotten her
body. She'd viewed the abundance for sale at the market with the same
appraising calm she'd once trained on the cold cuts at the German-
style deli at home. She'd again been a housewife and mother. She'd
repossessed her minor powers.

Now the town reverted to its prior opacity, with this new information that daily life was organized around religion. "We've stumbled into a cult!" she complained on the walk back, which complaint Tobias took too seriously, explaining to her with unassailable reason and erudition that the town's religion was not remotely a cult, for cults took captives while the townspeople here led free and very happy lives, enriched as they were by this one of Japan's many hundreds of folk religions, each of which was fascinating in its own way, as he was starting to learn. Of course, for him a life organized around worship did not seem so strange. It was how he'd been raised.

Anne's family had practiced a lapsed-Protestant indifference to religion that viewed demonstrations of faith as naïve; Anne mostly shared the family feeling, but sometimes suffered from intimidated awe in the face of such zeal and erudition as Adrian had possessed. Serk's past life, so far as Anne could judge, seemed to have been so untouched by religion that to call him indifferent to it was an overstatement. At least religion was a thing they never fought about. That night, after Louisa was sleeping, Anne said, "Did you know the school is religious? That the children go to the temple every morning, and bow to it from their classroom every afternoon? Louisa complained about it." In uttering this white lie, for Louisa no longer complained, Anne was aware that her motive was not concern for Louisa. It more had to do with how ignorant and bewildered she felt in this place, her husband's supposed homeland, which he regarded, at least it seemed to her, with dispassion and even distaste, like a diplomat tolerating a bad posting because he's been promised it will lead somewhere better.

"It was you who refused to consider the International School."

"Because it's too far away!"

"And *you* refused to take her. Her mother."

"What would I do in Osaka all day, every day?" she exclaimed, as if that were the reason that she had refused, and not her secret that her fingers, legs, cheeks were periodically numb, as if a cloud of death were wandering her body that would neither keep still nor disperse.

"So she should take the train alone. A child of nine."

"You say yourself this country is so safe."

"It *is* safe for a Japanese child, who's familiar with things."

"But not safe for your own child? And yet you dragged us here, so you could help your department chair out of a fix, when the other visiting professor left early because this place is a dump! And since when do you give a damn about helping your department chair with anything?"

"Don't call my goddamn country"—he had her by the front of her housecoat now—"a dump!"

"You call it a dump yourself all the goddamn time!"

There would be hissing and shoving, she might claw or bite—it was frankly sexual, this fury they had to expend, while conscious of the child just a few yards away behind so pointless a wall she was practically there in the room. What a luxury it would be, to bellow and shriek without restraint, to lay hold of real weapons and inflict real flesh wounds. Which was not to say they hadn't done this since Louisa had joined their household—certainly they had smashed plates, they had swung saucepans, they had broken toys of Louisa's, and they had broken skin—Anne had once bitten Serk so hard she'd had to drive him to the hospital. But they'd spent far more energy suppressing such eruptions. Had Louisa not been there to listen, how much worse, or rather how much better, those eruptions would have been.

The next morning, if Louisa noticed Serk's Band-Aids or Anne's bruises, she was soon distracted by a change of routine. Serk had canceled his class at the college. Anne was made up and dressed. Louisa was not going to school. Louisa was suspicious. "Where am I going?"

"We're all going sightseeing," Anne said. "To Osaka." Louisa made her dubious face but went to change out of her school uniform, then was suddenly back at the window, at the sound of her name being called from outside.

"Fuyuki!" Anne heard Louisa bellow, to somebody four stories down on the sidewalk. "Masako!" And then the unmistakable sing-songy sound of a good-natured taunt.

"What's she saying?" Anne whispered to Serk.

"She's saying, *Hey, dummy, guess what? I'm skipping school today!*"

Together, they walked through the white morning light to the train station, through all the mercantile tumult of delivery trucks and handcarts and filthy water being dashed onto the pavement out of battered white buckets. At a far corner two boys in the regulation blue shorts and white shirts and white sun hats and red leather rucksacks ran past, and Louisa rolled her eyes. "They'll be late."

"For the temple?" Anne asked, trying out her new knowledge.

"For *school*," Louisa said. "Temple service isn't for another hour."

At the train station, while Serk bought their tickets, Louisa asked Anne, "What sights are we going to see?"

"I think there's a park and a palace. And there's a place called the Osaka International School."

Louisa stopped fooling around with the box of milk caramels Serk had already bought her. "Why are we going to go there?"

"Why not? It's a very good school, for kids from all over the world. Who knows—maybe you could go there."

"*Why?*" Louisa repeated. "I go to school here."

Now Serk had rejoined them. "But this school might be better," Anne said.

"Why would it be better? I like the school here."

"You *like* it? But you cried every day when you started."

"And *you* told me I had to go back. You can't change me now," Louisa said angrily. "You can't change me to some other school just because *you* changed your mind."

"The train is boarding," Serk said.

"I'm not going," said Louisa. "You can't just make me do whatever you want!" Serk had taken tight hold of her hand and was towing her down the platform. "How would I get there?" wailed Louisa. "Like this? On this train? By myself?"

The train was crowded with commuters, tightly packed on the bench seats, and tightly packed in the space in between, dully bumping shoulders like so many human pendulums, hung by one hand from the dingy gray straps. A single gap lay between a plump woman who sat at the end of the bench seat and a salaryman in a suit. The gap was the width of a person, as if a person had just gotten up, but no one

in the tight-packed car moved to fill it. Both the salaryman and the
plump woman sat with their eyes closed, the salaryman's face impas-
sive, the plump woman's face strangely flushed and tumescent, as if
ecstatic energy were seeking escape. Anne couldn't stop staring at her
and wasn't sure why. If not for the woman's immobility Anne would
have thought she was having an orgasm. Louisa spotted the gap and
made for it, and Anne snatched her by her literal collar and yanked
her away just before she sat down. "What?" cried Louisa, her sense of
grievance, only briefly forgotten in boarding the crowded and intimidating train, now redoubled. A stain was darkening the worn red plush
upholstery from beneath the plump woman. It crept outward an inch,
then another. No one else looked at it or reacted.

"Look the other way," Serk said sharply to Louisa, turning her by
the shoulders to face out the opposite window.

The train ride was just over an hour. The train only took on passengers, it never seemed to let anyone off, so that the woman who
was bleeding, or urinating, or otherwise leaking somehow, was soon
blocked from Anne's sight. Through the narrow interstices that sometimes opened up, between a sleeve and an ear, Anne could glimpse
wires rising and falling, scalloping the morning sky again and again
as if creating a decorative border of light—and at the back of this she
saw the mounded dark hills, humped closely with their bosom-like
creases enhanced by a lingering fog. By the time they reached Osaka
and the train was disgorging its contents, every thought of the Osaka
International School, even of sightseeing, was gone, the precipitous
decision to come to Osaka made invalid in the execution, like so many
of the seemingly serious, seemingly responsible decisions that Anne
and Serk tried to make. They did not even leave the train station. Serk
bought Louisa a box of Pocky and a bottle of juice, and they boarded
the train to go back.

"What was wrong with that woman?" Louisa asked Anne dozily,
as the train started moving again. Now that the plan was abandoned,
now that the train was empty except for themselves and the strengthening light and they each had a comfortable seat, Louisa was again
warm and pliant and loving. She curled beside Anne, one arm flung

on Anne's lap, her face squashed in Anne's breast. Serk sat on Anne's other side, crisply folding and unfolding the newspaper like a change-able shield so that he never met her eyes.

"Sometimes people's bodies do things they don't mean them to do," Anne decided to say.

# Serk

**Just before they came** to Japan, Serk and Louisa had become movie-goers. They had seen *Star Wars*, which wasn't to Serk's taste except for the music, tolerable poor man's Beethoven he afterward bought for Louisa, the big black double album, and let her put on the turntable again and again. They had seen *Smokey and the Bandit*, again not to Serk's taste, but his enjoyment of sharing this ritual with her, the purchasing of the tickets and popcorn, the selection of seats, the quickening of anticipation as the house lights faded down, was so keen he did not really mind what they saw. From his arrival in the States he'd been a lone moviegoer. He had never wanted to share moviegoing with anyone, not even Anne in their earlier days. But his daughter, at age eight, abruptly revealed herself as the ideal companion for movies. It was nothing that she did, no request that she made. One day he simply realized he wanted to go to the movies with her. Then came the search through the paper for something appropriate.

By this stage of Louisa's childhood, their family life was represented by a simple Venn diagram, of the sort that he might draw for Louisa, though without using this example. Two circles overlap. In one circle, Anne. In the other one, Serk. In the zone of overlap, Louisa. Serk and Louisa saw movies and conducted explorations. When she was little they went to the zoo together, or ambled around the town park. Once she was slightly older they drove around in the car, sometimes all the way to Chicago. He took her to Mackinac Island, where they rented bikes and ate fudge. He took her to the Indiana Dunes, where they scaled the highest one, and sat at the top shaking sand from their socks, and afterward they bought salamis from a butcher whose store had sawdust on the floor. Once, in a past chapter of life, it was Anne and Serk who had such adventures, whose very togetherness was an adventure, the sort of electrification that illuminates mundane surroundings. But Louisa's transformation had taken place in tandem with Anne's, as if the same motion that drew Louisa into the foreground pushed Anne back.

From Louisa's birth Serk had monitored her development as a series of cognitive landmarks: learning her numbers, her letters, first recognizing certain printed words, first using such flamboyant modifiers as *actually*. But other amassments—of composure, curiosity, insight—would escape him in their increments, then ambush him all of a sudden. One day, she'd turned into a person he could treat to a restaurant meal, who would sit still, with her napkin and hands in her lap, and tell him funny stories, ask him funny questions. One day, she'd turned into a person he wanted to take to the movies. Of course he felt pride, but it was a strangely impersonal pride, more akin to wonder. He didn't feel he could take any credit for her. He felt if anything an admiring estrangement, across the growing distance of her greater maturity, and it was this that inspired him to treat her to special occasions, as if this were the best way to keep her in sight.

When Louisa breathlessly reported that posters had appeared everywhere along the shopping street advertising the opening of an American movie, *Close Encounters of the Third Kind*, he immediately agreed he would take her to a screening in Osaka. The movie, like the multicolored spaceship of its poster, seemed to have magically descended to distract Louisa from everything Serk feared she might notice and that it was intolerable to him she might notice: the shabbiness of their apartment and of his homeland in general, the lassitude of her mother, the bitter strain between himself and his "friend," a main source of which was the so-called friend's anger at being explained to Louisa this way. "I am her auntie," Soonja had said to him. "Just because your American wife threw her own family away doesn't mean you can throw *me* away."

"You don't understand the risk to me—to my daughter—if it's known that I have family in North Korea. This shitty college where I'm teaching has an exchange with my home institution! If the word gets around there it will follow me back to the States."

"Why are you so ashamed? *I'm* not ashamed."

"It's not shame, it's intelligence. I am not so stupid as to broadcast around the US that my family immigrated to a Communist nation."

"Don't you think I live with the same problem here?"

"You don't understand the difference between the US and here."

"'You don't understand, you don't understand,' this is all you ever say to me!"

"You *don't* understand—where are the travel permits, where are our parents? You said you had it all arranged, were you lying or are you just goddamn stupid? I don't know which is worse!" And this was the too-cruel, because too-true, final barb that Soonja only ever could answer with silence or tears, because their parents no longer sent word of travel permits, or any word at all. Sometimes he relived the argument exactly as it had most recently unfolded, sometimes his own part was honed to a superiorly devastating sharpness, such that Soonja's part would then include pleas for his forgiveness, that she'd made him false promises and all but forced him to upend his life. These were pleas the real Soonja never actually made. Their parents, perhaps even their brothers and sisters, were coming, the real Soonja insisted. He just had to be patient, this was not the US, where things apparently happened like clockwork for him, as if he'd turned into some kind of prince. "You forget yourself," Soonja had said.

"But *when*? But *when*?" a different voice was repeating. His daughter, for the past several moments unseen and unheard, while he obsessively rehearsed these arguments.

"Your next day off from school."

To his surprise, she didn't beg him to let her cut school, pointing out, as she could have, the number of times he'd recently pulled her from school himself. She only leaped gazelle-like from one end of the small cluttered room to the other while singing, "A movie! A movie!"

# Louisa

**She thought she'd lose** her mind from impatience, though it wasn't the kind of impatience she felt for pleasurable things like a good snack when she was hungry, or her friends' voices calling from the street when she was bored, or a beautiful unsharpened pencil in a design she had not seen before. The impatience she felt for the movie had more in common with dread, and the promise or threat that the dreaded thing, once it finally arrives, will at least release pressure. The ubiquitous posters tantalized and unnerved her. There was something decidedly more strange, almost sinister, in the dual-language nature of the poster, on which the title of the film, in English, was surrounded, as if to be consumed, by clamoring Japanese letters in all different colors. When the day of the excursion finally came she felt peculiarly unnerved and resistant to the Osaka McDonald's, though her father had brought her there at her fervent insistence. As soon as she laid eyes on the familiar molded plastic seats and tables in the familiar red and yellow colors, but unfamiliarly crammed with what suddenly seemed to be alien faces and bodies, all ringing with what now sounded like alien language and unbearably shrill alien excitement, she felt sickened, somehow violated. It was as if the Japan-like Japan, in its obvious difference from her, let her breathe, while this unruly Japanese approximation of Americanness seemed to poke and prod and threaten to smother her.

And there was much actual poking and prodding to deepen the

feeling. At the movie theater, as at the McDonald's, the crowd was astonishing, perhaps dangerous. She could see her father's jaw working
as it did when he was unhappy. Gripping her hand, he said, "Don't let
go. Don't wander away." As if she would, in her terror. They had taken
care to arrive very early for their chosen showtime but it appeared
that either the previous showing had begun very late or the show-
times weren't being observed in the first place. Unlike the multi-screen
movie theater at home, part of a brand-new indoor shopping mall,
this theater was an archaic single-screen, intricate and cavernous and
filthy. The outside doors and lobby doors were propped wide open,
and a crammed mass of spectators flowed without interruption from
an interior flickering darkness, through a dingy twilit lobby, clear out
to the midafternoon of the street. Yet the crowd, despite its suffocating
density, was utterly still, the faces of those at the outermost fringe as
attentive as must have been those of the lucky, indoors.

The people near them didn't protest when her father, holding her
tight to his side, began pushing steadily forward. She was reminded
again, by the swarm of countless faces, of the way her father always
looked different. Despite his looking more like all of the swarming faces
here than he did a single person at home, he still looked like a stranger.
The crowd seemed to agree; they flinched aside, pressed harder into
their neighbors to let him get by. Body by body he forced ahead until they'd tunneled through the lobby, then even through the theater
doors. Noise and darkness, the volume so loud she couldn't make out
words. At the obstacle of the rearmost row's seat backs her father
squatted in their compressed socket of space and, unavoidably kicking
both him and several people nearby, she climbed onto his shoulders.
Slowly he stood up again. She hadn't been on his shoulders for years,
knew she was much too tall for it. The soles of her shoes hung as far
as his waist. She was not the only child on an adult's shoulders; from
her new elevation she picked out other children held as she was above
the level of the mob like a scatter of puppets, their rapt, petrified faces
inconstantly lit by the screen.

There was the enormous spaceship, descending like a cosmic
emergency in a roil of blue and red lights.

Then suddenly the movie was over and the theater rippled to life in a strenuous thronging of cross-purposes, half the crowd trying to leave, the other half trying to get better seats, and a steady pressing in from outside to replace the escapees. Her father held his ground, was in one of the few spots, whether from luck or strategy, where this could be done. Yet Louisa sensed that being crushed was a real possibility as she watched her father's hands where they gripped the nearest curved metal seat back. His knuckles showed bulbous through his tautly stretched skin. She could feel his braced tension and resistance to the currents of force on all sides. She never doubted he'd prevail, but she was frightened. And then the house lights went down again and the crowd, as if submitting to a verdict, everywhere stopped where it was, and raised its thousand eyes to the screen.

Then she should have felt better, but unaccountably she was still frightened, in fact was even more frightened, as the movie recommenced in an ordinary daylit American world of moms, dads, and kids. The spaceship invader was unimaginably far away, but that much more terrifying in anticipation. Louisa squeezed her eyes closed and felt tears of fear painting her cheeks, but with closed eyes came a vertigo feeling. In shifts and tugs she made clear her panic, felt her father's bafflement as she came scrabbling down from his shoulders, digging into his sides with the soles of her shoes. Wedged beside him she buried her face in his side, but the film was equally irresistible and intolerable. For two hours she peeked and recoiled, the story stuttering along as if projected from the back of a truck driving down a dirt road.

By the time they escaped it was night. "Did you like it?" her father asked as they walked hand in hand to the train station.

"Yes," she lied, unwilling to risk that the next time there was a movie, he might leave her behind.

"I thought it was very good," her father agreed. "Much better than the one about the shark."

"*Jaws*," she corrected with delighted exasperation, her mute misery of the past two hours instantly forgotten. This was one of their moviegoers' jokes, that her father couldn't remember the unforgettable name of this film. Of course, Louisa had not gone to *Jaws*, it was too scary and she was too young. But she was familiar with not just the story but its particular iconography and mood. The danger concealed in deep water. The rough, uncouth yank, and the futile flailings and screams.

The rare times her father came home before she did, she heard her parents' raised voices down the whole length of the dank corridor. If, like today, she heard nothing from inside the apartment, it meant her mother was alone. And so she was deeply startled, sliding back the panel from the vestibule into the kitchen, to find her mother in the kitchen with a stranger. She faced an eerie tableau, a waxwork, and for a moment, in her mother's inanimate strangeness, Louisa saw the frightening changes wrought in her mother over just a few months—her hollow cheeks, her brittle hair, her tight mouth and ungainly gait—that dailiness somehow concealed.

Her mother sat in a chair facing the stranger, who stood with his fingertips touching the sides of her mother's head, just at the ends of her eyebrows. Sometimes, when reading at his desk, Louisa's father rested the fingers of his hands in the same place on his own head, as if aiding his brain. But those were his fingers, not someone else's.

The stranger's arms dropped and he turned toward Louisa. He was a young man but prematurely aged in some way, perhaps by his thinness, perhaps by the lusterlessness of his skin. He wore pleated trousers with the belt pulled so far through the buckle there was a dangling tongue of superfluous leather he'd had to bend out of the way. Above the pants was an age-grayed white button-up shirt hanging off the sharp points of his shoulders. He had the high cheekbones, sharp jaw, gloomy brow of a matinee idol, unsettling blue eyes. Something in him touched recognition and she twitched away. "Hello, little sister," he said.

"Louisa, you remember Tobias," Anne said, and she sounded very strange, as if playing the usual tune of her voice in a wrong, minor key. "You went strawberry-picking together."

"I don't remember," Louisa said, although, obscurely, she did.

Bright ribbons of recollection, each thinly cut from the overall fabric and beaten hard by the mind's wind.

"It was only two years ago."

"I don't remember," she repeated, and this wasn't entirely a lie. Those things that she did recall only made the memory more implausible. She shouldered her rucksack and shrugged past them, into the living room. But she didn't push the sliding door closed behind her. She knew this would be going too far, overt rudeness for which she'd be scolded, and besides, then she might not know what they were up to.

After a few moments they resumed their conversation very quietly. "It isn't your imagination," Louisa heard Tobias say. "It's not in your mind. But your mind *can* cure all these afflictions. The old cliché, 'mind over matter,' is true."

"I wish I could believe that."

"You're in a good place to start believing. The Japanese have it deeply ingrained in their culture. Look at the ways it's helped me."

"But are you well *really*?"

"How can you doubt it?"

They seemed to realize that, quiet as they were trying to be, Louisa in the next room was even more quiet. Their whispers grew so indistinct that Louisa couldn't make out the words. Then she heard a chair scrape. The next time she stole a glance, Tobias was gone and her mother had groped her way into the doorframe. She was wearing the kelly-green housecoat with the daisy patch pockets she wore every day, all day long, in one of the pockets of which she kept a large flaking metal barrette in the shape of a flattened oval, which periodically she would take out and work open, and try to clamp around the loose hair at the nape of her neck. The barrette closed with two long tines that flared outward a bit at the ends, and could be squeezed beneath a pair of little hooks welded onto the oval; it was a very large barrette, meant to hold a lot of hair, but Louisa's mother almost never could manage to close it. Sometimes she hardly managed to open it. Sometimes she was already in difficulties just fishing the stupid thing out of her pocket. And then there was the gathering of hair off her face into a single tidy bunch, around which the barrette might be clamped: she could not do this, either. Her clawed hands, seeking out the mess of hair to tame it, would rise uncertainly toward her crown as if in fear of going wrong and entangling instead with her ears. Sometimes her hands would shake as they sought out their target—her own head, in between her own shoulders! And the sorry spectacle would wring the breath from Louisa, and she would almost have to sit on her own hands to keep them from snatching her mother's hair, her mother's suddenly mysteriously dowdy dull hair with its unprecedented yet numerous kinky gray strands, and crushing it in the barrette as if its thickness were the neck of some small animal it would be satisfying to kill. When her mother in the course of attempting to grab her own hair dropped the oval barrette to the floor, as almost always happened, Louisa would pretend she hadn't seen, would punish her mother by forcing her to ask her to please pick it up. And her mother would ask in a defeated, hollow voice, rightly ashamed she could not do this trivial thing by herself. It was the voice of abdication, of giving up without a fight, intolerable and yet somehow preferable to the even worse, because thoroughly false, voice with which her mother now said, as she paused in the doorway and started to pat at her pockets for the hateful barrette, "Let's talk, sweetie. I know you have questions."

"Sweetie" was not an endearment her mother often used with Louisa. It always made Louisa feel her mother couldn't quite remember who she was. Now her mother was on the move to join Louisa at the table where Louisa had spread out her homework—trying to keep her balance, her mother actually stretched her hands out toward the table as if in supplication, those hateful hands that were no longer capable of putting hair in a barrette or even cracking an egg. For weeks her mother hadn't even made their dinner omelets—Louisa's father made them.

"I don't have questions," Louisa said. The living room, as they called it, as if they were still back at home, was furnished by an uncomfortable Western-style sofa and by a low square table that was larger than a Western-style coffee table, with heavy fabric flaps descending to the floor on all sides that concealed a small space heater bolted to the table's underside. The heater made a slab-shaped volume of warmth, just the right size for four floor-sitters to bake their crossed legs. Louisa had as always already taken the best side, the one nearest the sofa, so that she could both bake her legs and lean back against the sofa's front edge. This was also the only side Anne could have used; Anne could not possibly sit across from or adjacent to Louisa on the floor, unless she planned never to get up again. And so Anne painstakingly made her way onto the sofa, her unshaven blue-veined legs sticking out from the hem of the housecoat just next to Louisa's right shoulder. Louisa bent her fraudulently studious gaze on her workbook. She wouldn't turn and couldn't be made to, couldn't be made to bequeath her attention, not when her mother was clearly winding up to inflict information, just when it suited her, just the same way she withheld information when it suited her, either way never considering Louisa's preferences at all.

"When I was very young," her mother began.

"How old were you?" Louisa cut her off, feeling her mother in the instant grow stiff with impatience, that Louisa should already interrupt—her mother didn't merely want to tell it when she wanted to tell it, she wanted to tell it with no interruptions to the sound of her voice in her ears, as if she were reciting a script she'd made up.

"I was nineteen," her mother said after the slightest, admonishing pause.

"That's not young. That's twice as old as me. Plus a year."

"When you're older, you'll understand that nineteen is still very young," her mother said in another of her occasional voices, that of fond indulgence, which always sounded put-on, like a too-small coat that won't even button over whatever's underneath. Louisa wanted to say, *Oh, really?* in response to this new information that the age of nineteen was quite young, when she was frequently told, at age nine, that she was "too old" for any number of things, but delicious as it felt to refuse to submit quietly, interruptions also lengthened the conversation, which already in its inaugural seconds felt interminable.

"When I was very young . . . long before I met your daddy . . . I lived a very different life . . . among very different people. And . . . Tobias was a part of that life." And for that reason, of his being a part of that long-ago time of her life, which was very much over now, and of which she retained almost nothing, Tobias meant something very, very special to her. As their lives grew longer, her mother went on—warming to her subject, and seeming to find, as she went, a slightly different script that she preferred to the one she had first had in mind—they came to contain many chapters, all closed except the chapter of the moment, and all closed to each other, but sometimes . . . a character from one of those closed chapters wandered over the divide into the chapter of the moment, and was all the more welcome, for having been so unexpected.

Louisa wasn't going to permit this metaphor success. She prided herself on her reading—the reason, of course, that her mother had chosen to express herself this way. "Books don't change characters in every chapter," she interrupted, after having suffered in silence for what seemed like a very long time. "Books keep the same characters in all the chapters. That's what makes it a book."

"Perhaps it's more like the Narnia books, where characters from one world cross over into another, like when the children go through the wardrobe."

Nor was this fantastical analogy apt, nor was Louisa going to let her mother go on and on until she found the perfect fit, and congratulated herself on her ability to speak her daughter's language. "If he's so special to you, why doesn't Daddy know about him?"

"He does," her mother startled her by saying. Louisa wasn't sure she believed this. It seemed far more likely her mother was wronging her father by keeping a secret from him. If this was true then she, Louisa, held the power to expose her mother's lie. If this wasn't true, if her father was in on her mother's secret, then Louisa was shut out of an adult conspiracy by both of her parents, which felt somehow worse than finding one parent had shut out the other.

"Then why was he here on Daddy's day in Osaka?"

"That was just a coincidence."

"Why did he call me *little sister*?" Her tone was that of rising complaint—she was not aware of striking home but of grasping for straws, piling on the grievances to conceal her loss of standing. She could not see her mother's face, as she was still turned away, taking advantage of her mother's inability to seat herself in a better location, but a moment later she understood her own triumph, when her mother—after all the effort of getting herself on the sofa—tottered back to her feet and made for the tatami room, where her bedroll was always splayed open and her sheets and cushions slopped around— Louisa had entered the homes of enough of her classmates to know how aberrant this was. Louisa's heart was beating loudly in her ears and her eyes could not focus on the homework that she was pretending absorbed her attention. She was ready to resume their combat. She had felt herself winning. But her mother didn't get up again that day, even for dinner. Louisa's father made the omelets, and only the two of them ate.

Exactly a week after his first appearance, there he was again, but this time when she opened the door to the kitchen she found him alone. "Anne is resting," he said as she stared. He said it as if she ought to find his being in the kitchen, instead of her mother, the most ordinary thing in the world. "She said it was all right if I stayed and talked with you. I'm hoping I might be of service. She told me how hard you found the worship movements at the temple. It's complicated, and the children here have done it all their lives. That makes it very hard for you, trying to learn something all your playmates know so well they don't even realize they were taught. But I've learned it. I'll teach it to you."

After a moment she said, very coldly, "I learned it a long time ago."

"That's wonderful. Perhaps we can do it together, and I can tell you what each gesture means? You learned the dance from copying, so these are details you might not have been told. The townspeople here—adults and children—have performed this worship dance all their lives. Many of *them* don't know what each gesture means, because they can feel the whole. For us strangers, it helps to have each thing spelled out."

This time, Louisa was not going to let him get away with it: the maddening air of calm superiority, of self-assurance, as if he somehow owned her and her mother. She was certain he shouldn't be here. Today, this day that was exactly a week since his first appearance, was again a Thursday on which her father was in Osaka, and unlikely to be back before six. Tobias was wearing a pair of sandals that seemed to have been made from old bicycle tires, and a piece of cloth that wrapped around his waist like a towel, and over that a once-regular white buttoned shirt that was gray and yellow with dirt, and so distant in time from its last ironing that the sleeves appeared deliberately crimped, from being rolled up so often and sweated into so much. Assuming her enthusiastic consent to the lesson, Tobias was already moving the scant kitchen furniture out of the way. "Why are you here?" Louisa demanded. As usual she'd left her shoes outside the door but had not yet removed her red leather backpack, and its straps dug like blades into the fronts of her shoulders; it was as heavy as if it held bricks. She did not take it off. If he insisted on being at home here she would insist upon being a stranger.

"I wanted to see you. And Anne. We've been kept apart a long time. Now I want us to be together."

Nonsense words that were easily disregarded. "How old are you?"

"I'll be nineteen this fall."

"My mother says she was nineteen the last time she knew you."

"She was nineteen the *first* time she knew me. That's when I was born. She's my mother, too, you know," he said.

Crossing from ignorance to recognition required just the one step—yet she remained with a foot in the old territory, perhaps even an eye on each side of the line. It was possible to think, in the same dumbstruck exhalation, both *Of course* and *Impossible*.

"She is not," Louisa said.

He seemed genuinely surprised. "She said that she had told you."

"I said I was getting her used to it," came her mother's ragged voice through the kitchen doorframe, followed shortly by her ragged self. Perhaps she'd been making her pitiful way toward their voices from the distance of her bedroll, a mere one room away, the whole time that Louisa had been here. How Louisa despised her.

"I'm sorry," Tobias was saying. "I misunderstood."

"It's not your fault. I wasn't clear," her mother assured him.

Louisa so wished she had screamed at them both, to stop discussing her as if she weren't there, that she almost believed she had done this, so vivid later on was her imagined enactment. In fact she didn't even hurl her backpack in anyone's face, but felt the dull pain of its weight banging onto the base of her spine as she ran out the door, snatching her shoes off the bench as she went.


The metamorphoses of childhood are so swift, it isn't possible to retrace the steps. One day you're the new child, not just new to a school, but new to a country, it can even seem new to a planet. Every other child, every other living being, has the same glossy black hair, which reflects a band of light when the head is exposed to full sun, just like the band of light across one of your parents' LP records, which stays in place, at most rippling a little, as the record spins and spins. Your own hair, the straightness and darkness of which has always been a drawback at home, now isn't dark enough, or straight enough, or glossy enough, it marks you out as different just as if you were blond, but without the aura of international celebrity and wealth you would enjoy if you were blond. Your mother has white skin and blue eyes but she couldn't even manage to be blond, she sticks out like a sore thumb here too, she too is merely wrong without being exceptional.

The other children have not only matching hair but matching faces, which is not to say that they all look alike, or even that they all look like brothers and sisters. It's just a sense of the same materials having been used, though with impressive variation. Her first day in the schoolyard, ringed around by the glossy-headed same-seeming children, their group gaze at her solo strangeness tells her: *We are a tribe to which you don't belong.* Her dull brown hair, her wrong-shape eyes, her gangly height; there's no one thing that invalidates her, but over the next few weeks she'll try to alter or eliminate features, she'll hide her hair in her hat, she'll stoop her shoulders and believe she's grown shorter, and at night she'll pull the corners of her eyes back and try to fall asleep like that, without relaxing her fingers, in hopes that by morning the new shape will take. And it works, though not because she's grown shorter, or slant-eyed, or black-haired, but because, bit by bit, over days, the staring circle has eroded, parts of it drifting away, parts of it drifting near. Earnest monkey-like exchanges begin, with much arm-waving, lecturing, pointing. Louisa absorbs the information that she is wearing her hat wrong, that the white card in the small plastic window of the red leather rucksack is for her schedule, *Here, just give it over, we'll do it for you. Shall we trade pencils? You must get some with pictures, these are pencils for grown-ups. Have one of mine, for a start. Have you really never done this? You're hopeless! Stand behind us, you can follow along and we'll hide you. Oh my God, that fat Yuko split her gym pants, look at her, what a moron.* (The stunning implication: You are not as much of a moron as Yuko, at least one person is worse off than you.) *Hey, my mother made you this bento, you can throw out that weird stuff you bring for your lunch, she'll make it for you every day if you want.*

*Oh yes! Please!*

*Do you really like this food?*

*Yes!*

*Even this?*

*Yes!*

*Then come with us after school, we can show you where to buy this stuff and more. Have you got your own money?*

One day you're no longer the new child, not even any longer the Martian, and though that condition, while it lasted, had inflicted the worst suffering of your life, the cessation was just another of those constant fluctuations of childhood. You did not notice when it occurred. You are different, but the world has not changed, and the world is different, but you have not changed. Louisa doesn't remember learning the Japanese word for *blue* any more than she remembers learning the English word for it as a toddler, and perhaps she never does learn it, perhaps she points to Masako's fresh tube of blue paint when her own is squeezed out. Perhaps, when Louisa goes out alone to buy food in the market—in the beginning, before she simply stops cooking, Anne always wants meat, she wants beef just the same as at home, she wants carrots, she wants the packaged curry to which you add water, she wants spinach and eggs—Louisa merely points, says "That,

that, that." Though she also knows that beef is rarely to be found and exorbitantly priced when it appears, that all these things that look like spinach are not spinach, that her mother ought to cook with the tofu instead of the beef, *It goes just as well with the curry, you'll eat it, won't you, like a good girl? Yes, Auntie, I like tofu better than beef, it's less hard to chew*—perhaps she mimes displeasure at a gristly piece of beef, perhaps she knows *beef*, but not *gristly*, or not yet, the point is she's no longer thinking about it. At first she saw herself as a bug in a jar. Then one day the jar was gone.

Fuyuki and Masako live in her direction, and they walk to and from school together, raucous and rude; sometimes they're hailed by women through windows or doorways who offer them snacks, give them messages to carry, or reprimand them for one thing or another. The town dribbles off at its edges, from the back sides of houses where are slung coils of hose or erected pagodas of plastic and string from which a family's laundry is hung, into zones of piled dirt, piled refuse, discarded shingle and brick, beyond to broken meadows where the plants gradually outnumber the pieces of trash, and then at some point, in another of these unidentifiable transitions, one finds oneself in open country, scuffing the dusty gray road. There is the town in the distance, piled together as if dumped from a sack, the temple roof above all like a pair of dark wings. It's only from this distance that the temple appears clearly taller than anything else; from in town, half the time you can't see it. Louisa had thought the school building must be the tallest in town; from their classroom, on the topmost (fourth) floor, she can see to the tops of the distant dark hills, on clear days she can even make out crowns of trees that grow out of the crowns of the hills. The trees seem to float, like very tiny black clouds, on invisible trunks. If she can see to the tops of the hills, it must mean, standing in her classroom, that she's equal in height to the tops of the hills, mustn't it?—but from here, in the dust on the road outside town, she cannot see the school building at all.

Fuyuki has dragged some broken piece of fencing out of the weeds, two boards nailed to form a cross, with much rusty wire dangling off. Fuyuki stoops and gets it onto his back. "I'm Jesus!" he says, making a face of exaggerated dismay. Louisa laughs uproariously, along with her friends, because Fuyuki is very funny, not because she understands who Jesus is. She only vaguely knows he is religious. This easy mockery of another faith is the closest her playmates ever come to acknowledging their own faith, the faith of the town that requires daily dancing in the temple, daily kneeling on the cold classroom linoleum at the command of the bells. There's no more need to remark upon this aspect of their life than there is to comment upon the eating of regular meals. To Louisa the services in the temple, the classroom prostrations a few times a day, have run together with gym class and fire drills. She does them now without effort or thought.

Tobias's offer to teach her the temple dance had insulted Louisa not merely because she had learned it a long time before. She was insulted because it was him. His very existence insulted her, and all the ways in which he imposed that existence. Just by standing there breathing he seemed to be begging for something. She loathed his pale unwholesome skin, his greasy untrimmed hair, the confusing ruined handsomeness of his features, which seemed to have skipped over grown-up hardness, straight from a boy's freshness to dissolution, like a nice piece of fruit that abruptly is pocked, that will be brown and foul at the pit if you bite into it. Even after his ridiculous disclosure, *She's my mother, too, you know*, which Louisa felt proudly able to ignore, his physical resemblance to her mother remained invisible to her, yet it oppressed her without her realizing. He was uncanny to her, offensive. What she lacked in vocabulary to describe this reaction, she made up for with inflexibility. She wouldn't tolerate the sight or mention of him; all Anne's supplicatory efforts to talk about it were rejected.

She would have liked to tattle about him to her father, but the terms between them had changed in a way that made this feel impossible. Louisa's father seemed to have forgotten she was a solitary, English-speaking, American child. Her first day at school, before she could speak a single word of Japanese, before she even knew *hello* or *please* or *thank you*, he had walked her to the schoolyard gate and left her. "I went to school all by myself when I was younger than you," he explained. What he perhaps meant to say, or should have said, or in any case what she later felt she understood he had meant, was that she shouldn't want to be seen, her first day, arriving at school hand in hand with her father. He had done this before: come to school all alone, from a position of deep disadvantage. She had to get her footing on her own, for the other children ever to accept her.

But she had no way of knowing this yet, and this was nothing like her father had been all her life, up to this move to Japan. At home, her father had refused to let her ride the school bus until the stop was moved, from elsewhere in their neighborhood, to the foot of their very own driveway. He would stand on their front step in his white undershirt in all weather, a pipe clamped in his teeth, his arms folded, watching as she ventured the length of their driveway, watching as she waited with the rest of the neighborhood children, all of whom remembered when the bus stop had been someplace else. He would still be watching, his teeth around the pipestem and his arms across his chest clamped if possible even more tightly—a warning of dormant aggression—as the yellow bus huffed to a halt and she mounted its steps, lagging to be last, because he expected her to turn back and give him a wave before the door was pulled shut. The wave meant the usual driver was driving. Her father sincerely expected that one day the school bus would have been commandeered by some childnapping pervert, and only his vigilance would have saved her.

Then they'd come to Japan, and he'd simply left her at the schoolyard gate. He'd taught her one phrase before leaving: *Wakarimasen*. It meant: *I don't understand*. "Just say that if anyone asks anything," he advised, striding off.

Had he known that her sense of unfamiliar child's power would be superior—if she achieved it—from having so unassisted a start? Or had Japan somehow switched off his vigilance toward her, caused it to be discarded like the rest of their American equipment, their lawn mower and their dark-lacquered sharp-cornered dining room table, and their high, bulky, metal-frame beds, all of which had relinquished their claims, were at best the invalid detritus of dreams? Other times, her father's inattention had the opposite effect, and he seemed to forget she fluently spoke Japanese, fluently moved through the streets of their town just as he did, that, like him, though she might be different, she had somehow escaped being strange. The condition of being a stranger was like an illness: Louisa saw what had happened to her mother. Her mother still couldn't speak Japanese and now, in a transformation that to Louisa was as disturbing as it was logical, her mother couldn't walk and could barely stand up. Her mother was disappearing. Louisa, always uneasily aware that she was half her mother's child, knew the same might have happened to her, but for her father's hazing, or her own cleverness. It had been a close call. Had things gone only slightly differently, Louisa might also be trapped all day in the apartment, lying on the too-short couch under the window, staring at the dull glitter the ginkgo leaves made when they stirred in the breeze. Listening to Japanese radio shows and making pointless cassette tapes of them, to play back and "learn from," as if there wasn't the same kind of radio show every hour. No, Louisa had cast off her mother's specter. Louisa looked and acted like anyone else, she had the power to disappear among children, to disappear down the streets of their town. Yet, nonsensically, that power could be mistaken by her father, the very person who'd helped her acquire it. He would still seem to see her inside a glass jar, of as little account as her mother.

She knew this because he constantly took her along to see Mrs. Ishida, and then both adults would ignore her as if she were deaf.

"I've come all the way back here for nothing."

"Try thinking of them. They were promised the permits months ago."

"They're fools for believing it. We're fools."

"You don't even know how it is."

"And you do? I knew how it would be. I tried to tell them."

"Just because you didn't want them to go doesn't mean you knew better than them. No one knew. You're a monster if you think they haven't suffered."

"I'm here, aren't I!" This said banging the flat of his hand on the table, so the teapot's lid jumped and jangled.

Mrs. Ishida was slender and to Louisa looked younger than her mother, but her children had grown up already and gone off to school.

They'd left comics behind, thick dog-eared volumes in smudgy black ink on cheap rough-feeling newsprint, with only the cover printed in full color on stiff, glossy paper—a teasing deception, which Louisa fell for again and again, pulling these same comics out from the shelf. The stories were all too advanced, less confusing than boring, the heroines with fluffy clouds of hair and enormous dotted eyes like beetles affixed to their faces, the heroes toting massive swords and guns. Louisa read, or pretended to read, these turgid stories she knew perfectly well were for children much older than she, in full view of her father, while her father and Mrs. Ishida not only did not take the comics away, but at times even spoke of Louisa directly:

"Why haven't you given her sisters and brothers?"

"Her mother."

A silence: What exactly was meant was not said, or perhaps it had been said exactly. Silence was a language Louisa had not mastered yet.

"I can see that she's bright."

"Very bright."

"They're so anxious to meet her. They also want to meet your wife. Please say you'll let them. That you'll stop this ridiculousness."

"When they're actually coming—then we can discuss it. I don't want to have this argument again."

"Don't be cruel. It means so much to them that you've made a good life in America."

"My life in America is not what they imagine."

"Their life is not what *you* imagine."

Mrs. Ishida's town tumbled steeply to the sea. From the train station it was all downhill to Mrs. Ishida's, and from Mrs. Ishida's it was all downhill to the shore, which in most places except for the designated stretch of bathing beach was a concrete seawall, along the top of which ran a road. One day, instead of walking downhill from the station to Mrs. Ishida's, they were greeted by her waiting at the station in a car. Louisa was put in the back seat, which was so small, more like a spot to put a grocery bag, she had to turn her knees sideways to fit. She'd grown yet taller since they'd come to Japan but she wouldn't believe it, and her mother no longer stood her in a doorframe to mark her new height as the proof, and even the pencil-marked doorframe was gone, surely that house of Louisa's past didn't exist anymore. Mrs. Ishida drove, Louisa's father folded into the passenger seat, and Louisa couldn't hear them at all for the wind pouring into the car through the open windows. She felt surprising relief, despite the past effort she'd made to eavesdrop.

They followed the winding coast road, the unlovely gray sea to their left, the eroding hillside to their right. It was the kind of lukewarm, clammy day when the hard wind pulled into the car felt a little too cold, but when the car slowed, nosing through a coast town that always looked exactly like Mrs. Ishida's, the air was too warm, suffocatingly damp. The sky was the uniform white of a blanket of fog. Louisa nodded off, started awake with her chin thumping onto her chest. Buildings climbed the hillside, while the sea to the left was pulled into a dingy gray harbor marked by rotted black pilings that rose here and there, each supporting a single gray gull. They parked overlooking a pier, a black road of its own reaching into the water, weighed down on both sides with small boats at anchor. At the pier's terminus, farthest from them, was a much larger vessel, painted black, with beards of rust.

"That's it," said Mrs. Ishida.

"What's it?" asked Louisa, and they both swiveled as if they really had forgotten she was there.

"Don't eavesdrop," Louisa's father said, in English.

"I'm just sitting here!" Louisa protested, pointedly in Japanese.

"It's just a ferryboat," said Mrs. Ishida, the way Louisa's mother would, distracting attention from some failure of logic with a dull observation.

"When does it go?" asked Louisa's father, ignoring Louisa again.

"It's always changing. Sometimes it goes, and sometimes it doesn't. My old neighbor had a ticket and permit to visit her sister. The sister has been very sick. So she came down here and the ship didn't go. They told her to come back again, then when she did they said the permit had only been good for the day that the ship didn't go."

"That's so stupid!" interrupted Louisa. "She should sue them." Louisa understood *sue* as a sophisticated adult form of vengeance.

For whatever reason this time she was not reprimanded for listening in. "You see, she's an American," her father said with bemusement, as if he didn't threaten to "sue" all the time; Louisa had picked up the word from how often he used it to shout people down on the phone.

"Many things are like that," said Mrs. Ishida, of the ship that hadn't gone and the permit that hadn't been valid.

"She should be bringing the sick sister back here," Louisa's father remarked.

"Of course she would like to."

"The sister will be dead before she sees her again."

"I've asked about a permit for myself," Mrs. Ishida said with an air of disclosure. "Just a day permit, for Wonsan. Only if it won't work for them to come here. It would be better than nothing." Louisa's father looked uncharacteristically speechless. "Why not?" Mrs. Ishida went on. "My children are grown."

"You must not!" Louisa's father barked, as if Mrs. Ishida really were, as Louisa sometimes imagined, her mother.

"It's a permit of reentry, obviously."

"Why would you trust them?"

"But it's no use anyway, I heard they're only issued to old people, above fifty. Or sixty. My old neighbor is older than that."

"Japan will take the risk of sending old people because the DPRK won't want to keep them. The Japanese can then say they've been kind to a family. You shouldn't have asked after the permit. Don't do it again."

"There's no harm in it," Mrs. Ishida said mildly.

"You're naïve. You don't think the government keeps a list?"

"I didn't go into an office, I just asked a friend."

"What friend? Don't talk to people about this!"

"Just an old friend from the Organization."

"Especially them!"

"You've been gone too long," Mrs. Ishida complained.

When they all got out of the car, Louisa walked away from them. There was a dirty little beach, black with greasy crushed shells and torn ruffles of seaweed that formed a ragged line where the tide had left them. Mrs. Ishida had given Louisa a sushi roll and Louisa ate it sitting on a dry patch of a slimy washed-up log, out of reach of their voices, though aware of her father looking over the water.

They drove back the same way, the sea now to their right, the hill-side to their left. It was evening by the time Mrs. Ishida left them at the station. It was the last day of spring vacation, tomorrow she'd be back in school again. Louisa was glad. She missed school. These long days she spent with her father, which housed so much unease she couldn't name, made her lonely, though not for herself, exactly. "Why couldn't she have driven us home?" she asked, slumping against him.

"Our town is a long way from here. And we stayed late. It's time for her dinner."

It was also well past time for Louisa's dinner, but this went unmentioned. Louisa recalled, long ago, sitting down at the table to dinner. Plastic Tupperware tumblers the color of mustard, with water for her parents and milk for herself. Square paper napkins she folded from corner to corner to form triangles. The thin white dishes with the blue floral pattern that circled the rim. Many of these had been broken, one time or another, by her father in one of his fits. Somehow there were always enough matching plates. Perhaps her mother bought more. It had been Louisa's job to set the table.

"Is Mommy dying?" she asked him abruptly. He jerked upright, which made her sit upright also.

"No," he said after a pause, his voice oddly thick, as if his mouth were full of additional things he'd thought better of saying.

"Then what's wrong with her?"

Another long pause. He would not meet her gaze; he stared out the station's high windows.

"I don't know," he finally said. "But I'm sure that she'll feel better soon."

This was a cowardly dodge. He couldn't really think Louisa would believe it. His cowardice emboldened her. "Would you rather be married to Mrs. Ishida?" she asked. Louisa was careful in striking a casual tone; *she* would rather he be married to Mrs. Ishida. At the same time, she howled inwardly at their heartless betrayal of her mother. In her mind, she stood down on the sidewalk, craning her neck to look up through the ginkgo. Its rustling and shifting disclosed first this bit, then that, an unfinished mosaic. Her mother. She thought her mother, gazing down from the window, might see her. She thought her mother might smile. She raised her arm, waved as hard as she could. In her mind, her mother then smiled hugely, then waved hugely back—in brief stillness she saw the whole picture, before the tree, dense with brand-new spring leaves, closed over her mother again.

They had left her mother all alone, from sunrise to well after sunset. Her mother could not even walk.

When Louisa hated her mother, it was because the thought of her caused so much pain.

When she hated her father, it was because she was conscious of emulating his remoteness.

But now her father laughed into his hands. When he lifted his face, it was as wet as his palms. "Mrs. Ishida's not a lady I will ever want to marry," he told her.

# Anne

**In the early years** of their marriage Serk had taught straight through the summer because they'd always needed money. After Louisa's birth, there had been a few summers off, filled instead with toiling, unsuccessful recreation. They bought a Coleman tent and tried camping, but Serk disliked the presence of other people and the multiplicity of rules—he would want to bushwhack into the pristine forest and set up the tent in some spot that had never been used—and Anne, though she didn't admit it, disliked the outdoors, the small bugs flying into her ears, the omnipresence of grit, the profound darkness housing strange sounds. They had tried the shore once or twice but Serk would sit hunched on the sand, in his white undershirt and his khakis, appearing almost crushed by the weight of his fear that Louisa would drown. He didn't even like to see her caper through the flat tongues of foam that were left to subside once a wave had collapsed. He himself never swam, never even put on the trunks Anne had bought him.

By the time Louisa had turned four or five, Serk was back to teaching straight through the summer again, and the season became one for Louisa and Anne to share and endure. Whether a day was happy or tiresome, whether the lemonade stand turned a profit or the tadpoles died, it was a time of almost fevered duality. They quarreled, and embroidered winsome samplers. Anne sewed Louisa a fairy dress of pale yellow and pale blue flounces, and made her wings of white pantyhose stretched over bent wire hangers. Louisa took over Anne's front flower bed and constructed a rock garden, from rubble she made Anne help her steal from a derelict lot down the block. They spent hours at the park, at the pool, with other mothers and children, they both burned their palms on the hot metal slide, they knew as well as battlefield nurses the routine of bacitracin and Band-Aid. To Anne, this was motherhood—not her own mother's depleted benignity, nor the sharp exasperation of some of the other young mothers she met, but being playmates. Her own authority was perhaps sometimes lacking. But after all, she'd been raised by her sisters.

The most recent such summer was only one year in the past, a fact Anne could not keep tied down in her mind. Anne had with her a Kodak photo of Louisa in the flounced fairy dress and white wings, seated grinning at her lemonade stand at the end of the driveway where, Serk later declared, she could have been run over by a neighbor: the white border around the edge of the picture contained the small black number "77." Just one year, just twelve or perhaps only ten months ago. Anne was so fond of that photo she'd tucked it into her wallet with her money—it was too large for the little plastic sleeves—and brought it on this trip by accident. Now it was the only proof she had of that life. She'd brought no other photos from home. She hadn't anticipated a crisis of belief.

It was almost July, but the Japanese schools began summer vacation much later than American ones. While Louisa was still out all day, Serk and Anne made several trips to Osaka in secret. Each trip was arduous and expensive, requiring taxis each way from the stations, requiring Serk nearly to carry Anne downstairs and into and out of the taxi. This was the first time she'd felt him bent in wordless service to her, felt the touch of his hands, in more years than she wanted to count. Each pilgrimage to a new kind of Japanese doctor: a doctor of the eyes, a doctor of the hands, a doctor of the legs or the brain. Anne felt her helpless impassivity during these visits could hardly have been lessened had she spoken the language. Every part of her felt cut off from the others, the integrity of an able and obedient body that had once been beneath conscious thought had grown unimaginable;

had they been home, with a doctor who spoke her language, Anne still might have been mute. Yet the verbal gunfire that passed back and forth between Serk and this Japanese doctor or that made Anne feel murderous. Had her fingers not been numb claws, she might have strangled them with their neckties until their purple tongues hung from their mouths. Had her legs not been lead, she might have stormed out of the room. Her tongue still worked, yet she didn't use it until she and Serk were alone.

"Goddamn them!" she screamed in the taxi. "What the hell do they know? Goddamn fucking third-world shitheads!" For the first time in their marriage it was Serk's turn to withstand a barrage of profanity.

Black clouds wandered over her vision, yet the optometrist found nothing wrong. Her arms and hands, her legs and feet, didn't work—no, she couldn't be more specific! They didn't *work*, she raged, slapping the backs of her curled-up hands violently on her lap—she couldn't even manage to slap them palm-down, she could not turn them over, her least gesture was deformed and impotent. Perhaps she ought to see another specialist . . . or perhaps a psychiatrist. "I'm not the person in this marriage who needs a psychiatrist," she snarled at Serk, at the same time thinking, of course she was, but that had been true for years, for years she'd hidden all that underneath an attractive façade, and vastly worse than the deception was that the façade was now crumbling. They fed her into a machine and scanned her brain. Stiff with claustrophobic terror in the smooth, dark, plastic throat, which would have made a coffin feel roomy, she lay panting in fear, thinking of Tobias, and that insult to his brain that he now claimed had been his salvation. It would be the same with her, she imagined. Genes were a final frontier, more distant than galaxies, most esoteric in the schedule by which they released hidden freight. She'd always blamed Adrian for whatever was wrong with Tobias; now, with a sense of sacrifice that she realized was just as self-serving, she hoped to blame herself. She would be diagnosed with just the same growth, she would be rescued in just the same way. They had to wait for the results; the phone call came the following week. "Hai?" barked Serk. "Hai . . . Hai . . . Hai . . . Arigato!" That was all—he hung up. "Thank God," Serk said, almost trembling with relief. "They found nothing." He didn't understand when she wept in despair.

Serk and Louisa had used to be apologetic about going places Anne felt unequal to, like the famous park at Nara, where Louisa fed deer from her hand, or the famous towering pagoda, with the ancient coil of wooden steps that Louisa climbed all the way to the top. But when Louisa's school was finally out, the two of them went off every day without so much as telling Anne where they were going. She would come inching unsteadily out of the bedroom, willing her legs to wake up, and see their blank, deceptive faces staring at her, their excursion clothes buttoned and zipped, the egg yolk going cool on their plates. "We didn't want to wake you," Serk would say.

"Where are you going?"

"Sightseeing," Louisa would reply, poker-faced. Perhaps they really were.

The apartment, on the top floor of the poured-concrete building, had remained clammy and cold for weeks after summer weather had come to the world outside. The building entombed forgotten air, the same way it entombed forgotten Anne. Then one day the building was clammy and lukewarm, and the next day it was clammy and hot. Their rooms were all on one side of the hall, their windows all faced the same way, the collective effort of an army of tabletop fans could not muster a breeze. *No, no, no, no,* the fans shook their heads, while they traded the stagnated air. Anne's disorders grew worse in the heat. She hardly slept. Before, she'd had the energy to grapple with her limbs, even if the grappling ultimately failed. Now she had no energy at all. She could barely get herself to the toilet. She was glad Serk took Louisa out every day, all day long: she didn't want to be seen. In the winter, she and Serk had agreed on the lie that perhaps she would feel better in the summer, when it wasn't so cold. Now they agreed on the lie that perhaps she would feel better in the winter, when it wasn't so hot.

Despite their precarious finances—or perhaps because of them, because Serk couldn't stand feeling too poor for something—Serk returned from an extra-long day out with Louisa to announce he had rented a house by the sea, in a small fishing town about an hour due north on the train. He and Louisa had spent many days exploring up and down the western coast, he revealed, and this town where he'd rented the house was safe and inexpensive, and the air was much cooler. After dusk it was practically cold. Anne would sleep well. She might even step out the front door if she wanted. There were no stairs to keep her confined.

Anne knew better than to protest this expense that they couldn't afford. Also she was surprised and moved, that he'd done this for her. "Is that true, sweetie pie?" she asked Louisa, in a cheery voice that slightly overshot the mark. "Have you seen this little house?"

Louisa only nodded. "It's nice," she said after a moment.

"Did you help Daddy find it?" Louisa shrugged and lagged out of the room.

"She's tired," Serk said.

From the beginning Serk had insisted they not talk to Louisa about Anne's condition. They were never to say Anne was sick, only that she was tired, that something about the water, the food, the very air of this country did not agree with her. It wasn't serious, it wasn't lasting, it was sure to pass off any day. Children only knew what you told them, Serk maintained, and you did not tell them things that weren't meant for their ears. Money troubles and marital problems, illness and death, all were unfit for the ears of a child, or at least for the ears of Serk's child. "But she can see for herself something's wrong," Anne argued. "If we don't talk to her she'll be frightened. She'll come up with some wrong explanation of what's going on." No, no, absolutely not, Anne was not to spoil Louisa's innocence just because Anne was selfish and craved sympathy! Here was the threshold beyond which good sense was discarded, and plates flew through the air.

And so Anne found an unexpected but welcome discordance in Serk's having taken Louisa to rent the beach house. It was as if Serk and Louisa were momentarily the parents, making arrangements for Anne, the sick child. Serk's enlisting Louisa's assistance, Serk's speaking, in front of Louisa, about the benefits for Anne of the house's cooler air, and lack of stairs, might mean they were giving up secrecy. It was a policy Anne was already failing to keep, not by telling Louisa with words but by being the way that she was.

"Is the house furnished?" Anne asked him. "Will we need to bring bedding, or things for the kitchen?"

"You only need to pack your clothes," Serk said.

They moved into the small seaside house the first week of August. At home, there would have been corn on the cob and hot dogs, the summer concerts of Sousa and Copland in the little pavilion down-town. Here, there was the vendor who wandered the streets from the late afternoon until long after dark, keening like an injured animal jettisoned by its flock. When you summoned him, he poured eggy gold batter into greasy black molds, then turned the fast-baking cakes from the molds with his greasy black fingers and handed them to you. Anne ate the steaming hot, barely sweet cakes seated outside the door of their house, in a small plastic chair, while the last light died out of the sky. Across the gravel street was the sea. Tirelessly it assaulted an ugly breakwater of broken cement, pimpled thickly with sharp bar-nacles. It was not picturesque. It was not the familiar lakeshore, blue and white and smartly creased as a uniform. This water was vegetable-dark, like the sheets of black seaweed Louisa ate wrapped around fist-fuls of rice. But its breath cooled Anne. She did start sleeping better at night. And its varied continual noise, as of scolding, somehow soothed her inflammations. She was still weak, she was still made of lead, but she felt serene, propped in her chair. Old or ill people, at the ends of their lives, were often propped up in a chair by the sea; now, without resentment, she understood why. She felt included in the workings of the world, and in its movements among other worlds, and in whatever the great gyre was that encompassed them all. She felt, not quite that she could see beyond where she was sitting, but at least that she didn't feel blindered, as she had by their window frame in the apartment, which was always crammed full of the ginkgo, unless Anne pulled herself to the sill and peered over as if down the edge of a cliff. Some-times Louisa had called out to her from the sidewalk, and Anne would struggle to get in position to wave gaily back, like any mother, waving out any window.

A peaceful routine, when succeeding turmoil, after just a few weeks has the feel of an eon. The best kind of eon, untroubled and unmemorable. Dinnertime, though the sky is still bright. The husband, who has always arrived at a table expecting prompt service, instead serves: some cheap, tasty thing he and the child have shopped for together that only requires being put onto plates. As the child helped to choose it, she likes it. She eats avidly without any complaints. "Can we go back to the beach for the sunset?" she says to her father. "Just a short walk," he says. "Sunset is soon." Water and darkness combined make the husband nervous, the wife knows. He is relentless, you might even call him obsessive, about the child's safety. Before they set out, he helps the wife to her chair just outside the front door so she, too, can enjoy any colors that bloom in the sky. "Will you be cold?" he asks her. In this eon of peace that has settled—since when? ten days ago? two weeks ago?—the husband has reverted to someone the wife somewhat recalls from many additional eons ago. A man who is, if not exactly tender toward her, very careful and watchful. This is how he shows love, she believes. She also will try to show love, by not showing surprise at his solicitousness. "No, the breeze feels good," she says, and in any case, they both know that he and the child will be back soon, and he can bring her inside.

She watches them set off, the child skipping ahead but stopping short at the edge of the empty coast road. Her father still insists she hold his hand to cross the road, even if it is empty, and she still obeys him.

The swollen sun, sinking low in the sky, dull and orange as a persimmon, pours its warmth onto Anne and she closes her eyes. The air is the perfect temperature. She is not hot. She is not cold.

Nothing but the sea's exhalations; Anne startles awake in her chair, fingers and lips, legs and feet, numb, it must be from the actual cold and not just the nameless disease that runs its tendrils all the length of her body but hunkers its roots still nobody knows where. It's night, the sea made that much more enormous by the blackness in which it is hidden. Why is she still sitting here alone? Her teeth making a type-writer noise in her mouth. They've left her, is her first wild thought. For months Anne has feared that Serk thinks she's insane, whether willfully or helplessly it doesn't matter. Any loss of mental control is distasteful to him, distaste his constant emanation toward her, the only way he reaches toward her at all, this ethereal negative touch. He and Louisa have not returned from their walk, the house is cold and dark behind her, the sea is a black void in front of her, a single thought stands in her mind, that he has taken their child and left.

Lit by the bare porch light bulb, she is paralyzed in the folding chair, whether by her body or mind makes no difference. Twisting and struggling, expending her torso's last strength, she wrenches the folding chair more centrally into the doorframe and then is able to shoulder open the door. She's still confined to the chair, her arms and hands no better than dead, but she can see across the small, cluttered room to the clock: 9:40 p.m. The house has no phone, and Anne has no words in the language apart from *hello, goodbye, thank you,* and *please.* A child's good-manners words. Anne has no adult words. No emergency words.

The night diverged from its normal course around 9:00 p.m., the hour at which they usually come back, but deciding upon the diver-gence must wait until at least half past ten. You are a foreign invalid with a frail, fearful mind, pathetically suspicious of what, in this land foreign to you, is mere harmless everyday life. Say they have encountered a neighbor out walking and are enjoying a long conver-sation, say they are standing at a noodle vendor's cart, steam pulled sideways from their bowls by the wind like a pair of white flags. Most times, your husband is ferociously protective of your only child. He rages at you if you don't adjust her blanket in the night, if you crimp her depleted toothpaste tube and create a sharp corner upon which she might cut her hand, if you serve her canned soup that contains chemical additives. And sometimes your husband is unpredictably permissive with your only child, taking her to movies for which she's too young, or on an overnight excursion for which she'll miss a day of school. Always, this unpredictable permissiveness toward the child coincides with your exclusion as the unable, or uninterested, wife. You are too tired, too sick, too slow, too indifferent, you are told. Tonight must be an unadvertised version of this infrequent but habitual exclusion. That it was unadvertised doesn't make it unlikely. They are secretive, these two people upon whom you, their mother and wife, are as dependent as an infant—in fact, they've grown more secretive in direct proportion to your growing dependence.

Such thoughts, though in shrill and half-articulated form, take Anne through half past ten in the hard folding chair in the doorway beneath the porch bulb. The night further deepens and she feels the planet increasingly turning its back on the sun. The deepest depth of night doesn't come all at once as the word *nightfall* wants you to think. Its heatlessness and lightlessness are incremental, dialed by a merciless hand like the hand of the clock. When is night coldest and darkest? Logic tells us, midway between sunset and sunrise. Poetry tells us, just before the dawn. Experience has no opinion. The bulb-bewitched insects have given up killing themselves for the night. Nothing stirs but the irregular wind and the unseen ocean hissing and slapping its coils. The ocean, drowned in darkness on the far side of the street, sounds louder and seems nearer for being invisible. It is this amplification that at last detaches Anne's helplessness from herself. Empathetic speculation does not accumulate gradually. It electrifies with revelation. Anne understands all at once that Louisa and Serk have been plucked off the beach by the arms of the sea. Louisa is a child, Anne has never seen Serk swim and suspects he cannot. The tide has risen or the sand sunk without any warning; anything can happen onshore under cover of dark. Anne falls, or rather throws herself, out of the chair, taking the impact on her right shoulder, right brow bone, and right cheekbone, because her arms are too numb from whatever the cause to catch her. By dawn she'll have a lurid black eye, which will add its own substantial complication to the piecemeal narrative. Anne is moaning, or keening, she is emitting the strangled vocalizations of dreams as she undertakes the stymied locomotion of dreams, the agonized slow-motion running through molasses or drying concrete, not that Anne is doing even half as well as one does in one's dreams. She is not even upright but writhing around on the floor. What is she seeking? In what pitiful way does she think she can help?

Weeks ago, before they had moved to the seashore, a photograph of Serk and Louisa materialized on the small corner table where Serk tossed his billfold and keys, his spare change, other random detritus from pants and shirt pocket. A striking photograph, not only for its quality but for its anomalousness. Serk and Louisa both looked particularly handsome, both facing into a stiff breeze that lifted their dark hair away from their faces. Serk's trench coat billowing slightly like a cape, one half of Louisa's blouse collar standing up, Louisa wearing her school uniform, a windbreaker, her loose hair pulled out of the twin ponytails Anne once carefully formed every morning, which Louisa must now form herself. In the background, dun sand and gray ocean, perhaps the very stretch of ocean that crouches in darkness beyond the front door—but the appearance of the photograph had preceded their move to the coast. High gloss, vivid color—the photograph was entirely unlike the dismal, muddy scenes they produced with their Kodak. Who had taken this photo? Not the square format of their Kodak but rectangular, as if to better accommodate how much taller, how much prouder, Louisa appeared in this photo than in any others of her Anne had ever seen, let alone taken. The photo had been printed with a white margin in which appeared, in tiny print, "FUJI"—a Japanese brand of film—and this unending year of their exile, still just two-thirds gone, "1978."

"A friend," was all Serk said when Anne asked who had taken the photo.

"What friend? Where are you?"

"The beach."

"I see that, but what beach? When did you go to the beach?"

"You were sick." That was all. End of story.

Moaning, keening, writhing, Anne locomotes across the tiny living room into the bedroom, arms awakening under duress. As if hauling herself from the ocean, Anne achieves the high ground of her bed, achieves the hook from which is hung her fat, ugly, Naugahyde purse in the concealed inner pocket of which she has hidden that photo, along with her passport. Serk's secret from her, so carelessly left in plain sight, has for weeks been her secret from him. She has stolen the photo, if something discarded and unmissed by its owner can be said to be stolen. When Serk and Louisa have left her alone in the house, Anne has passed the hours in study of that photo as if long-enough staring might rotate the scene to reveal—not herself, but the rest of this alluringly alternate world, in which Anne has never existed.

Photo in the pocket of her housedress, Anne half crawls, half writhes into the night. She is disheveled, unable, effectively mute with her howling that cannot explain its cause. She is not alone long. Whether she finds, or is found, by the neighbor who calls the police will remain undetermined, but this indeterminate fact, unlike others, will not make a difference.

The next hour sees the beach being searched by the prefectural police and volunteers who stream out of their homes in the darkness, wearing house shoes pulled over their socks and old sweaters pulled over their pajamas, no one delaying even the minute or two it would require to properly dress, ready flashlights seized from their spots by front doors. A seaside town, before its halting beginnings—still far from complete—as a cheap summer place, a fishing town where everyone has known someone lost to the sea. Everyone knows about tides, rip currents, the locations of just-offshore rocks. The winds are light, the night air is mild, the water temperature in these dog days of August is as mild as it gets, conditions are exceptionally fortuitous. Before the tide has turned they've found Louisa, lying on her face in the tide margin, soaked to the skin. She is hypothermic, blue and gray, her small jaw grotesquely hinged open by the plug of sand filling her mouth. So obviously is she dead that the two townsmen who find her don't immediately turn her over. Rather, one waits, his flashlight solemnly trained on the back of her head, while the other, shouting hoarsely, conveys the discovery to the police. To an investigative eye the position of Louisa's body might have offered some indication as to whether she had actively swum or floated lifeless to shore, or never been offshore at all but been felled far above the tide line, so that the sea, in cautious ventures and retreats, only later curiously strokes her small foot and calf, as if to ask why she doesn't respond. An investigative eye might have been able to judge, perhaps from the depth of the indentations in the sand beneath Louisa's prone body where the tide achieves greater erosion, roughly how long Louisa has lain in this way, turning ever more waxen and blue. But there is no such investigative eye in any of the grave, pale faces surrounding Louisa, not even those that belong to the officers of the prefectural police. After all, there is nothing here that defies explanation. To find a drenched body hurled on the sand, some short distance from the ocean, is no more mysterious than to find a bloodied body hurled on the street, some short distance from an automobile. Here is the culprit now: as hands reach for Louisa's arms and legs, the sea, as if protesting the loss of its prize, unfurls a swift tongue of foam that overtakes Louisa's whole length, washing over her head, and Louisa convulses, gagging and spewing the grit-foam, the liquefied sand.

Instantly the solemn scene collapses into pandemonium. *Ambulance! Blanket! Turn her over or she'll smother! Don't turn her over or she'll choke!*

The chance to save; the risk of blame.

Once the ambulance is screaming for the hospital, the search for the father resumes at a gallop, night's funereal cloak cast aside. If the child could survive, the adult must have. The night rings with shouts as of a fervid congregation. Deliverance is at hand. Festooned with lanterns, the fishing fleet is moving out, their frail light breaking over the restless black water like a dissolving Morse code. The water's surface is infinite variation infinitely renewing itself and every variation appears to someone as a man's waving arm or bobbing head; on board vessels arguments are breaking out about which way to go, which chimera to pursue. Onshore, the damp sand has been thoroughly plowed by the townspeople's feet. If there were formed, earlier on this night, footprints or bloodstains of interest, they've been effaced as thoroughly as the water effaces the brief marks we make passing through it. By dawn, some of the searchers have fallen asleep on the sand. This vigil is equally unsuccessful. Their resolve leaks away with the strengthening light.

Later on when Tobias joins Anne at the hospital the two of them must present a strange sight: the white mother and white brother of the not-quite-white, nor-quite-Japanese, almost-drowned girl. Tobias in the ill-fitting good clothes he has borrowed from someone so his vagabond appearance won't draw unkind stares. His bony ankles and wrists protrude from too-short pant and shirt cuffs. Anne on the other hand does not even have the presence of mind to realize that she looks like a vagabond, too, in her raincoat put over her housedress and her rarely used sneakers shoved onto her feet without socks. That's what she had been wearing when the crisis swept her up, and the moment hasn't come yet when the crisis must readmit the ordinary, must allow for a shower, a snack, a change of clothes, all of which take on the solemn air of rites, and the obscene air of desecrations.

Tobias translates, Anne scribbles, miraculously her hands behave, and this ancient capacity, shorthand, blesses her with a task absorbing enough that the meaning of things can be shrunk for a while to the tip of a pencil.

—*went for a walk on the beach often did*

—*after dark?*

—*before and after dark. often did, watched the sunset then stayed for the stars. had a wheel that showed their names*

(Anne had not known this)

—*only on beach? Or also on the jetty?*

—*I slipped and fell, he tried to help me*

—*but Daddy couldn't swim?*

—*I never saw him swim before, I don't know if he could*

In other repetitions of the brief story, which Louisa told without complaint, without tears—without, it seemed to Anne, expression—many times over the handful of days she was kept in the hospital, it was Serk who had slipped and fallen first, Louisa who had tried to help him.

—*I hit my head and then I don't remember anything else*

*—you hit your head when you fell off the jetty?*

*— . . . yes. I hit my head and fell.*

*—you fell off the jetty, and then hit your head? On a rock?*

*— . . . yes.*

*—what made you fall? Did a wave come?*

It had been a calm night, the sort of night in which whatever light breeze has stirred the warm air while the sun is still up drops away when the sun does, leaving a sea that, for all its vast coldness, stirs intimately like a pond. Sound must have carried easily, fighting only the water's lugubrious sloshing, not a deadening roar. For Anne had cried out, and been heard.

Still, an accident. No less strange than small. A man and child, not despite, but because of the calm of the sea—they're seduced—walk too far on the jetty with no source of light, slip and fall. Someone slips, someone falls.

There had not been a moon, was that right? So this thing with the stargazing made feeble sense, though deep within, and disregarded by the outermost part of herself, Anne rebels against this. But perhaps this is only her jealousy. By the time of his death, the world Serk had shared with Louisa was far larger than the world in which Anne lived with either of them.

Had there been other people? In some tellings, there were other people on the beach at sunset, who faded away after dark. In other tellings, there were never other people on the stretch of the beach, far from the harbor, where Serk and Louisa had gone. In either case, no one had witnessed the mishap, no one had been there to help.

Anne's inner rebellion, however long it continues, is quashed. The water is combed through by boats, the shore either side of the town by grim strong-stomached volunteers, but no corpse appears. After two days the search is called off. It might be summer, but the water is cold. The water is presumed to have taken the body as thoroughly as it's taken the life. In this seaside town such an occurrence, though always dreadful, is also commonplace.

Serk, Anne knows, was reflexively suspicious, of inanimate objects no less than people, and fanatically protective of his child. He never even permitted Louisa to walk on the jetty in daylight.

Yet Anne says nothing. Well as she knows this, she also feels she has never known Serk, that her most confident assertions about him are wrong. When she was asked about his next of kin apart from herself, she was only able to say he'd lost touch with his family members before she had met him. How unfair it felt, the faintly disapproving expression her sad ignorance provoked from the local authorities, as if it proved a failing of hers, and not a policy of Serk's against which she'd been helpless.

Pointlessly fastidious in her helplessness, Anne translates her shorthand into legible phrases while her memory serves, though already, just hours later, the words she's notated rebel against her, don't make sense.

—*I hit my head and fell*
—*you fell, and hit your head?*
—*yes*

Anne does the best she can with it, impelled by the sense that some authority higher than these courteous, apologetic locals, who have already closed Serk's case, will require this transcription of hers for some great reckoning. And sure enough, the next year, when Louisa, under threat of being thrown out of school, is sent to the district psychologist, he will ask Anne if she has any notes that pertain to Louisa's near-drowning. How legitimate she'll feel as a mother to tell the man, *Yes*.

Returning home on that terrible morning, climbing wearily up the stairway to the top of the seawall, one by one the townspeople passed by the two pairs of cheap rubber sandals, one large and one small, neatly placed side by side on the bottommost step with their toes pointed inland. Nobody touched them. Later in the day, the sandals accumulated a glass jar of flowers, an apple, and a bowl of cold rice. Throughout that fall, through sun and rain, the sandals accumulated a bleached appearance, cracks in their rubber; they accumulated, nearly vanished beneath, a daily renewal of incense, small candles, figurine totems, local fruits of the season, occasionally handwritten notes, drawings, folded paper animals and stars, trinket bells, always fresh flowers and rice. In this way, several steps of the staircase in that little town where Anne and Louisa and Serk lived together for less than three weeks came to be largely obstructed, and the staircase itself, no longer a reliable beach access, came to be used more as a sort of bleachers, a place to watch the ceaseless action of the waves. Those who brought shrine offerings usually sat down and stayed, for as long as their day would allow.

Not until a violent storm of midwinter, more than half a year later, would the shrine disappear, overnight and all at once. It would not be rebuilt.

# Tobias

**The custodian remembered** Tobias, well enough to be visibly surprised by his altered appearance. Dark slacks belted over a respectable shirt, close-toed if cheap shoes. The slacks and shirt still hung from the knobs of Tobias's shoulders and hips, the belt was still drawn through the buckle to the inmost hole and the excess flapped like a tongue, the points of Tobias's collarbone were still sharper than those of his shirt collar. Yet he no longer resembled a beggar. He had made himself respectable, with these impoverished but mostly clean clothes that were free of gaping holes and unravelments.

"My condolences to your family," the custodian said, bowing deeply.

Tobias bowed in return, the way it was supposed to be done. His skin may have been white, but the volume of his being, he had come to believe, was Asian, most obviously in these graceful displacements. The torso levered smoothly from the hips, the even magnetism of the palms. He could still recall, but with remote wonderment, his unbalanced, twitchy teenage former self, his abhorrence of confinement whether it be the elastic band of his jock shorts or his father's expectation of reverent attention. That former Tobias had slumped and slouched, scratched and squirmed, in his thinking no less than his limbs. He had been a helplessly terrible student, a late and agonized reader, almost certainly an undiagnosed dyslexic. He had been incapable of repose even in his sleep; through the age of sixteen he had regularly fallen out of bed like a child of two, once even fracturing his wrist to the point that his mother—Norma—had put a rail on his bed (which his father had promptly removed).

"Will Mrs. Kang and her daughter return?" the custodian asked as they trudged side by side up the four flights of dank cement stairs.

"No. They've already gone back to America."

"To think these strangers came to my country and suffered a catastrophe like this. I'm just a stupid old man, but my heart is broken."

"That's because of the size of your heart. But, you know, my sister's husband wasn't a stranger to your country. He was born and raised here."

"Was he! I didn't know that. But he was Korean."

"His parents came to Japan from Korea to work, in the war years. After the war, they remained."

"I see. They were some of those stay-in-Japan Koreans. What prefecture and town did they live in?"

"I don't know. I didn't know my brother-in-law very well. How regretful I feel. I assumed there would be much more time."

"Death is the only sure thing, but we never expect it. Don't make yourself feel bad, young man. You're a good person, to help out your sister this way."

Tobias wasn't aware of deciding upon this imposture. He'd arrived at it by instinct, which belated consideration only ratified further. For one thing, it was a form of tact. Anne was understood here in exclusive relation to her late husband and to the child of their marriage, Louisa. Revealing himself as her son would have only exposed Anne to unkind speculation.

In the corridor they passed through the rich odor of the lavatories like passing through a cloud. Drenched rust, algal darkness, hardy microscopic flora requiring little human contribution to thrive. It was oddly an odor of human absence, of the living world indifferent to the comings and goings of people. These were Tobias's favorite sorts of places, abandoned and vibrant with invisible life. These were where he felt It, where he caught the fleeting Clue. His father's dogged insistence that every such clue had been dropped by a fatherlike God had done much to drive Tobias away from him—both the father and the fatherlike God—a circumstance Tobias would have liked to discuss with Anne but had not, and not just because the unspoken rule of their relations seemed to be that they didn't discuss Adrian. Nor because, even if they had discussed Adrian, in this imagined discussion she might have said, *All of this about* toilets? A smile—in fact it was Anne's smile—rippled over Tobias's face as he thought about Anne being puzzled by him. Unlike most people, she was not put off by the puzzle. Perhaps they would solve it together, Tobias and this late-arriving, second-chance mother of his. Tobias remembered Anne explaining to him that the college had given their family the entire floor of the apartment building so that, unlike the residents of other floors, they would not have to share toilets. "They're disgusting, but they're all ours," Anne had remarked of the toilets. This was the sort of blunt and funny thing Adrian and Norma had never said to him. They'd never joked in that or any other way.

In the vestibule, he and the custodian slipped out of their shoes and bent to put them on the shoe rack, which was partly occupied already. The scuffed oxfords with ragged laces were Louisa's school uniform shoes, abandoned for a month at the shore. By the fall she would have outgrown them. A pair of black rubber overshoes were obviously Serk's. Leaning in the corner, a child's clear plastic umbrella with a bright yellow handle. On the opposite wall from a series of hooks hung the deflated corpses of their winter coats. Even these Anne hadn't wanted—she and Louisa were not returning to their old home, they were moving to live with Anne's brother in Los Angeles. Anne and Louisa had jettisoned three households in less than a year, winnowing their things to a pair of suitcases. Tobias admired this, even as he worked to counteract it, briefly studying the yellow-handled umbrella—not merely counteract it, but countermand Anne's one request to him. "I don't want anything," she'd said. "Throw it all away." Even when he'd promised to do this he'd known that he wouldn't, despite having left everything of his own past behind. He was hard-pressed to explain why he felt unable to let Anne do the same. Perhaps because, unlike him, she was doing so under duress, reacting to the shock of unexpected

death. For Tobias, it was the shock of unexpected life that had compelled him, or inspired him, to be rid of the past.

"They had a lot of things," the custodian observed, after they'd
stepped over the threshold from the vestibule into the kitchen and
paused a moment in silence. The custodian was reluctant to leave Tobias alone, from some lingering need to be sure that Tobias was not
a con man. At the same time he was embarrassed by his doubt and
so pretending to enjoy their conversation. Tobias didn't mind this. In
fact he wanted the man to stay, to disrupt with his presence the atmosphere of uncanny absence. The apartment was the wrong kind of
abandoned.

"For American people, they had very few things. In general, American people own much more than this."

"You speak so well, I forget you're American, too."

"You honor me," he told the man, making quick work of the kitchen,
the one room in which he'd spent time on his previous visits. Anne's recipe box had gone with her to the shore; there was nothing else here of
importance. Tobias moved on to the family room, the custodian defer-
entially trailing behind. Here lay the challenge, the layered sediment
of family life, six months' worth no less daunting than six years'. In
a crammed bookshelf next to the window were stacked shoeboxes
full of cassette tapes labeled in Anne's hand with dates from March,
April, and May. There was no cassette tape player to be found, it must
have gone with them. All the tapes would have to come along, there
was no way to pick and choose between them, no way to rule them
out as a whole. The same proved to be true of the pile of Louisa's
schoolwork, the many stapled and stitched and decorated and plain
workbooks and notebooks in which Louisa had recorded vocabulary
lists or practiced her kanji or done her American "phonics," whatever
these were. The books, no less than the tapes and the schoolwork,
were unsortable; after the books, the clothing. The wardrobes were
stuffed full of non-summer clothes, Louisa's thick wool tights, her
blue uniform sweaters, her weekend plaid kilt with its gold safety pin,
her corduroy jumper, Anne's rarely if ever worn "special occasion" silk

blouses, some with large floppy bows, her everyday polyester slacks, her small box containing a set of clip-on earrings and broach made of blue metal flowers, all these items no less harrowing for their wearers' continued existence than the tangle of Serk's black dress socks, the limp ranks of his white and blue dress shirts, his empty gray suit. Tobias couldn't find a basis for picking and choosing, he'd lost sight of the goal or perhaps never had a clear goal, in a blind trance he placed item atop item in a mounting heap, straightening with small yanks and caresses, as if tenderly laying each discarded cloth husk in a grave. And how was he going to get all this back to wherever it was he was planning to keep it? The custodian had been drawn into the work, he, too, was piling, folding, sorting. At Tobias's request he absented himself to run to the market and returned somewhat later with empty bags, boxes, and sacks. Toward the end, having forgotten the vestibule where they began and having used all of their containers, Tobias and the custodian tied the winter coats and shoes into a bedsheet and stuck the umbrella through the knot as a handle.

Entirely outside Tobias's consideration from the start had been the items of actual value: the furnishings, futons, floor mats, and cookware. The custodian had made silent note of this, all his doubts about Tobias forgotten. As Tobias regarded, with dismay, his own handiwork, the custodian departed again to arrange affordable storage, or transport, or both. The custodian insisted upon providing this service, it was the least he could do. Tobias nodded his consent, hardly hearing the man. He'd been alone with his thoughts for some time. When the man was gone Tobias's last strength went also. He practically crawled to the sleeping room, and lay curled there on the tatami, staring into the gathering dusk. The tatami, as they always did, smelled deliciously of fresh hay, of a lost but unforgotten country life. Tobias must have dozed; he started awake, his heart galloping. His body felt battered and helpless, as if cast down from a height, or as if the floor had reared up and struck him. He heard the movement of the outer door: the custodian, returning. This must have been what woke him. Yet he couldn't dismiss the feeling that something else had occurred in the room.

He was on his feet and had found the light switch in the moment it took the custodian to rejoin him. He asked the man, "Was there an earthquake a moment ago?"

"An earthquake? I don't think so."

"Maybe just a mild tremor?"

"I don't think so. I didn't feel anything."

"I must have been dreaming."

Before they left the apartment for the last time at the end of the night, Tobias returned to the sleeping room and on an impulse lifted the edge of the tatami. He was almost unsurprised to see a little sheaf of paper, several sheets from an extra-small notepad that had been further folded in half so as to barely span his palm. Unfolding, Tobias saw a child's rickety hand densely crossing the pages. Pencil, English. Even without these clues he would have recognized Louisa's writing at a glance from his long study, earlier on this day, of her tedious schoolwork. Nowhere in those numerous notebooks had he seen anything like this, a hurried but lengthy outpouring of thoughts. Tobias refolded the small sheets and slipped them in his shirt pocket. Later that night, alone in his hostel, he read them.

*I had a weird dream. I was at the beach with my dad but it was really pretty, not like beaches here. We were standing on the beach but at the same time we were standing on top of a hill with the water below us. The hill was smooth and green and really steep, like a wall coming up from the water. There were cars on wires going down from the top of the hill out over the water for as far as you could see. I can't remember what those kinds of cars are called. I looked far out to where they got so small you couldn't see them anymore and there was something sticking up out there, small like the size of a mushroom. But it was getting closer until I could see that it looked like a tower of water. The water in the tower rushed up like a waterfall turned upside down. The tower moved closer and closer, gliding the way people walk if they're wearing a skirt that's too long that you can't see their feet. I'd never seen anything like that before. The tower got louder the closer it got, making a noise like a storm.*

*Then I was in the water and I could feel how the tower was sucking
me in. I tried to scream but I couldn't make noise, and tried to swim
but couldn't move. The ocean was roaring and shaking like when a
train passes. Then my mom woke me up and said, There was just an
earthquake, did you feel it? It felt like when a train passes by. And
that's how I remembered the dream. The first second I woke up, I
couldn't remember. Now I remember it all as if I had been there.*

Nothing about the account suggested why it had been removed from
its notebook and hidden. Nor was there a clue as to the date, although
of course it had been prior to their departure for the house by the sea.
The earthquake was no aid; throughout Japan such minor tremors
were mundane. Tobias reminded himself it didn't matter when the
pages were written, or why they were squirreled away. Their youthful
authoress had surely forgotten, herself. *Now I remember it all as if I had
been there.* Tobias, too, remembered it all as if he had been there, even
before he reread the pages, which he would do many times. The uncanny feeling they gave him derived from himself. He was frequently
forced to conclude this, about all sorts of uncanninesses.

"You are not so special," his father had said to him, not long before he left home, "that everything that happens to you is a sign or a
wonder."

"No," Tobias had agreed. "I've just inherited the tendency to think
so, from you."

By the time Tobias's flight lifted off it was October 11, 1978, one
week into his twentieth year, and more than four weeks into the time
he'd intended to spend helping Anne in Los Angeles. One thing after another had seemed to conspire to delay his departure, people and places
he'd been unable to part from without visiting one last time; things,
most often insignificant, to which he'd paid tender tribute. The weathered shrines by the roadside; the sample soups, grown congealed and
buzzing with flies, in the noodle house windows; the tattered plastic
tents within which wizened men tended wizened bonsai. He'd found
himself suffering the sensation of leaving a homeland, he who'd felt no
such thing for the actual homeland he'd left. That harrowing day he'd

seen Louisa inert on the cottony slab of her hospital bed, he'd thought
of the wisdom-struck faces of the young Egyptian dead, painted, as
if to serve as a wordless unspeakable label, on the face-ends of their
mummies. He had stood in line the previous year with Adrian to see
King Tut's tomb contents at the Field Museum. Louisa in her hospital
swaddling had not even been as expressive as an Egyptian memorial
portrait. Louisa, who had defied death by drowning, had not seemed
alive. For two days bereaved Anne had kept a solitary watch on this
enigma from the hard-backed chair into which police detectives had
deposited her without once offering her food, a cot, clean clothes, an
English-language interpreter, let alone condolences. Then Tobias had
come, as if assuming a role that had always been waiting for him, as
if those little services by which he'd paid his temple board, by which
he'd drawn closer to Anne, had been mere preparation for this solemn
appointment. The feeling had carried Tobias through the settling of
Anne's affairs, the packing of her abandoned apartment, but now it
deserted him. As the plane rose away from Japan it shook violently,
eliciting gasps from the passengers as it sliced through invisible, powerful currents of air. Tobias could almost imagine that these emitted
from him. His seatmate was an elderly Japanese man who had intro-
duced himself during the boarding in painstaking English: "I visit sister, Los Angeles. First time US!" When Tobias had answered him in
Japanese, the man's voice dilated like his smile. "How will I practice
my English on the flight, if you speak Japanese so well? It's just my
luck!" "Then we'll speak English all the way," Tobias told him in English, "because I need the practice as well." As the plane continued
to struggle upward, like a senseless fish butting its head through one
hostile current after another, the man peered thoughtfully in Tobias's
face, and then took his hand.

"Don't cry, my friend," the man said in English. "If this plane crash,
you and I, brave." Tobias clasped the hand back and laughed through
his tears.

"Thank you. We already are brave."

"Ah! We *already* are brave," the man repeated, nodding his appreciation for Tobias's reminding him of such a useful time expression.

# Part III

# Anne

**Anne's brother and his wife** waited until Louisa finished fourth grade to kick Louisa and Anne out, on the literal last day of school, when Louisa came home with a smile on her face and a messy stack of schoolwork in her arms she'd apparently been proud enough of to show off. Both behaviors, the smile and the pride in schoolwork, had been absent from Louisa's repertoire since the trip to Japan and would be absent for a long time again after this day. Anne couldn't have been the only one of the four adults to wince, in guilty anticipation, as they sat together in the front parlor—Anne and her brother Gerald and his wife Dina and Louisa's school psychologist Dr. Brickner, whom Gerald and Dina had called in as some sort of referee—listening to Louisa shout "I'm home!" and "Guess what!" from the front hall as she audibly kicked off her shoes, *bang, bang,* against the wall. At some point earlier that spring Gerald had led Anne into that front hall to show her the many little gray marks that had come to decorate the baseboards. "Here, and here, and here," Gerald had unnecessarily pointed out, while Anne, who struck those baseboards often enough with her wheelchair—though not in this particular locale, as she almost never used the front door—could do nothing but sit and try to look sufficiently contrite for both her child and herself. Louisa's smile had disappeared the instant she saw them all sitting there, though she hadn't, as Gerald and Dina likely expected her to, simply dropped the load of

schoolwork on the floor. She'd kept it clutched to her chest all through
the terrible conversation. Anne couldn't blame Gerald and Dina for
throwing them out; they were retired people, their sons had long since
left the house, and Gerald and Anne had barely known each other
growing up. By the time Anne learned to tie her own shoes, Gerald
was already off in the infantry liberating occupied France. But the way
it all happened—the school psychologist appearing at the door, Dina
pouring out her grievances to him as if he were *her* therapist, all of
it no less an ambush on Anne than on Louisa, but Anne having to sit
there, as she always now had to sit there, as if she were one of the
powerful adults and not, herself, an equally helpless child—that part
was especially hard to forgive.

With Gerald's guilt-money, as Anne thought of it, Anne was just
barely able to rent an apartment, in the kind of neighborhood where no
child safely walked to school, where there were no parks, where the cars
parked at the curb had their windows smashed in, and where the neighbors all seemed to be furtive young men, angry-eyed and fast-moving.
There were no other families, no children. The apartment was dark
and dank with matted carpeting and a too-narrow tub that did not fit
a shower chair, so that for years Anne had to shower sitting with her
limp unmuscled butt precariously planted on the cold rim of the tub,
shower curtain sticking to her shoulders and quantities of water escaping onto the floor so the vinyl peeled up at the edges. They had
been so poor. Gerald's guilt-money, Serk's tiny university pension that
paid out to her, had been so little and Anne's medical bills were so large.
At thirteen, Louisa lied about her age to get a job at a pizza restaurant
in the strip mall, and every shift she worked Anne "let" her bring them
the throwaway pizza for dinner, ostensibly because she, Anne, was too
tired to cook, a truth that concealed the more pertinent truth that Anne
had no money for food.

But somehow Anne eventually found her job at the MS Foundation, after first having gone there for help. What a nice surprise, to
find she could also help them. Apparently there'd been some cultural
decline in the Art of Typing, evidenced by Louisa's not caring when
she failed it at school, typing class being to Louisa a joke—but joke or

not, people still needed things typed, and since the start of her current remission Anne's hands worked okay at most times. "Okay at most times" was "great" in the Foundation context. Many of the other MS people the Foundation liked to hire had crabbed useless hands paired with still-okay legs, instead of Anne's combination—though how Anne would have traded the hands for the legs, those slender strong uncherished legs of her youth! Gliding her over the earth! Sometimes she awoke with a phantom sensation of walking, residue of a dream. If Louisa had already left for the day, Anne would let herself cry, even scream. She never so much as misted an eye when Louisa could see. She was aware that Louisa regarded her as an unfeeling person, a sort of robot whose heart—if she even had one—must be made of the same dull aluminum, cold to the touch, as those hideous crutches all but fused to her arms.

Let her think it. Anne would rather be hated by her daughter than pitied, having experience of both.

After Louisa left home for college Anne found that by switching to a one-bedroom she could afford to move to a nicer place. At the old apartment, her back windows had looked out on her parking space, roofed with corrugated tin, and her front windows had looked at a wall. The new apartment was washed in sunlight. The actual building was nothing special, just a two-story box of orange brick holding four small units, two down and two up. But the freestandingness of that box meant that each apartment had three sides of windows—each was almost its own little house. Each had a back door that opened directly on so much yellowish but neatly mown crabgrass it could feel like a pasture, the way it stretched out in front of the building all the way to the faraway street, and to the sides all the way to the neighboring buildings set far enough apart the builders could have put a few more buildings in the spaces between and yet hadn't, and most narrowly behind the back door, where it ended at the driveway across which were the carports—the apartment manager gave Anne the carport nearest her place. This still made a distance of about thirty feet from the seat of her car, across the driveway, up onto the curb—very tricky, no railing—across the narrow sidewalk onto the grass, level but spongy, and finally to the back door, which had a step of its own and again no railing (though Anne learned to come around to the side of the step and grab the outside doorframe and the drainpipe). It was not the worst obstacle course Anne had faced, but other places she'd lived had more clutter, more things to cling to, the sides of buildings or the poles holding up a breezeway. Yet that perilous wide-open vastness was just why Anne moved here, because she'd sooner die tripping over the curb than live another day without sun streaming into her rooms—the small living room with the big picture window, the snug bedroom, best of all the kitchen, where she'd sit at her table eating whatever little thing she'd cooked, as she perched on her chair by the stove.

The generous feeling wasn't just in the light. The widely spaced boxes of brick that made up the complex—which was a large one, with several streets of its own wending through it—were actually decently built. The cupboards in the kitchen weren't particleboard but gold-stained solid wood. The shiny bathroom tiles, in a pink and black pattern, resembled the bathroom tiles of Anne's childhood home. The window frames were not warped aluminum and unopenable; they were wood, and they opened and closed. And all this simple quality, which had so long been gone from Anne's life, seemed to emanate a good feeling, or absorb it, or both, from all the other ordinary people who lived in the other brick boxes scattered at their odd angles across the carpet of grass that even sprouted the occasional shade-giving tree. People left their doors standing open when it wasn't too hot—another thing, like the tiles, Anne felt she had not seen since childhood. Almost no one drove the streets but the people who lived there, and so the littlest kids safely rode bikes and trikes, and men propped hoods open and worked on their cars. Sometimes a family would set up a barbecue grill and carry chairs and a card table and a radio outside that would be tuned to the rock stations Louisa had played as a teen, or to something in Spanish. And when Anne came click-clacking along—slow as the snail but without the snail's grace, and with her shopping bag wildly swinging off one of her crutch handles—often some neighbor, some young man from one of the cookouts, or some college girl, would stride over without the pitying smile but what Anne could swear was a regular smile, and take the shopping bag off Anne's crutch handle so it no longer banged on her leg, and walk Anne, at Anne's glacial pace, all the way to her door.

Which was how she met Walter, although he wasn't a young man from a cookout or a college girl or wearing any kind of smile.

She'd made her usual pilgrimage to the grocery store with the sit-on-top scooters—it was her very own Foundation that had made the store get them—to pick up her usual couple of things. One of the many ironies of being so helpless was that you only could carry a couple of things, so that although going to the grocery store was a major exhausting production, it also needed doing almost every other day. On this day, the haul was a high-effort bag with a pound of ground beef, a single onion, a can of tomatoes, a box of spaghetti—Anne still made Louisa's favorite meal at least once a week, she hadn't had a new cooking idea in decades. She'd almost completed the trip without killing anybody or dying herself, the last obstacle the turn into her carport without hitting the metal supports. Slooooooooowly she did it, white-knuckled and jutting her jaw until the car neatly sat in her slip. Anne glowed with pleasure each time. They made it! Organizing herself to get out took forever, but there was nobody waiting. *Bang-rattle-accidental-whack* as she threaded the long clumsy crutches between the front seats, the small interior of the car and long inflexible crutches always a maddening mix, at last got them onto her arms. She had already opened her door, lowered the left foot, flapped it around on the pavement a bit, awaiting some sense of connection that did not always happen. Proceeded to the right foot, which required a twisting-in-place to get the hips faced the right way. Shopping bag was already hooked to the right-hand crutch handle, purse was already hung like a bib around her neck, car keys were already inside it. She did the twist, and that was when she saw his feet, then looked up to see the rest of him. Where had he come from? It gave Anne a start, the way he'd materialized in the spot on which she was just concentrating so hard, to avoid running into the pole. But that might have been as many as ten minutes ago.

He was a big man—he looked down at her from a great height. Long solemn red face, long ginger-haired arms dangling from the short sleeves of a clean-enough, no-iron, button-up shirt. Chest like a barrel and long skinny legs, saggy pants. She realized she'd seen him before, ambling unhurriedly over the grass.

"This sure is a whole lot of work," he observed.

*Everything's a whole lot of work when your legs don't*, she wanted to snap back, but he was so awkward standing there, without either a normal or a pitying smile. Very carefully, as if reaching into a thorn-bush, he took her shopping bag off her crutch handle and then stood gripping its handles in his big hands like a trained bear that had forgotten its trick. He was really more trouble than help, blinking anxiously down while she readied herself for the Big Heave. All at once he grabbed her by her left upper arm and pulled her upright without even asking. Riding the momentum of her outrage, Anne threw herself toward her back door, *click-clack-click*, set off without looking back.

"Should I lock it?" he called after her, about the car door.

"Yeah, lock it," she yelled, hell-bent on getting over the curb and then up her back step before he'd caught up. But this was a hopeless ambition. He was already at the curb, grabbing her by her forearm again, which might have actually saved her from pitching onto her face because she'd been going so fast she'd let her top half get ahead of her bottom.

Once she'd finally unlocked her door she dropped into the chair waiting directly inside. Her back door opened into her kitchen, same as every other back door here, presumably including his, and her fridge faced the back door, same as all the other fridges, again including his. Still he hovered in the doorway, awaiting permission. "Just stick that in the fridge, thanks," she said of the bag, hoping to be rid of him, but he carefully unpacked the bag on the counter, placed just the beef in the fridge, looked at her questioningly for the rest. "Leave those out on the counter, I'm going to cook in a couple of hours," she told him impatiently. He seemed to really want to put these away but he followed her orders. No one could ever understand that putting that onion, box, and can more properly away would just make more work for her later, wasting the precious energy she needed to cook. There was nothing for him to do but leave. The tide of adrenaline that got her to the store and back had receded and she needed to rest. But he was still standing there.

She was literally drawing the breath to say *Thanks, you can leave now* when he said, "You're Anne Kang." He mispronounced her last name, not saying it like *"bang* but with a *K,"* her decades-old explanation to people of how to pronounce it, but some way more muddy and dull. Before she could correct him, he added, "It says on your mailbox." She wanted to know why he'd been peering at the tiny mailing label she'd typed and stuck on her tin mailbox, which happened to be on her side of the vestibule, inches from her front door, meaning she could open the door and hang on to the frame and unlock and empty the mailbox with her free hand without even an extra step needed. That mailbox was a luxury to her, she was as proud as if she had put it there herself. Now she had to picture this galoot squinting at it. "How come you're reading my mailbox?" she asked, feeling he'd earned her unfriendliness.

His long red face got redder. "The young lady, Ginger Matthews, who lives upstairs from you—she told me there's a new lady living downstairs, her name's Anne Kang's how she said it, like *bang.* Just checking I heard Ginger right, I looked at the mailbox and I read it, 'Anne Kang'"— he said Anne's name in that wrong way again—"and I was, uh, very interested someone with that name should move in around here. But that was—that was back a few months ago, now. And I kept my eye out, but it seemed like . . . I didn't see anyone named that."

"I don't get out much because it's a real production, as you can see."

"You get out quite a lot," the man contradicted her. "You move pretty damn good on those things. Sometimes too fast, it looks like to me, and with too much stuff hanging on you. You should let people help you out more."

"You should" this, "you should" that, how she hated hearing this from busybodies in her life, and now from this wouldn't-go-away stranger! "Well, I let *you,* so thanks—"

"Walter," he put in.

"So thanks, Walter, and now if you don't mind—"

"What I meant was, I kept my eye out for Anne Kang"—still saying it his way—"but I kept seeing you. And I finally figured, you're her."

"For Pete's sake!" Anne broke out. "I *am* her, do you want to see my driver's license? Special Cripple's Edition?" Of all things to do, Walter cracked up.

"'Special Cripple's Edition'—that's a good one," he said, turning even more red, but it seemed with pleasure. Most people wilted when Anne said "cripple" and "crip," so she said them as much as she could. Something dawned on her, without any lessening of her annoyance. "Is it because I don't look Oriental? If that's what you're puzzling over, you're right. Kang was my husband's name." Poor Walter's face stayed red, but the chuckles drained out.

"Um, it was—"

"He's dead," Anne clarified. Her arms were still in the cuffs of the Canadian crutches, which stuck out to either side like the legs of some huge metal spider. Anne shifted her forearms and gripped the handles in readiness—she was going to stand up, make her way to her bedroom, and lock the door behind her. He could let himself out.

"I'm awful sorry," stricken Walter said.

"Thanks, but it was a long time ago."

"I would have liked to talk to him," Walter bizarrely continued. "Are you going somewhere?"

"I'm going to lie down. What's wrong with me makes me real tired, and I've been tired since you got here."

"Well, I'm a goddamn idiot," Walter cried. "What a damn shit-for-brains! I was just so damn curious seeing that name." Anne was on her feet again now, pointed toward her bedroom, while Walter did a motionless dance in which wanting-to-help-her was counteracted by being-scared-he-might-trip-her. This ought to keep him occupied until she was out of the room. "How about I cook that spaghetti," Walter suddenly said. "That's what you got going here, right? Fry the onion and beef and throw in the tomato—I could do that, and you could just sit there, or keep lying down." Anne couldn't see his face anymore—she'd rounded the corner, out of the kitchen with its slidey linoleum into the more-grippy carpeted living room, where she took on some speed, just a few yards to go. If this Walter tried to follow her into her bedroom, she'd take out his eye with a crutch—the joke was on her, imagining this. No man, even some dumb galoot, would ever want her again, when one hadn't in half her lifetime. "How 'bout five?" Walter called after her.

"Okay, okay, five!" she called back just to be rid of him. She sank gratefully onto her bed at the same time as the back door clicked shut finally.

Then he came back at five.

Practically at the stroke of, like he'd been standing outside her door peering down at his wristwatch so that he could knock the same instant the second hand crossed the line. Later on, when she knew Walter better, she'd be sure this was just what he did. Walter was scrupulously on time, as if afraid of some punishment handed down from on high. Walter was always a little afraid—a big man like him!—and this knowledge, once she acquired it, would make her heart actually ache in her chest, the way her calf muscles ached long ago when she ran, when she really used them to their limits.

But that was a long time from this day when they met. Anne still didn't know Walter, and in fact had forgotten his insistence, three hours before, to intrude on her dinner. In those three hours she'd barely had time to marshal the resources, by lying very still in her bedroom where the blinds were always down in readiness for her to collapse, to get herself upright again, contend with all the indignities—before, during, and after—of using the toilet, and then at last to relocate herself, in a clean and decent state, to her small living room and turn on the TV for the news, her nightly habit and pleasure. What's-happening-out-there. How-bad-is-it-now. Back when she could still walk, Anne was never one for the news. In fact, she'd intensely disliked Serk's dedication to it. Dinner preparation had better not interfere: if she banged pans too loudly or ran water too hard so he couldn't hear, there would be hell to pay. If Louisa had a little friend over and they made too much noise—he would never scold Louisa, but his ears would turn red and he'd snarl at Anne about something. In their old house—that unlikely

mirage—the kitchen, dining area, and "den" where their faltering old
Zenith lived were one continuing space, though the den had a step
down and carpet, while the kitchen and dining room were floored in
linoleum. It had been a very modest-sized house, a one-story ranch
like almost all the others around it, but on the inside despite the low
ceiling there was a sense of openness from that absence of walls. Anne
standing at the stove or the sink could see the Zenith's screen two
rooms away, see the glossy stubborn back of Serk's head—how it managed to so convey stubbornness from the back was amazing. To Serk's
left, out the sliding glass doors where all their neighbors had a stone or
wood-plank patio, a few outdoor chairs, a barbecue, they had none
of this but only the lawn coming right to the threshold. Serk was obsessed with that lawn, he would not hear of covering so much as a
square inch of it with a nice patio, he would have put the house on
stilts if it meant he could plant more grass seed. It might have been
the most American thing about Serk, how fiercely he tended his lawn.
And he'd been good at it; sometimes the other husbands up and down
the road came and asked him questions. A strange sight, those pink
and white men in their belted beige shorts, pretending to have just
happened to be walking by when Serk was mowing out front, so they
could just happen to ask him what fertilizer or seed he was using without seeming to actually care. Men who otherwise never spoke to him,
looked straight through him with a blind smile while complimenting
themselves, probably, that they let their kids play with Louisa.

Anne is deep in the past now, standing unaided with her bare feet
sunk into that lawn, at 4:59 in real time as Walter's fisted hand is rising
toward but not yet making knuckle-contact with her door. The grass is
really something. The way it feels against the soles of her feet reminds
her of her fanciful idea of shrinking to Tinkerbell-size to take a walk
on Serk's skull. Serk's spectacular hair is another thing she would bet
that the neighborhood men hate him for, most of them not even forty
and already bald.

Why's she on the lawn in bare feet? It's an exciting day, a long-
forgotten day of actual shared anticipation and cooperative work. In
preparation for their trip, Anne has signed up for an adult-ed Japanese

class. The timing is terrible for her; she has to make a cold dinner beforehand so it's ready to serve the instant she gets back. But the teacher
is marvelous, handsome and young—Mr. Ogawa!—that's exactly his
name. His English has no trace of Japaneseness, close your eyes as he's
speaking in English and you'd think he was just anyone. This however
doesn't help Anne with the Japanese part. She toils over the katakana,
cannot tell the kanji apart, and worst of all sounds like a perfect idiot
when she opens her mouth. There is no conceivable connection between the stuttering noises she makes and the bewildering artillery
fire that will spill out from Serk on those alarming occasions he gets a
long-distance call—always snatching the receiver from her as if there
were a chance she could eavesdrop on him. But despite her hopelessness as a student, the injury to her ego—Anne has always been a quick
study, this is her first genuine intellectual failure—her pleasure in the
class is undiminished. In fact, it only grows as the class ebbs away, until
she realizes her pleasure is linked to a cautious idea. Late in the semester, time having almost run out, Anne lingers after class as handsome
Mr. Ogawa is packing his briefcase. He's much younger than Serk—he
might just be a kid, Anne realizes, passing for older in his starched
shirt and tie. "How can I help?" he asks Anne in his easygoing English,
which never ceases to surprise her, as well as to cast into starker relief
the forbidding cliff-face of the Japanese language. His patient recep-
tiveness, so unlike Serk, almost defeats her English, too.

"My husband . . . I'm taking this class because he comes from
Japan—in a few months we're going to visit—I wonder if you'd come
to our house and have dinner? I think it would make him so happy, to
speak to a real Japanese."

Mr. Ogawa laughs with delight—he is honored. The day and time
are set.

It must be October—the weather is exquisite. A deep blue sky, as
if the stars might wink on in daytime. Cool and breezy. Anne's purple
clematis scales the trellis as if wanting to touch its star-petals to the
ones in the sky. The lawn is in its full glory, cool and enfolding to the
touch, a lake disguised as grass. As nice as it ever gets. Serk as well is
as nice as he ever gets, if solemn and even the slightest bit anxious. It

might be a long-lost relative they expect. They'll eat outdoors—Mr. Ogawa will like that. When Anne tries to point out they have no patio, Serk brushes her off—there's no need. Together they carry a card table into the middle of the backyard, set it under the walnut. Put a tablecloth on it, bring chairs—Anne is in charge of this, nothing else. More astonishing even than Serk's manner is that he has insisted on shopping and cooking, activities she has never seen him perform, not even in their earliest days. This emergence of his hidden competence doesn't anger but moves her. Watching him mix up a soy sauce marinade for the steak and asparagus, set the coals in the new-bought hibachi—where have these skills been hiding?—Anne is riven for perhaps the first time by how alone and lonesome Serk must be. Even, or especially, with her.

Louisa has been sent for a sleepover with the across-the-street sisters who are her most frequent playmates. Anne has put on a dress— she can't remember the last time she wore something nice. Surprise, it still fits. She's noticed she's losing weight lately. Serk has traded his summer uniform of white Hanes undershirt and lawn-mowing shorts for his school-year dress shirt and slacks, although he rolls up the sleeves carefully so as not to mar them while grilling. It's as if he has just gotten home from teaching—and what would that be like, Anne allows herself to wonder, if there were days when Serk came home, rolled up his sleeves, and made *her* dinner—rather than wrenching open his can of Black Label and turning his back to her, to watch the news in strict silence while expecting to find dinner waiting for him on the table the instant Walter Cronkite signs off—but there's no time to think of this now. Mr. Ogawa has arrived, in a jacket and tie. He and Serk, two of a kind, shake hands, take a step back, *and bow to each other*—while Anne stands to one side in her nice dress, pair of clip-ons, even lipstick you'd be forgiven for not noticing, since her jaw's on the ground. But she's on the outside of this, a spectator. At the beginning Mr. Ogawa does his best to include her, both translating himself into English—"I'm telling him I can't believe he got his doctorate in only four years—I'll be lucky if I get mine at all!"—and picking out

some easy bits of Japanese for her—"*Oishi*—right, Anne? Delicious!"
But as the food goes down and the beer goes around, this effort trails
off, and Anne doesn't mind. They talk and talk, these two handsome,
sort-of matching men, although the longer she watches them, sometimes touching her lips to her half-glass of beer, which will last the
whole meal while the men seem to go through a beer every couple
of minutes, the more different they appear. The glowing red-brown
of Serk's skin, as if he were constituted somehow of the same stuff as
the coals in the hibachi, beside Mr. Ogawa's marble-like paleness; Mr.
Ogawa's pen-and-ink features and Serk's carved-clay ones; Serk's impatient shoulders chafing his dress shirt while Mr. Ogawa is so narrow his
form is less constrained than created by clothes. A volatile man and a
languid man-boy; no one who actually looked would mistake them for
brothers. Yet they talk and talk and talk, about what, Anne will never
find out beyond a scant handful of facts that could not fill five minutes,
let alone nearly three hours. The sun, which seemed to have stretched
out its setting an extra-long time, finally sets. Cold dew lies over the
grass. Mr. Ogawa helps them carry the dishes and bottles inside and
thanks Anne profusely for her hospitality, as if she's done something
besides sit there watching them sing in a language from which she
cannot even pluck the occasional word. Yet she's been enthralled, as
if at an opera.

The next meeting of Japanese class is the last. Mr. Ogawa keeps
Anne briefly after, to thank her again for the wonderful evening.
"It was so great to have to keep up with a genuine native Japanese
speaker," he tells her, and at first she thinks she has misheard him. It
was so great for *him*? Yes, exactly! he explains happily. He's from Davis,
California, born and raised. His parents also. *Their* parents came from
Japan, but they both died before he was born. He's been studying the
language since his teens, hopes to travel there someday, sure does envy
Anne and Serk their forthcoming trip. "And keep up studying, Anne,"
he tells her. "It's a hard language but you'll get it. Look at me."

What do you know, Anne thinks, driving home.

Someone's knocking—Anne's no longer standing unaided and

barefoot on that plushy cool lawn. Coming back to herself at such
moments, she thinks, Life is over. But apparently not. There are more
things to cherish and lose.

Once she finally opened the door to him, he stood there blinking as if
lost. He was looking at her photos, she realized. "That's my daughter,"
she said of the framed photograph perched on top of the TV, Louisa
from when she was in the ninth grade. Somehow that year the eyeliner
was not an inch thick. Also unique to this photo, Louisa was smiling.

"She's half Oriental," Walt observed.

"Well, yeah. I told you my husband was Kang. That was her dad."

"How come I never see her helping you out?"

His tone of reproach annoyed Anne. "She's at college. Having her
own life is the best help I could ask for."

Walt wisely retreated, then blundered in another direction. "Who's
that one—a brother of yours?" Uh-oh. The only other photo in the
room was a recent-ish one of Tobias, standing she had no idea where—
for the first time Anne wondered who took it. What was centered
wasn't his smile but the sag of the skin where his ear met his cheek,
like the skin of a much older man. The photo had arrived in a letter
a few months ago, and Anne, lacking a frame, paper-clipped it to her
calendar.

"That's my son," Anne said, "and no, you haven't seen him, either,
because he lives overseas, but he's a big help to me, too, even so far
away, and no, *he's* not half Oriental, so you've got yourself a good
puzzle to solve."

"Well, it's none of my goddamn business," Walt said miserably. "I
just came here to cook that spaghetti."

"No one's stopping you." Anne felt worse by the second—was she
always this much of a bitch? "It's right where you left it."

Just a bit more went wrong—he offered her help getting into the
kitchen, she replied that she'd get there the same way she usually did
if he could get himself out of her way—but once they moved rooms,
if things didn't begin to go right, at least they didn't get worse.

Anne's kitchen was small by regular standards and too large for Anne—when she was alone her chair traveled all over the kitchen obeying her needs. It sat right inside the door as a launchpad for leaving and a collapsing-spot for returning. It sat just to one side of the door, square in front of the stove, while Anne sat in it cooking. It sat in front of the fridge, while she rooted there for items to cook. Rarely did it sit at its spot at the table, which occupied the corner opposite the stove so that its spaces for chairs were just two. When Anne followed Walt into the kitchen she saw her chair had been pushed all the way in at the table, which got it out of the way of the stove and made it wholly inaccessible to her. But—but!—Louisa's chair, the one farther away from the stove that never saw use anymore, was pulled *out*. This person Walt, who was already making headway with the onion, had apparently, before Anne finished her trip from the sofa, located the knife and the cutting board; put Anne's chair in; pulled Louisa's out; and even set it at an approachable angle. Anne click-clacked to it and sat.

She was looking not at her kitchen as it usually existed, but at her kitchen transformed. Someone else doing the cooking, herself seated in a spot where she never sat, and doing a thing she never did, which was nothing—nothing but gaze idly out her back door. Walt had stood it open, the same way she did, so the cooking heat didn't build up. Outside, over and above the strip of crabgrass, the band of sidewalk, the driveway, and carports, was the sky, plum-purple and apricot-orange from the now-absent sun. It was December, sunset came early, though the temps would stay mild. Even at Christmastime here in the depths of the night it would rarely get colder than forty degrees, something Midwestern Anne couldn't get used to. In her mind, yes, she knew that the absence of snow and ice helped her symptoms. But in her body, and all the more strongly for how weak she was, this absence of hard cold and stripped trees and white crust on the ground reminded her of her hospital stays: the non-nights blazing with fake light and noise so you never knew how many days had gone by.

"This the right oil?" Walt was asking her, holding up the Wesson's. No, use the good stuff, the little bottle—olive oil. But just a touch— just enough to keep the onion from sticking before it gets soft and you throw in the beef. Because that beef's going to put out a lot of fat, and then you need to skim some of it off with a spoon before putting in the tomatoes, and those tomatoes will need to be crushed, not chopped with a knife, crush them up with the edge of that wooden spoon there—no, not that one, the one with the edge that's more slanted.

Walt suffered all this minute direction without an eyelid twitch of irritation. Satisfied that he was doing it tolerably right, Anne went back to staring out her back door at the now-dark-purple but no-less-mild night, focusing on the line of the freeway, just above and beyond the carports like a river of light, and off at the edge of her vision the rock arena where Louisa used to sneak out for concerts under the hubristic impression that Anne didn't notice. It had been toward that same arena that, one remarkable day, Anne saw an elephant walking—because on the far side of the carports, but this side of the freeway, was a railway track down which trains never came except this one time, when the train for a circus arrived and all the animals were ferried from the train to the arena in closed trucks or vans except one, the biggest and heaviest one. For this one all interfering traffic was stopped, so that the elephant could walk off the boxcar, and onto the street, and over the highway bridge Louisa must have used on those delinquent concert nights, to the arena. It had been the middle of a strangely quiet day, and there had been few drivers that had to be stopped to enable this vision, but Anne, on her way home from the store, had been one of them. And so she'd seen the elephant, its ancient flanks as otherworldly as the moon, its eye as bright, the four stupendous steles of its legs bearing its hulk easily as the sky bears its clouds.

That was the sort of thing you stayed alive for.

The next day, Anne had found a photo of the elephant in the paper, taken not during its transit over the bridge but at the slightly later moment of its arrival at the loading dock of the arena, where it had been welcomed by a press corps. Anne was glad she hadn't seen this pomp and circumstance but also appreciated the photo it produced, which proved that she hadn't been crazy. She had cut it out and taped it to the wall.

Walt had the sauce going and Anne could smell all the things

wrong with it, each of which took a moment for her to spell out in
her mind. It needed oregano and basil and most of all salt, it needed to
move to the back burner turned low, it needed that beef fat skimmed
off as she'd warned earlier. Maybe it even needed, Anne surveying in
her mind's eye those items of her pantry she only took the trouble to
reach for when she had the excess energy, some canned black olives
sliced into rings or some canned mushrooms sliced into quarters. Perhaps Walt could put in those little extras Anne liked that she'd almost
forgotten about, because they asked too much effort from her. Back
when Louisa still lived here, Anne never asked Louisa's help getting
those extras put in because Louisa disliked them. For Louisa, just the
smooth meat sauce spooned on the pasta and shake cheese from the
shiny green can, carrot sticks on the side a begrudging concession to
health. But Louisa sure did love the sauce; Anne still made it so often,
she suspected, in quest of that too-rare sensation of pleasing her child.
Not far into her first year at college, Louisa had called to ask Anne to
write down the recipe for her and Anne had discovered the recipe existed nowhere in her brain. She couldn't write down the shopping list,
let alone the instructions. Should the onion be "medium" or should
it be "large"? Anne only knew how the right onion felt in her hand,
the same way she knew how the number of shakes from the saltshaker felt in her wrist. She couldn't put these quantities into words
any more than she could describe how brown the meat should get or
how crushed the tomatoes should be. She had tried—she had gone
to the trouble of finding her measuring spoons, she had stopped herself after each step to write down what she'd done, notepad balanced
on her thigh where she sat in her chair, left arm reaching up to keep
the pan's contents moving around while she scribbled so the sauce
wouldn't burn. And it had come out completely, mystifyingly wrong,
the wrongness just as impossible to put into words as the ingredients
and actions had been. Was the sauce too greasy or too watery, had the
onion been too small or too large? Anne's store of culinary knowledge
was, she knew, smaller than that of many women of her generation—
yet by mere dint of existing it dwarfed Louisa's. Why hadn't Anne
taught Louisa the first thing about how to cook? None of the obvious

answers—that Louisa styled herself a feminist and equated kitchen ignorance with liberation; that Anne's illness rendered any extra effort impossible, even an effort that might save her effort in the long run; that Anne and Louisa so disliked spending time with each other that such extra transactions as cooking together simply never occurred to them—seemed to quite touch on the actual truth that Anne sensed but that, like the sauce recipe, receded from the words with which Anne tried to snare it. After Anne sent Louisa the dubious recipe they never discussed it again. Anne was afraid to find out that Louisa had tried it and found it bad, so that this one thing Louisa liked from her childhood was spoiled; and Anne was equally afraid to find out that, after all of her effort, Louisa hadn't bothered to try it at all.

These thoughts made Anne reluctant to further boss Walt, but she could see he was just standing there stirring the sauce needlessly when what it needed was to simmer awhile left alone. She'd made him scared to turn around, with her viperish tongue. Give this poor frightened man something to do. "You can shove that to the back burner awhile. In that cupboard where the olive oil was? There's some Italian seasonings and there might be a can of black olives—that's it. You could open that up and slice up a few olives to throw in the sauce. The same with those mushrooms—if you want. Those are just extra things. They don't need to go in."

"That sounds real good," Walt said. "I never would have thought of that."

"My daughter never liked that extra stuff. Just the meat and some cheese."

Walt nodded, his back still turned to her as he worked open the cans. "I guess kids like the basics. I grew up on a farm and my mother grew all sorts of stuff in her garden, but I didn't care for eating any of it." After a long pause in which Anne could only imagine he was weighing whether or not to pursue this confessional vein, Walt finally added, "I never got a taste for vegetables until I went overseas."

Anne owed him some normal, polite chitchat, she knew. "Where was that?"

"Korea. That's how come your name caught my eye. Or I guess

I should say your husband's name." Poor Walt, resolutely turned toward the task of the mushrooms, was nevertheless showing Anne a renewed sunburn glow on the back of his neck.

"It's my name too."

"I just meant—before I met you, I assumed you must be from Korea. And, big and nice as this apartment complex is, I've never seen any Koreans move in. I thought you were the first."

"Even if my husband came back from the dead and moved in, you'd still be waiting for the first. He was from Japan—born there and died there. His parents moved there from Korea."

"Oh, that's real interesting! A Korean but born in Japan? I sure wish I could have met him—but you must have learned plenty about his life, too," as if Anne might be feeling offended. So this was what Walt really wanted, someone to jaw at about the Mysterious East. It was almost too easy to rebuff him.

"I don't know a thing about his life. He was a very uncommunicative man."

Luckily the sauce was finished—it had turned out, to tell the truth, somewhat better than Anne usually made it—and the pasta was cooked and they could concentrate on the embarrassment of situating themselves, perfect strangers, at her undersized table and eating together, so as not to concentrate on how their hours-old acquaintanceship had been based on thorough misunderstanding and was likely, once they got through this meal, at an end. Probably feeling bad about it all, Walt made an unwelcome further insistence on doing the dishes. Definitely feeling bad about it all, and really wishing he would leave, Anne permitted her dishes to be washed and then felt further bad about how begrudging her permission was and so told Walt he could heat up the dregs of the coffee she'd made that morning, and then felt even further annoyed at how her guilty feeling from being annoyed by him made her invite him to stay even longer, so he could annoy her even more. Finally the reheated coffee was drunk and the coffee cups were also ponderously washed and the debt of Anne's rudeness, she felt, had been paid. "Well, good night," she started to say, when the orange cat sauntered in through the still-open door with a haughty tail-flick.

"Hey, what's this?" Walt cried out in delight.

Of course it turned out that Walt, like perhaps every other first-floor resident in the entire complex, had been feeding the orange cat under the false belief, somehow conveyed by the canny feline, of his being a stray despite his large bulk and high gloss. The cat passed through the kitchen without a glance at his delighted patron—his food and water bowls and box, which Anne maintained with gritted teeth and frequent profanations, were located in Anne's small bathroom the better to keep bad smells corralled in one place. A few moments later, doubtless having emptied the food bowl and his bowels, the cat stalked out again as he'd come. "Orange Tom is *your* cat?" Walt was saying, amazed.

"That's what you call him? He's my daughter's," Anne said, and because it was unavoidable went on to tell Walt about Louisa's coming home with this cat sometime in June or July of the previous year, shortly after which, having established the cat as Anne's dependent against all Anne's objections, Louisa went off to college, never again lifting a finger to care for "her" cat. "She named him Holden after the kid in that book," Anne went on, "but I call him You, or Damn Cat, especially when I'm trucking his Kitty Chow home."

"Well, you don't have to do that anymore," Walt declared. "I'll move his stuff over to my place. I already feed Orange Tom—sorry, whatever you call him—most days. I got my own bag of Kitty Chow under the sink." But just as Anne was forming her lips around Hallelujah Walt mistook her astonished gape for censure, and repentantly told her, "I don't mean to take your kid's cat!"

"Are you kidding? *She's* never going to take him."

"I'll just take care of him for you. He's still hers anytime she comes home."

"She rarely comes home, and when she does, I doubt she'll notice a change. You can call him whatever you want and consider him yours, but I don't think you'll want to. He comes and goes as he likes—sometimes he's gone for a couple of days and then I get worried sick for him, and I don't even like him."

"He's a solo act," Walt said. "I know how that is." But Anne suspected Walt only lived like a solo act—and so perhaps he especially admired a creature with solitude in its actual nature.

Anne had been out of cat litter awhile because it was so heavy that buying it meant not buying anything else, and as a result the orange cat's litter box was disgraceful. She refused to let Walt so much as examine it, but undeterred he appeared the next morning to show her the new setup he'd bought, to throw the one in her bathroom away, and additionally to inform her, as if they'd discussed this, that he'd gone ahead and picked up steaks and why didn't she come by at six, once she'd watched her newscast. "That oughta help Orange Tom understand how we've changed his arrangements," Walt explained, but who was helping Anne understand her own changed arrangements? How had it come to be that less than twenty-four hours after she'd finally gotten rid of this man, and her unwanted cat in the bargain, she was standing outside his front door, in the role of the visitor? On first arrival Anne was afraid she'd have to double the effort she'd already made walking the ten yards or so from her front door to his, in going around the outside of the building to try at his back door instead, because the front door appeared impassable. The modest space of Walt's living room—a square footage allotment that in Anne's version was exhausted by just a sofa, coffee table, and TV—was given over to bookcases so numerous they didn't stand against the walls but in rows perpendicular to them, and so close together that Walt—appearing out of his labyrinth to greet her—could only squeeze himself sideways. But once he had the door open and was leading her on the path to the kitchen, apologizing all the while, Anne made it at record speed— there was no way to fall over because there was nowhere to fall!

The kitchen was only slightly less un-fall-able than the living room, due to an armchair Walt had shoved next to his dining table, for reading, which made use of the light from the window, all the living room windows being blocked by his shelves.

"Sit right there," Walt urged Anne. "Best seat in the house." She watched him mix a few things into soy sauce to marinate the very thinly sliced steak, then lumber in and out the back door to do the cooking on one of the complex's shared outdoor grills, and finally serve her with lettuce instead of a fork. "My husband made steak like this once," she exclaimed, recalling that long-ago night when she brought home her Japanese teacher.

"It's the Korean Way," Walt said with what Anne feared was his trademark pedantry on this subject—but Walt was otherwise so un-assuming that even this pedantry came across as the shy offering of a child. While announcing the "Korean Way" Walt had also set a sauce-pan of Minute Rice down on the table and demonstrated how to put a spoonful of the rice and a strip of the meat on a leaf of the lettuce, roll it all up, and pop it—far too large for a single bite—into his mouth, where the mastication it required silenced him for a moment.

"You know a country's not doing well when they're still using leaves to grab food," Anne remarked with her trademark meanness. She sawed up the steak with the knife and fork Walt had begrudged her, and with more energy than she usually brought to a meal, be-cause she found each bite so surprisingly dense with strange tartness and sweetness, like the meat had turned into a fruit. In this unexpected situation with this neighbor named Walt, Anne was also starting to suspect of herself that she did not have the habit of praising the food others cooked. She deduced this absence in herself from its presence in Walt. Walt appeared to be so reflexively appreciative he had thanked her the previous day not only for the food—which he had cooked—but for permission to fill himself a glass of water at her sink: "Thanks a whole lot, Anne—I was damn thirsty." Or, later, of the sour coffee he himself had reheated: "That sure hit the spot—no, I don't mind it was on the cold side. A cold coffee goes down easier." And capping it all off: "Thanks for letting me wash up those dishes—gives an old in-the-way somethin' to do." What made Walt so determined to express gratitude for even things he had no business thanking her for? And what made Anne so slow to *ever* say thanks, even under circumstances that really called for it, such as this incomparably luscious steak Walt had made for her? What other nicenesses did Anne lack, and where had she lost them, or how had she never acquired them to start?

"'Using leaves to grab food!'" Walt chortled, while doing the same. "That's a good one. But you know the Koreans use chopsticks same as the Chinese and Japanese do—they just have foods they eat by hand, too. Same as us with our burgers and hot dogs. Come to think of it, eating by hand's pretty all-American, and our country's doing all right."

"That's what I want to know: how an all-American guy like you ends up so interested in Korea," Anne said, unaware that she wanted to know this until she had said so.

"It was just survival," Walt said. "I was such a dumb greenhorn when the army sent me to Korea. I figured, better keep my mouth shut and eyes open so nobody guesses how stupid I am."

Walt was far from stupid, Anne suspected, what with his book-shelves every possible place. How a big man like him managed to wriggle himself among all of those books Anne couldn't fathom, even watching him do it. He'd even managed to find little bookshelves to fit in the john: "Sure as hell gotta have books in the crapper, that's where I do most of my reading!" crass Walt would say, once he dared. Anne didn't yet know how compatibly crass they both were, that was still in the future. There was life in the future, absurd as this seemed, Anne almost fifty and with her bum legs. In her dark moments she'd think, Well, who else could a lunker like old Walt have found? But this would be scorn for herself, not for Walt.


From his farm childhood through his army service in her own hus-band's ancestral land and right up to the day that they met, Walt had lived a life, it appeared to Anne, of impenetrable solitude. The rare times he wasn't at home staring into a pan on the stove or a book in his hands, he was staring into a beer glass at the bar down the street where men who just barely knew him despite his regular attendance talked over his head to each other. In his invisibility as in countless other ways Walt was different from Anne, and yet Anne kept seeing sameness. There was Walt's family—or complete lack of one, despite the qualifying persons existing. Like her, Walt had grown up in a fam-ily to every appearance equipped to keep hold of its members. Two parents who stuck with each other and trained up the kids with hard

work and the focusing presence of poverty. A house Anne might have
lived in herself—though it sat among fields and not, like her childhood
home, in a town—with the same absence of softness, the same water-
worn floorboards the ridges of which Anne still felt in the soles of
her compromised feet. Like Anne, Walt had living siblings with whom
there had been no particular rupture but just a lifelong weakening of
the fibers. So that neither of them, at this point in their lives and for no
clear reason, had any family relationships at all.

Then there was the equally enormous realm of marriage. Unlike
Anne, Walt had never been married, though he'd been jilted once at
an altar he himself had approached with reluctance. This should have
looked like a difference to Anne, she of the two children by two different men. And yet even here Anne felt a sameness with Walt. An
inherent unfitness for marriage, an unspoken but obvious failure on
both of their parts to hold marriage in awe, lay in both of their hearts,
or so Anne, as she came to know Walt, also came to believe.

And finally, though Walt was the star student, and Anne the lag-
gardly and lazy one, both had only attended the School of Life. Both
had gone off the tracks before finishing high school, both—despite intelligence that, if disregarded by those nearest them, had later caught
a more discerning eye—had hovered uncertainly in the vicinity of, but
never managed to keep themselves enrolled at, a college. Both had
managed to glean tutelage some other way. Anne had her years with
Dr. Grassi. Walt had years behind desks in the army, where his lousy
vision had kept him out of combat but his "knacks" for things—what
things, Anne would learn only slowly—had gotten him *in*: to the kind
of military work that turned a "greenhorn," as Walt derided himself,
into a student of things. Every sort of thing, judging from his bookshelves, but mostly the histories of nations and their many conflicts
with each other.

The one real difference that Anne saw between them was children. Not only did Walt have none, but he insisted on elevating Anne's
children to the intimidating status of gods—the fickle kind, as much
to be resented as appeased. Walt held fast to his first impression of
Anne's children as unforgivably unloving and neglectful of her, and

Anne refrained from arguing with him for fear she would find he was right. But at the same time, Walt seemed anxious, if not to win their favor—for clearly he dreaded to meet them—at least to deflect their displeasure, as if they loomed over him like taskmasters, whether military or divine.

The following spring, Orange Tom stopped coming to both Walt's and Anne's, nor was spotted by anyone else in the complex. Many of their neighbors joined Walt in searching those square yards of crabgrass and driveways and tin-roofed carports that made up the known world, they assumed, of Orange Tom. But it was Walt alone who drove an ever-wider territory at ever-later hours, his car's windows rolled down, calling the cat's several names. It was Walt who made up LOST CAT signs and posted them in the complex's various laundry rooms, in the entrance vestibules of the other complex buildings, and even in the windows of neighboring businesses, all of which, due to the complex's sprawling size, were a lot farther than either Walt or Anne could picture the cat having gone. The longer the cat stayed away, the farther Walt ventured, until the day that Walt, following an awful intuition, drove the perimeter of the opaque plywood fence that had recently enclosed the enormous vacant tract between the back of the complex and the old railway tracks. Bordered on its long sides by the tracks and the complex's corrugated-tin carports, on its short sides by utility towers, it had been a void utilized only by weeds, noticed by Walt—when he noticed it at all—for its resemblance to abandoned pastures of his boyhood. A nothing to humans but an untamed savanna—rich with glitter-eyed skittering rodents, with songbirds bobbing a moment at rest as their claws clamped the stalk of some weed, with the sugar-scent of flowers and the spice-scent of seeds—for a solo-act, wandering cat.

The featureless wall of plywood had replaced the view into this vacancy sometime earlier that spring. By the time Walt noticed the change, the whole wall was complete. So Walt did what he'd somehow never thought to do before, driving west a good quarter mile along the new wall where it ran parallel to the back of the complex, then turning north for about half that distance, then turning east for about the same distance again before finding an opening in what he saw was chain-link fencing with sheets of plywood attached to the outside. The opening where Walt stopped was a gate allowing a small army of backhoes and dump trucks access to what the lot had become: a gouged moonscape of raw red dirt clods.

On the far side of that waste, Walt's imagination saw the tiny orange dot of a strong nimble cat alight on the upper edge of the plywood enclosure, briefly survey the scene, then drop down, amid the steel jaws, out of sight.

Walt equally plausibly saw the tiny orange dot popping up at the base of the fence, from having squeezed underneath—just as easy for the cat to go under as over.

Walt saw the cat variously called Holden, Orange Tom, Damn Cat, and, by Walt lately, Buddy, picking his unconcerned way through a landscape of death that had been stripped of every vole and weed stalk and sparrow and pill bug, that shook with the deafening thunder of crushing machines. Walt both saw this with a certainty that flooded his eyes, and of course didn't see anything but the big machines inexorably about their business.

Still, when he drove back to the complex and told Anne about it, he felt as though he'd laid the corpse of the cat at her feet. They both did.

Anne started to cry angrily. "That asshole cat! That's just the kind of place he would go!" And though there wasn't any evidence of it, their shared intuition that the cat had found both his death and his grave in that lot was so strong that it took on the status of fact.

A few days later Anne picked up the phone to hear Louisa's voice backgrounded by a hubbub of college kids; she was using the pay phones out front of the library. Louisa so rarely called home Anne immediately understood the call as a moment of reckoning, even if Louisa did not. Some premonition of loss had impelled Louisa to dig the little-used long-distance calling card out of her wallet, though from the impatience in her voice—as if Anne had called her—Louisa had mistaken her premonition for guilt. Anne hardly heard Louisa's inventory of all the important things that had kept her from previously calling, so unready was Anne to deliver the news. "Honey," she finally interrupted. "I have to tell you something. About Holden." When

Anne's phone had rung that evening, Walt had been planted on her living room sofa waiting for a basketball game to come on, but as soon as he'd grasped it was Anne's daughter calling, he'd fled the apartment. She might have liked his helping presence in the moment, although, given his awestruck fear of Louisa, it perhaps would have just made things worse. Anne told Louisa about Holden's not having come home, for more than three weeks. She told her about the vacant field turned vast construction zone. Holden's going in there to explore, and not coming back out.

"NO!" screamed Louisa, the sound so piercing and sustained that Anne flinched from the phone.

"Louisa!" she urged. "You're at the library!" But Louisa kept screaming that note of protest, which, even when it changed into words, still continued to ring in the air.

"There's not a single fucking thing you can fucking take care of!" screamed Louisa at Anne. "Not even a *cat!*"

Louisa's calling card must have run out. The line clicked. The neutral, monotonous song of the dial tone poured into Anne's ear like a salve.

Afterward Anne sat on the sofa as if she'd been nailed there, waiting for Walt to return. But Walt, it turned out, had been waiting for Anne to phone him and let him know that her call with Louisa had ended. It never crossed Anne's mind to do this. She was too afraid to touch the phone again that night, as if Louisa's scream had rooted there, like the sound of the ocean in shells.

A few days later Louisa called Anne again. This time there was no screaming. Instead Louisa's tone was rigid with censure, as if the walls of her throat had become petrified. "You said Holden went into that construction site and died there," Louisa intoned. "Did you *see* that? Did you see him go in? Did you see him get—run over? *Crushed?*" At these cruel evocations of the cat's final moments, Anne's eyes spilled tears which raced so quickly down her cheeks, jaw, and neck that before her clumsy hands could absorb or divert with a tissue, the tears had entered her collar and then, unbearably, her bra. The coldness made her break out in gooseflesh, as if it had snowed on her chest.

"Oh, honey, I'm so sorry. But he was an outdoor cat—he was that way from when you first brought him home."

"No. No! That is not what I'm asking. You can never just listen to me. Did you *see* my cat die?"

"Oh, honey! What an awful question!"

"What an awful *question*? Just answer! Did you see Holden die?"

"Of course I didn't *see* him die—"

"What about his body—where is his *body*. Do you *have* it?"

In the moment this felt to Anne like a gruesome cudgel wielded to shock, not an actual question. "Honey, please listen. My neighbor— he knew Holden too—he drove all around. He looked everywhere. A whole bunch of the neighbors helped look. And then he saw that construction site, it's as big as this complex. And it's being dug up everywhere—"

"So you don't even know," Louisa cried, triumphant in grievance. "You told me he'd been killed—you told me my cat had been *buried* or *crushed*, and you don't even know that he's dead! Why would you do that? What kind of person does that? What's the *matter* with you?" And here the screed took up Anne's faults, a ground so familiar to Anne as to serve as a shelter, so that even before Louisa hung up on her, Anne felt herself alone with, and able to ponder, these questions flung at her like knives. Why had she told Louisa the cat was dead? Because he *was* dead. To say otherwise—that he might be alive—would be fantasizing. Which Louisa would persist in for years, claiming that Holden had found himself a more congenial home—not a difficult thing to have done, went the implication, for a cat who'd been living with Anne. Enlightening Louisa that Anne had pawned the cat off on Walt would not, under these circumstances, have been an amelioration. Well into her twenties, until finally Holden faded from mention entirely, Louisa would refer to the cat's having run away, not the cat's having died. As for why Anne told Louisa the cat had been killed while exploring the construction excavation, here again Anne could only cite the overwhelming plausibility of that death, as compared to the plausible others. That the cat's body had not been found, and never was in the remaining years Anne lived in the complex, was in itself a kind

of proof: that the cat must have died and been buried in the excavation. The likeliest other death, by a car on the road, would have left
its unbearable trace. And Walt, fearful as he had been of encountering
the little body—no longer glossy orange but dingy gray, deflated and
almost formless, barely distinguishable from the jetsam of trash that
lined the larger and more dangerous roads—nevertheless had searched
tirelessly, with his heart in his throat, but determined in finding that
horror to avoid the worse one, of a little corpse subjected to such indignities as time brings at the side of a road.

Anne knew that despite what the absence of a corpse proved to
her, it also proved nothing. It rendered both the death, of which Anne
was certain, and the survival, on which Louisa insisted, mere stories.
Anne believing hers true only made it more false for Louisa.

Throughout that spring of the cat's death Walt buried his grief beneath study. Walt was, Anne had begun to understand, a man for whom
the autodidactic imperative served in place of all the other imperatives:
the worshipping of God, the raising of a family, the pursuit of a wage.
Walt had only ever paid attention to the wage part, and only until his
veterans' benefits gave him enough to survive. The rest of his life he
intended to spend reading books. It had long since evolved that if one
day they had dinner at Anne's, the next day they had dinner at Walt's.
On those days—even though they were usually spaced just one day
apart—Anne noticed the heap of books on the tabletop next to the
armchair would have changed composition. A few of the books Anne
would have seen strewn there before, but many more would be new.
Anne would sit like a visiting queen in the armchair browsing this
book or that while Walt cooked and pontificated in his Fibber McGee
of a kitchen. Anne had loved Fibber McGee as a child but only remembered it at all on first seeing Walt's place, with its atmosphere
of being about to explode from its surfeit of Waltstuff. "It's a whole
lot more organized than Fibber McGee ever dreamed of," Walt objected the first time Anne made the comparison, delighting her that he
knew what she was talking about—but, of course, he was just eight
years older than her, and he'd grown up in this country. Anne had
forgotten—perhaps had never really known—the pleasure of sharing

childhood associations with another adult. And Walt was right in his
affront at her comparison. His place might be full to the bursting, but
it never did burst, and Walt really could lay a hand on whatever he
wanted, or direct Anne to it. The books might spill over the table—but
they always returned, like the workers of some teeming metropolis,
each to a permanent address Walt knew by heart in his labyrinth of
bookshelves. "If you muster up the energy, Anne, third shelf from the
bottom and three or four books from the left in the blue bookcase by
the door to the john there's a book about Hirohito," Walt might say,
"that was real interesting to me for the context of Japan's rivalry with
China over who got to boss the Korean Peninsula—I don't know how
I ever thought I could understand Korea without going in deep on
Japan. I guess because I took to Korea so much, I took on their bad
feelings for Japan, too, but I should have known that's just all the more
reason to learn what Japan's all about. And I keep finding out more I
don't know." This was, Anne observed, Walt's main problem in life—
his tireless quest for knowledge only pointing out to him more things
he didn't know.

"You must have keepsakes, like photos," Walt realized one night, as
they were sitting at Anne's place, on her sofa, waiting for the basketball game to begin. Walt had taught Anne about basketball—how to
understand who was winning and why, the strengths and weaknesses
of the different teams and players, the different names for all the brash,
balletic movements those players could do, and most important of all
about Magic and Larry, and the transcontinental rivalry that had wired
the whole nation for the same inexhaustible thrill—and Anne found
she'd gone bonkers for basketball. She never could have imagined she
would like something so much—especially something she'd expected
to hate. All that bodily capability—all those extra-long, extra-strong
legs, like the legs of a whole flock of fleet, vengeful, mischievous
gods!—just look at them surging from one end of the court to the
other as if a mere painted rectangle could contain so much force, and
with that wily ball connected to their hands. Anne could not believe
that the players were mere young human men, that the ball was not a
sentient poltergeist. Far from feeling her crippledom more, Anne felt

as though she levitated off the couch and flew through midair keeping
pace with the players, as if she rode a magic carpet right over their
heads. How she loved basketball—and it was that love, even more than
her love of not having to cook her own dinner, that had startled her
with the embarrassed understanding that she might also love Walt.

But when Walt suggested she must have some keepsakes or photos
from Japan, Anne was only exasperated with him—the Lakers were
about to play the Celtics, and he still had his mind on *Japan*?

It wasn't until the game was over that Anne used one of her Canadian crutches to point Walt, in a manner that might have given him a
black eye had he not nimbly ducked out of the way, to the high shelf
of the narrow coat closet where sat a box that had been there since
Anne had moved in and that had been taped closed since Anne and
Louisa had left Gerald and Dina's, almost ten years ago. It was the kind
of box that had long since ceased being a container and transformed
instead into an enigmatic solid it would have caused Anne more effort
to throw away than to ignore. Walt eased the box off the shelf and
lowered it onto the coffee table in front of Anne's sofa. Even closed,
it somehow exhaled a scent of the past. That scent of exile, of being cast away from her own body, returned to Anne in the space of
a breath, even before Walt asked, should he look for some scissors?
The drawer next to the fridge, she must have said, through the mem-
brane of this scent of the past closing over her face. For a moment she
could barely breathe through it, or perhaps she had stilled her own
breath trying not to dispel it. She remembered, as she hadn't in years,
that for all of their time in Japan she had believed that her symptoms
were psychosomatic. That it was all a mental failing of hers, an unconscious willed weakness so powerful that no conscious imploring
of hers could unseat it. *Please,* she remembered begging herself, on
those long afternoons on the uncomfortable, too-short, rat-scratchy
Japanese sofa. *Please, just get your fucking feet on the floor, and get your fucking legs and your butt up above them, and* walk, *just get up! Just get up!* She
had thought she was crazy. So had everyone. The Japanese doctors. Her
husband. Her child. They had all thought it was some hysterical protest
of hers against the alien culture because she hadn't told anyone about

the symptoms she'd already had before they'd taken the trip, about
the bouts of loss of feeling in her fingers and toes, about tripping and
falling in the middle of a flat pavement because her feet had suddenly
forgotten what it meant to find the ground. It hadn't been until after
Serk died, and she and Louisa were living with Gerald and Dina, that
the neurological specialist at Cedars-Sinai had seated himself on the
exam-room footstool and, taking Anne's two useless feet in his hands,
asked, "Can you feel this, Anne?" And when she'd said no, he nodded
confirmation and said, "Because your nerves have stopped doing their
job."

Not her fault, then, if her nerves could be considered not-her—and
what else could they be, those shredded nebulae whose feeble glow
reached Anne's imagination across light-years of the void of her ail-
ing insides? Anne had sobbed into her hands while the poor doctor,
whose experience of suffering to that point had left him unprepared
for such a moment, struggled to put on Anne's socks. He hadn't realized that her tears weren't of despair but of relief. It wasn't in her
head. She hadn't made it all up. She was not a hysteric but the victim
of a disorder that could be explained in the simplest terms. Anne had
always liked changing her own car battery, rewiring her own lamp,
dismantling her own sewing machine and lubricating all the parts and
reassembling them so that they meshed and made stitches again, so
that when her body's rebellion was finally explained in such tangible
terms it marked a break with her previous life as complete and un-
crossable as the abyss the doctor explained lay between her nerve end-
ings. Continuity between the new Anne and the old one was no more
possible than communication between her isolated nerves—yet it was
this clean severing that had made it possible, somehow, to go on.

Walt had scarcely touched the ancient seam of tape with the points
of Anne's scissors when it zippered open as if the contents of the box
were pressurized. The scent of the past grew in strength. But when
the flaps were folded back, the box seemed more opaque than before
it was opened. It contained nothing but two more containers: a red
leather backpack and a dingy shoebox. Anne remembered: This box
hadn't been packed in Japan, but at Gerald and Dina's. Into it had

disappeared the last reminders. The shoebox was full of cassettes Tobias had brought, in defiance of her order he throw everything away, because he'd thought they held an audio diary. The school back-pack Louisa had insisted on bringing with her on their flight home to the States, alternately gripping it to her chest as if she expected to be robbed, and scrabbling through its boxy interior with her back hunched against the possibility of Anne's prying eyes—what on earth besides novelty pencils and scented erasers had Louisa kept in there?—but no sooner had the plane touched the ground than the backpack had lost its allure. Not long after they moved in with Gerald and Dina, Anne found it pitched into the back of Louisa's closet. Anne had ex-pended considerable effort from the perch of her wheelchair and us-ing a broom to extract it, all for the pleasure of throwing it into the trash, but then she'd made the error of looking inside first to be sure it contained nothing useful. It was perfectly empty—whatever Louisa's hidden treasures were, they'd been squirreled away someplace else. But lifting the flap had revealed to Anne the clear plastic pocket into which was inserted a white cardboard square on which Louisa had laboriously written her name. Their first weeks in Japan, for hours on end Louisa had knelt at the living room table, her narrow back crossed by the giant blue X of the straps for her blue pleated school pinafore, practicing writing her name. Anne's own Japanese textbook and work-sheets lay untouched at the bottom of a half-unpacked suitcase, while her nine-year-old child, with the fervor of a monk, repeatedly formed the strange jumble of lines. Only after Louisa had satisfied herself that her facsimile was perfect did she nervously remove the clean white identity-tag square from its clear plastic pocket on the new red leather backpack that bore, to Anne, a bizarre resemblance to the accoutre-ments of the fascistic military state Japan claimed to no longer be. Exquisitely cautious in her effort to put her name on the tag, Lou-isa miscalculated her spacing, attacked the error with a substandard eraser, created an even worse smudge, and fell finally into paroxysms of grief further aggravated by Anne's suggestion she turn the card over and start fresh on the back. "But the *lines* aren't there," Louisa sobbed and raged at Anne's stupid idea, as if it were Anne who had

ruined the front side of the card. As Anne gazed on the card again at
Gerald and Dina's, that crisis of the name tag felt no less unbearable
for belonging to an unlikely past. Then it was Anne's closet in which
the backpack was hidden, having become an early example of those
objects easier to hide from oneself than to dispose of, just like the box
within which Anne would eventually hide it, and just like that box's
other contents.

Walt immediately recognized the backpack as connected with that
fearsome person, Anne's daughter, of whom he never dared speak.
He set it aside like a bomb. The shoebox, by contrast, made him look
to Anne's face for approval. "Go ahead," Anne said. "I have no idea
what junk is in there," although of course she did. "Just some stupid
idea of mine," she went on, as with exaggerated care Walt removed
the cassette cases from the shoebox and peered down at their labels.
"If listening to Japanese radio all day long never helped me learn the
language, taping the broadcasts was not going to help, either. But if
you're a language idiot, then you're other kinds of an idiot, too." Anne
was conscious of mimicking Walt's trademark style of vigorous self-
deprecation, and as she'd known that he would, Walt disputed her
words. But he also said, "Maybe recording the radio didn't seem useful
to you at the time—but it's useful to me. When have I ever got to listen to Japanese radio? Can I play them, Anne? I can't imagine anything
more interesting."

"Play them at your place when I'm not around." It pleased her
enough to please him that the memories associated with the tapes
lost some of their hold over her. Only Tobias could have believed in
a version of Anne not only sufficiently self-reflective, but sufficiently
organized, to keep an audio diary. Anne had never kept a diary in her
life. Why were there people like Walt, who knew where each of their
countless books lived on their shelves, and people like Anne, whose ir-
regularities of existence were not even redeemed by a diary? Walt was
a man who maintained his own scorebook throughout every basketball game that he watched on TV, who, when his family farm had been
sold, retained all the yellowed and crumpled receipts that he found in
his father's desk drawers and organized them by item and date in a

scrapbook, so that he could study, belatedly, the tidal motions of his father's meager fortunes, how much was spent on hardware wire and seed and new tires for the tractor. Walt was a man who'd never met a shred of ephemera he didn't like, and who was, in the most tactful way, seeking out Anne's—while aware there might be none to find.

After Walt carried off the cassette tapes Anne got Louisa's backpack on her lap—she'd told Walt not to pack it back in the box, not to put the box back on the shelf, because the time had finally come, the thing was finally going in the trash. Not once in the past decade had Louisa asked for it. She was practically a grown woman, off at college with some larger backpack or perhaps no backpack at all, perhaps she had some more sophisticated way to schlep her books. As she'd done all those years ago, Anne lifted the flap to make sure that within there was nothing of use, no perfectly good pen or pencil; as she'd been all those years ago, Anne was pierced by the sight of the name tag. But unlike all those years ago, this time the backpack wasn't empty. It contained a school subject folder, a piano practice book, and a sketch pad, all three dog-eared and doodled-upon and outwardly mundane, but they were not mundane. Anne remembered Dina declaiming each word, refusing to stop even when Gerald tried to pull the subject folder, practice book, sketch pad out of her hands: . . . *SHITHEADS! chop your heads off it might make you less stupid    cut you in half with a chainsaw    your own children never come visit they probably hate you    when you smile that fake way I want to kick you in the mouth . . .*

Louisa had left the "threatening letters," as Dina called them, scattered all over the house, but only in the same way she'd left all her belongings scattered all over the house; Dina had discovered the "letters" when she'd picked up the sketch pad, left lying open to an incriminating page on the floor of the TV room, where Louisa spent her afternoons. After the first discovery, Dina had gone through all Louisa's practice books on the piano bench, all Louisa's school subject folders scattered on her desk, until she'd found the additional passages. Dina hadn't denied she'd gone looking for more "proof," as she called it. Nor did Dina view the way she'd found the "proof" as grounds for leniency toward Louisa. It had been clear to Anne they weren't "letters" at all but verbal doodling, shocking and vile as it was; the very fact that Louisa had left the writing carelessly strewn around seemed to attest to her innocence. Louisa had said as much when she managed to say anything, through her snot-streaming sobs—Louisa and Dina had almost been two of a kind. In the end—after Dina's and then Louisa's hysteria, after the doctor's ineffectual effort to "lead a discussion" and Gerald's cutting that short—Anne had been left with the documents dumped in her lap. She had no memory of hiding them in the backpack, or of why she'd done this. Perhaps she'd been too embarrassed even to use her brother and sister-in-law's trash can to throw the "evidence" away.

The worst of it, Anne thought, was how awful *she'd* felt. Awful to be humiliated that way. Awful to be exposed as a terrible mother. Of course, she'd been angry at Gerald and Dina—what a pompous ass Gerald had been, what a judgmental bitch Dina had been. But Anne's greatest, if unspoken, anger had been at her daughter.


In the days after they opened the box, Anne found herself avoiding Walt. The next day should have been a dinner-at-Walt's day, but when Walt called her, after she failed to turn up at the usual time, Anne said she was feeling too tired. The day after that, a supposedly dinner-at-Anne's day, Anne said through her front door, to Walt's knock, "I'm still under the weather, okay?"

"Have you called up your doc?" Walt anxiously hollered on his side, so that the specter of Anne's failing health was broadcast up and down the stairwell of her four-unit building.

"I'm not *that* under the weather, I'm just not up for dinner!"

"I got minute steaks. All you need to do is eat one."

"I don't *want* to eat one." But the next day Anne was out of milk for her ritual breakfast of one shredded-wheat biscuit and half a banana. Since eating dinner every day with Walt, Anne never had to go to the store anymore, because Walt picked up whatever she needed while doing the shopping for dinner. Anne found herself having to gird for that grocery-store battle, which the loss of habit made all the more overwhelming to face. First she couldn't find her checkbook and went clicking through the apartment until a second claw-through of her purse revealed it sitting on the far side of some interior fabric divider she'd never noticed. Then she couldn't find her car keys which should have been in the purse and spent a half hour shifting every last item from the purse to her kitchen table before noticing the keys sitting right on the table itself. Then when she had the purse packed up again she got afraid she'd be cold in the store and went click-clacking back to her bedroom to dig up a sweatshirt, but she was already wearing the reassembled purse as she always did, with the strap over her head and crossing her chest so it wouldn't fall off while she plied the crutches, so she had to get the purse off again to get the sweatshirt on, and then she had to get the purse on again over the greater bulkiness of the sweatshirt, and all this extra effort exhausted her so much that she lay back on the bed where she'd been seated and actually fell asleep, for almost half an hour, from which nap she was awoken by her stomach literally roaring with hunger, because not only had she not had her breakfast that morning, but she hadn't had any dinner the night before, after lying to Walt about not wanting the minute steak. Light-headed indecision stymied Anne; getting into a car wreck, a likelihood even on her best days, seemed inevitable. But what could she do? She had nothing to eat! It was a wonder she didn't pitch forward onto the walkway when she finally got herself out her back door and commenced the walk to her car. She was hardly halfway there when Walt materialized beside her. "Are you headed to the doctor? Are you still feeling bad?"

"No, Walt," Anne said through gritted teeth, "I'm just grabbing milk from the store."

"What the hell are you doing that for? I can zip over and grab it for you before you can say, Walt, you are getting on my last nerve!"

"Walt," Anne said with a stab at the concrete with the right crutch, which sounded with a furious *clack!*, "you are getting on my last nerve!"

"But why? What did I do, Anne, that's making you so mad at me?"

"NOTHING!" Anne yelled, pivoting so as to cast the full heat of her fury on him, abruptly halting her momentum to do so, and in the

process falling over, but with what must have been the look of a me-
dusa on her face, so total was the terror she saw in Walt's eyes just before he caught her. And then, of course, he had to fold her up in his big
meaty arms, so that the mingled Old Spice, Downy, and lunchtime's
airborne hamburger grease smell of him, which she already knew so
well, now became her complete atmosphere, and any one of their
neighbors who happened to look out the window just then could have
seen not only big Walt clutching withered small Anne so that her ugly
metal crutches hung uselessly from her forearms, but then Walt *swinging Anne into his arms*, purse and crutches and all, and carrying her like
some helpless crippled child home again through her back door. "If
you ever do that again," Anne said at long length, after recomposing
herself while lying down on her sofa with a wet washcloth over her
eyes, "I will bludgeon you to death with my crutches."

"Oh, I know it," Walt said humbly, having already gone all the way
to the store and back again for Anne's milk as well as thick-cut pork
chops and red bliss potatoes for dinner. With her eyes closed Anne
listened to him put the milk in the fridge, put the chops on a plate and
salt-and-pepper them, and put them in the fridge with the milk, and
scrub the potatoes clean at the sink. Anne could even see the expression
on his face with her eyes closed. His eyebrows were slightly bunched
up because he felt perturbed at how strange she was being. Finally he
came back into the living room and she could tell, still with her eyes
closed, that he was looking at the box and the backpack that she had
told him not to put away, the last time he had been there, because she
was throwing them out. "I notice you still got that box and that backpack you were going to throw out," Walt said, as she'd known that he
would. "You want me to carry them out to the dumpster?"

"No," Anne said.

"No?"

"No. I want you to open the backpack and take out those things
stuffed inside." Anne directed Walt to the relevant pages and told him
to read. "I'm not explaining," she said with the washcloth still over her
eyes. Then she waited for Walt's attentive, reading silence to deepen
into shocked silence. Instead he started to laugh.

"Wow. Hell of a potty mouth."

"*That's* what you have to say?"

"Well, what am I looking at, Anne?"

It took her so long to tell him that Walt cooked, and they ate, and Walt washed the dishes, and then they were back on the couch again with the offending materials and the backpack in front of them like Exhibit A before she was done. And even then, Walt had to sit in his thoughtful, silent way for so long Anne wanted to kick him. "I don't know why it should make you feel bad about yourself," he finally said. "You didn't do anything wrong. It seems more to me like you did everything right. You had no one to help you at all and look what you did. Your daughter's alive and kicking and in college. She takes you so much for granted she dumped her cat on you without so much as asking."

"And blames me for him dying!"

"She's gotta blame someone. Just like when things were tough and you were living at your brother's, she blamed *them*—she was good and mad, and why shouldn't she be? Her dad dies, her mom's sick. Scary stuff. So she got good and mad and that got her through. She's a fighter. She must have learned that from you."

"Stop complimenting me, Walt. It's annoying."

"You want me to stick this stuff back in the closet now?"

"*Now* I want you to throw it away."

Walt considered again. "I'm not sure that you do. That stuff's making you feel bad—throwing it out just might make you feel worse. How about you wait on it a couple of days?"

"I've been waiting on it for ten years already!" But she didn't object as Walt, like the librarian she sometimes suspected he wished he could be, carefully repacked the offending materials back into the backpack, and the backpack back into the box. "I'm not putting the box in the closet yet, because we've still got your tapes out—and I'm not letting you throw those out, either. I'm sure glad you never threw them out before now. I've got another surprise from the past for you, but I hope this one won't make you feel bad. I hope it just makes you intrigued. I sure got a kick out of it."

Walt told her to be patient as he slotted the tape in her player, got it going, and quickly dialed down her volume to blunt an onslaught of static—that noisy enactment of silence that had always, those nights she startled awake on the sofa, sparked physical terror in her, as if the weight of a blizzard or sandstorm were about to close over her head. It would be the witching hour too late or too early for broadcasts. She would not have meant to fall asleep on the sofa, with the radio on and still wearing her housedress. Louisa fast asleep in the tatami room, and Serk simply away—paying one of those unexplained overnight visits to "a friend" that became so common toward the end of their time in Japan. When Anne accused him of having a mistress, his eyes flicked upward in a gesture the brevity of which communicated that Anne was beneath even emphatic disgust. Perhaps no one but Anne, who had lived with him and tried for so long, could understand how impossible Serk made it to know the least thing about him. A constant wretched privacy had radiated from him, more powerful and more wretched the nearer you got. Anne surprised herself with this new insight, that Serk's bristling fortress had also pinioned him like a prison. Had he hated her for having come near? Or for not having come near enough?

Static was also the way Anne envisioned her nerves: *We have ended the broadcast.*

"Just another second," Walt said. "I rewound it too far."

"Just another second and what?" But then the static cut out and was replaced by the voice of a woman, speaking in a language Anne could not recognize. Walt had a notepad on his knee already covered with writing that he was emending with quick little scribbles. "Hang on, it's almost over," Walt said, and as he promised the voice stopped and was succeeded by static again. "Isn't that a hell of a thing?" Walt cried. "Do you remember recording this stuff?"

"No! I still don't even know what it is!"

"I bet the same thing happened to you while recording as happened to me while I was listening. For most of the side it's all Japanese music and talking—when you were too mad at me to have dinner, I had plenty of time to listen. And then, you know how it goes in the recliner, I fell fast asleep. The next thing I knew I was half waking up because the sound of the tape changed—the broadcast was over, there was probably an end-broadcast message I'd missed, and now nothing but static. But I was too damn groggy to turn off the tape deck. I even had the thought, *I bet Anne, when she was making this tape, fell asleep just like me before the end of the broadcast, and then I bet the static noise woke her back up just like I've woken up—but I bet she was just too damn groggy—just like I am right now—and maybe she reached for the tape deck, like this, but it was too far away—and I bet she fell right back asleep.* And I fell right back asleep. And then just past the forty-minute mark, the sound changes again, and when it did *that*—I nearly flew out of the armchair."

"But why?"

"Because, Anne, this is a numbers station—a message for spies, for any agents behind enemy lines, in what you call a denied area, a place they're not supposed to be. This is how spy agencies send directions to spooks in the field. That's what you've got on your tape. Their boss would've said, *Tune in to such-and-such station at such-and-such time,* and they don't even need special equipment. Just an ordinary radio like anyone has."

Anne remembered, many nights when she could not fall asleep, slowly turning the radio's dial; remembered the particular serrations on the edge of the dial, and the meshing of these serrations with the calloused, dry skin at the edge of her thumb, so that she was able to maintain great control while turning the dial, as she no longer could with most tasks. A hairbreadth at a time, she drew the indicator forward—into the future, as if along a timeline, or into remote atmosphere, as if released from entrenchment on earth. The traversing of vast physical spaces was somehow contained in that small plastic box, and perhaps that was why she'd clung to the radio literally, holding it on her chest as she lay on the sofa; why she spent the better part of her days and her nights with the flickering beam of its voice playing over her body. And she remembered Serk, coming back to that house by the shore where they lived at the end, and hearing the radio, which to Anne was as usual unintelligible but which to him was apparently otherwise—"Why are you listening to this *shit?*" he had thundered at her. In the night, when she could not fall asleep, it was true that she sometimes traversed hissing voids such as separate us from dead stars, before a portal of sound opened up, any harbor of speaking or song. Anne would stop there, never knowing if she'd been there before, never knowing if she'd be there again.

"But where's it coming from? Who's the broadcaster?"

"That part's easy. It's Radio Pyongyang. North Korea."

"How do you know?"

"Because that was my job." Walt finally looked up from his note-pad. "You think this nearsighted galoot was an army foot soldier? When I served in Korea, I sat at a desk. And I listened to this sort of stuff all day long."

Whenever Walt came over to Anne's he always brought books, as if he expected to suffer boredom in her company, or as if—this was the real reason, she knew—he just felt better with a few books at hand. One of the books Walt had brought this evening was a Korean-English dictionary through which he paged forward and backward as he worked his way down his notepad—double-checking his translation of the message. "First the lady says, 'Here are the questions.' Then come the chimes and the tone. Then what I think is a new woman's voice starts reading out numbers, like this: 'Page four-fifty-six, question thirty-four. Page two hundred, question eleven. Page one-twenty-two, question seventeen.' It goes on and on like that. Always 'page,' then a three-digit number. Then always 'question,' and a two-digit num-ber. On and on like that for a total of a hundred and twenty sets of numbers! None of the numbers repeat, if you take them as two-digit numbers and three-digit numbers, and of course they don't repeat if you take them as five-digit numbers—but who knows if that's how they're meant to be taken? Maybe the first digit of each three-digit set is a sequence, maybe the second digit of each 'page' plus the third digit of each 'question' are meant to be taken together—there's no way to know. Or maybe it's not a code at all but just a load of non-sense that's not intended for an agent in the field at all, but for all us eavesdroppers—psychological warfare. Make us think there's agents out in the field when maybe there's not—or not in that field, but in some different field. Make us bust our brains trying to crack a code that's uncrackable because it doesn't exist. Confuse us with chaos—you can't win a game if you don't know which game's being played."

"So you never cracked a code?" Anne asked after a moment.

"Wouldn't know if I did. I found patterns sometimes. Then I handed those off to the guys above me. If we'd won the war because of some little pattern I found, no one would have told me. Pretty unlikely, even if somebody had won that war, and you know no one did."

This was something Anne did not want to admit: that "Korea" was hardly more than a meaningless word from her girlhood, from her father's newspaper discarded on the dining room table. In all her years of being "Anne Kang," she hadn't even connected that place with herself—until the Koreanness of her own name had brought Walt to her door. Walt also lapsed into silence. A moment before, the notepad on Walt's knee, the pencil in his right hand, and the tented-open dictionary in his left, all had seemed caught in the same living current. As if Anne were promised the answer to a question she hadn't yet posed. Now this feeling dropped away. It had only been Walt's excitement, Anne knew, that created the false impression of connections that didn't exist. Walt's army service on the Korean Peninsula decades before; Anne's pitiful vigils, on the coast of Japan, one decade before. The same sort of nonsensical radio broadcast, reaching Walt's ears in one decade, Anne's tape deck the next, and making them both feel unmoored in 1987. It didn't mean Walt and Anne shared a past, or that Anne's past was somehow more legible, added to Walt's, than it was on its own. It meant nothing but that the Cold War had gone on for a very long time. Anne wondered if these nonsense broadcasts were still crossing that body of water for which each nation had its own name. Koreans called it the East Sea, because it lay to their east, while Japanese called it the Sea of Japan. This long-forgotten piece of geographic trivia unexpectedly dawned in Anne's mind. Serk had told her this, on a rare night he hadn't left her alone with only the radio for a companion. What had made him stay with her that night?—the two

of them, as they rarely were, seated together outside, on the cracked
little apron of concrete separating their door from the street on the
far side of which was the seawall, at its slimy base the margin of sand
where Louisa and Serk would go walking at sundown, leaving Anne
behind. But on this night, Serk is sitting there with her, having brought
out a second of the cheap plastic kitchenette chairs. Louisa must be
inside and asleep. Rare rearrangement of their trio. Anne cannot see
Serk's face, or she can't see it well—he has unscrewed the light bulb
above the front door. And, in doing so, brought the night into view, in
all its purple gradations. As never happens when Anne sits alone underneath the light bulb—an invalid on spotlit display—she can slowly
discern the coast road, strung with small, sleeping structures, curving
away to her left; and across its dark pavement the line of the seawall;
and beyond this the sea's undulations, betrayed here and there by the
cold silver light sifted down by the moon. As Anne watches, a needle-
point of extremely bright light winks at her, but no sooner has she
glimpsed it than it's gone.

Serk has been saying to her, with a gesture she barely discerns in
the darkness, "The Japanese name means 'the Japanese Sea' but Korean people all call it 'East Sea.' When I was a boy and I first went to
school, the map in the textbook said Japanese Sea. I said, 'Isn't that the
East Sea?' and the teacher hit me on the ear."

How can Anne only now be remembering this? What else had Serk
told her that might have seemed unremarkable—dull, even—for not
being cast in relief on the background of his days-away death?

Or no—Serk has said this in response to a question—stupid question—of hers. The sun goes down over the ocean—watching this is her
consolation, it is even a luxury. This, too, she'd forgotten. On this night
Serk has stayed to watch the sunset with her, and she's asked him—she
must have asked him: *What's that way? Straight across the water?*

*Korea*, he has to have said.

*North or South Korea?*

*Both of them*, he has to have said with impatience, *they're both over
there*—making Anne feel stupid, and perhaps Serk—who is not, Anne

admits, a monster—is aware she might feel this way. He adds, *The east coast of the peninsula, that's what's over there. North Korea, South Korea. They share an east coast. That's what lies straight across this water. Which is called . . .*

And that's when he explains it, about the two names for this sea.

The needle-point of bright light flashes out—or perhaps it has flashed out already, perhaps this is why Serk unscrewed the light bulb from above where they're sitting, to try to seek the origin of this bright light on the water, expressive and distinct as a star.

"There," Serk says.

"What?" Anne asks, or perhaps she has already asked. Who was it who noticed the bright light, who was it who said, "There," when it flashed out again? "That's not a fishing boat," Serk says, but not in his usual, lecturing voice. His voice is low and questioning. It is almost as if he hadn't meant Anne to hear.

"The fishing boats go out all night long," Anne says, daring to present her invalidism, the hours she has spent sitting here in this chair staring out at the sea, as expertise. But Serk is so distracted, his gaze so fixed to the indistinct faraway spot where the light had appeared, that he does not even react with annoyance.

"None of the fishing boats have a light that bright—that powerful. That's something different," Serk says.

"Like what?" Anne pursues. They so rarely have conversations like this—or rather, it has been so long since they've had a conversation like this, one in which they both seem to be on the same side, even if she doesn't know what they're talking about. With caution, yet hope, an inward part of her is starting to dilate, to bloom with curiosity. To be less—as she has been for so long—exclusively defensive and absorbed in herself.

What she remembers, sitting quietly with Walt on her sofa, as Walt with one of his giant yet dexterous hands depresses the eject button and takes the tape from the hinged-open mouth of the tape deck and slots it back into the clear plastic box, is that Serk watched for that tiny, bright light on the water, as it flashed out and vanished at irregular intervals, as if it were a code he was trying to crack. "That's not a fishing boat, that's something different." Anne can't remember how long they sat there, but she remembers the feeling she had, of curiosity more than unease, that Serk himself was made so uneasy, by this trivial thing that he could not explain.

# Louisa

**Because Anne was incapable** of driving on highways, the day Louisa left home for college she took a bus to the airport alone, in predawn darkness. By the time her plane had landed on the opposite side of the country, and she'd found the bus to her campus, and her residence hall from the bus, complete darkness had fallen again. Four of the five other girls with whom she'd be sharing the three-bedroom suite had long since finished with the rites of arrival and vanished into a shared understanding. They left behind beds neatly made by their mothers, walls hung by their fathers with enigmatic posters in languages Louisa couldn't recognize, desks embellished with tented framed family photos and lamps piously bending their heads over squared stacks of books Louisa hadn't read and mostly hadn't heard of, like *Persuasion* and *Letters to a Young Poet*. Louisa's single suitcase contained no sheets, blankets, or pillows—she hadn't known she would need these—let alone framed photos, posters, desk lamps, or books.

She learned that the four girls had gone out to dinner only because the fifth girl, Amalia, had waited for Louisa. Amalia seemed to have made it her duty to guard the naked mattress, naked desk, and naked wall pierced by the nail- and tack-holes of the poster-hanging tenants of the past that by default were Louisa's share of the suite, as by default Amalia was Louisa's roommate. Amalia apparently had been waiting and guarding for hours, flanked by her watchful parents, with whom she shared a truncated build, melancholic and enormous black eyes, and quantities of wildly curly hair—Amalia's lashed into a braid, her mother's into a bun, the father's glued to his scalp. In every case the shared family hair had sprung upward and sideways from its moorings due to the length and anxiety of their vigil. Amalia was from Spain, she explained to Louisa, confirming the impression that she and her parents were also from the past, from some discredited European realm of the Latin mass, serfdom, frequent illness and death, which Louisa, if she really knew anything of it at all, had only gleaned from a movie. Even before having met the other four girls with whom she would share that suite—and nothing else—that first year; even had she never allowed Amalia and her family to take her to a nearby greasy spoon for a burger, nor yielded to their uncertain and gloomy questions about her origins and name, Louisa would have grasped the lowliness of her status, the depth of her disadvantage, simply from looking at Amalia, who showed her all this in reflection. It was even possible to sense, from Amalia's tentativeness and resignation, the strangely irrelevant fact that, if Louisa would prove to be the least-prepared student in their freshman suite of six, Amalia would prove to be the most: the most broadly and deeply educated no less in the sciences than in the humanities; the most naturally gifted; the most fluent in the most languages (four); and most of all, the most hardworking, by a spread that would increase every week. Yet they were both somehow marked out as lesser, an association Louisa bristled to escape. The next day, Amalia and her parents accompanied Louisa to a discount store walking distance from campus and observed as she purchased herself the cheapest-possible sheet set and foam-rubber pillow; they broke the pact of their taciturnity only to insist that Louisa also buy herself a blanket lest she perish, as they clearly feared Amalia would, in the Northeastern cold.

After classes began Louisa almost never saw Amalia again, despite their sharing a bedroom that measured six-by-nine feet. Amalia slept in library carrels and computer labs. Louisa slept in a series of short-lived boyfriends' beds. They weren't avoiding each other so much as living in such different worlds it was hard to remember the other existed. Toward the end of their first semester Amalia walked into their room while Louisa had a boyfriend in her bunk, cried out in mortification, and fled. If Louisa had chased after Amalia that day, made the moment a shared story they could laugh about later, things might have been different between them. Things might have even been different between Louisa and college. With Amalia as a fellow outcast, allowing her to feel that at least with one person she was not second-rate, Louisa might have learned how to learn things, starting with admitting to the things she didn't know. What was "Baudelaire," she might have learned to ask; what was "Comp Lit"? But showing she was making an effort, as Amalia did, took a courage that Louisa didn't have.

Besides, there was a different kind of gain to be made from disguising her vast ignorance. One day in the late fall while she was sitting in the common room waiting for dinner to start, a fellow freshman entered with a bang of the doors and began distributing a fistful of leaflets. Tamar was red-haired, green-eyed, wore enormous peasant dresses, combat boots, and what Louisa much later in life would recognize as a keffiyeh looped around her neck so that its tassels hung symmetrically brushing her breasts. "Schubertiade! Schubertiade!" Tamar hawked, handing out her leaflets. "Schubertiade," she repeated as Louisa took a leaflet which read: *Schubertiade!—tonight—piano end of Common Room—11pm–expulsion.* "You look like you could use some lieder," said Tamar.

"Who couldn't?" countered Louisa, with the nimbleness of one recognizing that every other person in the room and perhaps in the world must already know what Schubertiade was. Nor would she ask about *lieder*, nor be able to guess even after that evening was over, and she had sat in the Common Room in a cloud of acrid cigarette smoke, passing a flask with the jagged-haired crowd she'd to that point only studied from afar, while Tamar, accompanied by a young man wearing lipstick and a mohawk, sang warbling dirges in what Louisa guessed, again from movies, was German.

But it couldn't be allowed to matter what *lieder* was, any more than it could be allowed to matter what "Baudelaire" or "the MoMA" or "conservatory" or "Schubertiade"—no less mysterious for Louisa's having attended one—was. Tamar and her accompanist who was also her boyfriend ("conservatory casualties," Tamar unhelpfully explained) took Louisa with them to Manhattan. ("Don't look up," Tamar said as they mounted the steps from the subway, and Louisa, humiliated, snapped her gaze back to the level.) Little by little yet quickly, after meeting Tamar, Louisa found her people, or the people she felt should be hers. Every last one a New Yorker, incurious by training, secure in the knowledge that their city, and their status as its natives, would always matter more than any school, no matter how ancient or elite. They ignored all demonstrations of ardor for school, to a great extent ignored school itself, fleeing back to Manhattan on weekends and, once their freshman year was over, to decrepit rental apartments off campus, in which they resurrected the rites of their homeland, the dinner parties and drugs and the difficult books not assigned for their classes. Because their parents were painters, professors, and Freudian analysts, they considered themselves to be the genteel poor, and because their city's fame largely came from its hodgepodge, they considered themselves above noticing those differences that might draw the attention of such unsophisticated servants of convention as they were surrounded by at school, the entitled rich prep-school jerks no less than the starry-eyed strivers from the vast hinterland that was anywhere outside the northeast. Somehow, despite being from that hinterland herself, Louisa managed to escape this identification. Her new friends never asked where she was from, "really." With unerring instinct, if not understanding, she adopted their nonchalant scorn toward some things and their unabashed passions for others. She studied French and discovered the MoMA. She moved off campus and slept with pale, gloomy men whose disinclination to do their laundry marked her bed with a permanent odor of cigarettes and scalp oil despite how often she did laundry herself. She agreed that Freud was a rank misogynist and, at the same time, somehow so important that his rank misogyny must be fiercely prosecuted, rather than his theories simply ignored.

In the spring of her junior year Louisa informed her mother during one of their lightning-fast, widely spaced calls that she would be spending the summer in Europe. It had taken her more than a year saving up from her work-study jobs just to pay for the ticket, and no, she didn't have money left over to pay her expenses once there, but she'd find a job, just the same as she'd done at school. In addition to her dining-hall job she waited tables on weekends, did Anne imagine there weren't restaurants in Europe? And Louisa had already received her summer student visa that made her employable, maybe Anne had never heard of such things, having not gone to college? Despite the ease with which she served such insults to her mother, Louisa was in fact terrified of the upcoming trip for which she'd worked so hard and waited so long. The days counted down in her mind like those remaining before her execution. Yet when her mother ventured that the trip sounded expensive, like it might put Louisa in the hole for her whole senior year, Louisa was as enraged as if Anne had called her too incompetent or timid to travel, perhaps because Louisa feared that she was.

Louisa had to go almost as far back as Schubertiade to measure how long she'd understood the importance of a summer in Europe, the importance of finding her way to those unimaginable places that for her friends were mere street-corner landmarks, the Left Banks and Trevi Fountains and Uffizis. But despite hundreds of nights with her skull in the vise of a language lab headset, Louisa dreaded speaking French to an actual French person. Tamar would be spending the summer in Paris and had shamed Louisa into joining her with not persistence but its opposite, the blithe assumption that Louisa had already agreed. "I can't *wait* to be hanging out together in the Left Bank!" Tamar would say, without explaining how the two of them would be inside what Louisa felt certain was the edge of a river. The prospect of speaking French in France was overwhelming enough; seeking a job in France was unthinkable. Louisa told Tamar she was starting the summer in London and would get to Paris as early in August as possible. "If you want to see someplace besides Paris I have *no* idea why you wouldn't choose Rome," Tamar complained, relieving Louisa with her mistaken belief Louisa only had poor taste, not a shortage of courage and funds.

The last week of the term, between taking her finals, turning in final papers, and agonizing over how and what to pack, Louisa hardly had time to eat or change clothes—and this was when, uninvited, unannounced, and unwanted, Tobias appeared at her door. He could only have gotten the address from her mother. It was the first time they'd seen each other since what Louisa snidely called his First North American Tour, back when she'd been thirteen or fourteen. He'd lived in Japan before then and since but never, from what Louisa could surmise, found a job that suited his particular skill of doing nothing, if very serenely. Louisa had long suspected her mother supported him. She disregarded his too-frequent letters and could not even feel interested enough to hate him—but seeing him on her doorstep ragged as a hobo and beatific as a saint she was so angry her mouth literally gaped while she struggled to change fury to words. "Did she send you to *talk me out of it?*"

"Not at all, not at all! I had a flight to the US already—I was planning to go to her first and then come to you later this summer, but when she told me your plans, I reversed mine. I'm so glad I did! Look at you, my God, a bona-fide college student . . ."

He declined the single filthy sofa as she'd known he would, in favor of what must have been in better days the house's dining room and now was furnished only with a few abandoned boxes and a bicycle missing one wheel. "This is perfect. This is marvelous. It's like the chamber for a king, *mais je ne suis pas un roi—roi-pas-moi.*" Already she was fighting the urge to scream at him. It was incredible, his ridiculousness—literally not to be believed. Surely an act. Yet she could never catch him snide, making fun of her—never anything but crushingly earnest. Just as when she was a ten-year-old child, then a thirteen- or fourteen-year-old adolescent, now as a nineteen-year-old and vastly changed adult, she still found him insufferable.

The next morning coming down to make coffee she heard a strange noise from his room—a continuous shuffling and shifting; an accompanying sighing and intermittent, tuneless humming. Turning the corner she found herself staring at him through the dining room doorway—he had not even bothered to pull the door closed.

Without stopping he wove into his motions a gesture of welcome—
"Join me"—as easily as unfurling the smile on his face.

"No thanks," Louisa said, turning on her heel, but not before yank-
ing the door shut between them.

Later on he made it worse with explanations. "I don't need an explanation," she said. "I'm just amazed that you still do that voodoo b.s."

Of course he would take this the wrong way and make her feel
even more of a bitch than she already did. "Voudou is also a remarkable example of syncretic religion, unfortunately caricatured far more
than understood—if understood at all—and the caricatures clearly
prompted by a racial animus. But in both cases—"

"I withdraw my flippant use of 'voodoo.' I should have just said
'b.s.'"

The searching gaze was extra-intolerable because emitting from
that uncanny double of her—their—mother's face. "'Bullshit,' yes, cat-
tle crap, malarkey," Tobias was appreciatively agreeing, "way to John-
Wayne-it, my straight-shooting American sister"—she prickled all over
to hear him say "sister"—"I do like the way that you talk. You get to
it! If I could be half so concise. But was it really always b.s. to you,
even then? When you first learned it, young as you were, maybe less
burdened with knowledge-as-burden—was there never a joy in it, too?"

They were sitting in a burger place where she had brought him
for breakfast despite his confirming he was still a vegetarian. "I was
humiliated by not knowing what it was, let alone how to do it. That
wasn't joyful."

As if discovering the habitual gesture for the very first time, Tobias
drew his palms toward his sternum very slowly, then, with a lyrical
circling of both wrists, inverted his palms to face outward, and pushed
them away. "Sweeping the dust from the heart," he said, as if reading
the name of his gesture for the first time, maybe written in the smoke
above the grill. "It's such a beautiful idea. I'm so grateful for it. Every
day this idea saves my life."

He didn't just promise to leave her alone but went about it like a
sacred duty, full of admiration for her sensible refusal to introduce him

to anyone, show him anything, which, after all, he seemed to imply, would have deprived him of the pleasure of discovering it for himself: her often-robbed house, separated from her campus by a long, danger-ous walk on which he delighted in conversing with the locals—perhaps some of the very same people who smashed the house's windows—and who responded to ghost-pale rag-clad Tobias with his overstuffed filthy backpack chatting them up about their lives with not just benign tol-eration but actual warmth, as if he were just the mad holy man they'd hoped would enliven their days. Most of all Tobias was enthralled by the campus and its castles, its chateaux, its turreted fortresses—so he gushed—of books—every book one could imagine, and there for the reading! His pleasure in her campus perhaps grated Louisa the most. It overturned her own laborious indifference to the outlandish luxuries and privileges of her school, which she had forged in imitation of her peers. Arriving there almost three years earlier Louisa had been sur-rounded by people her age who uttered words she had not even been able to place categorically let alone know what they meant, and she had worked furiously and secretly both to learn the words' meanings and to appear she did not care about them. Tobias, whose not having gone to college was so far as Louisa could see his own choice, nothing besides his own irregularity having stopped him, was gawping all the amazement Louisa had not been allowed, by her own sense of what was required. Unlike Louisa, Tobias enjoyed everything, without the slightest inhibition. During the days, while she took her final exams and toiled over her final papers, bewildering even to herself as she wrote them, he wandered the campus in a daze of pleasure and espe-cially wandered the libraries, reading whole books while seated un-successfully concealed amid the real students—she once even caught a glimpse of him and quickly changed her direction. He had looked like a vagrant. It was true there were some grad students who affected the tattered, seasonally inadequate clothes that were for Tobias his only wardrobe, and the battered backpack, mapped with stains, which was for Tobias his only possession and which he always carried with him as if he expected any day to return to Louisa's door and find her no longer willing to open it. But none of these graduate students who wore their jeans and sweaters gaping with holes and rolled Drum and cultivated purple under-eye bruises to indicate sleep deprivation could affect Tobias's starkly apparent malnutrition, the unwholesome plaster shade that concealed that alabaster complexion he alone had received from their mother. He was not even thirty years old. Louisa would turn twenty this year, Tobias twenty-nine. "My half brother," she persisted to say, the rare times she had to explain him, always conscious of the needless punctiliousness of the "half," always explaining—to herself, no one else was asking—that she shouldn't make false claims of intimacy. Other people had brothers or sisters, and this must feel different, in ways she couldn't guess at or imitate. Louisa would never be fake, this was the most important of her values or maybe her vanities, its inconsistency with her countless impostures at school somehow the proof of its preeminence. All those impostures after all were geared to her goal of appearing to not try too hard, which was perhaps what being "fake" meant to her. In any case, "my half brother," she said if she said anything. Tobias only said "sister."

He had timed his departure to hers—they would even take the train together to New York, although once there thankfully they would finally part, their flights leaving from separate airports. Their last night he offered to cook, and so she led him to the grocery store, a many-blocks' walk through the "wrong" part of town where Louisa had previously only gone, with a boyfriend who had an ID, to buy beer. "Oh, marvelous, marvelous," Tobias exulted without irony, "look, Louisa, they have soy sauce!" Was there ever an element of condescension in these effusions of his? Dazzled by the profusion of treasure at the grocery store, where the freshest vegetable was a bowling ball of iceberg lettuce wrapped in plastic, Tobias finally purchased a bag of rice, a bag of lentils, a bottle of soy sauce, and, for Louisa, a six-pack of beer. As the four items moved up the black rubber belt, Louisa already holding her wallet, Tobias surprised her with one of his own from the depths of the backpack. The wallet was dangerously swollen with money. Louisa glimpsed so many twenties tightly folded together she guessed it might have been close to a thousand dollars. A throb of heat dampened her scalp.

"You shouldn't carry around so much cash," she said as they walked back through the sadly impoverished and hideous not-campus streets to her house, herself carrying the bag with the rice, lentils, and soy sauce, while Tobias carried the bag with the beer ("Better let me tote the contraband—how could I endure it if your student life were ruined by a charge of underage drinking," he had said in utter, ludicrous seriousness).

"My bank is on my back. There's nowhere else for me to put it. But you're right that it's a burden. I'd prefer not to use money at all."

This piety she would not even dignify with scorn. "What if you get robbed? I've told you this is a big town for mugging. Almost everyone I know has been mugged. Please don't," she forestalled him, "say something about the thief needing it more than you do."

"The mother of theft is necessity," Tobias disobeyed. "But I'd feel terrible if our mother's money were stolen due to carelessness of mine. It's not easy for her to come by it."

There was the heat-throb, the scalp-damp, again. Of course, she'd already suspected Anne's ironclad Rule of Adulthood—that Louisa was On Her Own no less when it came to paying for an Ivy League education than for a six-pack of beer; that she should further be grateful for this because it set her apart, had made her already so capable and would continue to do so such that the only response was *Thanks Mom* ("Completely on my own from the age of eighteen just like all my brothers and sisters") and *Thanks Long-Dead Dad* ("Your father never had help from his family, after leaving Japan he never even saw them again")—did not apply to Tobias. Anne had secured some sort of pity job that involved light typing, filing, and answering the phone, was part-time and paid very little, and so far, at least so Anne claimed to Louisa, had provided just barely enough to outfit the beater Honda with hand controls of some kind Anne used to drive herself the three miles to and from work rather than accept rides, as she'd had to do ever since she'd been sick, which was nearly a majority of Louisa's almost twenty years of life. That Anne could have earned enough to bankroll Tobias's travels, Louisa couldn't have imagined.

"I'm surprised you accept it from her," Louisa said unkindly, of their mother's hard-earned money, through the nimbus of heat pouring out of her scalp.

"I didn't want to, beyond the barest amount needed to accomplish the travel. But she insisted, in a series of very forceful and excellent letters. You know how she's stubborn, Our Mother."

*I know she's very stubborn about not giving me a dime,* Louisa somehow could not bring herself to say.

"And her argument was sound," he went on. "If my motive, after all, was to see the two of you, for as much time as possible, then my original plan, though it saved a great deal of money, also wasted a great deal of time."

"What original plan?"

"I was going to make the trip by merchant steamer—not as a seaman, my God—imagine this bag of bones swabbing a deck!—but as a passenger, which it is possible to do for very little money, but the crossing can take weeks, and then there would have been the bus travel from whatever port of entry—"

"Oh for God's sake!" Louisa tried to interrupt him.

"—but I do ardently wish I didn't have to take her money at all. It makes me feel the worthless parasite I am."

He had these moments of self-laceration, casual and startling. "I read *The Pillow Book* in such a wonderful translation," he had told her a few days earlier of whatever this was, "and it was so transporting!— even for a know-nothing like me. I've tried to read it in the Japanese but my Japanese will never be good enough, there's only so far that a half brain can go . . ." He said things like this constantly, she realized, weaving the self-denigration into his loopy elocutions with the same facility, and almost the same camouflaging effect, as he'd woven that gesture of welcome to her into his morning worship dance.

"It makes her feel better," Louisa said, with nothing in the words beyond the sudden apparition of their truth.

They were in her house's kitchen by now, Tobias making lentils and rice. "So she says," he answered surprisingly.

"So she says what—that giving you money makes her feel better for abandoning you?" She seemed to have wanted to say this for years, as if in vengeance of an injury, but whose? His? If so, why did she long for a sign of the blow having landed on *him*? Which it hadn't—there wasn't even a dent in his smile as he watched his burbling lentils.

"I was hardly abandoned. But yes, she has said it eases something in her heart, to help me when I need it. And, shambler that I am, I often do."

"I can't believe she says it *eases her heart*."

"You're right, those are my words. The way she says it is blunter and sadder. You know how she's plainspoken, Our Mother."

Louisa's scalp was still a furnace, but even through its waves of distortion she was aware of something having shifted, as if the old house had revealed a new trick and silently revolved her and Tobias into a hidden room. Her reflexive hostility, his reflexive tranquility, the saucepan and lentils, all were here. But the view out the window had changed.

"Why are you so nice to her?"

At last Tobias raised his gaze from the lentils. Our Mother's Eyes: surpassingly beautiful, slate-blue, ideally wide-set, framed by eyebrows and cheekbones like delicate wings. As also seen in Renaissance paintings and on the sides of Greek urns. Louisa's avaricious gaze was always feasting on these unless, as now, met. "I love her," Tobias said, and even this, in this new room, was bearable. His poverty and homelessness, his ruined handsomeness, and above all his way of floating through the world like a mote: these were what was unbearable.

"That's not what I mean. You can love someone and still not be nice to them. In fact, it's more common. You're *nice* to her. You go out of your way to be *kind*. It makes her feel worse, but that's not why I'm asking."

He was stricken—how was it possible for this person almost ten years her senior to be so naïve? "I make her feel *worse*?"

"Of course you do. She'd be more comfortable if you hated her. But like I said, that's not why I'm asking. You shouldn't change—you shouldn't act different." She was surprised to hear this reassurance issue from her, and more surprised to feel it was sincere. "But *why* do you?"

"I've never chosen a way to feel toward Our Mother. I just always have. Felt a tenderness and love for her. *Filialis felicitatus*," he tried to joke.

"But she gave you up. Without thinking twice."

"We don't know that she didn't think twice."

"She never came back for you."

"She was nineteen years old, Louisa."

"I'm nineteen right now!"

It threatened to vanish their room—she wished she hadn't said it. The tranquility-fog came back into his gaze. "If only we could all be nineteen as you are."

"Don't—*don't*. You can't just say, *She was nineteen. She didn't know what she was doing!*"

"But I can." He showed his pallor to her in profile—he looked more like Their depleted, Their lifetime-sick Mother in her forty-eighth year than even a third-world almost-thirty-year-old, as if he hoped to close the gap between his youth and her deterioration, as if this were his motive all along. "I might have been angrier, when I was younger," he allowed finally. "But I honestly don't remember. After everything changed for me—when my brain cracked its pan and they taped me back up—I always felt the same way I feel now. And . . ."—here he paused and stared before him as if reading out the words in advance—"not long ago I was nineteen myself, when I was left to settle up your affairs after she and you—and your father—were all in Japan. I felt terribly tested. I felt then, if I didn't already, so much compassion for her. I can't judge her."

He was clearly so wrong. Just look at him! Standing up for oneself, making others repent for the harms they had done, was justice. Anything less, cowardice—if sometimes dressed up as enlightenment. But this desire to hector him into making his claims, while proving to them both she wasn't merely venting hatred of Their Mother, wore her down and confused her. Tobias took refuge behind clouds of steam, heaping rice and lentils on plates and anointing them heavily with the soy sauce. Louisa was on her fourth beer. She ate her entire serving, which was surprisingly good. Tobias ate all of his, then all the rest, then appeared as if he'd fall asleep with his face on the table.

"Tested by what?" she demanded before he actually did fall asleep.

"By what happened to the three of you. When your father died."

With such an unexpected answer, she could hardly help if nastiness came first to hand. "*You* were 'terribly tested' by *my* father dying," she said. But again he only gazed more thoughtfully at her.

"Not the way you and Our Mother were tested, and still are. Of course not. But I think there was a role there for me. A way I was supposed to have helped you. And I failed."

Her earlier thoughts about false claims of intimacy returned to her. Here was one. Perhaps her test was not to point this out to him. Perhaps the greater kindness was to allow him to believe in this imagined failure, rather than know his irrelevance. "Greater kindness"— this was not the kind of thought Louisa generally had. Tobias must have been coming off on her like mildew. But they were parting soon—he winging off to Their Mother bearing news of her, Louisa, as one more of his filial gifts.

"Our Mother always says you *were* helpful," Louisa offered in this novel spirit of greater kindness, with no small amount of pride in herself.

"She would," Tobias said tiredly.

The next day was a blur of anxiety. Midway through the long walk to the train station past the cratered public housing and the massive windowless concrete police station like a Nazi bunker Louisa had to stop at the side of the road and almost entirely unpack her duffel to reassure herself she had her passport and student work visa. Tobias was no help at all and even made things worse with his unending questions—did she have a prepaid calling card, did she have travelers' checks, didn't she know anybody in London, when was she going to Paris and how and what for? His nervous-Nellie-ing exasperated her so much she began to forget to be nervous herself as she tried to imagine him on the ship he'd intended to take and formed a theory that he hadn't just been attracted by the cheapness but the slow rate of movement, the absence of sudden transitions. As if she were not herself about to embark on a trip she'd been fearing for months, Louisa became overwhelmed by the hopelessness of being responsible for Tobias, because he had stayed these past days at her house. His getting lost on his way to LaGuardia and missing his plane and being mugged of all that cash of Their Mother's and treated rudely at every turn not despite but because of his childish kindness was all her terrible burden to somehow avert. She was so upset with him she could barely speak as they rode the clattering commuter train through town after town toward New York.

When they finally arrived at Grand Central they spent a long time disagreeing about not only who should take which train or bus but also who should have the subway map, which Louisa wanted Tobias to have because she had long since memorized it so as not to be exposed as a visitor on her trips to New York and had only brought on this trip for his benefit, and which Tobias wanted Louisa to have because apparently he refused to accept a single thing from her, even a thing she didn't need. She was on the point of walking away from him with the hope she never saw him again when he said in a tone of surprise, "My God, I almost forgot I have something for you." Then he was the one half unpacking his backpack all over the terminal floor in the midst of impatient crisscrossing commuters. What he finally unearthed was a small envelope. Inside was a thin sheaf of small sheets of paper. "I found them in your family's apartment when I went back to clean it—they were hidden beneath the tatami. I wondered why you'd hid them and wanted to give them back to you. But you were still in the hospital then. And as soon as you could travel, Our Mother took you back to the States. And I've never seen you very often afterward, to my painful regret."

Even without the pale gray staggering cursive, of one who clearly rarely sharpened her pencil, and expended great toil in crossing the page despite how unusually short the distance, Louisa would have recognized the paper. Round-cornered, pale-blue-ruled, triply perforated, made to match the preciously tiny three-ring binder she used as a diary when she was nine. Unremarkable red plastic cover. The teeth of its three little rings never failed to connect with a menacing *snap*. How she'd loved it, how faithfully she'd contributed to it. Like so many things, lost.

But she was having trouble, standing there in the middle of Grand Central with her ears ringing, with the sound of the trains somehow inside her skull, recognizing the words. *I had a weird dream. I was at the beach with my dad but it was really pretty, not like beaches here. We were standing on the beach but at the same time we were standing on top of a hill with the water below us.* Something fleeted through her mind—as if it ran behind her eyes. *Come back here*, she thought. She gasped, her lungs sucking themselves full of air. She'd forgotten to breathe.

"Louisa," Tobias was saying. "This upsets you. I'm sorry."

"I don't know what this is," she said angrily, though her voice sounded questioning rather than angry.

"I admit that I read it—long ago, when I found it. Then I felt that I shouldn't have read it, and haven't looked at it in a long time. But I should have, before simply handing it to you."

"Read my diary? Why would you do that? You should have just thrown it away." She had the impulse to do this herself—it was just like him, to make worthless scrap paper into a relic. She was aware there was some jagged edge grinding at her attempt to keep calm. "My flight!" she said. "Fuck, I have to go catch my plane!"

In fact, it was Tobias's flight from LaGuardia that was leaving first; hers from JFK wouldn't leave for another five hours. Still, they both became frantic as if she might miss it. She wrenched open her duffel bag's zipper again and desperately clawed through its contents, coming up with Mary Shelley's *Frankenstein*, which she'd chosen to read on the plane. She stuck the little pages in their little envelope into the book, repacked the book, and then struggled to reclose the zipper as if the featherweight addition had inflated the duffel past its outermost limit. Finally it was closed again. Tobias had also repacked his backpack and wore a panicking look as if he had something more he was determined to say. Louisa couldn't take the chance he'd say it. "I have to go!"

"Call us when you get there," he insisted as he rushed alongside her, the "us" so strange to her ear it took her until after they parted to realize he'd meant him and Anne. "Don't use up your calling card for it, tell the operator you want the charges reversed—"

When she promised to do this, perhaps she was not really lying. It took great effort to keep such a promise, but none at all to break it.

Despite those elusive memories of transpacific travel in her childhood, she was terrified during the flight. All night long as the plane shuddered through a transatlantic windstorm that was apparently completely ordinary, Louisa kept a white-knuckle grip on her armrests while the rest of the passengers snored. The morning light of London smote her eyes. Only her inability to understand how to use her calling card from overseas stopped her from calling her mother and sobbing into the phone—it was all her mother's fault, was Louisa's strong feeling if not her clear thought, and the impossibility of calling Anne to inform her of her culpability felt unbearable. Louisa sat on her duffel and cried from exhaustion as the legs of busy London morning people scissored past. Eventually, the feeling of not having been able to call and yell at her mother changed from unjust deprivation to vague pride at having withstood this temptation. She found the youth hostel after asking many strangers the way. But even once there, in possession of her own cot, in the coward's gateway to Europe where the language was English, she knew she was an amateur. That night and every night after, she could never sleep well. Three years at college had done nothing to counteract the profound influence of her childhood's solitude, so that unlike the rowdy backpackers her country sent to London in such great numbers, the Jamies and Brads with their spirit-wear sweats and their baggies of weed, she was incapable of sharing a room. Her superior refinement, as she wanted to view it, was in fact a rigid hypersensitivity.

One night the other girls in the quadruple-bunked room decided to hold a séance because the hostel was reputed to be haunted. "That guy Justin was brushing his teeth and he saw a *face* watching him in the *mirror*," cried one of the girls, like all of them blond and to Louisa indistinguishable. To this report was added rumors of a floating woman in a long dress and the constant disappearance of small objects, which at least to Louisa did not require a paranormal explanation. The one blond girl whose name Louisa had learned was Vanessa. Vanessa had walked the Scottish Highlands by herself and would soon be similarly conquering Spain. "Let me get set up," Vanessa marshaled them all with her perpetually hoarse, bemused voice as she dug through her backpack. Vanessa was not just the one blond girl Louisa could distinguish; she was the only person in the entire hostel whose acknowledgment Louisa pined after. Like Louisa, Vanessa was alone at the hostel, which might have marked them out for friendship, but the point in common only magnified their contrast. At college Louisa had followed the cue of her Manhattan-bred friends to whom "Deadheads" and "hippies" were little better than idiots; now, having traveled so far that the Northeastern US itself appeared small and provincial, Louisa for the first time recognized the authority of an earth-mother type like Vanessa. Vanessa was radiant, content, competent, and at ease in her body in a way Louisa sensed, but at this time of her life couldn't name.

Vanessa had found what she was looking for, a red plastic flashlight. Sliding from her bed onto the room's tiny floor space, she arranged herself cross-legged and balanced the flashlight before her with its light pointing upward. Just these few economical motions of hers had commanded silence from the rest of the usually boisterous girls. It was very late, long past the hour of the final Tube train. Upstairs, on the floor for boys and men, no doubt the shit was still being shot, the lagers still popped, but the heavy old walls of the house—stuffed with horsehair and plaster, somebody had said—blocked all this. It was still as a tomb.

"Jenny," Vanessa said to one of the indistinguishable blondes, "hit the light?—but stay at the switch, I'm gonna ask you to turn it back on." The blonde called Jenny turned off the room's light and they heard Vanessa click the flashlight's slider as its beam landed without force on the ceiling, a sifting of light. "Batteries are running down, but it's enough for our uses," said Vanessa. "Actually, it might be even better the light's not too strong. We need a calm feeling in here if we want to get through. Jenny, mind turning the light on again?" Louisa closed her eyes before the overhead light could shock her, before seeing the flashlight's pale cloud disappear.

"Vanessa, what are you doing?" asked one of the girls in a small, compliant voice. Such was Vanessa's charisma. They had no idea what she was doing or what she was talking about, but she held them enraptured.

"I learned how to do this from a couple I know. Spirits have energy, like we all have energy, but they have less, and they've lost their main tool, their body. We have our bodies and they don't, that's the main difference."

Louisa could not keep her eyes off Vanessa; she watched with the rest of the room while Vanessa, with the same sort of small dexterous movement they'd seen her so often use to roll Drum, loosened the head of the flashlight by the slightest of increments. Without having opened the flashlight but seemingly satisfied, she asked Jenny to turn the light off again. "Close the door all the way, too." The darkness was total.

"This is freaking me out!" wailed a new, slightly accented voice.

"Shhhhhh, Lena," soothed Vanessa, who somehow knew everyone, "everything's cool, you're okay." Wherever she was in the darkness, Lena seemed to accept this announcement; all of them did. In the renewed silence the flashlight beam sprang up and Vanessa reappeared, the light ghoulishly striping her face; she'd apparently tightened the torch end just enough that the batteries met their connections. As Lena began to whimper again Vanessa gave the flashlight's head an imperceptible turn and the light blinked back off, leaving them in a darkness only marred by afterimages, those drifting, throbbing blobs of orange or green.

"Okay, the flashlight's still where it was but I'm scooting back," Vanessa told them. "I don't have my hands anywhere near it, I'm holding Lena's hands now. Right?"

"Vanessa's got my hands," Lena whispered shakily in confirmation, adding, "I'm scared!"

"Shhhh, Lena, everything's cool. Whoever else is here, they're scared, too. They're scared of *us*. We're just here to talk and invite them to answer. And no matter what happens, I'm not going to freak out and scare the spirit even more, because *they're* the one who doesn't have a body."

So quickly it was possible to feel, afterward, that it might not have happened, the flashlight blinked on and off, disclosing itself like a candle at the center of darkness, no Vanessa's chin or finger or corkscrew curl caught by the glow—all this happened with such suddenness that by the time they had all gasped air into their lungs in preparation for screaming, the darkness was total again.

"No one scream," Vanessa snapped in the same instant with such authority, despite her voice's low timbre, that their screams somehow stuck in their throats, although Louisa could hear someone panting, probably Lena.

"Spirit," resumed Vanessa in a new voice like a low incantation, "is this your house? Flash the light if it is."

Nothing happened for so long that someone whispered, "I need to pee—maybe I'll see the spirit in the bathroom," and someone else or the same person muffled their giggles in a pillow, which digressions Vanessa did not even dignify with a *Shhh*. Then the flashlight blinked on again. This time it held its beam steady as they all crushed their lungs with their intakes of breath and felt their hearts slam—once, twice, and again; or at least this was how many times Louisa's own heart continued to pump, before the light blinked back off. A scuffle broke out, they heard scrabbling and clanking, Vanessa calmly said, "Someone turn on the light?" They all now saw a sobbing Lena struggling in Vanessa's arms after having apparently sprung from her bed to assault the flashlight, the component parts of which—shaft, torch, and batteries—had rolled in different directions and vanished into the regions of dust hidden under the beds.

"You can't just *do* that," Lena was sobbing, "you can't just summon spirits, you *can't* . . ."

"It was a trick," Louisa heard herself say. The statement landed far more censoriously than Louisa had conceived it—she realized too late.

"If that's what you need to think," said Vanessa without perturbation, still shushing Lena, actually rocking her, an almost-stranger, like a child.

"I'm not saying *you're* trying to trick us. But what happened isn't supernatural. It just has to do with how temperatures affect the little bits of metal inside the flashlight. And how electricity works."

"I actually know how electricity works, but thanks for your explanation. Electricity is a part of nature. And the supernatural, whatever different people want to believe, is part of nature, too."

"I'm not saying it isn't. I'm just saying that what happened just now is because of the way flashlights work."

"That's why the light came on *just* when I'd questioned the spirit."

"That was a coincidence. Inside the flashlight, parts of it were cooling off from when you'd had it on before. The cooling makes the parts shift, especially if the flashlight isn't screwed together tight. And when the parts shift the electrical circuit can close again, and the light comes on."

Vanessa's voice had also cooled. "Like I said, I appreciate your explanation."

"I'm saying this for Lena. Because she's so scared."

Lena tilted her tear-streaked face toward Louisa's upper bunk. "Spirits are real," she said with surprising hostility.

"I'm not saying they aren't, I'm just saying—"

"How do you *know*?" demanded a girl from an opposite bed. "How are *you* so sure that what you know is right and what Vanessa knows is wrong?"

Everyone had turned on Louisa. Vanessa grew generous. *"Heyy,"* she cautioned the others, "what she's saying could make scientific sense. And I know belief in spirits, for most people, seems *unscientific*."

"But I never said I don't believe in spirits," Louisa insisted, as if this were the misunderstanding most urgently needing correction. How could she make Vanessa understand that she, too, had felt something, if not exactly a lonely Victorian ghost? She had felt a depth of loss. And she'd felt a strange envy, of the horsehair-stuffed walls (if that detail was true). Some small number of people—a family—had lived here. But the hive had already buzzed and resettled, with Louisa on the outside, the same place she'd begun.

A few days later, as she was packing to move out of the hostel—she'd already found a job at a nightclub waiting tables, and now had finally found a room for rent she could afford—Louisa saw Vanessa heading to the women's bathroom and followed her in. Ever since the séance Louisa had felt a tension between them, but when she burst out with, "Hey—I'm sorry," Vanessa showed her a face that was utterly uncomprehending.

"You okay? You need something?" Vanessa asked in her casually nurturing way.

Louisa realized how wrong she had been. If Vanessa even recalled the "dispute," she didn't recall it was Louisa with whom she'd disputed—didn't recall Louisa at all.

"Just—the other day, during the séance, I said it was a trick. I didn't mean it the way that it sounded."

"Ohhhhhh, right! Did you think I was mad? It's no sweat, I forgot all about it." With the deft movements of a master sculptor, Vanessa had begun piling her spectacular hair—"Janis hair," Louisa had heard her call it—into a topknot, but when she sensed Louisa was still standing there, she paused and glanced at Louisa as if to say, *Is there some further help you require?*

"Okay—that's good—maybe it was some of the others who felt offended, but I didn't mean to offend anyone."

"Everyone's free to believe or disbelieve, right? No one's ever gonna offend me by not believing the same things I do. Just don't try to *make* me believe like *you* do. I don't mean you, particularly. I mean anyone."

"Of course. I totally agree."

"I mean"—and now Vanessa, though she'd gone back to work on her hair, gazed thoughtfully at her reflection—"it's like when kids are little, and their minds are so open, and that makes the world so magical for them. And then there's always the one kid who's like, *Santa Claus isn't real!*"

"Oh my God!" Louisa groaned, eager for confession, absolution. "*I* was that kid!"

"Really? Bummer." Vanessa had finished her styling and regarded herself with contentment. "My thought with kids like that was always, *Who ruined* your *fun?"*


Louisa's rented room's best feature was its view, but she almost never got to see it by daylight. Her shifts at the nightclub ended in the wee hours of the morning and then her new boyfriend, or it might be more accurate to call him a man she'd met at work who "fancied" her, tended to follow her home so as to launder his clothes. "It's me best suit," he observed gloomily the first time he did this, sitting in his boxers and socks on the edge of the shared boardinghouse tub at three o'clock in the morning, poking at the suit jacket, trousers, and shirt as they swam listlessly. While the suit drip-dried, Louisa and her admirer would grapple on the room's narrow iron-frame bed in the embrace of its lumpy stained mattress, on which it was impossible not to imagine a long succession of the British fighting force of two world wars dying of their wounds and diseases. Her visitor never removed his last layer of clothing, never entered her, never ended their encounters other than by falling asleep, his face squashed in her breasts. Trapped there as he snored, Louisa would feel her face pricked by the tines of his lustrous black hair, which he wore standing straight off his head like a broom. His hair was his signature, often discussed at the club. "What *is* it you've got in your hair makes it stand up that way?" Louisa once heard him asked by another of the servers, the dirty blonde whom Louisa suspected her admirer also admired, or perhaps was already done with. "It's spunk, innit," he'd said.

The rare times she was awake in the room before the sun had gone down, she sat in the window and pored over that view, the slate-gray and redbrick jumble of Kensington rooftops, so many closed box lids hiding an ancient city life she'd never know. Although the window had a dirty curtain, not blinds, for some reason she remembered her mother's story of the first apartment she and Louisa's father had rented, where the landlady had taken a cleaning deposit "which you'll get back if the place is spotless, and I mean spotless," or at least these were the woman's words as Anne told it. Which Anne apparently had taken as a personal challenge when she and Louisa's father vacated the apartment, cleaning it fiercely and flawlessly, climbing a ladder to wipe the upper frame of every door, crawling on hands and knees to vacuum every mote from every cranny, hauling a bucket of soapy water and then mashing up fistfuls of newspaper to wash the windows, inside and out, and polish them dry—the windows that were hung with blinds Louisa's mother had pulled into their highest bunched position, to get at every inch of window glass. When the landlady arrived to inspect, she carefully lowered the blinds, opened them so that the slats were horizontal, then ran her finger the length of each slat until her fingertip was pale with dust. "And wouldn't you know she penalized me a dime for every slat, and, added up, it came to the amount of the deposit exactly."

For Louisa's mother, the story's moral was that the good always lose by their efforts. For Louisa, who had never known a version of her mother capable of such feats of cleaning, the story's moral was more of a question: How could the woman in this story, and the woman telling it, possibly be the same person? And where was Louisa's father? Not helping, surely, or even observing; Louisa drew this conclusion not from unique memories of her father, of which she felt she had none, but general observation of men. No man, certainly not a man of her parents' benighted era, was going to stand around watching his wife work herself to a frenzy in pursuit of a measly ten dollars or whatever the deposit had been. In fact he might even yell at her—did she think they were poor?—then stalk off in a rage. So incisive was Louisa's imagination, no sooner did it give her this scene than her memory claimed it as one of its own. It was often this way, what had actually happened and what she could imagine had happened being equally vivid. She would not just forget which was which but why it mattered to know.

One of those rare daylight days in her room—she was always so tired in London, she'd still seen none of its sights except what could be glimpsed from the bus on her way to her job—Louisa looked at the diary pages again. The dream the diary pages described had its aspect of nightmare, obviously having to do with Louisa's father's drowning and her almost-drowning—*I was in the water and I could feel how the tower was sucking me in. I tried to scream but I couldn't make noise, and tried to swim but couldn't move. The ocean was roaring and shaking*—but it was just as obviously a wish fulfillment: *I was at the beach with my dad but it was really pretty, not like beaches here.* Where was "here"? LA, obviously. Tobias had said he'd found the pages in the tatami room at their Japan apartment, but this made no sense at all; Louisa had no memory of him poking around in the bedrooms on his visits to that apartment, of which her memories were distinctly unpleasant, and she had no reason to believe he'd ever been there when her family wasn't. The date on the pages also didn't make sense: January 18, 1978. That was when they'd first moved to Japan. She'd been a punctilious little fanatic about dating her diary pages, but she'd also been a kid, and kids made mistakes. The date had to actually be January 18, 1979. Her dad would have died, she and her mother would have moved to LA, at the end of the previous summer. Louisa had had plenty of nightmares all throughout that first year—these diary pages clearly came from that time. How Tobias had ended up with them she couldn't imagine, but that he believed he'd found them in Japan would be explained by the erroneous date. Louisa hadn't had some dream predicting her dad's drowning and her own almost-drowning eight months in advance; she didn't believe in psychic powers, let alone possess them. Vanessa, if she'd become Louisa's friend, might have gotten a laugh out of that.

Still, something about the diary pages made Louisa feel panic, as of something neglected, done wrong. She had trouble, her hands suddenly clumsy, getting the little pages back in the envelope. She stuck the envelope back in the book, which she still hadn't started—she hadn't had time.

When August came she kept her promise to Tamar and quit her job at the nightclub—her admirer did not even ask for a private goodbye—gave up the rented room, and took a train and ferry and train that eventually brought her to Paris, to a filthy terminus where she stood

paralyzed before a wall map of the Métro, three years of college
French dead on her tongue except for *parlez-vous Anglais*. Those were
the words with which she turned gratefully to an approaching man
who turned out to be offering not help but the wad of flesh that
was his scrotum and penis, which he stood pumping with a hairy-
knuckled fist.

That night the station pervert became Louisa's hilarious French
Welcome story when she had finally found Tamar's brother's apartment. She and Tamar were taken to dinner by Tamar's brother Daniel
and his French fiancée Christiane, who regarded Tamar and Louisa
out of blue eyes so exquisitely set in her face by eons of French ge-
netics they brought to mind the work of ancient jewelers. Tamar was
reduced to howls of laughter by Louisa's story; Louisa's gratification
came full circle and became embarrassment that she might have been
showboating.

"*Calmes-toi,*" chided Daniel.

"I think," uttered Christiane, while continuing to eye Louisa and
Tamar, "the US must be a difficult place to grow up."

"OH MY GOD, what did I tell you?" persisted Tamar from half
under the table. "Is she fucking HILARIOUS or *what*?"

Daniel was Tamar's senior by a decade; brought together by some
process of parental divorce and remarriage that was never explained,
Tamar and Daniel shared no blood and perhaps had never overlapped
under the same childhood roof, but there seemed to be no fastidious
parsing, no thought, whether uncertain or affirmative, assigned to their
bond to each other. It seemed to go without saying that Daniel, and the
forbiddingly beautiful Christiane, and the equally forbiddingly beautiful apartment like something out of a movie with its towering rooms
garlanded in plaster roses and flooded with air and light that poured
through the *actual French* doors twice as tall as Louisa that opened onto
a vast cobbled Parisian courtyard, all belonged to Tamar, as the Grove
Press paperback of Breton's *Nadja* Tamar pulled from Daniel's shelves
to loan Louisa, the ever-replenished wine in the fridge, the sofa cushions Tamar uprooted and scattered over the floor for herself and Louisa to sleep on, also belonged to Tamar.

Mostly Tamar badgered Daniel ("How is it possible you've always been so square?"; "He got his BA from Harvard in butt-kissing"—even cracking up Christiane), but sometimes Daniel also grew antic, as if by a process of gradual infection, and then he and Tamar would roast all their other extended-family members, convicting everyone of crimes of personality while speaking in a shorthand Louisa thrilled to and Christiane protested. ("*Who* is Kauffman—it's like I have to listen to a baseball broadcast during dinner.") They ate in a different restaurant each night, but every meal was somehow the same, a bewildering succession of courses and bottles of wine, at the hazy end of which, as Daniel and Christiane lit cigarettes, Tamar would drag Louisa off to yet another party of yet another kid Tamar somehow knew ("Nick went to Fieldston, then got thrown out of Brown—I don't know how you *even* get thrown out of Brown"), while Daniel, by way of farewell, admonished them to be careful when they came back home drunk not to wake up his neighbors. Did Louisa acquiesce—to a king's banquet each night, to a burglar's return every morning at dawn, to a carefree drunk's belated awaking every afternoon, sprawled across the archipelago of Daniel and Christiane's dislocated cushions amid a litter of her and Tamar's dirty panties, splayed books, and crushed pastry bags? To say she acquiesced would suggest there'd been some other path to consider, that she hadn't simply, on arrival, found herself enveloped in Tamar's Parisian life. One night Daniel told them, "I'm taking you to the job site tomorrow—we leave the apartment at ten sharp, so no carousing and making me have to drag you out of bed, do you reprobates understand me?" No less a reprobate—no less a little sister, perhaps—than Tamar, Louisa laughed as Tamar did, reassured Daniel as Tamar did. She was suddenly so happy—she felt that she had never been so happy in her life.

The next morning she and Tamar were ready, clean, sober, and fed on stale baguette before Daniel had even emerged from the bedroom. Christiane, in her thin silk kimono, bade them a sleepy goodbye: "She's seen the site a thousand times," Daniel explained as they awaited the cinematic cage elevator that so recently had astonished Louisa and into which she now stepped with the casual posture of ownership. They

descended through the alternate sunshine and shadow made by the
building's marble staircase as it twisted its way to the distant skylight.
Daniel's car was an Audi convertible with leather seats in the front and
a sort of afterthought niche in the back into which Tamar gallantly
slotted herself to give Louisa the passenger seat—Christiane's place,
was the thought that briefly crossed Louisa's mind as the glamorous
car shot into traffic.

Daniel's boss, Daniel shouted to Louisa as he drove, was the world-
famous architect who had scandalized all of Paris by designing a space-
age glass-and-steel pyramid for the Louvre; the excavations for the
project had uncovered castle moats and walls and artifacts by the tens
of thousands. "And the archaeologist who's showing us over the dig
has become a real friend—Tamar, we're having lunch with him after
because he came to archaeology via art history, and he knows everything about the grad programs you're looking at, so don't say I never
did anything for you."

The car raced through a Paris Louisa realized she was seeing for
the first time—dove-gray and glittering with a morning light that even
far from the Seine held the brightness of water, of the translucence
and freshness of a summer day before the onset of heat. Where had
Louisa been, why did she feel she was just now arriving? Then they
passed through a palace gate into a realm of trenched dirt and mazed
plywood teeming with hard-hat-wearing people as single-minded-
seeming and as unified as ants. Daniel parked and produced a hard hat
of his own from beneath his car seat. "Let's find Yves."

"Do we have to do lunch with this Yves guy *today?*" Tamar said.
"That's going to be so boring for Louisa."

"We're going to drop Louisa at the apartment on our way to meet
Yves at the restaurant."

"She's not coming to *lunch?*"

"I'd rather not," Louisa offered honestly. "I don't know Yves."

"*I* don't know Yves!" Tamar said, adding, "Dude: you know I'm not
even decided on art history grad school, you said yourself it's a totally
random thing to be doing."

"I never said 'totally random,' that is not my argot, and if you're on the fence, how much better to get some inside information from someone who knows that field."

"Why is *on the fence* your *argot*? Do you guys have some kind of workplace rule to speak in the blandest clichés possible?"

"*Pay*"—this was the enigmatic syllable Daniel constantly uttered—"isn't exactly the type to impose workplace rules about how we can speak. He's not exactly a fan of authoritarianism. *Pay* was born in China," Daniel broke off to not exactly explain to Louisa.

Tamar said, "*Pay* isn't exactly a household name despite the fact that your little planet orbits him and you worship him like a god."

"Unmix that metaphor," Daniel parried as they hurried through the regions of dirt.

"For your information the astronomic and the religiosic were one and the same in many ancient cultures, so my metaphor isn't mixed!"

"Religi*ose*."

"Why can't Louisa just come to lunch and be bored stiff with me?"

"My God, Tamar, are you twenty or twelve? I'm *networking* for you. And you just said you didn't want Louisa to suffer the boredom of a lunch to discuss your professional future."

"I'd rather go back to the apartment," Louisa said as Daniel's visible annoyance with Tamar made this more and more true.

"*Et voilà*," Daniel concluded, as they reached a man with a tripod whose sun-bronzed and muscular chest was not concealed so much as emphatically framed by a linen shirt missing half of its buttons—a Gallic Indiana Jones and apparently Daniel's friend Yves.

"*Bonjour tout le monde!*" Yves said.

Louisa tried hard to understand what she was meant to be seeing, but there were so many layers of imagination required. The discovery by Yves and his team of whatever shard had to be imagined, the intact thing before it turned into a shard had to be imagined, the person who'd used the thing and their clothing and occupation and whole way of life had to be imagined, and only after all that might a phantasmal Paris—monotonously dusty and clay-brown, an enormous French ant farm—even in the most fragmentary way be imagined. Louisa couldn't do it, she couldn't find in herself the least feeling of

interest for the yards and yards of dirt or the homely stacks of filthy
rocks that were apparently impressive castle walls. Dust coated her
eyeballs and lips, her sandals seemed designed to trap sharp rocks between their soles and the soles of her feet, the sun hung in the blue
sky directly above like a punishment. Whatever Yves might be saying,
Louisa couldn't hear it, trailing as she was behind the trio of Yves,
Daniel, and Tamar, whose whining about lunch and Louisa's exclusion
had died on contact with Yves.

Finally they descended from the trenches into tunnels and the heat
of the day was snuffed out. A damp breath of raw earth chilled Louisa's bare skin. She felt the weight of a flashlight put into her hand
and dutifully she thumbed the button and followed in the wake of its
light and Yves's voice, but she wished she could stay in the dark. Too
soon daylight poured around a corner and the respite was over as well
as the tour. For the first time Yves spoke directly to Louisa. "I hope I
was able to time-travel you," he said kindly, repossessing the flashlight.
"But I've learned nothing about you, Louisa-Friend-of-Daniel's-Sister-
Tamar, I talk too much. I hope at lunch I will learn more? I must go
home now to shower, I have been in this sandbox since dawn, but at
lunch we will drink wine and have a real talk." His eyes met hers as if
to say *Yes, I really am talking to you.* His eye-creases deepened a bit as
he smiled. Then he broke off to wave over her shoulder. "*À bientôt!*
Daniel, you have the address, right? I'll see you all there in an hour."

The drive back to Daniel's was silent and seemed to take longer.
Yves's words, his clear expectation she was coming to lunch, trailed
after Louisa, along with the sense she had made some mistake, mis-
led Yves in some way, by not saying she wouldn't be there. It was impossible to tell Daniel she thought she should come. That would be
putting the mistake onto Daniel. As Daniel pulled up to his building,
Louisa's mind raced to retrace the error to the obscured place where it
had begun, but her chance to fix it had already expired. "Thanks," she
managed to say, her throat and lips feeling clumsy and thick. "I hope it
wasn't a hassle to bring me all the way back."

"Not at all."

"How's she going to get in?" asked Tamar as Louisa got out of the car and Tamar climbed between the front seats to replace her. "Should I give her my key?"

"Christiane's home—she'll let her in."

"Have a nap for *me*," Tamar said with a laugh as the car drove away.

It took a moment to understand, once Christiane had opened the apartment door and was leading Louisa through the vestibule and into the sun-splashed dining room/parlor, why the room looked so different. The cushions had all been reinstalled in their sofas and chaises. The spilled LPs and paperbacks and pastry bags and underwear and skirts and sandals and leggings and blouses and tank tops that had littered the floor had vanished. Louisa's panicked inventory, of the absences of all her belongings, turned her fully around, and then she saw her duffel sitting by the door—coming in, she'd walked past it.

"I made you salad," said Christiane. "So you can eat before you go."

The salad comprised many items Louisa had never seen in a salad before, the only one of which she could identify was cheese—long ribbons of a pale flexible cheese that resembled wood shavings and tasted less like cheese than dirt. Maybe Louisa's mouth was full of actual dirt. The leaves in the salad were very large and natural-looking, as if Christiane had just ripped them out of the ground, and Louisa couldn't understand how to eat them; she had never learned to hold her fork in her left hand and her knife in her right, deftly cutting little pieces of food as she went, and she was too ashamed, eating her unasked-for salad alone under Christiane's gimlet eye and the sinuous thread of Christiane's cigarette smoke, to rip all the leaves into pieces at the outset, with her knife in her right hand, and then swap the knife for the fork, which was the method she normally used. Leaving the knife out of it, she tried to daintily fold a leaf with the tines of the fork to the point where she might fit the leaf in her mouth, but the leaf kept springing open, once flinging a drop of salad dressing into her eye. Her fork hand was trembling, though perhaps not enough to be noticed. Christiane crushed out her cigarette and took a long pull from a bottle of the bitterly stinging "*eau gazeuse*" Louisa found undrinkable, which was the only water sitting on the table. Louisa was desperately thirsty, her lips and tongue were coated with dust, but getting up to fill herself a glass with tap water as if she lived there and asking Christiane to do this for her were equally impossible. "Tamar's mother has never paid a moment of attention to her, Tamar knows nothing of how to behave. I'm not here to learn your explanation, however. Do you have money?"

"Yes," Louisa said, although she had no idea how much money she had. She hadn't looked in her wallet in days.

"Don't eat the salad if you don't want it. I have already had the pleasure of feeding you every meal for two weeks."

"I had a sandwich," Louisa needlessly lied as Christiane took the salad from under her fork.

"*Alors, au revoir,*" Christiane concluded.

Back in the Métro for the first time since the day of her arrival, Louisa blindly stared at the map. Two weeks on Daniel and Christiane's living room floor, in their restaurants, in their car, at Tamar's side at some party, or tumbling in the back of a Citroën cab she now understood Tamar must have paid for with money supplied by Daniel, and Louisa had learned nothing of the Métro or the city except the lesson of her very first hour, that if she stood still too long, a man might expose himself to her. Tidal movements of Parisians came and went, trains swept in and out. Aboveground it was a spectacular late summer day and the Parisians carried it with them in their erect postures and brisk movements. Louisa also held her head upright and stiff in her effort not to let her tears fall. After an unknown length of time, she walked like the others to the edge of the platform and, when the train came, dumbly stared until a girl near her elbow uttered a noise of disgust, reached past her, and slapped open the latch so the doors would slide open. Even this Louisa hadn't learned. On the train she gripped a train strap with one hand and her duffel's strap, hooked over her shoulder, with the other. The duffel's strap bit her shoulder and the duffel's clumsy horizontal weight made Parisians who tried to move past her have to cringe around her because she took up too much space. Parisian place-names came and went, one as abstract as the next. She had no sense of moving north or south, east or west,

into the center or out to the periphery. The discovery of her imposture
was inevitable. When she saw the officious little man making his way
down the car, she knew he was coming for her.

At the next station, on the platform again, with fingers as clumsy
with francs as they had been with her salad fork, Louisa surrendered
the larger part of her money in exchange for a sheet from the officer's
citation pad. The shame of fare evasion was only eclipsed by the stupidity of losing so much of her money this way. Her mortified sobs
broke free and the officer, heaving a sigh of forbearance, steered her
to an underground office where, eventually, another officer was found
with more English. "Where are you traveling?" How could she answer
this? "You're an American?" he tried again. "You will return home?" All
of this was undeniable. "Do you have a plane ticket?" Her affirmative
answer finally won some approval: "You have a ticket from London,
you're going to London. Please show me your money. Is that all?"

The horror of her situation, but also a thread of familiarity, had
begun to have a sobering effect on Louisa. Her tears had dried. "I just
paid half my money for this fine," she said, adding the citation to her
display of paltry funds.

"Because you paid no fare."

"I didn't know. And now I'll be sleeping in the Métro because I
don't have enough to leave Paris."

"Sleeping in the Métro is strictly prohibited."

"Then you should give me back my money so I can go sleep in
London."

"Impossible. Fines for fare evasion cannot be returned. You will have
to take the overnight bus from Paris to London. It is the cheapest, slow-
est way, and very uncomfortable. Often there are drug smugglers and
thieves." While thusly promising, the man swiftly flicked Louisa's coins
from one pile to another. "In fact you're still missing two francs for the
bus."

"Can you give it to me?"

"Me?" said the officer. "For what reason would I give you two
francs?" As if it required great effort, he leaned back in his chair and

dug with a hand in his pants pocket, then emptied the hand on the table. "I have more money in my single pants pocket than you apparently have in the world."

"You don't have to brag about it."

"Just take it," he said, flicking his hand at her with impatience.

The overnight bus to London didn't leave until eight at night. Even after the ordeal of discovering which bus station it left from and buying the right Métro ticket and making her way there, her duffel strap chafing her shoulder raw, Louisa was hours early for the bus—almost half a day early. Those with no care in the world might still be smoking post-lunch cigarettes. Somewhere under a forest-green awning at a round marble table bearing an enormous sizzling bottle of eau gazeuse Tamar might still be sitting with Daniel and Yves, as effervescent as her beverage in the crosshairs of their attention. Maybe she was talking about the *Book of Kells* and how fucking *crazy* it was, but what did you expect from a bunch of guys wearing hair shirts and prostrating themselves to Jesus as the time off from their unprecedented achievements in drawing the world's most elaborate pretzels? While Louisa, no more conspicuous in absence than in presence, "took a nap." What would Tamar think, returning later with Daniel to find that Louisa had vanished? Would Christiane and Daniel admit to having thrown Louisa out? Or—had *Tamar* asked them to do it?

The station was less a structure than a sooty gathering of buses whose deafening vibrations and choking clouds of exhaust filled the indoor waiting area no less than the outdoor loading area, which equally resembled the bowels of a highway. Just beyond the station was a wide black trench of oily water that was somehow the Seine. It seemed to Louisa that there were two Parises, the famous and beautiful one to which Christiane held the keys, and the other, where the cigarette butts and empty eau gazeuse bottles and people like Louisa belonged.

In a remote corner of the waiting area with bolted metal seats shaped to make sleeping impossible she carefully counted the rest of her funds. Before leaving London she had hidden the last fifty pounds from her nightclub job deep in her duffel with the plan of only changing it to francs in case of emergency; this was the kind of stratagem Tamar had never had to dream of. A rage at Tamar that was also a shame at herself boiled the length of her body. She had ample time to confirm the pounds were still there as well as that Christiane had balled up her clothes and crushed most of the art postcards Louisa had bought along with a profusion of scarves, bracelets, leather goods, French paperbacks vastly beyond her comprehension level, and, worst of all, more precious French notebooks in Tamar's favored brands, in every color and style and size, with and without elastics, with and without spiral bindings or little paper pockets inside the back covers, than Louisa would fill in many lifetimes of far more diligent writing than she had ever demonstrated. All spendthrift mimicry, the humiliating proof of her desire to be Tamar.

The notebooks were a main reason her duffel was so much heavier, and she willed herself to throw them away but her helpless frugality, one of her least favorite inheritances from her mother, would not permit it. She repacked everything, keeping out only a stiff, small leather purse with an extra-long strap, the twin of one Tamar had bought. ("Now we can be like those Medieval Jews and carry our money hands-free without breaking the Sabbath.") The purse was barely large enough for her passport and bus ticket. Then she was ready and it was barely three.

The hours stretched before her. Outside the bus station a wretched dusty park lay shriveled beneath the Parisian sun that was also shining on Tamar wherever she was. There had to be at least one tree in that park with enough leaves, at least one bench with enough slats, for Louisa to have somewhere acceptable to sit for the rest of the day and the evening while she filled one of her untouched notebooks or read untouched *Frankenstein* while already living slightly in the future, a future in which she said to some unknown admiring person, "My last day in Paris I was so broke I just sat in the park reading *Frankenstein* while I waited for the bus." Slightly in the future, the vision had a flavor of proud solitude, but here in the present it was impossible. Standing up and walking outside to the bald ugly park so as to claim a future in which she described her last day in Paris with some scorn and bravado

was impossible. Tamar was one of those magnetic people who reorga-
nized a room just by stepping into it, but maybe this charisma had to
do with Tamar's intense dislike of ever being alone—while Louisa intensely liked being alone, she was very good at it, she'd had a lifetime
of practice with it, and so perhaps the social invisibility she sometimes
felt was just the outward sign of this great talent she possessed for
solitude. But here on the hostile chair in the hostile bus station of the
hostile city, her talent for solitude vanished. She had never wanted to
travel, she had a bone-deep aversion to travel, she'd only traveled this
summer at the unspoken but no less aggressive behest of Tamar. Accusation by accusation she built her case against Tamar, who by virtue
of merely existing made Louisa feel ashamed of her three campus jobs
and not having learned French in grade school. Then she was in the
apartment, in an alternate past, possessed of the admonition she had
neither felt nor voiced as Tamar scattered clothing and ashed in a cup.
And as she scolded Tamar—earning expressions of solidarity and gratitude from Christiane and Daniel—her voice was that of a much older
woman, and as Tamar whined in protest, hers was that of a much
younger girl.

In this way Louisa—who was also exhausted from two weeks of
poor sleep on couch cushions—left the bus station and even her body
because in the same way that she often couldn't sleep when she most
needed to, she also sometimes slept when it was most important she
shouldn't, as in a bus station that was said to be rife with drug dealers
and thieves. Startling awake, she would clutch at her duffel and snake
her hand inside to touch the folded wad of pounds.

Sometime between eight and nine the bus was finally there to be
boarded. Louisa staggered to it while her body cried out to return to
the hard metal seat that had come to feel as necessary to her as the
shell to its snail. In half a day Louisa had become a nomad. She no
longer thought of the beautiful Paris apartment that her phantasm
scolded Tamar to keep clean. Nor did she think of London and what
she would do when she got there. Her horizon had shrunk to the
rubber-treaded steps of the bus and then to the stained velour seat
perforated with cigarette burns that she crawled into while keeping

the duffel in the seat next to her so that no one would try to sit with her. She put her arms through the straps, hid her face in the bag's side, and tried sleeping again. Then someone touched her shoulder.

"*Scusez-moi? Puis-je mass-war ici? Le bus ay completement plane.*"

"Oh, sorry . . . *bien sur* . . . *scusez-moi*," Louisa mumbled as she stood in her seat and tried to heave the duffel into the overhead rack, the girl with the good French and bad accent who had asked to sit with her attempting to help as a succession of other passengers shouldered impatiently past. A boy forced his way into the aisle from the opposite seat, the people he displaced shrinking from him as if from a leper. He wore explosions of sun-bleached, wind-whipped hair on his scalp and in his armpits, no shirt, and a combination sunburn/suntan of such depth and complexity he gave the impression of having slept outdoors for months. He smelled as if he hadn't bathed in as long—a swoonily potent smell such as Louisa, who had no immediate experience of this, imagined horses made in their stables. The boy nimbly tossed the enormous duffel into the overhead rack, where it would barely fit, punched it in securely, and withdrew. The fellow passengers he'd interrupted, a numerous family with dark hair and skin who gave the impression of being usually cautious and meek, cast censorious glances all around at the boy, the girl who had joined Louisa, and Louisa herself, before moving away.

The girl, Gabby, was pugilistic and merry. She quickly established that she and Louisa were fellow Americans, even that they were both returning to London to catch flights home to the US—Gabby to San Diego, where she would drop in on her parents before continuing to Cal for her last year of college. Louisa only said that she was flying to New York. She didn't mention that she was almost two weeks early for her flight and had nowhere in London to stay. "And his name is Roman," Gabby went on, "and I have no idea where he's from or where he's going because nothing he says makes any sense." The boy laughed and Louisa watched his face alternately eclipsed and revealed by the buttocks and torsos of those passengers still jostling in the aisle. His face possessed the sort of ideal symmetry that makes ordinary faces appear bulbous and lopsided. His untrimmed many-days'-worth of beard was the color assigned by Louisa's mind to the phrase "spin-ning straw into gold." He'd seated himself yogi-style entirely sideways, the better to take part in the conversation, and in addition to lacking a shirt also seemed to lack shoes.

"Everything I tell you is true," he told Gabby, "you just can't accept any of it."

Gabby and Roman had been traveling together since they'd met in Tangier, Gabby having "gotten so tired of the way the Moroccans treat women," Roman having been robbed or perhaps just attacked—perhaps he had already been dispossessed or perhaps he'd never had possessions in the first place—in either the mountains or the desert, or it might have been while surfing off the coast of Tunisia—their account of their adventure, separate and joint, was laconic and teas-ing and suffered either from what Gabby said, that nothing Roman said made sense to her, or from what Roman said, that Gabby dis-believed him, and either way, as Gabby did more of the talking, the deficit wasn't supplied. What was certain was that they teamed up in Tangier because, with Roman, Gabby was less a target of male ha-rassment, and, with Gabby, Roman was less a target of law enforce-ment harassment, "although he still might be more trouble than he's worth," Gabby said, "because he literally stinks."

"I tried to bathe with the dolphins," Roman said, unoffended, "but Gabby wouldn't let me jump overboard."

"We saw dolphins from the ferry we took from Tangier to Gibral-tar," Gabby explained. "I was so happy to finally get out of Morocco and get to drink beer."

"I wasn't even going to come to France," Roman said, "but when we got to Barcelona there weren't any boats that I liked."

"His plan supposedly was to get hired on a boat and sail to Italy from Spain."

"'Supposedly.' I'm a very good sailor."

"Yet here he is, on the bus."

They were speaking now in whispers; after bellowing several times, *TAIS-TOI! TAIS-TOI, C'EST UN BUS DE NUIT!* the apparently in-censed driver launched the bus into the night through which it lurched as if the driver hoped to expel passengers through the windows. The bus was clearly full, and yet no one sat down with Roman. "It's our system," Gabby whispered. "I find a person to sit with, Roman gets a double seat because he smells, and then we take turns in the double seat, sleeping."

"So I'm the sucker," Louisa whispered.

"No, we liked you," Gabby said.

When Gabby announced that she wanted to sleep and she and Roman changed places, his pungency enveloped Louisa less like a smell than a nimbus of warmth. Louisa had been starting to shiver in her thin T-shirt, but with Roman in the seat beside her the rattle drained from her bones. She felt real sleep, Tamar-free luxuriant sleep, spreading through her like a drug. "Are you sure you don't mind?" Roman said. "That I stink. I don't notice."

"I don't, either," she said, which was true in a way she could not have explained. She did notice his odor, but she wasn't repulsed. Her cells craned toward that smell as if it answered a question she couldn't have put into words but had been bothering her for a very long time.

"Lean on me and sleep," he urged her.

Across the aisle Gabby was reduced to a pair of knees tented under a jacket. Still Louisa wondered, "But won't Gabby mind?"

"Gabby?" He was clearly surprised. "Oh! No. We're not—no."

Louisa fell asleep like stepping off the edge of her life.

The bus must have squealed to a halt at Calais, trundled onto an enormous car ferry like a waterproof parking garage aboard which it lurched across the English Channel to Dover, its engine must have reignited briefly so it could roll off the ferry and almost immediately stop in the parking bay of a customs and border facility, but Louisa didn't know any of this. She was transmigrated in an instant, sealed in an unconsciousness that even Roman, shaking her with last-resort urgency, struggled to pierce. She grew aware of the bus driver yelling again. "Louisa," Roman said, "hurry, we've got to show passports." The bus was empty, the bus driver's yelling was somewhere outside. Louisa tumbled off and she and Roman caught up with Gabby amid an exodus of bleary passengers from many different buses that idled with impatience at the edges of a building's sickly light. It was still dark, Louisa couldn't have guessed what time it was. Inside the building uniformed people shouted them into this or that line, and only then did Louisa really think about her passport. Her heart surged in panic—but what was this against her hip? It was the bandolier purse she'd been wearing all the time that she slept and that she'd carried off the bus without thinking or using her hands. And there was her passport inside.

Louisa felt a rush of love for Tamar. She was so lucky to have ever known Tamar, she was so lucky to be alive and have friends. Solitude wasn't an absence but a sort of magnetic condition in which friendship formed—it wasn't just Tamar who was magnetic! Louisa almost laughed as the ache of her grievance dissolved just as viscerally as when her monthly cramps were vanquished by aspirin. She was having some sort of religious experience at the gateway to England—she turned eagerly to Roman and Gabby just as a uniformed agent who was sorting the mass stepped between them. "You, that way," he said to Roman and Gabby, "and you"—to Louisa—"over here."

The larger current of travelers pulled Roman and Gabby with them as they called back, "We'll see you on the bus," Roman grinning reassurance to Louisa over one muscly brown shoulder at the same time that she noticed a large tear in the seat of the olive-drab pants that were his only clothing, through which flashed a generous glimpse of his pale naked ass. She burst out laughing, and Roman seemed to hear her and wink through the many jostling bodies filling the space between them as Louisa was corralled into her line.

Her line seemed to be much shorter and slower than the others she saw forming up deeper into the room. Deeper into the room there were podiums at which agents stamped passports, and conveyer belts like you had at an airport; Louisa's much shorter almost unmoving line had a podium with an agent, but the agent never seemed to stamp anyone through. Just past the agent at a set of plastic tables Louisa saw the same dark-skinned, dark-haired family from her bus who had glared because of Roman, arrayed helplessly before their disemboweled luggage. Object after mummified object was rudely yanked free of extensive swaddling in cloth and paper and bubble wrap to reveal another enormous glass jar. "What is this," Louisa heard an agent repeating, with undisguised contempt. "What is *this*. What is *this*." Then Louisa stood before the podium, the agent staring at her passport.

"Where are your bags?" he demanded.

"My bag's on the bus."

"All the luggage from the boot of every bus comes through customs, this is British *customs*. You're in *Britain*."

"My bag wasn't in the boot, it's *on* the bus."

"Then it's hand luggage. All passengers must bring hand luggage through customs. That can't be your only hand luggage."

"It's not, I said my bag is on the bus—"

"But it can't be on the bus. You have to have brought it through customs."

"But I didn't know!"

"Did you know your bus came here to Dover from Calais? Are you aware that Calais and Dover are in different countries? Anyone mention that to you?" He took a different tack abruptly. "Who are your traveling companions?"

"No one. I'm traveling alone."

"Who are your traveling companions?"

"I said no one!"

"No companions. No luggage."

"I do have luggage! On the bus!"

"You can't leave luggage on the bus when you're entering Britain. All passengers must bring hand luggage through customs."

"But I didn't *know*. They said just bring passports!"

"Did they? 'Just bring your passport, your luggage can walk through on its own.' Is that what they said?" The agent had waved over a female version of himself, with a skirt for the bottom half of her uniform; without a glance he handed her Louisa's passport as if tossing it into the trash. "Next!" he said.

"Where's she taking my passport?" cried Louisa.

"Follow my colleague, don't stand there gaping, is something the matter with you? *Next!*"

The woman agent strode rapidly paces ahead. "Wait!" Louisa said desperately. "Wait!" The rupture was total, everything familiar had fallen away. The dark-haired family and their jars had disappeared, the lines of passengers had disappeared, there was only a scattering of the weary and disheveled reassembling themselves as if entirely alone in their bedrooms. Time, which had seemed to be standing still, roared to life and Louisa understood as if she saw it from above that the last member of the dark-haired family had heaved himself onto the black rubber treads at the door to the bus, clutching the violated suitcase closed against the sliding, knocking weights of the many glass jars that had prompted such scorn but were not, in the end, what the agents were seeking. "My bus is leaving," Louisa tried to make the woman agent understand, as she herself was trying to understand, as difficult as it was to comprehend, that through nothing worse than a moment's relaxation of her vigilance, her almost pious belief that what can go wrong will, her disaster was decisive. The expulsion from Christiane's had been nothing, it might have even been a lark, she could have gone to the Paris youth hostel, she could have gone to the Louvre excavation in pursuit of what she now recognized was Yves's genuine interest in her, she could have told Christiane to *Fuck off, you Parisian rich bitch!* because then she'd still had everything and now she had nothing. "Please," she implored the woman agent who'd led her into a windowless room with a wall clock, a bare metal desk, and a chair. Her voice was husky and commanding, the tears she felt washing her face didn't interfere with it. "My bus is going to leave and then I don't know what I'll do."

"If you cooperate, you might catch your bus. If you argue, you'll just waste more time."

The wall clock said it was almost seven a.m., but no matter how fervently Louisa reconstructed the moment of awaking to Roman's voice and touch and smell, she couldn't guess what time it had been when that happened. "Undress," the woman agent said, "and be fast about it." As if she were a doctor, the woman left the room before Louisa could shape her shock into a question. Alone in the room Louisa could hear the clock's second hand twitching from one to the

next with a sound like a very tiny door, in the very far distance, closing again and again. She could hear nothing else. Clumsily, because
her fingers felt numb, she lifted the long purse strap over her head.
Then it was almost like a fight with a straitjacket to get her T-shirt off.
While trapped inside she realized it held Roman's smell. She pressed
the fabric against her face, drinking his smell in and blotting her tears.
The door opened as Louisa tore herself out of the shirt and stood
crawling with gooseflesh in her jeans and her bra. "Everything," the
woman agent said with annoyance. When Louisa was entirely naked
the woman yanked on a pair of rubber gloves and approached with
distaste. "Arms out and legs spread. Cooperate and we'll get it done
with."

What else could it be called but cooperation as the woman knelt
down with her face averted and jammed her rubber-clad fingers,
squeaky and dry, into Louisa's vagina, where they poked and pushed
as if expecting to find a trapdoor? Louisa bit her lip hard enough to
taste blood and fresh tears hotly flooded her eyes but she made no
sound apart from a grunt that escaped her as if she'd been punched
in the guts. Without warning or any decrease of friction the woman
yanked her hand free and transferred it to Louisa's asshole, with such
force Louisa almost lost her footing. Louisa felt her skin tear and the
raw sting of blood. "Hold still," the woman complained, again jog-
gling her hand side to side as if angry the space wasn't larger. With a
final exertion the woman uprooted her hand and through the renewed
pain Louisa squeezed her sphincter for everything she was worth.

"You can dress," the woman said as she left the room again and
then immediately returned to drop Louisa's passport on the desk,
while Louisa still stood clutching herself. "Weren't you rushing for
your bus," the woman added by way of goodbye.

With almost useless hands Louisa clawed herself back into her
clothes, wincing as her underpants and then her jeans touched her
crotch. She couldn't get her passport back into the bandolier purse
or the purse's strap over her head and rushed out of the room clutching them against her chest. Somewhere at the back of things there was
daylight, there was the terrifying brightness of a morning that was

well under way. Louisa rushed toward it and a man shouted at her, "You! Passport!" and in mute astonishment Louisa stopped before him and struggled to hand him her passport from where her hands were clutching it and the purse. "Please," she managed, "I think my bus might have left and I don't know what to do, I don't have any money." Hardly looking at her, the man opened her passport and stamped it.

"Maybe you ought to go see and not stand there whingeing about it," he said.

Then she was outside the building beneath the tauntingly high and bright sun of a rare summer's day and an asphalt parking lot stretched before her, empty but for a single idling bus whose driver stood toeing a cigarette butt into the pavement with the thoroughness of someone reluctant to resume his labors. It was a betrayal of weakness Louisa's animal self sensed and lunged for, far ahead of her mind deciding. Breaking into a run she shouldered past the driver and flew up the steps of his bus, where, panting, she faced total strangers—even the unseen strangers of a bus on which she'd slept had made themselves familiar to her, so that she knew at a glance these were not the same people—but she'd already known this was not the same bus.

"Get off!" cried the driver as he came up the steps behind her. "You weren't on this bus!"

Louisa quickly backed down the aisle. "I was."

"The hell you were! Show me your ticket."

This driver was British, not French—it was like being armed with the same strength of weapon. "They took my ticket—they took everything from me and they even strip-searched me."

"Because you're a fucking drug runner, aren't you?"

"Just let her ride," a weary voice called from the back.

"I *had* a ticket, how else do you think I got here?"

"Not with me, and you'll bloody get off."

"Just let her ride," someone else said, "so we can fucking leave already."

"She has no ticket," the bus driver appealed, whether to the one passenger, or to them all, it wasn't clear, but in this second betrayal of his weakness Louisa spotted an old woman sitting alone, frowning furiously, helplessly conscious she'd soon be a victim. Louisa dropped into the seat beside her and sank out of the driver's sight line.

"Get off!" he shouted again, but he had not moved from where he stood next to his seat. Louisa's seatmate pressed her lips in a tight line and closed her eyes, not in solidarity, Louisa knew, but to signal both her opprobrium and her demand that Louisa leave her alone.

"Just drive, would you," and "What bloody difference does it make to you, just take us the fuck to London already," and other such mutinous comments were rising from different parts of the bus, until finally the driver slammed on his handle to close the bus door, and slammed into his seat.

"I'll be fetching the authorities to you at Victoria Coach Station!" he shouted, but his threat passed almost unheard over her bowed head where it had dropped against her knees. Now her animal courage was used up and she sobbed into her jeans, while trying to be as quiet as she could so her seatmate would not open her eyes. Her duffel, that embarrassing burden, was gone. Gone with it weren't just her wasteful Paris purchases and her hoarded pounds but her plane ticket home to New York. Her mind was a windstorm of half-formed ideas. The most recurrent, US Embassy, was also the vaguest. She didn't know where the US Embassy was or if it owed rescue to someone like her. What had happened to her felt like violence, and yet she couldn't escape the sense of her own stupid culpability, which must have been located somewhere specific, must have consisted of a moment or an act that if she tried hard enough she could skewer on the point of her self-blame like a juddering moth. Irresistibly she was led back to Gabby and Roman, and their faces glancing back at her as she was pulled aside to be questioned. Roman, against whom she'd swooned like a bee in its flower. And he had been carrying nothing, not even his bare ass in a pair of underpants . . . the very depth of her inexplicable trust in him, in them both, showed how far she'd been fooled. Perhaps he'd somehow planted drugs in her duffel? When the agent had accused her of traveling with someone, was this what he'd meant? And somewhere ahead of her on this same road, Gabby and Roman each reclined gloriously in their own double seat. Maybe they'd divided up

Louisa's blank notebooks, or more likely laughed at her for having so many of something so useless.

A few hours later the bus pulled into Victoria Coach Station and the driver planted himself just outside the bus door and could not be avoided. Louisa only flinched slightly as he seized her upper arm and propelled her roughly toward the station building. "Ride without paying," he fulminated. "Threatening and mouthing off! As if I have time for it!"

"Hey," shouted another driver, "you can't leave your coach there, move it on if you're finished unloading."

"Unload where you are, why don't you?"

"It's not the loading and unloading zone, is it?"

"Can't you see I've got a fare-evading criminal here!"

"Put her back on your coach and drive her to prison then!"

Whether it was hearing the word "prison," or feeling the driver's grip barely perceptibly loosen as he continued to shout at his colleague, though her mind stalled and stammered, Louisa's animal body tore free. The bandolier purse flapped and slapped against her side. There were shouts—but whether she was their cause she didn't wait to find out, running for the second time this day as she hadn't since she was a little kid pounding through dust on a playground. She wasn't a runner, she wasn't a physical person of any kind, her body generally felt more like an antagonist than an ally, but it was as though her mind, that strange little capsule she thought comprised her whole existence, had broken apart like an egg so her body could revel in the sensation of the hard pavement shocking her bones, the sweat between her breasts and under her arms and in the roots of her hair, the glances of barely engaged passersby mere flares of color at the edges of her vision. She kept running even once the driver and the other driver and the entire area of loading/unloading and even the station, an obstacle course of lumbering humans and trash cans and benches, had been left behind; she kept running out the far side of the station because the sheer momentum of her running was better than anger, it was intoxicating, who could stop her from running? Cutting across the sidewalk dodging late-morning pedestrians, she was drawn simply by the brightness on the far side of the street, that place where the station building's shadow gave way to the light. That was where her brain-less animal-body was running when the shouting rose around her yet again, along with a blare of car horns and her name—yet again someone had her by the arm and she wrenched herself away while hurling something like a snarl at him, this unfamiliar man in a jacket and tie. "You almost got yourself killed!" he cried before rushing away, as if to make up for the second he'd wasted in saving her life. Louisa caught her breath as the traffic she had tried to interrupt continued surging past, all of it objects and colors without meaning. "Louisa!" she heard again, "Louisa!" and then people were running toward her from opposite directions, one was tall and resembled a god, one was short and resembled a twelve-year-old boy, but when they converged on her she understood that the tall one was Roman and the short one was Gabby. Like refugees from an overseas war they shrieked and clung to each other.

"We had such a fight with that prick of a driver!"

"We've been circling and circling the station for hours, Roman went clockwise and I went counterclockwise to double our chance we might spot you—"

"—we *begged* him to wait–"

"—we were really about to give up and then we saw each other coming for like the thousandth time—"

"—and you shot out the doors right between us and almost got hit by a cab!"

"We almost gave up, but you're *here*!"

"And *you're* here!"

"I can't believe it!"

"*I* can't!"

And they were laughing and crying and hanging on each other and falling into annoyed passersby for so long that finally a station officer came shouting at them to stop blocking the way, and Louisa told Gabby and Roman that she was a wanted criminal at the bus station, and in a sort of crabwalk because of being unable to let go of each other they made a clumsy rush for the station's bag check, where Roman

and Gabby had stored Louisa's duffel for safekeeping while they conducted their seemingly hopeless search for her, and Louisa sobbed and
hugged them both again at the sight of her duffel, and then they all
went together to have English breakfast and Louisa said, "I can't afford it," and Gabby laughed and said, "Haven't you worried enough?"
Somehow their enormous breakfast of fried eggs and bangers and
ham slices and broiled tomatoes and mushrooms and baked beans
and stacks of bread fried in butter was paid for by Roman despite his
still lacking shirt, undershorts, and shoes, and then with Roman toting Louisa's huge duffel as if it were a dinky handbag they rode the
Tube together to Paddington Station with Gabby so she could get to
Heathrow in time for her flight and Gabby wrote down her address
in Berkeley and gave the slip to Louisa and when Roman said, "What
about me?" Gabby rolled her eyes and ventured that the two of them
could probably share the one slip. And then so suddenly and strangely
Gabby was gone in the crowd.

Roman set down the duffel and picked up Louisa. He was just
enough taller that the tips of her toes brushed the ground. He tasted
like sour mouth fuzz and the grease of their sumptuous meal and whatever else made up the compost of however long he had lived indigent
on the road. Louisa, long used to herself as a finicky person, devoured
the sticky softness of his mouth the way she'd devoured the breakfast,
which she was to some extent having again. She said so to Roman,
something she never would have said in her previous life to a boy that
she liked, but she knew he would laugh, as he did.

"I'll brush my teeth at the flat," he said, "and we can have a bath."

"What flat?" said Louisa.

She must have said other things, too. She must have asked many
questions, whether with timidity or astonishment or a pretense of already knowing the answer, but later she would never remember how
the enigma of Roman transformed into his thorough familiarity, as
if despite everything that was strange and unprecedented about him,
at the same time she had known him already. She would no more
remember how she learned his scattered family and homes and former schools than she would remember his hobo stench, once they

had taken their baths, and he reappeared to her as a smooth-cheeked young man in a clean suit of clothes.

Love is, perhaps, the sensation of expertise that erupts out of nowhere, and as time goes on accumulates enough soil at its feet to be standing on something. Louisa's expertise, though, resisted this process. She *understood* Roman, which was better than knowing him, which was perhaps conditioned on her not entirely knowing him. There was a lot in that locked box of his she had an instinct was better untouched. It was clear to Louisa almost from the beginning—although she didn't have words for it until much later, until The Age of Therapy, by which time, being a person who could pay for such things, she could barely remember the person she'd been that the therapy-words described— that what Roman most cherished in her was her naïve and credulous image of him. It was important to safeguard this image against the erosions of too many facts. "But *whose* flat," her mother persisted, a child's bewilderment distending "whose," a child's petulance protesting "flat," although perhaps, to be fair to her mother, some of this was the effect of the long-distance line. In the arrogance of love, Louisa had inexhaustible patience for redirecting her mother's attention, for cajoling her, not into accepting vague answers so much as giving up her attachment to questions. The "flat" was in his family, or belonged to his family's friends, or was his eventual inheritance—it didn't matter, Louisa didn't know, she understood that her value relied in large part on her continued not-knowing. And she, in turn, became adept at rewarding not-knowing in her mother. In this way she retrained her mother to stop asking such questions as when would Louisa return to the US, or when would she go back to college, or when at least would she visit—rewarding only the humblest inquiries with any reply.

Three years after that summer, clambering on all fours through the metal tubes and chutes of a complicated seaside play structure, Louisa stood up and, misjudging the play structure's size, slammed the crown of her head on a railing. Her vision went black and she reeled and almost pitched to the ground—the structure was designed for people much smaller than her—before catching hold with one hand. Swearing, she palmed the throbbing spot on her skull. It was a long moment,

what with half her attention on the all-fours infant shuffling at her feet
and the other half on her possibly concussed and swelling brain, before she felt herself being watched. Her gaze met that of a dark-eyed
young woman with dark, curling hair in a topknot—a young woman
like almost every young woman in Barcelona, except for the way she
was staring.

"Louisa?" Amalia said.

Roman was still at the boatyard and might be there the rest of the
day; it was impossible not to end up in a nearby café, enduring that
beseeching gaze again, darkly glittering as if Amalia were just about
to cry. Amalia didn't know to glance away during conversation; she
never had, Louisa realized, and perhaps this was the source of her air
of supplication and alarm. It was just the same conversation as Louisa
had already mastered tolerating, and abbreviating, on the phone with
her mother: yes, she was married, yes, this baby squirming in the cage
of her arms with increasing desperation was her own, yes, she had no
thought of finishing college, and no, that wasn't because of the baby,
obviously she'd blown off college well before she had him, their graduation was two years in the past and Julian was not even one. Amalia,
Louisa learned, was in Barcelona for the wedding of a colleague; she
lived in Madrid and worked for a pharmaceutical company, whether
curing AIDS or cancer Louisa didn't ask. It was all so predictable an
outcome of Amalia's anguished, lonely doggedness, her notoriety for
sleeping on the computer lab's floor and eating her meals alone behind a battlement of science textbooks of the sort Louisa had thought
it was the point of college not to have to ever look at again. So un-
protestingly did Amalia reinhabit Louisa's scorn that it never crossed
Louisa's mind that Amalia's unease might be other than a product of
her welcome shock at Louisa's bold rejection of their childish college
world. It didn't cross Louisa's mind that Amalia, of all people, might
feel sorry for her.

"Madrid is nice because I get to my parents so easily," Amalia was
saying, "it's just an hour on the train, I can see them as much as I like.
You must have been to Madrid if you're here?"

"There hasn't been time, with Roman trying to get his boat ready."

"Perhaps you could come? I could show you around. It's a beautiful city."

"We traveled a lot before this one was born—mostly the Eastern Mediterranean, Turkey, places like that. Roman grew up in Western Europe and he's sort of over it, honestly. And we went so many places together, lately I've been relieved to stay put." Perhaps more than any other aspect of what she thought of as her wildly nonconformist life, it was this sort of offhand comment she thrilled to. Even while she'd endured it—all the sleeping on beaches for the sake, apparently, of not spending money *because* it was so plentiful—Louisa had told herself that her discomfort would be worth it, for the eventual telling. This was what she had proudly told herself about a great many things she had done recently.

"Think about it—perhaps you'll want a break? My parents could come up and stay with the baby while I show you the city. They love little children."

"That's so nice."

"They still ask about you."

Louisa found this hard to believe but reiterated how nice it was; Julian was squealing and huffing, working himself up for a good sustained scream, and with relief she started readying to leave. Something in Amalia's face changed; she seemed to give up a pretense. "I'm so surprised," she said, helplessly. "I thought . . ."

"What?" Louisa said, cloaking the challenge behind a bright smile.

"My parents were so impressed by your independence—they always talked about it, how you arrived with that single suitcase, all alone. So different from us, who were scared to death, and we'd all arrived there together! I'm just surprised you left school," Amalia concluded abruptly, as if there had been more that she'd wanted to say, but then thought better of it.

But that was all Louisa needed—Amalia's surprise, not whatever the reason for it. When she thought of figures from her past, like Tamar or even Anne, she felt an angry craving—to surprise them. To do the thing they least expected.

# Part IV

# Serk

**"Look at you.** No wonder you think you're so special."

Accusation? Affection? A little of both. He can't see what he knows he is seeing, though he knows it so well. Or did, once. "Like a little prince." Again there are opposite sides to the tone. *You are special, I am awestruck by you. You are ridiculous, I am tired of you.* "Put it back in the box before the others can see it, or they'll ask why we didn't make portraits of them. Our mistake was making this one of you! That was our vanity."

When are these words said? By whom? What about?

In dreams, there is sometimes the knowledge of knowledge, without the knowledge itself. And it's very like waking, with the knowledge of the dream, but no clear recollection. Some phantasm, flirting its tail as it whips out of sight.

No: "Like a little emperor." That's what it was. "No wonder you think you're so special."

He sees it, as if at the back of his mind: more feeling than sight, what impressions were made but still not quite the image itself: the bump of a nose barely human, more like that of a bear. Yet the miniature features have somehow amassed a gigantic expression. *Look at you . . . special . . . ridiculous.* The expression of a haughty little tyrant, affronted at having been born. Laughable miniature emperor's robes, a prop provided by the studio, part of the cost.

It's a portrait, of a baby, at the age when if set on its bottom, it can hold itself upright just long enough to create the exposure. Not his recent baby brother, but himself, now a long-legged boy. "Put it back in the box before the others can see it." A secret shared with Mother, long ago. So long ago it has been long forgotten.

"Let's try again. I admit it has been entertaining to call you Your Highness, but we're growing impatient."

*You are special, you are ridiculous.*

*Where is that portrait?* he would like to ask, did his mother keep it in that box long after he forgot it existed?

Though even if these thoughts could find words, the words could not find sound. As his mind stirred and tried, his throat gagged. He found a silvery eye staring at him.

"What is your nationality?" the voice repeated, not in Japanese or English but Korean. He had been gleaning the meaning for some time before recognizing the language in which it was made. The language of Mother. Not her voice as he had dreamed.

He had not produced sound. He gagged harder and shuddered all over, as fingers entered his mouth and his gorge beat against their wet mass, and his throat detonated in coughing and the rest of him in pain. A dense cold wetness like a piece of his flesh was pulled out of his mouth but the knifelike sensations only split his jaw and tongue once the flesh piece was gone. It had not been a flesh piece at all but a sodden wad of gauze from which heavy black droplets rained down as the hand removed it.

"Still can't talk?" the voice noted. "I am sorry for the difficulty, but you lost several teeth. That could have been avoided if you had not attacked. This operation was carried out very poorly, and there were many mistakes, and the persons who made those mistakes have been relieved of their duties, but even so, you would not have been attacked if you had not attacked first. You're very lucky you weren't shot to death. The object of the operation was to take you unharmed, but you made that very difficult. You were really a savage with *this*." Serk flinched violently in surprise; the silver eye had nudged forward and tapped him between his eyebrows where he lay, he was coming to understand, with one cheek and one temple adhered to a sour-smelling lump that perhaps was a pillow. The silver eye was in fact the round end of some cold hard object, which pressed against Serk where his third eye would be were he Buddha. It pressed as if trying to press that eye into existence, then relieved him of the pressure and withdrew, again taking the form of a silvery eye.

"What is your nationality?" the voice asked again. "You came here from Japan but sometimes you curse in Korean, with an accent no one recognizes and profanity either unknown or laughable. The clothes you were wearing, and this, have English letters. What does this say? Can you read it?"

The silvery eye grew and shrank, approached too near so it blurred in Serk's vision and then receded too far, but Serk did not need the object to pause at the right focal distance to realize what the word was that was etched on its round end in sturdy block letters. The letters increased in height toward the word's middle and then decreased again so that the word, and the box etched around it, resembled a house with a shallow pitched roof. It said EVEREADY, Serk could not say, and with this he remembered everything that had happened, and though he still could not move he lunged off the bed, seized the other man's neck in one hand, and, grabbing EVEREADY, bludgeoned the man's skull until it cracked open, and then mashed up and scattered his brains.

Much later he would return to these earliest moments. His first captor, the man who asked him to read the flashlight, would never have been so stupid as to lay EVEREADY within Serk's reach even if Serk hadn't been tied to the bed. The man had been on his guard even as Serk, electrified by delusions of murder, weakly and helplessly writhed. From the man's vigilance, far more than from his words, Serk understood that he had given his captors a great deal of trouble already, yet for some reason wasn't dead. He understood he had some kind of value but not what it was. He understood that EVEREADY also had value. His captor had taken EVEREADY in his grip and demonstrated enjoyment of its heft, the smooth motion of its on-and-off slider beneath his

thumb pad, its obvious and rare quality. He'd turned it on, so its halo
of light met the opposite wall, and indicated with his eyebrows respect
for the fact that it still worked, despite so much exposure to salt water.
He gazed on it as on a trophy, which perhaps it was; as on a symbol,
which perhaps it was. What did it tell him? That Serk had bought it
at a hardware store in the United States, where he held a green card,
and gladly participated in that country's exploitative capitalist system?
At some point, amid his shackles and stained sheets, Serk again lost
consciousness. He would remember the man holding the flashlight,
and then the man being gone. What had happened in the moment of
transition was irrecoverably lost.

What, if any, words had Serk bellowed and shrieked when they
seized him? How had they learned he knew English? Had they learned
Louisa's name from him, or from Louisa herself? They knew her, they
spoke of her; their trouble with her starting consonant was reminiscent of his own, the first weeks of her life, when he'd sit with her
asleep in his arms and whisper her name to her over and over again,
taming the tip of his tongue to the blunt, firm contact of the L. Despite this difficulty in pronunciation, they use her name constantly, to
threaten or inspire him, to reassure or bully him. Is their use of it a
proof that she really exists, as they constantly claim that she does? Or
did they glean it from him in the first place, then add to it little details
he had recklessly scattered before he grew wise—"She's just a young
girl!" he must have begged them. "You can keep me, send her back to
her mother!" Later they tell him Louisa has said, "I wish my mother
could come here as well!"

"Please bring her to me," he begs, too exhausted by his longing
even to rage, even to cry. Even to hurl at them the old-fashioned exple-
tives they find so amusing.

"But the difficulty is your incomplete reeducation. Your indoctrination by the Japanese and American imperialists is bone-deep. You
are so unreceptive, we must be certain of you before we bring you and
your daughter together again. How can we risk your daughter's flaw-
less consciousness? It was so much easier with her: She is after all so
bright, and so young. Despite her American birth, her mind is so pure.

And she's more and more worried about you—she has told us you're stubborn and proud."

Had she? Well, she would know, wouldn't she? he thinks proudly. And so he must cooperate, but no, cooperation is like eating poison, he must resist, but no, resistance endangers Louisa, he must keep her safe, if she really is here, if she actually lived.

Her screaming, as they'd thrown them in the boat. The bag a perfect darkness through which the blows came; they were angry at him that he'd managed to land so many blows of his own. Her screams were the last sound he heard.


It took a long time for his body to heal enough that he could sit up by himself, then stand and walk short distances, then squat over a toilet instead of the humiliating effort with the bedpan. Even once he could sit up, stand, walk, and squat, he only did so with pain. Only forty and he felt like a man twice his age. It was the persistent cold and damp, it was the untended mess of his mouth, most of all it was the meagerness of the meals they provided, poverty meals of millet and the occasional shaving of pickle, which were arbitrarily punctuated by a feast day of pork or beef on which he would gorge uncontrollably and which renewed the intensity of his hunger pangs when the austerity diet resumed. Like every unpredictability, this must also be deliberate. He almost wished the meat days never came. He sometimes wept into his bowl as he wolfed down his food, mortified by his inability to moderate his intake and by the fear, often realized, that he would vomit and lose this protein that for all he knew might never come again. Louisa had always been a wolfish eater and it had horrified him, he had flinched at his own aggrieved tone as he snapped at her, "Slow down! No one's going to take it away!" Was Louisa, at this same moment, helplessly devouring her meal like a starved dog? Or perhaps they were giving her meat every day? "In our country," his handler of that day would pontificate as he struggled to not eat his food like a dog, "owing to the perfect workings of our economic system, and the perfect harmony that prevails throughout the social body, we eat meat every day in the proper proportion to maintain perfect health—but your imperialist indoctrination gives us concern that a taste of our excellent meat will return you to gluttonous ways. And so we must be very careful with you. Meat only sometimes—and, sadly, you're still gluttonous." Of course it was torture. Might it also be a way of concealing an actual shortage of food? His handlers were gaunt, with poor complexions and poor teeth. He thought of Yeonja so long ago, writing to ask him for seeds. The meat days lingered in his nostrils' memory as a torment and in his guts' memory as daggerlike pains, but despite this outsize role the meat played in his mind he knew his body's underfeeding was steady, that his body had turned from its scant stores of fat to his muscle. His healing faltered short of true restoration and his mind roamed in circles.

After he could sit up, stand, walk short distances, and squat, he was hooded and moved in the back of a vehicle the struggling engine of which was so deafeningly loud, and that crashed with such agonizing violence over what felt like a continuous field of rubble, that he feared his barely knitted bones would break again, or that he would fall through the vehicle's apparent lack of floorboards and be crushed by its wheels. He fainted from pain and awoke in a small room with one door and one window through which he saw, from where he lay on a mat that did not blunt the cold of the room's cement floor, a gray sky. A strong gasoline smell emanated, he realized, from himself, from his filthy stained and torn Hanes T-shirt and his equally degraded slacks, from which the belt had long since been removed. These rags of his that had also transited from an unlikely parallel universe stank of gasoline from his ride in the vehicle that had lacked floorboards, shocks, and probably an exhaust pipe. Lying on the mat he was overtaken by the memory of his American garage, a space in which this room would fit twice. The garage, so little thought-of before, unfurled fully preserved in his mind. Lawn mower, garbage cans, pegboard of tools, right down to the smell of the gasoline stain on the concrete underneath the Toyota, the smell that had delivered him from his unlikely present to his unlikely past. That a space so well built, amply sized, and replete with all the armaments of the prosperous property owner was ever his to disregard is incomprehensible, as in, he cannot comprehend or even withstand this idea and so, intact and detailed as it is, he removes it from his plane of consciousness, back to wherever it came from.

Here, too, are handlers who extol the comforts of his new home. What palatial conditions, and all to himself!—with hot plate and, most dazzling of all, a sink and floor toilet boxed into a closet (with a door but no lock). Even if he fails to express it to his handlers, he is grateful for the private commode over which he squats for hours in the agonizing effort to move his locked bowels. Out the single window, which is set so high he can only see out balancing for brief exhausting moments on his toes—and he is surely taller than the inhabitants this room's creators had in mind—are rampant weeds, a razor-wire fence, and beyond this an almost pastoral landscape of gravel roads and trees and, in the distance, the back side of a little square structure like his. His handlers tell him this is a village for esteemed guests, like him.

"Is my daughter here?" he asks, desperate for the answer to be yes, desperate for the answer to be no.

"Oh, your daughter! Such an inspiring student of our national philosophy! Don't you understand that being moved here is a sign that you're making progress? She's so anxious for you to catch up to her. Isn't it something, when the parent is taught by the child?"

While his captors showed awareness of Louisa from the very beginning, they never spoke of his parents and brothers and sister. He was careful not to mention them. His captors' discovery via EVEREADY of his years in America only bent them with greater ruthlessness to further extractions: that he was Japanese-born, that even after the peninsula's liberation he had followed his rotten imperialist's heart to the US rather than come "home" to the DPRK. He understood that he couldn't win favor by revealing his family's story. Logic didn't prevail, favor didn't exist. His one clear source of utility to his captors, his deep knowledge of the languages of their two foremost enemies, was equally his crime, a proof he could never be trusted. It must be the same for his family, not despite but because of the promises they had been made. *Why*, he imagined the taunts being hurled at his parents, *did it take the promise of an* indoor gas cooker *to bring you finally back to your homeland, after so many years in Japan? Was it merely the lure of material goods—not your love for your homeland itself?* His family must be marooned in the "hostile" class just as he would be, if he survived, despite his captors' promises, which were no sooner made than revised or retracted: that they would make him a film star, he was so tall and handsome, and who better to broadcast to the world than a man who'd abjured *both* Japan and the US, and finally "come home" to the DPRK; that they would restore Louisa to him and give her a gorgeous stepmother to be his new wife; that they would make him the head of a top-secret military research and development unit where all his engineering know-how would be finally put to good use, unlike in the racist imperialist US, where he'd been made to teach a mere introductory class. That they would give him power and pleasures they were not even at liberty to describe, so reserved were these for the elite. At the very least, they would take him to the national stadium, where he would witness Louisa performing a flag dance.

At the same time, he could never rule out that his captors knew all about his parents and siblings already, that whether or not he revealed their existence was a test.

This terrible thought spawned another: that his family weren't just known to his captors but were why he'd been taken. It had been Soonja who gave him the number of a friend of hers who was starting a real estate business, renting cheap houses in shore towns to people wanting to escape the summer heat. Like all Soonja's friends—like everyone his family had ever known—the woman was an ethnic Korean and a member of the Organization. Did she promote her business through the Organization? But everyone did. That was what it was for. The Organization, which had once been so struggling and small, and now had its own banks. The Organization, which in recent years had been accused by the Japanese government of undisclosed business deals with the DPRK.

They hadn't even spent three full weeks in the house on the shore. Not wanting Soonja to visit, Serk hadn't told her where the house was. But Soonja's friend could have told her. Soonja's friend could have told any number of people.

And then he thought he had finally gone mad, because he spun stories like this. Always with the same theme of how special he was, how special his disaster was, when what had happened to him was not special at all. It might have happened in the same way had he been an illiterate fisherman, or a restaurant busboy, or a college kid hoping to score with his girlfriend on a dark stretch of sand. Eventually, he met an example of each kind of man. They differed from him only in that they didn't believe, as he did, that their disaster was tailored for them. But this belief was a form of resistance. Over time it left him, or he allowed it to die.

For a long time, while he lived in the "village for guests," he was "re-educated" by his "comrades." His hut was suffocatingly hot, then bone-piercingly cold, so he knew seasons passed.

Different versions of the same woman came every day with his meal. All wore ill-fitting pants and a smock, were the size of an American five-year-old child, had face-creases so deep they looked cut by a razor. The women were indistinguishable from each other, except for the one who one day, as she banged down the bowl, said, "Stupid, your daughter is dead."

This lowest-down woman—the only tyrant without a lackey. Or perhaps her lackey was at home—some child she beat. Off she went past the expressionless guard at the door while Serk shoveled the food in his mouth, then promptly vomited into the toilet, where it sat in a heap, each grain distinct and unchanged by its journey.

Of course his daughter wasn't dead, his reeducators assured him. His daughter—smart like him!—had recognized the paradise in which she found herself, his daughter had a thoroughly revolutionary consciousness, his daughter's voice was the loveliest in the youth choir, his daughter's light step was the most graceful in the patriotic dances performed by her school. Were these visions possible? Were they impossible? He remembered how obsessed she'd been by her Japanese school uniform, how besotted with the fascistic bars and ribbons of rank, and how this had startled him as being un-American, some primitive race-memory for which he was to blame. But this imagined Louisa who was singing the songs, dancing the dances, and wearing the pin also gave him hope. She was surviving and he must do the same.

He improved in his so-called reeducation, memorizing the dicta of the dictator, the lists of commandments and maxims, the dates and locations of their pronouncements, the "guidance" on every possible subject from the planting of seedlings to the mending of pants, the hagiographies of the dictator's family members, and, most difficult of all, the dictator's infinite numbers of speeches, which approached such incoherence as to almost defeat his shrewdest schoolboy tricks of rote memorization—even these, he managed to parrot.

Then he was rewarded with a student of his own. The lock was thrown and like Pavlov's dog Serk's mouth flooded with saliva and his mind with the insipid exhortations of this day's memory work, but instead of one of the scowling bent old women who brought him food, or one of the rigidly grinning young women who lately gave him his "political instruction," the guard admitted a young man, like his uniformed counterpart well-fed and hard-muscled but wearing civilian clothing and armed only with a notebook and pen. As the door banged shut and the clang of the bolt came again, the young man seated himself opposite Serk with the desk between them, set the notebook on the desk, opened it to a blank page, and took up his pen. Serk stared dumbly at the notebook, which replaced the enormous bound volumes of the dictator's output that were usually presented to him at this hour of the morning.

"I have the honor of learning Japanese and English from you," the young man announced.

Serk didn't know if it was an inappropriately long time, or an appropriately brief time, before he replied, "Your request honors me. But I have no ability to teach languages." His parrot-voice had been well lubricated by recitations, but it had been a long time since his mind had supplied it with words.

"You speak fluently. That will be enough for me to learn."

All three languages, including the one he shared with the young man, withdrew into silence. His thoughts, barely articulate, raced beneath language. That this must be a test or a trap. Every transaction contained hidden meaning. Humility was reliably safe, but it could also be seen as evasion. "I am still a student of your country. How can I be trusted to teach someone like you? I may offer poor guidance."

"You express your hesitation in a very nice way. I'm already glad to be learning from you."

Serk felt a movement within himself, like a quiet earthquake. His eyes, he feared, glittered with weakness. All this unquantifiable time and he still hungered for kindness like a little child. Remember the power of questions, he reminded himself. In the role of teacher, he was perhaps permitted questions. "Shall we start with English, or shall we start with Japanese?" he asked in English. He then repeated the question in Japanese. Asking these questions, he forced himself to look with seeing eyes at his new interlocutor. The young man's nose and jaw seemed insistent beneath his faintly shiny skin, as if they'd recently grown into masculine hardness and the skin hadn't yet stretched to fit. His scalp was brown and taut beneath close-shorn hair. He held his head erect and his shoulders bulged slightly beneath his new-appearing shirt. The gaze he returned to Serk was composed, but something flickered in its depths as Serk posed the one question two ways: partial recognition, frustration to find oneself tongue-tied. "Did you understand my questions?" he asked, returning to Korean.

"You spoke of Japanese and English. That's all I could catch."

"You speak a little of each. They're not completely unknown to you."

"I studied them both in university. But never enough to speak."

"You're a graduate of university, then."

"Yes, our Great Leader has blessed me with an excellent education. Still, I'm not as learned as you. You speak three languages. You must have studied hard, to learn them."

"I'm sure you will study even harder and prove a much better student than I ever was. The question I asked was which language you'd like to begin with."

"Let's begin with Japanese, Teacher."

To be addressed as "Teacher" in his current position was almost too much. He recoiled as if mocked, but the young man's face remained calm. Serk again reminded himself to make use of the power of questions. "Because Japan is nearer your home than England or the US?"

"Because I've studied more of it already. Perhaps I'll make quicker progress and gain greater confidence for the challenge of English."

It was possible for courtesy, persuasive humility, and the use of honorifics to electrify with suspicion the tiny hairs at the base of Serk's neck. But the unfamiliar sight of the quiet young man and blank notebook had also gusted open his mind from its state of inert emptiness. Even if it was a new sham, the enactment of this ritual, teacher and student, was as irresistible to him as the cruelly sporadic meals of meat. Perhaps the young man would never appear again after this day. Or perhaps he would come frequently, and Serk would learn something from him, as the young man claimed to want to learn something from Serk.

That first day, they had barely time to establish the manner in which they would address each other, and the beginnings of a method, before someone outside sharply banged on the door and the young man gathered his materials, sprang to his feet, bowed, and stepped through the flash of daylight made by the briefly opened door while Serk was still shifting his weight from his buttocks to his knees in preparation for standing. "Thank you, Teacher, stay well," the young man said as he vanished, and the sound of his voice persisted in the empty room until it was obscured beneath the labored, wheezing sound as of a broken fireplace bellows that was, it always took Serk some time to realize, the sound of his tears. His sobs and tears were a purely physical event like his other secretions; they were no longer accompanied by thought. When he finally got on his feet, he began his slow circles around the tiny room's perimeter, first supporting himself with his

right arm, then, once this was painful, reversing direction and supporting himself with his left.

The young man came back, whether the next day or several days
later, Serk was no longer able to judge, and he continued to return,
frequently if unpredictably. "Byung Ho *shi*," Serk addressed him, as
he might any student, and this singular intimacy alone was enough to
mix into his fear and suspicion a genuine curiosity, which he tried to
both conceal and gratify with instructional questions. "I will be a better teacher to you if I understand what you hope to achieve with the
language," he explained. Any greater specificity required great care,
that he not appear to probe or, most fatal, accuse. It had been his first
thought that Byung Ho had been selected for the spy services—that
for the sake of Serk's own mental freedom, he was willingly training Byung Ho to snatch more skillfully someone else into captivity. It
was precisely the perversity of the scenario that made it seem likely.
At other times Serk imagined he was facing the son of some powerful
official who spared no effort for the son's education, even the effort
of kidnapping a Japanese tutor. Then Serk further imagined Byung
Ho, because possessed of a uniquely free mind, finding Serk's situation intolerable and demanding Serk's freedom. And so Serk would be
seduced, by the chance that Byung Ho was someone he could trust—
and then alarmed, by the very sensation of trust. He would remind
himself that, because Byung Ho was the one person he ever spoke
with, he was the one to trust least of all. There was no middle ground
in Serk's thinking, as there seemed to be no middle ground in his situation: Byung Ho would cause either Serk's salvation or Serk's final
destruction. The entire incalculable conundrum had deafened Serk's
mind in the moment between his saying to Byung Ho, "I will be a
better teacher to you if I understand what you hope to achieve with
the language," and his adding, "For example, do you hope to someday
continue your studies in a Japanese university?"

But Byung Ho parried each question of Serk's with a scrupulously
polite one of his own. "Would this be a wise course, do you think? How
would you say, in Japanese, 'Is this a wise course,' or 'Is this a good
idea'?" This was the method of instruction on which they had settled:

the exceedingly cautious conversation in Korean, like making their way through a minefield, while encountering occasional phrases for which Byung Ho asked for translation. It was neither conventional nor efficient, yet each translation question Byung Ho asked led to useful yet safe-seeming words. The question about "wise course" and "good idea" led to the many words for good and bad, which led to everyday innocuous examples: This food is very good, those directions were bad, when will this bad weather end, is this the best way to the station, have you been feeling well, I wish you a good night. Byung Ho's notebook filled rapidly. Watching him write—Serk still was not allowed any paper or pen of his own—Serk found those Hangul characters of his earliest childhood speaking to him, even across decades, and even, from where he sat as always facing Byung Ho, upside down. And so his knowledge of his very first language, which had been stunted so long ago, reached full flower in this unexpected way. He might not have realized, in these quiet moments during which Byung Ho wrote, and he watched his own words appear upside down, that his reflexive distrust of Byung Ho was being slowly eroded, by the earnestness of his student's note-taking.

When at length they returned to the place their exchange had left off, Serk was ready with a careful non-response of his own. "You've said your education has been excellent. What more could a Japanese school have to teach you?"

"The Japanese schools must have taught *you* well, Teacher." But though his emotions kept stirring to life, Serk's mind also kept pace, and it muzzled his yearning to speak and be heard. He would not be so easily tricked into confirming he'd been educated in Japanese schools.

"Perhaps your hope is not to attend a Japanese school but simply to visit and travel? This could be instructive." Serk knew better than to use their lesson words *good* or *bad* when describing such potential instruction by an enemy nation. He could no more do this than ask, Are you hoping to pass yourself off as a Japanese person, for the purpose of espionage? Or, Are you hoping to escape your homeland, where your freedom is perhaps not so different from my captivity?

Unsurprisingly Byung Ho replied, "Have *you* found *your* travels instructive, Teacher? I understand you have seen many parts of the world."

"Of your country I have only seen this small room, and a previous one, even smaller, and without even a small window like this one to let in the light." But when Byung Ho next spoke, he surprised Serk by breaking their pattern.

"I hope that will soon change, and that you'll be able to see my great nation. In fact, I hope to be able to show you myself. What is the conjugation for expressing hopes, in Japanese? I don't believe we've addressed this."

After the lesson Serk was left with the torment of interpreting Byung Ho's comment. It was clearly a signal, but was it sincere, or was it a sham of sincerity meant to deceive? What if Byung Ho was, as Serk longed to believe, a young man of conscience who wanted to help? On the side of the door with the dead bolt was the guard who let Byung Ho come in and go out, as well as the higher authority, whatever this was, that allowed the arrangement. At any moment that higher authority might bring the arrangement to an end. Always, his extreme caution was at war with his fear that he might miss a chance. The next time Byung Ho came, in addition to the notebook and pen he had a pack of cigarettes and a box of matches. "The guards gave permission," he said, tilting his head toward the door that had already banged closed behind him. Serk was ashamed of his trembling hands that could not pull a cigarette out of the pack nor a match from the matchbox. Byung Ho handed a cigarette to him and, when he'd pressed it between his lips, lit it.

"Thank you," he said.

"Please don't thank me for such a small thing."

"It's not a small thing for me."

"I'm sorry not to have brought some before."

Serk had to believe this additional signal was earnest. "Byung Ho shi," he began. The cigarette made his blood swoon. "I've sometimes sensed you're curious about me."

Byung Ho was smoking his own cigarette. He hadn't yet opened his notebook. He pinched the cigarette in his lips, opened the notebook to a blank page, carefully tore out the page, and laid it on the desk between them so they had a place to deposit their ashes. Then he closed the notebook again. "It's true," he said. "I've learned a lot from you, for which I'm grateful. But I've wished I could learn more about you."

"Did you know I have a daughter?" With difficulty he forced himself to watch Byung Ho's face, afraid he might see evidence of deceit.

"I didn't know this, Teacher. I know very little about you. Congratulations on having a daughter. I hope to also have a family someday."

"You're a young man, and I'm past forty. In a different life, you could have been my son. But my daughter is much younger than you are. She's just a little girl. She was brought here with me, but the people who keep me here won't let me see her. I haven't seen her since I arrived here. Can you help me with this?"

After months of self-restraint, he'd leaped forward—precipitately. What if he'd misread the signal and spoken too much? He startled as the cigarette scorched him—he'd let it burn down to his fingers. Without any change of demeanor Byung Ho took the butt from him, extinguished it against the floor, placed the butt on the sheet of notepaper, and lit Serk another. "What do you mean, that your daughter was brought here with you?"

"We were brought here by force. In the summer."

"It's summer again, seon saeng nim. But what do you mean, 'brought by force'?"

Serk almost lost hold of his delicate faith, but he fought to retain it, to keep it intact. "My daughter and I were attacked, while we walked on a beach in Japan. Our attackers—your countrymen—brought us to this place, or at least they brought me. I haven't seen my daughter since that night."

Byung Ho's calm was uninterpretable. "I'm sorry, seon saeng nim," he said after a moment. "Such a brutal action is hard for me to reconcile. But I appreciate your confidence in me. I'll try to find news of your daughter."

Serk's emotions broke free of his mind. Tears and hoarse groans broke free of his body. While this happened Byung Ho watched with concern but not pity. "I apologize," Serk finally said. "How can I thank you?"

"Keep telling me more of your life. The more I know, the better able I'll be to find news of your daughter. But, if you'll forgive me for making a suggestion, we should continue the lessons, so I keep making progress." It was a moment of explicit alliance, and Serk felt an almost-forgotten sensation course through him. It was akin to energy and alertness, though not as simple as these. He could only have described it as the sensation of being a human, with a body and mind, and the will to survive.

As if his captors had agreed with this will to survive, his circumstances improved in new ways. Byung Ho continued to be his most frequent student, and now that they had a shared topic—whatever part of Serk's life in which Byung Ho took interest—their lessons had greater depth and focus, and Byung Ho learned even more quickly. And perhaps because whoever sent Byung Ho had noticed his progress, Serk acquired new students. They were young men with guarded expressions and hard musculature, only missing the uniform and the weapon to confirm them as soldiers, but unlike Byung Ho none of them was curious or even noticeably intelligent, and Serk could hardly remember their names. He found himself becoming an actual teacher, for these new students were so passive they didn't ask questions, so that he had to design lessons for them, an absorbing challenge and even a pleasure, because now he was given his own paper and pens. He was also rewarded with a thicker bedroll, a cushion for sitting, and a second pair of pants. These material improvements were so dramatic he felt like a beggar turned into a king, but their reward was insignificant compared to the conversations he had with Byung Ho. They began their meetings, once the door was closed and the bolt thrown and they knew that they weren't overheard, with any update Byung Ho had in his search for Louisa. Byung Ho's inquiries, Serk knew, could not be overt. Though Byung Ho never admitted that he was a recruit to the intelligence services, his systematic approach told Serk that Byung Ho possessed not only understanding of the workings of power, but increasing access. Byung Ho sometimes arrived to

their lessons in a suit, decent if visibly cheap. In time he completed a
quiet survey of the capital's orphanages. He told Serk he was making a
friend who worked in a bureau that handled adoptions. He found pre-
texts to visit children's special schools for music and dance, pursuing
the story Serk's earlier captors had told, of Louisa's precocity. Though
each investigation so far had led nowhere, Byung Ho's loyalty to the
quest—which Serk knew must put Byung Ho in danger, even more as
his star rose and he grew that much more useful to Serk, and also that
much more vulnerable to downfall—gave Serk a sense of progress.

After they had talked about Louisa, and Byung Ho's newest
thoughts about where she might be, they would continue their talk
about Serk—not just the events of his life, but their meaning. For it
had become clear to Serk that what Byung Ho hungered for was less
Serk's biography than his viewpoint. Serk the double exile, not just
from his parents' Korea but the Japan of his birth; Serk the climber of
ladders and getter of visas and ideal embodiment—as it now seemed
to Serk, all his past petty complaints about his American life invalidated and even absurd—of the American Dream: these were the topics that formed the core of their lessons. Serk talked to Byung Ho
about topics as broad as his view of American culture versus that of
Japan, as narrow as favorite movies he'd seen. He described the way
Americans socialized with each other, viewed outsiders, protested
their government, owned many duplicates of the same thing. Most
gratifying of all, he described his own American, Louisa. He described
the sorts of things she'd learned in her American school and the sorts
of views she had seemed to be forming, the games she'd played with
her friends and the shows she had watched on TV, the swiftness of her
adaptation to Japan and his conclusion that this proved her American
essence, for the Americans, Serk told Byung Ho—he had found this a
favorite subject—were somehow less bound, by their very young culture, by ideas of how they should be. They were chameleonic, in some
ways perhaps had less integrity and shallower values and were selfish,
"everyone for themselves," but it was these very qualities, and their lack
of apology for them, that let Americans seize power over the world.

These were the sorts of unrestrained talks Serk found himself having with Byung Ho as their alliance deepened across the seasons. Byung Ho grew fluent in Japanese, conversant in English, and not just comfortable with but clearly partial to the US system of free markets and liberal democracy, judging from the astuteness of his questions. For his part Serk learned the hierarchies of the Great Leader's capital, though he never received any clue as to whether his cell was within, near to, or far from that city. Serk learned of the privileged party elites who might have adopted Louisa, and of the youth academies and party cadres to which Louisa, joining one of these families, might belong. He learned of the rigid hereditary caste system, which categorized citizens based on the political behavior of their parents and even grandparents, and which would have judged his own parents imperialist "pigs" for the very fact they had lived in Japan, despite the poverty that drove them there during the time of the Japanese Empire, and kept them there after the empire's defeat. His parents, his sister, and his brothers would be barred for life from party membership in a country in which party membership determined everything, yet in itself wasn't even enough. There also had to be total loyalty, obeisance, compliance, self-sacrifice, and worshipful zeal. And so his family—if they even any longer existed, those luckless fools Serk did his best not to think of—remained a blank in his accounts to Byung Ho, because it would certainly compromise Byung Ho to know about them. And Serk's fear, that Byung Ho was compromised already, that he would one day soon recognize and reject the increasing risk to himself of their friendship, was another blank spot in their otherwise ranging and deep conversations.

Serk had long since reached the end of his personal story, though only the beginning of his opinions about the DPRK, now that Byung Ho had reciprocated him with so much information. "I find it hard to believe your Great Leader would not make use of my daughter for propaganda purposes," he said one day, as he and Byung Ho smoked as usual, and also shared a packet of rice crackers. Byung Ho had recently made a habit of bringing Serk crackers, dried squid, or some other small snack, telling Serk to keep any leftovers in his pants pockets, to avoid irritating the guards, who would turn a blind eye so long as the snacks were not flaunted. "When they first brought me here," Serk went on, "some of my so-called political teachers told me they meant to use me in a propaganda film. 'Former US Resident Praises DPRK.' Even if I did become an obedient mouthpiece for such sentiments, my face is still Korean. It wouldn't make the same impression. But this must be part of my daughter's value. Her appearance is clearly foreign."

"Though crude to say, it's undeniable that a white face, or even a half-white face, would make a greater impact in this context. Or would I say 'in this case'?" They had taken to speaking Japanese almost exclusively, because it removed any lingering fear they might be overheard.

"Either phrase makes your point equally. I said this because I again feel concerned, though I know we've discussed this, that Louisa is not in the capital city. And you've told me yourself that living conditions outside of the capital aren't comfortable."

"Conditions are less modern. More rural. And yes, as I've said many times, I don't think your daughter is outside the capital. But, seon saeng nim—today I'd like to be forthright with you."

"It's my hope that you always are forthright with me."

"Yes. And forthrightness consists, in my view, both in sharing facts once they're established, and in sharing convictions, even if they are not confirmed fact. I have a conviction I need to share with you."

"Please," Serk told him, and the sound of his own voice, calm as a bell in that moment, would afterward linger so long in his mind that its tone was deformed into sharp dissonance.

"Your daughter is not in this country. Those who have said otherwise have been lying to you. Please understand they did so with the purest of motives. In their sincere hope of redeeming your consciousness, your earliest handlers spun a fairy tale of your daughter for you. In that way they hoped to inspire you, but they were wrong to do this: not only wrong to deceive you, but wrong to let you believe that agents of our nation would ever attack, let alone kidnap, a child. We're not animals. I hope the friendship you and I have shared, which has been my great honor, has proved that to you." Byung Ho gently removed Serk's burned-down cigarette from between his immobilized fingers

before it could scorch him, the same way he'd done on that long-ago
day their alliance was formed. Serk's hand continued to hang in the air,
paralyzed. A stale inhalation still hung in his throat. He could not de-
code Byung Ho's words. "My further conviction is one for which you,
seon saeng nim, hold the proof in your heart. I believe my colleagues'
theory, that when our agents found you, in your small craft, very far
from Japan's territorial waters and very close to our shore, your inten-
tion was to infiltrate our country, to spy for your adopted country of
the US. You're an incorrigible imperialist-capitalist. Your passion for
your adopted nation has dominated every conversation we've shared
and withstood every effort of our finest instructors to reeducate you,
but the time we've spent together hasn't been in vain. I've not only
learned Japanese and conversational English, I've learned the depth
and breadth of your intelligence. I still believe you capable of service
to my Great Leader and Nation."

Somehow Serk was holding another lit cigarette. He flung it onto
the floor. "I've never driven a boat in my life! Are you insane? What has
happened to you?"

"I've tirelessly advocated for you. I've insisted that your reeducation is in fact possible, but merely requires different methods. Please,
seon saeng nim, if you really do have a daughter somewhere under
this sky, remain calm now and be grateful for the future opportunities
offered to you. Spies in this country are usually shot."

"You are *all* animals!" Serk screamed as the two guards, who had
entered the room, pinned his arms behind him. Impotent as a child in
the throes of a tantrum, Serk tried to kick Byung Ho's shins or head-
butt him as the younger and stronger man, nimbly evading, pushed
a full cigarette pack into each of his pockets, then seized hold of his
windpipe to make him hold still.

"I'm sorry," Byung Ho said close to his ear, in the Japanese Serk
had taught him. "Please believe I did my best to spare you an even
worse outcome."

The next morning Serk was handcuffed and hooded again. Outdoors the shock of wet cold stung his nostrils and numbed the bare
soles of his feet. Winter was coming. He smelled evergreen sap and

understood that this place where he had been, however long he had been there, wherever it had been located, with whomever he'd shared it, was better than wherever he was going.

He traveled again in the deafening vehicle that lacked shocks, floorboards, and an exhaust pipe, again over endless expanses of boulders, his lungs again smothered in gasoline fumes, his bones again rattled to fractures and his guts surging into his throat. Then he was flung to the bottommost bowels of the country. Then he learned what real suffering was.

# Anne

**Anne couldn't remember** when her energies had turned from accumulation to reduction. At some distant time in the past she must have been an accumulator, like everyone else. Once her body went rogue, she'd not even bothered to shop for new clothes. She had a tendency to wear what free T-shirts the fates sent her way. To get her reading from the library and her furniture from people who'd tired of theirs. On the rare occasions that she had to make a purchase—for example of her motorized scooter—the fuss and anxiety overwhelmed her and the process took months. She couldn't comprehend people who lived for new things. "We had to downsize from a thirty-eight-hundred-foot home to this eight-hundred-square-foot apartment," Bob at dinner would often introduce the favorite topic, for all the others to take up with gusto, airing again their sad stories of bending lifetimes of accumulation to the dreadful requirement of reduction. The dining sets and credenzas and collections of China sacrificed to fit into a new home that was almost too roomy for Anne and that the others regarded as a cruel rehearsal for the ultimate unfurnished box.

It all made her miss Walt terribly. Big Walt, who was supposed to have taken care of her to the end, who instead was the one who expired in a hospital bed while Anne sat sobbing and cursing in the visitor's chair. "Goddammit, Walt!" she had sobbed. But by then he could not even hear her. They'd had barely ten years together, not much less than the time she'd been married to Serk. Strange how her marriage to Serk had seemed endless and the time with Walt felt like a blip. A bright, chiming blip like the noise from her computer when someone has recalled her existence and sent her a message. *Yippee! You've got mail!* Or as it had been: *Yippee! You've got Walt!*

Better to have loved and lost, etc.—she always hated those prim platitudes. Walt would have had a good comeback to that one. "Spare me the Hallmark-card crap!" That's something, that she still has his voice in her ear.

And his books in her bookshelves, which is more of a grief. Of course, she only kept a few dozen, consigning epochs of the world to Goodwill. No American Civil War, First or Second World Wars, no Age of the Ottoman Empire or the Roman one or the Austro-Hungarian one or however many other ones, no thanks. She mostly kept his reference works, a few books about basketball, a few about Korea, and a few about the West Texas where Walt had grown up. The Korea books had been for Louisa—"They're a way to remember your dad," Anne had said. Anne couldn't really blame Louisa for rejecting them, though as always, she could wish that Louisa was nicer about it.

"They weren't his books. And he was born in Japan. He wasn't any more Korean than you're, what, Scotch-Irish? You don't even know. Just because he wasn't *white*, you think his heritage was somehow painted all over him when yours is so irrelevant to *you*, you've never learned your own grandparents' names. That's called othering. It's a form of racism." Could Louisa at least berate Anne with words Anne understood? Would Walt have known what Louisa was talking about? But Walt had never gotten over his fear that Louisa was some kind of Fury sent to pluck his eyes out.

"The boys might be interested someday," had been Anne's last attempt.

"If the boys feel like seeking their roots, I'll spring for books that weren't published four decades ago."

Needless to say, Louisa had not been one of the little army Anne had needed to make it through that ordeal of a lifetime of ordeals, emptying out Walt's apartment. All of her neighbors had helped—so many nice people had lived in that place, which now was as much of a lost paradise as Walt himself. Even after losing Walt, Anne would never have moved, she would have stayed forever tending to the ghosts of Walt and Orange Tom, but hardly had Walt died before they all had to leave, all the nice young men and women—always new ones—and all the wonderful families—always the same ones—who had shared that, as it turned out, too-nice place where there had been so much grass between buildings and so much room for the spreading oak trees. Anne should have known that nothing like that was allowed to survive. When the residents received notification that the same developer that had paved over the huge lot across the way ten years before and erected a strip mall was apparently so pleased with the result that the same was now going to happen to all of their homes—every last little box of gold brick demolished, every old oak cut down, and every blade of grass converted to concrete—Anne could only be glad Walt had not lived to see it.

So Anne did what Louisa had been nagging her to do for several years already, and "downsized" to one of those so-called assisted living places—"assisted dying" is what Walt would say. The truth was, though it had been perhaps the worst move of her life, when it was finally over Anne did feel a bit of what Louisa, always lecturing, had scold-promised her she would feel. Not "relief," but at least a dumb numbness. A passive plopping-down and not-thinking. She liked that the new place was so small she'd had to jettison half her belongings and cram the rest so tightly together that normal people couldn't understand how she managed. To which she would say that she managed just fine—until now. Now all the indescribable hard work Anne had put in, days spent just getting one box of books unpacked into a bookshelf, weeks spent corralling a single slippery haystack of paper into the regimentation of hanging files—no one who had not spent hours in her company understood how long it took Anne to perform even the lightweight tasks to which she was limited, how each separate book, each handful of paper, had to be cajoled into place by hands and arms that were starting to insist on their own cajoling, after decades of uncomplaining compensation for those bum legs and feet—had been erased at a stroke. Anne's tiny apartment, which she had filled to her satisfaction to the brim, overflowed on all sides. More boxes: a murder of boxes. Boxes Anne had never in her worst nightmares feared seeing again, let alone unpacking. Though the boxes were "only" paper— "That's all," Tobias had reassured her, somehow not understanding, as Anne did, that a single box of paper was like ten boxes of anything else—it might as well have been the whole house that had forced itself into this latest and tiniest of Anne's homes.

The invading house was the one she'd bought with Serk, the only home she'd ever owned. Now with undesired vividness Anne recalled lying in bed the night after their closing, too horrorstruck to sleep. Serk, by contrast, snored with particular ferocity, as if to say, *See? You thought I couldn't do it, but I did.* Everywhere they had ever paid rent, Serk had seethed with resentment as if he'd been indentured. He dismissed as typically feminine and irrational Anne's view that tenancy was the more privileged condition, wherein all the anxieties of leaking roofs, frozen pipes, iced sidewalks, and cracked windows were the landlord's to endure, in exchange for mere money. And so their purchase of a two-bedroom home represented another triumph of Serk's values—which he labeled American—over hers, which he often implied were almost socialistic.

Anne had to remember all this because of the astonishing thing Tobias had called to tell her just the very instant, Anne felt, when she had finally taken the last little thing from the last too-big box, and finally called the nice maintenance guys to flatten the boxes and take them away.

"You *what?*" she cried.

Two decades ago, after Serk's death, while she and Louisa were still living with Gerald and Dina, Anne had sent Tobias armed with the necessary empowerments to settle with the tenants, dispose of everything the house contained, and sell it. Now in this most unexpected phone call Tobias informed her that all those years ago he had instead put "just the things" he knew she would someday "be glad to have back"—all her papers and letters—in a storage unit on which he had then somehow paid the bill for two decades—until now, when the storage unit had suddenly been sold in order to be torn down and replaced with something else. "Is every damn thing being torn down this year and replaced with some other damn thing?" she cried.

"It's only eight boxes—they're not even large, though they're heavy," Tobias went on soothingly. "Alternatively I can ship to Louisa—"

"No—NO!"

"I'm sorry to say I just can't ship them here to myself, the cost of overseas shipping, especially with the weight of each box, is prohibitive. But you don't have to touch them! Just have a helper stack them in some out-of-the-way corner and the next time I come I'll help you go through everything." He said all of this kindly—he always said everything kindly, even as she interrupted him to yell that there *was* no such thing as an out-of-the-way corner, he did not understand where she lived!

What she'd been too shocked to say to Tobias, or to even recall, until they got off the phone, was that Louisa had never forgiven her for getting rid of all the things they'd left in storage when they'd gone to Japan. Louisa's realizing Anne had done this had not exactly been the end of their trust in each other, because this had already been drawn out to a transparent thinness. But it had been the end of Anne's thinking the trust might return. Louisa had accused her of giving no thought to Louisa when she got rid of all of their things, and Anne had made no argument because this had been true. It had never even occurred to her that Louisa ought to have a say. Now the unintentionally un-got-rid-of stuff mazed itself in heaps all around Anne not like a second chance but like the proof of an indictment. Anne knew her daughter well enough to predict that the restoration of these things would only be a repetition of Louisa's dispossession. It crossed Anne's mind not for the first time that she could still get rid of everything, could pay the maintenance guys to put it all in the dumpster, from which it would vanish irrecoverably. Louisa would not be the wiser. But Tobias would know.

So far, she had opened just one of the boxes, the one that turned out to contain the tidy archive of her carbon copies of her letters of more than a decade. Like the first one, from 1966, most were to

Dr. Grassi. Just after her marriage to Serk, as they were readying to
move to the town where Serk had a postdoc, Dr. Grassi had given
her the gift of an electric typewriter. *Now I see your clever stratagem*,
she'd written. *By your extravagant gift you mean to turn me into a person
who writes her friends letters. Despite the evidence you hold in your hands,
don't imagine you'll ever succeed.* But he had; she and Dr. Grassi had
exchanged long, confiding letters, one every couple of months, up
to the time that she left for Japan. Anne's letters to her siblings, now
that she looked them over, were at moments as frank and funny as
she had once imagined them to be, but for the most part they were
dutiful and factual. Anne's letters to her friend Marguerite were
chatty but formulaic, as were Marguerite's to her; Marguerite had
been a friend of the moment, of the warm nimbus formed by spontaneous conversation, and their loyal letters were a tribute to this,
but no approximation of it from afar. By contrast Anne's letters to
Dr. Grassi were far more voluble than Anne had ever been in Dr. Grassi's
presence. They were, she realized with a mixture of pride and acute
embarrassment when reading them again, *literary*—at least in their
aspiration. Dr. Grassi, who had loved literature so much, and had tried
so hard to create it himself, seemed to have most succeeded in drawing forth a literary flowering from Anne, however briefly it had lasted.
Reading her own words to him, Anne was actually transported—she
lost track of the time, which moved so slowly most afternoons that
she filled it with a hundred tiny duties, like taking her scooter down
the hall to check her mailbox, which almost always resulted in entrap-
ment in doddering conversation with some other resident, or listening to the radio news when it started at four, or turning on the TV
news, which started at five, or swinging by the tiny library, for whatever transaction, on her way to dinner, which started at six. All these
ironclad rungs of the day's ladder went unscaled, and Anne was only
startled back to the world by her words' melting into the purple background of the page, because the room had grown dim—it was past six
and her fingers were stained from the carbons and she had forgotten
to turn on a light.

*October 24, 1966, "Ypsilanti." Esteemed Doctor: No, I don't have
the hiccoughs and I'm not even cheating at "Scrabble." "Ypsilanti"
is the name of the town where we live. Who would have thought,
when we set out for Michigan, we would find such exotic place
names. Another place not far from here is called "Kalamazoo" and
no, it does not house wild animals. Other than the names which
seem especially made up to torture Serk's tongue Michigan is not so
different from the Valley. You would be pleased with the roses that
go over a little wood arch in the yard of our sweet little house. Sweet
half-house, to be precise. We rent one-half and the landlady lives in
the other, we get the view of the roses and she gets to tend them. Is
this not the ideal arrangement? Serk, however, hates sharing a wall
with a stranger and has already taken his "Eastern Michigan State"
ID card down to the local credit union to ask them to give us more
money we haven't yet earned. It's The American Way.*

*Feb. 8, 1967—Happy New Year, Better Late Than Never? Dear
Doctor G., thanks for your letter of last November and thanks
especially for the story. I'm sorry I've sat on it so long but it wasn't
your writing but my own that slowed me down. I like the story
very much and I disagree wholeheartedly with whoever called it
"sentimental." I'd call it "realistic" and I'd call that Good. The
character of the young wife I thought was especially realistic—I
sure would not like to trade places with her. I also disagree with
whatever blowhard it was said that you don't write a plausible
female. As a plausible female—I hope—I say yours is far more
plausible than most. I put a few thoughts on the ms (enclosed) but
not many because I liked it so much as it is. As for what's kept me so
busy, I wonder what Waku would think of his young friend Serk's
interest in Christmas. Now that we have our own place he has to go
the whole hog: tree, wreath, pile of gifts for little ol' me. If only they
weren't all items for use in the kitchen! Ask Serk who the "Christ"
in "Christmas" was and he couldn't care less: I think he's more
American than either of us.*

Except for the discussion of his stories there wasn't much difference, that first year, between her letters to Dr. Grassi and her letters
to her sister or even to a person called "Fran" at whose identity Anne
could no longer guess. Newly married Anne of 1966–67 did a lot of
reportage about the roses in the yard that she got to enjoy without the
bother of tending them and about the abundance of cookware her so-
generous husband gave her for Christmas. (Another letter of the same
day in Feb.—she must have been on a guilt-ridden roll—to this "Fran"
revealed the cookware as specifically a four-piece cook set, an oven-safe
casserole, and an electric hand mixer—clearly she had less to say to
"Fran" and was padding things up.) Anne wondered about the prom-
inence of the roses, the comedy of the cookware. She had no more
access to her true thoughts of that time, if such true thoughts existed,
than to those of a stranger. But the manuscript-helper in her—the part
of her that had known so well, not how to make Dr. Grassi's stories
truly good, but how to know how he'd meant them to be, and reflect
this back to him—told her that her young self had seized on those
roses and that cookware as the perfect devices. Just idyllic enough, just
comedic enough. Just enough *Dick Van Dyke Show* crossed with just
enough *I Love Lucy* to persuade any onlooker, even herself, that her
marriage was happy. Anne didn't even like roses. Their four years in
the Campbell Hill Road house, when Anne had seriously gardened—
for in fact this was one of her skills, now lain dormant for two-thirds
of her life—she had grown blooming shrubs, clematis on a side trellis,
and a riotous bed of annuals by the front steps—no roses.

In the years that followed, her letters to Dr. Grassi drew away from
the others. No salutation was needed to tell them apart. Though they
weren't any more frequent—Anne had always been an all-or-nothing
correspondent, alternating silence with apologetic torrents—they were
far longer than her earlier letters to him or her letters to anyone else.
Their content was different. It consisted of the sorts of stories no one
else would have found interesting, but he must have—and his interest
must have helped her make them so. That vibrant exchange, in which
spectator makes spectacle, just by giving his ardent attention. From a
distance of decades Anne could see it had been a subspecies of love. Its

lack of sexual heat hadn't been a deficit but a requirement, along with every other kind of distance, between her new home and her old one, between their ages, between his confirmed bachelordom and her rash lust-provoked love affairs. Perhaps Dr. Grassi had known from the time they'd first met that they'd be an alchemical pair. He had only been waiting for her to drift off, tethered by the typewriter.

She so dreaded the end of the series she skipped forward to it, as if she might find a different outcome, and not those blithely unsuspecting letters leading up to the trip to Japan.

*September 27, 1977*

*Dear Dr. G,*

*If you ever opined that I married Serk in hopes to avoid social life, I admit you were right. Serk has astonished and dismayed me by making some friends. Perhaps "friends" is the wrong term. They are countrymen or rather country people of his, a couple like us, man and wife. The man's name is Tae-something but he asks that people call him Tom which Serk is snide about outside Tom's hearing. "Tom" is a Korean but unlike Serk born and raised there. The difference in their upbringing—remember Serk was born and grew up in Japan— seems like it makes for some tension or at least not-so-nice jokes. Serk calls Tom a "ninny-boy" (out of earshot of course) which is an insult I think Serk invented but the meaning I am sure you can grasp. For his part Tom, at least according to Serk, has said Serk must have caught his conceited attitude from growing up among Japanese. These nasty sallies go back and forth between two smiles as perfect as knives. "Tom" is a solemn long-faced fellow who looks as though he might need cookware in his house more than we do but like his countryman Serk he has excellent teeth that change his face completely when he smiles. I am told (by Serk) that my admiration of his (and his countryman's) straight strong white teeth is an insult as it apparently suggests I expected the opposite so don't tell him I said so.*

*I've been no better than the menfolk in ignoring, to this point, the wife. The trouble is I still don't know her name. Every time we're to*

*see them I ask Serk to tell me her name—write it out on a piece of
paper?—and every time he says it so dismissively I can't even get the
first letter. I call her "Would-you-like-some-more-tea?" In her absence
I call her Tom's Wife. I think she is doomed to have no other name on
my tongue unless I get help that is not forthcoming.*

How remarkable that Anne had forgotten about Tom and Tom's
Wife. Anne closed her eyes against the kitchen light she'd turned on
and tried to remember their faces. It was past seven now; she had entirely missed dinner. If she got on her scooter and went straight to
the dining room she'd find no one but Luz, clearing up the dishes,
and maybe Carmela emptying the steam table. "Oh, Miss Anne, did
you doze off? Are you feeling okay?" Carmela would fuss—she was a
very nice woman, but she treated Anne just as she treated the older
inmates, the ones whose physical incapacity had come with age and
was accompanied by the fuddles. In general, Anne didn't mind being
thought on account of her dead legs and scooter to be at least ten years
older than she actually was. And her face had not weathered time well.
Only Bob had ever had the insight to say to her, as his dumb deaf wife
was clicking toward the salad bar heavily leaned on her walker, "You
were a beauty, Anne, weren't you—you looked like Rita Hayworth
once upon a time."

"I certainly knew how to get into trouble," Anne had replied,
making Bob throw his head back and roar and his dumb deaf wife
come clicking back to the table all pink and excited by whatever the
unknown festivity was.

Any moment now Anne's phone would ring and Bob would ask
where she'd been during dinner—he maintained a harem of the paid-
attention-to, the goosed and teased and flattered. Her eyes were still
closed, her moth-eaten memory still trying to knit up the holes. Her
memory was actually very good for a person of any age, and a whole
lot better than Louisa's—Anne remembered things about Louisa's
boys, things they had done and said and asked for, of which Louisa retained not a shred—but the sheer span of things to be kept organized

was unmanageable. That her age made her a mere child next to some of her neighbors didn't fool her into feeling young.

Even if it did, her true youthful image had emerged from the box to correct her. She knows she'll hate looking but can't help a peek: seated smiling at her own knees, one slim leg crossed over the other, wearing some kind of navy blue dress. It's not a posed picture, although Anne, despite that her gaze is cast down, seems aware it's being taken; she has a self-conscious, preening look about her that annoys her descendant, the aged Anne of now. Who took the photo, and why had Anne wound up with it? The nice dress makes Anne think it's a holiday party, it must be at the school, for where else had they known anyone? All the young professors and their wives, even the odd pair of Serk and Tom, the two Koreans, what a strange coincidence. But it was not so strange, Anne remembers—the presence of darker-skinned men with unusual accents, at least in these small college towns. It had been the same way in the Valley, in Northampton and Amherst; there was always the one Nigerian, the one Chinese, the one Pakistani. Always a man, very carefully dressed, very carefully spoken. He had always brought a wife, and she always smiled and was silent as the eager white wives of the American professors exclaimed over her delightfully colorful sari or her glossy black hair—"What I'd give to have straight hair like that!"—or her unique jewelry. Only Anne and Serk failed to fit into the pattern, Anne the odd white woman who had married the foreigner, Serk the odd foreigner who had married a white woman. Their oddness consigning them to friendlessness—to wary courtesy from the other foreigners, to excessive arm's-length chattiness from the other white people.

A very long, the longest yet, of the letters (Anne remembered, as she hadn't for decades, Dr. Grassi, when she still worked for him, interrupting her typing one day to read to her from Homer's *Odyssey*: "'. . . across the wine-dark sea': notice, Anne, the way that Homer's sea is *purple*, not, as our culture says, 'blue'!" Sweet Dr. Grassi, incandescent with amazement; and the many purple carbons of her letter bring his voice back to her from across the wine-dark sea of decades):

*December 12, 1977*

   *Belated Happy Thanksgiving and thanks for the account of your feast.*

(There must have been a letter from Dr. Grassi to which Anne was replying with rare promptitude; having relocated now to the kitchen table's tiny amount of available surface, annoyingly cluttered with her pill and vitamin bottles and the many sheafs of notes she was always writing to herself on different-size paper usually gleaned from those charity solicitations in which they try to rope you in with a free memo pad, Anne had pillaged the box and still could not find a late November letter from Dr. Grassi; that was the trouble with regaining the lost and forgotten, once you got a little back you wanted it all.)

   *Whatever wise person it was who said be careful what you wish for, I should have listened more closely. Remember how much I complained about Tom and Tom's wife? Rather tactlessly I shared with you (thank you patient listener and friend) my lack of enjoyment of Tom and Serk arguing in their shared tongue which I cannot comprehend until they were red in the face while Tom's wife just sat as if deaf (though she was not actually). Left with nobody to talk to I would drink gallons of tea until the bladder protested and be the only one to sample the cookie's [sic] I'd made. Such are the trials of the faculty wife. Wickedly I wished Tom would go away on a sabbatical or otherwise vanish from our lives. And now he has.*
   *I must warn you in advance not to find this too interesting. All the details I know were extracted from Serk, by the same process other folks use to get blood from the turnip. So I can assure you the holes in this story aren't going to get filled.*

(Anne looked up from the carbon already frustrated. The long-forgotten incident hovered just outside the brightness of thought. It promised to come into view if she could grasp, without trying, one

true-seeming thing. But faith is the flip side of doubt; there must be
something here she recognized. She read on.)

*Of course as you're used to with me I have to go back to go forward.*
*A bit before these events I'm about to describe Serk and Tom had*
*a quarrel I was able to get the gist of. It was about a piece of mail*
*we'd received here on sleepy ol' Campbell Hill Road. Now I have to*
*go back even more and tell about the piece of mail. Why should mail*
*be so controversial? Was it a check for a thousand dollars? No, but*
*it was almost as strange. It was a letter for Serk, in Korean. I mean*
*what I assumed said his name, and the return address, were in the*
*Korean script which I had never even seen to recognize, but our street*
*address was neatly written in English and the postmark was New*
*York City, USA. I was thunderstruck when it came. Serk has never*
*received a single piece of personal mail in the dozen years I've known*
*him. I thought it must be from his family, who he says were all lost*
*long ago. I thought Serk would be thrilled! He sure wasn't. "That*
*goddamn sumbitch ninnyboy Tom!!" he yelled (!!) "I'll kill him for*
*this, sunnuvabitch!" Have I mentioned he said all these swear words*
*in front of our innocent child?*
*You could have knocked me over with a feather. As you know Serk*
*has a terrific temper but this I wasn't prepared for. "What? What*
*is it?" I cried in great alarm but instead of explaining Serk went*
*raging out the door—to go and give Tom what-for, I supposed.*
*Later on Nancy Drew here went picking through Serk's waste*
*paper basket (did I mention we made our little dining room Serk's*
*study? Which means we eat in the kitchen which is also where*
*the typewriter lives but that's all right, I'm used to making my*
*"study" wherever I can fit a chair, pardon this divagation) looking*
*for the letter but I never could find it. I sure wanted to know what*
*it said. I couldn't very well ask Serk (and I think I've told you Serk*
*even claims, at times, that he CAN'T speak Korean—he and Tom*
*quarreled about this—in Korean, I can only assume!). So I decided I*
*would try to ask Tom, who speaks English perfectly well, as he was*

*hired hear [sic] to teach, but hardly ever speaks it to me. But now I had a reason to speak to HIM—if I could ever get him alone.*

*I have been writing you this letter through a pot roast, shrimp "jambalaya," and breaded pork chops, having to stash the typewriter in the pantry (Serk never sets foot in there) every time I am interrupted and now it is the Thursdayafter [sic] the date you see up at the top so I had better wrap this up if I can.*

*I hadn't yet got the chance to ask Tom, out of earshot of Serk, what the mailing had been, but one day Serk was in a good mood so I asked HIM and he seemed like he'd forgot all about it. "It was just some stupid propaganda," he said. I said, "Then why were you so mad about it?" He said, "I didn't want them sending that trash to me." I said, "Who?" He said (hand wave), "These people." I could see I wasn't going to get far in that direction so I said, "Why were you so mad at Tom?" And he said, "I thought he gave out my address. But that was stupid I thought that." Then he said, getting that disgusted expression he gets, "Ninnyboy Tom is afraid of these people." End of conversation.*

*Skip to last week. Our phone rings, quite late. I pick it up, and hear—the voice of Tom's wife! Somehow I know it's her, though I've only ever heard her say "yes" and "thank you." Now she's crying to beat the band and talking a mile a minute in their language. I can't understand a thing so I hand off to Serk. To my dismay he seems to launch into an argument with her. "Stop!" I say. "She needs help! Don't yell at her!" Serk slams down the phone and shouts, "Stupid woman!" But he puts on his coat. Then I asked if I might come with him and surprise, he said yes.*

*Tom and Tom's wife had the upstairs of a house where the landlady lived downstairs. When we got there, Tom's wife was downstairs in the landlady's sitting room, with the landlady holding her hand. The landlady said that earlier that day the phone had rung and when she picked up a voice asked for Tom—probably. The landlady said she hadn't actually been sure what the voice said, but she knew it was a foreign accent, so by the process of elimination she figured it must be for Tom as her other boarder was from Cleveland. She went up and told Tom and Tom's wife they had a call, and then because she'd been on her way out anyway she went out. When she came back a couple hours later she found the phone off the hook just the way she'd left it, and Tom's wife in a state of hysteria. I've had to take more time off to do some desperate preparation for a trip we are suddenly taking that I don't even know how to begin to explain so that will wait for my next letter if I can ever get this one wrapped up. As far as the landlady could figure it out, after taking the call Tom had gone out of the house without so much as hanging up the handset. And so far, he hadn't come back. Tom's wife was in such a state that when the landlady went to put the phone back on the hook Tom's wife got even further hysterical. The landlady had to explain that there was no one on the line—that was why it was beeping.*

*The landlady was a nice woman but all Tom's wife's carrying-on had tried her patience. As soon as she'd told Serk and me the above she excused herself to bed. Then it was my turn to be bewildered as Serk resumed just the same scolding tone with Tom's wife and after thrusting what cash he had in his wallet—perhaps fifty bucks—in her hands he had us leave. I was appalled. "Is that all you're going to do?" I demanded. But, "She's crazy," Serk said. "Tom probably went to a girlfriend." "He had a girlfriend??" "I don't know, probably he did." "Is that what she says? Is that why she's upset?" "No. She thinks someone came and took him, she keeps saying, 'They got him,'" and here Serk made a gesture like somebody snatching the mouth of a bag closed, maybe after they've stuffed someone in it! "Who would take him??" I said. "The people who sent you that mailing?" And then Serk looked at me like he'd forgotten I'd been there all along. I think he might have even forgotten I'd been there when that mailing arrived. Then, "That was nothing," he said. "Tom ran off on his wife. She'll have to face it." I said it didn't seem like something Tom would do, but what did I know?*

*So far, Tom hasn't come back, and now his wife is gone too—Serk told me just the other day she's gone back to Korea.*

That was the end. It had been Anne's style to pull her letters off the carriage and add a handwritten sign-off, to make up for what she'd felt was the too-impersonal habit of typewriting her letters. Had she written to explain the Japan trip? No such carbon appeared in the box. She knew she hadn't written once she got there. Of course they hadn't brought the typewriter, and physically writing a letter was already too much for her hands.

And where were his letters? Not a single one had surfaced in the box. A physical coldness poured through her, a first-ever experience of what must be meant by one's blood running cold in one's veins. She had probably thrown out his letters. There was nothing she couldn't be persuaded to throw out, and also nothing she couldn't be persuaded to keep. She had no system for it. A freak of mood coinciding with an opportunity, and she either pitched it or cached it away like a precious gemstone.

Perhaps they were in one of the seven other boxes, but Anne was afraid to look. She was afraid to confirm they were gone. And she was tired; the lie she'd told Bob when he'd called, interrupting her reading (that she'd skipped dinner because she was tired from not having slept well the previous night) now came true. She was so tired she could not even move from the chair. Sightlessly she gazed on the senseless, uncurated museum of her life. Anne wished for Dr. Grassi's letters because they might tell her what to make of the episode with Tom and Tom's wife. Surely Dr. Grassi had known what this episode meant. Surely his reply would confirm if it meant anything. By the end of that month, callous as it now seemed, she and Serk had forgotten about Tom. They were borne away on their own journey, toward Serk's own disappearance—a disturbing coincidence, that both men, with so little warning, should cease to exist. But Anne reminded herself that she knew nothing about Tom's existence or nonexistence. He and his wife were likely doddering around their own old people's home, with even less recollection than Anne of this tumultuous night of their lives. His story was only a mystery to someone like Anne who'd been left in the dark.

Yet it wasn't so easy to banish the ghosts that emerged from these boxes. Without Dr. Grassi, for he was decades gone now, Anne tried to play Dr. Grassi herself. She must have spent at least a week toiling over that letter, judging from the number of meals and errands she'd mentioned. As she'd told Dr. Grassi, she would have stashed the typewriter on the pantry shelf in between writing, and not feared Serk's looking in the pantry himself—that had been no exaggeration, he expected Anne to open his soup cans no less than to fry his pork chops. Even so, she would have tossed a dish towel over the carriage, concealing the letter in progress. She'd felt herself transgressing in writing this letter, despite her light tone. Tom had been forgotten not because she and Serk were so busy with trip preparations, but because Serk decreed this amnesia. Tom must not be discussed.

*Shouldn't Tom's wife go to the police?*

*Why? She's ashamed to be left by her husband.*

*But you said she doesn't think he* left. *You said she thinks he was* taken.

*By who? What goddamn person takes him?*

*I don't know, Serk—you said that she said it.*

*It's a crazy person talking. Stupid woman.*

*What about the department? Don't they wonder?*

*Of course they wonder! Always asking me these goddamn questions you're asking—just because he's a goddamn Korean, how the hell should I know where he went?*

And now she recalled something else. It's Louisa who first sees that letter, comes running inside with it from the mailbox. Louisa, just turned nine, is deeply ensconced in the childhood development stage Anne will call, if she ever gets around to writing Dr. Grassi about it, "Postalphilia" (that will give Dr. Grassi a laugh). Everything postal charms her. She has created mailboxes all over the house—for Serk's study; for Serk and Anne's bedroom (where they sleep separately in a pair of queen beds that leave almost no floor space); her own room; the kitchen; and even the den; every member of the family receives mail in every room he or she frequents, most of the mail authored by Louisa, but some of it authored by Anne to encourage Louisa and keep the game going. Envelopes elaborately addressed (*TO DADDY THE STUDY 10 CORRIDOR WAY*) and decorated, stamps hand-drawn and colored and glued on with Elmer's. (Serk's way of playing along is to lecture Anne, after Louisa's bedtime, on the in-house postal system's proof of Louisa's enormous intelligence, and its proof in turn of Anne's poor mothering, for Serk believes Louisa's public school is beneath her and that Anne should have found a more suitable place.) Louisa has pen pals, her fevered production of letters (*I am eight years old I live in Rolling Prairie Michigan my favorite actress is Pamela Sue Martin of the Nancy Drew mystery series my favorite flavor of ice cream is mint chip*) would seem to leave no time for anything else but Louisa has also become a fanatic philatelist. It goes without saying that any sent or received correspondence involving the actual USPS is Louisa's to bear to or from the mailbox. Louisa is reverent in raising the red mailbox flag.

When that envelope arrives, it must seem to Louisa like a magical response to her efforts. She's a meteor of joy as she comes running inside with it. "Can I have the stamps? Can I have the stamps? Can I have the stamps?" she cries, springing up and down like a pogo stick in her cable-knit tights and plaid jumper, her hair divided in two ponytails that fly up and down with her movements. Serk denies Louisa nothing, often he is outraged at Anne for her reluctance to serve Louisa a third slice of cake, or buy her the fifth iteration of some toy the first four of which Louisa carelessly broke. But today Serk curses, grabs the envelope away from Louisa, and turns out of the room. When Louisa hangs on to his elbow, he shakes her off roughly. A beat later, the door to his study slams shut.

Not despite but because of her familiarity with her father's temper, Louisa is stung. The angry father is her mother's fault and problem, never hers. Anne sees Louisa's eyes welling.

"For heaven's sake, don't nag him," Anne snaps. "It's his letter. He'll give you the stamps when he's done with it." But he never does.

Tom's wife, Anne reflected now, had been treated by everyone, not least Anne, like a child. Whether because of her not speaking English, or being an Asian, or being a woman and wife, or all those things added up—when each one separately was disadvantage enough—Tom's wife was ignored. Even or especially because of the strange thing she'd said—that "they got him."

Abruptly Anne's appetite for the old letters died. She reordered the pages, squared their edges, and packed them away. Closed the flaps. A consultation with the maintenance guys whose names she learned were Reynaldo and Hector—names as noble and nice as their bearers— revealed that for just another ten dollars a month Anne could rent a bit of a shared storage space that was located down some hallway or other—she was careful to not pay attention as they assured her she'd get her own key and could visit her items whenever she liked. Anne hoped to never see the boxes again. She still had not admitted their resurrection to Louisa despite realizing from the labels that some of the boxes included Louisa's drawings and scribbles and schoolwork from babyhood to age nine. Anne's guilt—at having gotten rid of these things, at having gotten them back, at not telling Louisa about them—only made her want their disappearance all the more, but the breathtaking spectacle of Hector and Reynaldo bearing all eight boxes away at the same time, a stack of four in each man's enormous arms seeming to give him no more trouble than a single sack of trash—still didn't quell Anne's unease. The past would not be past that easily.

No sooner were the eight boxes gone than the photo appeared.

Unlike the boxes rescued by Tobias, the photo owed its survival to Anne's miserliness, which was also the lifelong enemy of her reduction campaign. The photo had been smuggled to the present in Anne's filthy old purse. She could so little stand the thought of purchasing something again that if an item retained functionality, she held on to it, whether Ziploc bag, pillbox, or purse—and for her, the functionality of a purse was a serious matter. If the purse worked, Anne kept it, no matter how ugly or old. For a long while, when her MS had been so bad she'd been in the chair most of the time, she'd used a little backpack Louisa had rejected: Anne would wear it on her front, which kept her arms free to haul at the wheels. "That looks dumb," child Louisa had said, mortified. After Anne's MS improved—it was both a blessing and a source of madness that the progress of her MS was nonlinear—so that she frequently had crutches days, she'd wanted a purse again, with a long-enough strap to put over her head. Rooting around in her closet—voilà!—she found the ugly old clay-colored purse she had bought for their trip to Japan.

The unprecedented prospect of the journey had inspired Anne to the rare purchase: She'd liked all the zipper compartments inside. She'd imagined these concealing their passports and cash as they busily took in the sights. She'd imagined she and Serk and Louisa remade by exotic adventure. Instead she had sat through the year, her legs turned into lead, and come home a widow.

That long-ago day of putting the purse back in service, for the first time since leaving Japan, she'd roughly shaken it upside down at the kitchen sink to remove foreign grit—almost funny, that the grit literally was foreign. A splash of sand acquired she didn't know how, as she'd never set foot on the beach. But the sand had gotten into everything that summer, creeping into the house like a tide. One final, hard shake to dislodge not just grit but these unwanted associations, and without further investigation Anne plugged the necessaries of the moment, wallet, keys, et cetera, into this vessel reclaimed, and moved on. A handful of years later yet—Louisa in high school or perhaps even college—an episode of a lost something sent Anne rooting back into the grimy old purse, to the point of turning it upside down once again so that handfuls of spare change rained onto the table, Louisa observing the search with distaste. The distasteful face couldn't help date this event, as Louisa put on that face in the mid-1980s, and hadn't removed it to date.

"You need a new purse," says teenage or college Louisa. "Jesus, how long have you had that?"

"Quiet," Anne mutters, as if the lost thing—it is probably a check—might be trying to communicate with her. The empty purse is pulled open as far as possible to expose its depths to the light—"Have you searched all the pockets?" Louisa asks, involved in spite of herself.

"Never use the pockets."

"If you're going to look, *look*," condescends Louisa. Further bickering and traded condescension in all likelihood follow, Anne unzipping and rooting inside every never-used pocket with many nasty flourishes of superfluity until—surprise—she feels a thin glossy square. Not the check. Out comes the photograph of Louisa and Serk, preserved, all these years, by an inner cloth pocket against an interior wall of the purse. Though it bears a few creases, its edges are sharp and its colors almost pornographically bright. Louisa and Anne stare at it, for a moment attuned by their equal surprise. Then:

"Why were you hiding this?" Louisa demands.

"I wasn't hiding it. I must have put it in there and forgot about it."

"You just said that you don't use those pockets."

"I guess I must have used them *once*." Anne is angry that she still can't withstand Louisa's anger without feeling a threat to herself. She is angry that she can't absorb the anger and return it to Louisa as love.

"I've never seen this photo," says Louisa at last. Anne is surprised by what seems to be Louisa's effort to infuse the words more with question than accusation.

"I've always wondered who took it," Anne replies, and she's done just what Louisa avoided: her words hold far more accusation than question.

"I have no idea who took it. I assumed that you did."

"I never went to the beach with you two. I never went anywhere that you went."

"That can't be true." Louisa goes into Anne's desk for an envelope and makes to put the photo inside.

"Put that back," Anne says sharply. "Put that back where I found it."

"I want it," says Louisa.

"It's not yours."

"It isn't yours, either!"

They'd fought bitterly—with what exact words it hardly mattered to remember. However the argument ended, Anne clearly had won, because the photograph had returned to exactly the same zipper pocket and lain dormant until this morning. Evenings, Anne was unable to resist the baked treats that were always laid out on a table in the salad bar section, but she was also unable to eat them—like many of her fellow inmates, despite her relative youth, Anne's appetite was sadly diminished. She was constantly disappointed by her lack of hunger, and equally hopeful of hunger returning. Hence she'd adopted the really bad, widespread among her fellow-inmates habit of squirreling baked goods away in her purse, then forgetting about them until whenever her hand, reaching in, met a substrate of crumbs. Cleaning the grubby purse out this morning of the eight boxes safely disappeared again, of the past pushed back into the past, Anne noticed the deep-buried zipped inner pocket and knew what was there. She hadn't meant to leave the picture in the pocket all this time. The only reason she'd returned it there at all was likely because, all those years ago during the fight, she'd gotten stuck with demanding the photo get "put back where I found it!" After Serk's death, for the rest of childhood and much of adolescence Louisa had been an incorrigible thief, often of Anne's rare keepsakes. The handful of photos from her and Serk's wedding; the Holy Land earrings; a silk scarf of the sort Anne apparently wore in her beautiful, dangerous youth. If Louisa came across it she would appropriate it so unhesitantly it was not even clear if the word *theft* applied to the act. To Louisa, it didn't. In Louisa's view, what appeared to be Anne's unsentimental willingness to part with anything made her an undeserving steward of everything. Nothing existed that didn't deserve being rescued from Anne. "At least I'll take care of it," Louisa once said, arguing for ownership of a chunky pendant Adrian had bought Anne in Jerusalem several hazardous lifetimes ago. Anne had been surprised to see Louisa come home one night wearing this meaningful and, Anne had thought, secret possession she usually kept in a souvenir box in her underwear drawer.

Louisa had even tried to steal Anne's name from her—by suggesting that *Anne* was the thief. "Why do you still have his *name?*" Anne remembered Louisa screaming, as if Serk had been some helpless mark Anne had killed and disposed of in order to make use of his name. "It was easier to keep it," Anne lamely said, and—for some years—believed. Easier to use the same checks from the same bank account, easier to fund that account with the widow's benefit from Serk's pension, easier to sell the house and the car—the only things of real value either of them ever owned, and both things owned by them jointly—than to stop using that ill-fitting name. But weren't all of these reasons the same sort of innocuous lie? Wasn't the actual reason that, if she gave up this name that she shared with Louisa, Anne gave up all proof that Louisa—who looked nothing like Anne, and appeared to despise her, for example screaming "Why do you still have his *name*"—was Anne's own and no one else's child?

Perhaps it was always this way with a mother and daughter. Anne wouldn't know, having barely caught a glimpse of her mother in her own childhood. But because she was so accustomed to regarding Louisa's childhood as uniquely unhappy, it comforted Anne to imagine their estrangement as inevitable. Even had she married a kind, steady, comprehensible man who had lived, he'd now be giving her shoulders a jostle and telling her to *ignore the little Hecuba, Anne—she's always been a tough nut.*

Anne realized that she had cast Bob in the role of the husband and father, absurdly—no Louisa could have sprung from Bob. Bob's own daughters were happy red-faced blondes who wore smocked blouses and hooted at their father's outré jokes and cooed over their dim-witted mother.

Long experience had taught that there was never a good time to phone, so Anne called Louisa whenever the mood struck without allowing premeditation. "I'm sorry I never sent you that photo," Anne launched in without explanation. "I meant to get it copied. I'll try to do that soon. Maybe there's somebody here that knows how." She should have realized Louisa wouldn't know what she meant. Once she'd explained, Louisa said:

"The picture of us at some kind of pagoda?"

"No, you're standing on the beach."

"The beach where we lived?"

"I suppose," Anne said, studying it. But, no: now the mystery of the picture returned to her mind. It wasn't the beach where they'd lived, because she'd found the photo before they had moved to the beach. In it, Louisa is wearing her school uniform, which they'd left behind in the apartment, as she wouldn't have need of it over the summer. Serk is dressed in long pants, a trench coat. A stiff wind lifts their hair, the sea behind them the color of pewter, whitecapped. "No, it's some other beach," Anne amended. "The weather looks cold in the photo. You're wearing your school uniform."

"We'd gone to see a friend of his," Louisa replied easily, as if hearing the picture described was like hearing her cue in a play. Then she was silent. Anne had the sense she was as surprised by her words as was Anne. Serk hadn't had friends.

"What friend?" asked Anne after a moment.

"I don't know. I don't even know why I said that."

"I wish you'd tell me."

"I'm not *not* telling you. I just don't remember. I was a child."

"Was it a man? Or a woman?"

It might already be the longest conversation they've ever had about Serk. Anne remembered Louisa, an indentation in a hospital bed. Thin wrists venturing out from the shroud of the sheet, then creeping under again. Once Louisa regained consciousness she had always looked cold. And much younger, reminiscent of the watchful baby who'd so rarely cried, just a pair of dark eyes gazing out from the pillow. As she hadn't for three or four years, she'd let Anne hold her hand; Anne shocked herself with the keen recollection of that long-vanished, frail child's hand, as irrecoverable as if Louisa had died in the sea with her father. Anne had sat in the chair into which they'd installed her, by Louisa's bedside, and held on to that hand, its slight warmth her only clear sign that Louisa was there. Slightly warm, soft and dry. Unresisting. Louisa yielded her hand but would not say a word—until the authorities, cleared by her doctors, came to interview her. Then, to Anne's astonishment, Louisa had answered their questions—quietly but readily and fluently, in a language that Anne couldn't speak. "What are they *saying*?" Anne had implored Tobias.

"I feel like it was a woman," Louisa said now, "though I'm not sure what makes me think so."

"Was she a girlfriend of Daddy's?" Anne couldn't stop herself asking. But surprisingly Louisa didn't swerve to mockery or offense. She protracted the rare moment, fragile as a soap bubble.

"I don't think so. I remember it feeling . . . dreary."

"But he brought you along."

"I don't know why." She didn't say this in a tone of defense but more as if clarifying the fact to herself.

"Was she old? Young?"

"Just a grown-up. The age that a parent or teacher would be. I don't recall anything special about her. I don't know who she was. I don't know what she looked like. I don't remember her taking the picture, but I guess she must have."

Every moment, Anne expected Louisa to say she couldn't talk anymore. Louisa was always already impatient when she answered her phone. She always warned Anne right away: her boys required their dinner made, or their homework checked, or their brawl broken up and self-reflection induced and better values instilled, in other words Anne had clearly forgotten how difficult parenting was. And indeed Louisa's manner of being a parent was unfamiliar to Anne. For a life so free of care as Louisa's appeared—no one sick, no one dead, no one yelling who wasn't a child, as far as Anne knew—Louisa always was anxious, aggrieved, fending off some impending disaster that Anne was an idiot not to discern. But for the moment, and for the first time in Anne couldn't think how long, Louisa seemed willing to linger in silence.

"I remember feeling as though Daddy and I had a secret from you, and I liked feeling that, and felt bad about liking it," Louisa finally said. "But then I realized it was also a secret from me."

"How did you realize?" asked Anne, only when Louisa's fresh silence had lasted so long Anne was more afraid Louisa had hung up already than she was of making her hang up by speaking.

"I don't know. I don't know what makes me think that. I hadn't even remembered that woman in I don't know how long."

"I don't think you ever talked to Dr. Brickner about her."

"Was that the shrink? Oh, God. I don't think I ever said a word to him that wasn't a lie. That was not your finest moment."

The spell was broken. Anne had nothing to gain from reminding Louisa that it was not herself, but the school, that insisted Louisa see Dr. Brickner. But it also seemed she had nothing to lose in asking, now that she could feel Louisa's impatience returning, "What was the secret?"

"How should I know!"

"I mean the secret that you said you kept from me."

"Didn't I just say the woman? If there was even a woman."

"Was she a Japanese woman?"

"I guess. It would have been strange if she wasn't."

"And did they talk? Do you remember anything that they said?"

"I get the feeling you want me to make things up. Even if I remembered them talking, and I don't, because this happened decades ago and I was a child, I wouldn't know what they'd *said*. I don't speak Japanese."

But you *did*, Anne wanted to say. But didn't—the boys were fighting, hungry, bored, required some other service that only Louisa could provide. Whatever the reason, Louisa cut short the call—a long call for them, anyway.

At lunch that day Anne asked around the table if anyone knew how to reproduce a photo that she didn't have a negative for. "I want to send it to my daughter," Anne explained, which set off a lively and unfocused conversation about photos—everyone at this place was obsessed with their photos, mostly of their grandchildren.

"You can just scan it," said Julie, the nice tenants' services girl who often joined them at lunch. She had to repeat herself to be heard above the deafening chorus of unhelpful and irrelevant comments.

"You mean on the computer?" Anne once so prided herself on her computer savvy, but since she'd retired from her Foundation job she'd been lapped a million times by the new advances, and now barely could locate her email.

"I can do it for you," said Julie. "Is your daughter on email? Just bring it on by after lunch."

It felt terribly strange, sitting in Julie's office having handed her the photo with its particular edges and creases and its sad otherworldly brightness, as if the past would always have more life than now, and seeing Serk and Louisa pop up on Julie's sleek monitor, their image grainier, the colors muddier, the child and the man more convincingly invalidated. Anne felt a foolish stab of fear, that the photo might somehow be gone, but Julie lifted the lid of the scanner and handed it back to her and it was still, or even more, alive. Anne put it back in the stiff envelope, which she'd even gone so far as to furnish with two squares of cardboard to sandwich the photo between.

"What a pretty girl and what a handsome man," Julie complimented Anne.

"My daughter and my late husband." How simple it could sound.

Anne found Louisa's email where she'd written it in her address book, and read it out to Julie, and just like that, the picture had gone to Louisa—was already there.

# Tobias

**Tobias met the group** almost by chance. Because he had banking errands that day that he couldn't put off, he walked downtown, an area he otherwise avoided, intensely disliking its charmless aspirational high-rise glass buildings and its wide level sidewalks obsessively swept by old women and men as if this canyon of capitalism were the holiest temple. Unlike a native Japanese, Tobias was unabashed in his sentimental attachment to the old, and in his affronted aversion to the new. Though Westernization had already been well under way the first time he set foot in the country, Tobias still held the Japan of his youth as authentic, or at least more authentic than now. He knowingly fed this delusion by living only in dilapidated neighborhoods and even by inducing in himself a sort of blindered hauteur when he ventured elsewhere, literally looking down his nose so as not to discern the new chain stores and bus shelter ads and the other offenses that made his heart ache. But the protest, though like most Japanese "protests" so orderly as to require a different term—a Meek Assertion of Collective Dismay?—was still anomalous enough to attract his attention.

"Here's the would-be savior who cannot even buy his own food," Tobias's father had characteristically greeted him the previous year, when Tobias, having flown eighteen hours, visited his deathbed.

His father always knew how to find the soft spot. Tobias did have a lifelong weakness for the suffering of others. What his father failed to understand was that, unlike in his own case, Tobias's weakness didn't arise from belief in himself as a force of salvation, but from obscure and infinitely adaptable feelings of guilt.

The protest resembled, as they often did, a combination public lecture and craft fair. A microphone and speakers had been set up, before which a dozen or so people sat at attention on two neat rows of cushions. A young woman, perhaps in her thirties, was at the microphone. "It was such a beautiful day," she was saying. "How could she have known what was coming? Remember, she had just been at tennis-team practice. She was thirteen years old. She was walking home, from her own school, down her own street, in her own town." The audience members nodded quietly, a few blotting their eyes with tissues. Preaching to the choir, thought Tobias. No one listening seemed confused or surprised by the story. They all seemed to have heard it before.

A little off to one side, near enough to be clearly allied with the lecture, but sufficiently away that conversations there wouldn't distract, sat a table spread with a pretty cloth, under a sun canopy. Neatly arrayed on the table were fanned-out flyers, weighed down with gay figurines of characters and animals. Hung from one corner of the canopy to the other was a string onto which the same flyers had been clipped, along with vertical strings of origami cranes in different colors that swung back and forth in the breeze. The cranes, the figurines, the merry splashes of color all seemed to have been calculated to draw the attention of children, and there was indeed a lone child standing in front of the table, accompanied by a woman with shopping bags who looked impatient to be on her way. Behind the table sat a gray-haired couple of the sort who over decades of marriage have come to resemble each other despite being physically different.

The man had completed a pale orange crane. "There!" he said, holding it out for the boy. "Now you can tell everybody that Yumi's dad made you a crane. Okay?"

"Okay," the boy said.

"Tell him thank you," the mother said. As soon as the boy had done so with a bow she pulled him away, though the wife had been trying to give her a flyer.

"Please read!" the wife called after her, waving the flyer, but the pair hurried off without taking it.

"May I?" Tobias asked.

And that was how it started, with Tobias's too-ready pity. Before they'd even launched into their story he was already almost in tears for this pair, who so haplessly betrayed their sadness with the efforts they made to festoon their small table with cheer.

"BRING YUMI HOME!" said the flyer. It pictured a pensive, dark-eyed girl of, Tobias would have guessed, sixteen or more. For she was tall, and projected composure that would not have looked out of place on a woman of twenty. But she was wearing the standard school uniform, the bright white blouse and pleated blue skirt, the blue blazer bearing its pins.

Within the trifold, not an inch had been wasted. At first Tobias felt he should skim, so as to sooner turn back to the oldsters and make conversation. But he could feel them watching his own face with such intensity he surmised they more wanted him to read it thoroughly.

"Our daughter Yumi," the flyer said, "is a straight-A student and gifted athlete, the star of her school tennis team. Her life is full of friends. She loves frogs and collects plushy frogs and frog figurines of all sizes, each one with a name. Yumi's dream is to attend veterinary college to help animals. A loving daughter, she makes her parents proud every day.

"On October 14, 1977, Yumi went to school as usual."

Tobias blinked over the date, but he hadn't misread it. More than two decades ago.

> It was tennis team practice day. After practice, she said goodbye to her coach and went to walk home as always. There was still light in the sky. Yumi liked to walk along the park although sometimes she took a different route to buy a snack at the store. The store owner did not see her that evening. Yumi did not come home. By eight o'clock that evening the local prefecture began their search. The search continued

for many days and weeks. They found no trace of Yumi.

She had her backpack and gym bag with her when last seen. She would have been wearing her tennis uniform, as it was a warm evening and her coach described her wearing it still when she left. Her schoolbooks, school uniform, and bento all would have been in her book bag or gym bag. Her book bag had her name and address on the card. Her gym bag had a plastic frog key chain. None of these were ever found.

Since January 1, 1977, more than thirty Japanese citizens have gone missing without explanation from coastal towns up and down the west coast of our nation. Our government has explained each one differently. Runaways, suicide, drowning. No bodies have ever been found. WE KNOW YUMI DID NOT RUN AWAY. YUMI DID NOT COMMIT SUICIDE, OR DROWN. WE KNOW YUMI IS ALIVE.

BRING YUMI HOME!

Thus related the inner panels. On the back, Tobias found a list in two columns, the first headed NAME and the second DATE LAST SEEN. At the bottom, a plea: "PLEASE DONATE TO THE FAMILIES OF THE DISAPPEARED GROUP."

The hair on the back of Tobias's neck had stood up in the course of his reading. All his life, even after his tumor was found and removed, he'd had episodes of dizziness and nausea that resembled the onset of a migraine. He credited their management to daily meditation and strict vegetarianism. But now came an onslaught like a freight train, so that he snatched at the table for balance, upsetting its careful arrangement.

"Please, no, I'm so sorry," he inadequately tried to repel their assistance as these elders whose pitifulness had derailed him leaped to their feet, interrupted the storyteller's recitation, commandeered the too-many cushions required for his comfort—for everywhere that he went in this country, he was taller than everyone else—and then seated themselves on the pavement either side of his head, fanning him with the same document that had brought the attack. Back and forth, back and forth went the young girl's face over his.

He wasn't sure how many minutes passed before a more normal feeling crept into his blood. The microphone and speakers, the table canopy and the table's contents, were being packed up by the same group, it seemed, that had made up the audience. Perhaps they were less a protest than a portable church.

"How old was your daughter when she disappeared?" Tobias eventually asked. Lying flat on his back on the sidewalk was a peculiar meditation. There were the squared-off glass tops of the commercial high-rises he hated, now seeming to lean over him with concern as the old couple did. In the treeless sky framed by the buildings, birds streaked back and forth like small missiles.

"Yumi was thirteen," answered the father. He must have seen the shock in Tobias's face. "She was tall for her age."

"Today she would be in her thirties," Tobias misspoke, too astonished to avoid the conditional tense.

"Yumi is now thirty-five," corrected her father. "She's grown up so much since the last time we saw her."

He never made it to the bank that day. Instead, he found himself accepting tea at the home of the storytelling woman, Saho, who was hosting the elders, Fumiko and Koji. But, "Please just call us Yumi's Mom and Yumi's Dad," Koji said. This seemed not an accommodation to Tobias's foreignness but rather, like the use of the present tense when speaking of Yumi, a matter of form.

Once they had gathered in Saho's small apartment in a relatively new building of just the sort Tobias hated—"I like how clean it is," she told him as they went up the lift—Yumi's parents asked Tobias to tell them his story, as if he were a traveler arrived from afar, which he supposed that he always would be. Never in Japan did new hosts fail to ask for his story, so that he'd long since codified a reply. "I first came to Japan on a backpacking trip, and I just never wanted to leave."

"Because you met a girl?" asked Yumi's Mom teasingly. They all laughed. By this time of the afternoon, though the real conversation had only just begun, they already felt comfortable with each other not despite but because of being strangers—strangers who had shared a small adventure that had turned out all right: Tobias's fainting spell.

Yumi's Mom's question was another unvarying aspect of Tobias's encounters with Japanese strangers: the probing of his marital status. He was far too old to be anyone's prospect. Most Japanese imagined he must be a widower, and further imagined he must have some children. All of these imaginings Tobias tried to dispel while not causing his questioners any embarrassment. "I am one of those weird Western people who is enamored of the lives of Buddhist monks, but lacks the discipline to actually live like them. So, I teach English and French for a very low wage, live in scruffy solitude, and of necessity know how to make my own noodles and mend my own socks." After they had all laughed again, and the tea was replenished, Yumi's Mom carefully opened a scrapbook and they rearranged themselves in the small room so that Tobias could sit on the truncated sofa, with Yumi's parents flanking him as they paged through the scrapbook together.

It told the story of a missing child, a meandering and ultimately futile search by the police. And the irrelevant, magical acts by which communities try to reclaim what they've lost. Yumi's schoolmates, as related by the small local paper, after she'd been missing a week set the goal to fold ten thousand origami cranes. Hundreds of children from all the grades of Yumi's school were pictured, in the grainy newsprint photograph, seated at long tables in the school gymnasium before tidy square stacks of paper, determinedly folding cranes as if the more swiftly and precisely they did it, the sooner their friend would return. "That's where I got the idea for doing the cranes," Yumi's Dad put in. "The kids made up a song, about how the cranes would fly out from our town, and with their sharp eyes they'd find Yumi, and with their feet pick her up, and with their wings fly her home. It's a beautiful song."

"He likes to sing the song, but it makes me cry," Yumi's Mom said. Tobias had noticed that she'd remained silent while her husband explained that they ought to be called Yumi's Dad and Yumi's Mom, and not their given names or any other title.

In the scrapbook, the first anniversary of Yumi's disappearance was observed in the small seaside park of her town. Despite the lack of positive confirmation, the park had come to be presumed as the site of Yumi's disappearance. At their ceremony the members of her tennis team dedicated their season to her, and planted a red star-leaf maple. "It keeps its bright color all year round," explained Yumi's Dad. "So she can always see it, and find her way home. It's a symbol," he acknowledged.

"It's huge now," Saho said.

"We set up under it," Yumi's Dad went on, "when we're home, and we set up the table. It's gotten so big that we don't need the sun canopy."

New as the catastrophe was to him, Tobias could not imagine its urgency fading, and retrospectively the sparseness of the protest surprised him. But even more surprising was Yumi's parents' story of becoming, in the eyes of their town, if not exactly divisive, at least a source of unease. After the first year, their local police stopped investigating. Yumi's parents were urged to accept the official conclusion that Yumi was a runaway or a suicide. For obvious reasons Yumi's parents refused to believe this, and they also refused to believe she was dead. "Parents just know," explained Yumi's Dad. "We're not superstitious, or crazy. I used to work as a bank manager. Yumi's Mom taught preschool. We're very regular people. But we know our daughter better than anyone else, and we know she didn't disappear from choice." Like other parts of the world, Japan had its share of cults and of lone psychopaths. Unbearable as it was, Yumi's parents believed that a person or people had recognized in their daughter her unparalleled value, and seized her for themselves. Increasingly unlikely as it was, they also believed that their daughter continued to survive her ordeal.

The years passed. The news stories became few, brief, and obligatory. For many years, they traveled with their table and their cranes only on holidays and weekends, while Yumi's Dad still held his bank manager job. After he retired they were able to spend all their time seeking Yumi. They aged. Yet in every photograph, in contrast to other Japanese people of their generation Tobias had known, Yumi's Dad and Mom smiled. On both their faces it was an increasingly similar, shy, hopeful smile. For Yumi, Tobias realized. As if each photograph were a window, through which they were looking, for her.

The room had gone quiet. Tobias realized he was pinching the bridge of his nose with his thumb and first finger, down which streamed his tears. Reaching his wrist, they fell free, and struck the clear plastic sheets of the scrapbook. Yumi's Mom tactfully pulled it to safety, and Saho offered them both paper napkins.

"Thank you for your tender heart," said Yumi's Mom, patting his knee. Yumi's Dad was patting his shoulder. Twice in one day he had allowed himself to be comforted by these people who were both elderly and bereaved.

Saho found them through their table, too. In the spring of 1979, when she was fourteen years old, Saho's older brother Takashi, twenty-six at the time, confided in her that he'd decided to propose to his girlfriend. The couple had been dating seriously since university days, and so their marriage was taken for granted by both families. But because there was such an age gap between Takashi and Saho, he'd always made her his pet and coconspirator, and let her feel crucial to his plans. Takashi told no one but Saho about the proposal, and asked her help choosing a ring. The evening of the planned proposal, May 12, 1979, he'd given Saho a wink as he headed out the door to pick up his girlfriend for what she assumed was a regular date. It was finally warm, and Takashi had told Saho he was going to take his girlfriend to the beach to watch the sunset and propose to her there. Neither Takashi nor the girlfriend returned home that night.

In the confused morning hours of the next day, Saho came under pressure from both families. It was as if her special bond with her brother, of which everyone was aware, rendered her not only somehow responsible for his disappearance, but also able to reverse it. Saho felt she must have forgotten some part of her brother's surprise. Had he meant to take his girlfriend to a hotel for the night, or on a spontaneous trip? But no bag had been packed; Takashi had not consulted her about a suave outfit. Takashi and his girlfriend, both university graduates, were living at home to save money; that they might take themselves to a hotel would be uncharacteristic but hardly a scandal. Takashi's swearing Saho to secrecy had been meant to preserve the surprise to his girlfriend, but Saho could only assume that the secrecy had to continue. Surely this couldn't take long. Soon he'd be back, with his flushed, laughing girlfriend on his arm, the new ring on her hand.

"You saw him last," insisted her parents, and the girlfriend's parents. "What did he tell you? What were his plans?"

"Nothing special!" Saho said over and over again.

By sundown that night, she confessed—the beach, the sunset, the proposal. Without hesitation the four parents called the police. Takashi's car was found parked at the beach outside town, doors locked, the remnants of a picnic, including an empty beer bottle, sitting on the back seat. There was nothing wrong with the car—with the spare key, it started right up. Nothing appeared on the beach but the usual flotsam. It had been a long, cold winter, and though the weather had finally turned enough to make a beach walk by daylight appealing, it was still too cold for swimming or hanging around in the evening. Few people could be found who had been to the beach on that evening, and none who had seen the young couple.

The authorities suggested a suicide pact or accidental drowning. Perhaps the young couple had been using drugs. Perhaps the young couple, fearing parental disapproval of their plan to be married, had run away—on foot. "Disappearance demands explanation," Saho concluded, "and no explanation is too ludicrous. This isn't death, where the body can always give some explanation. A disappearance is so inexplicable that any explanation at all will seem reasonable." The desperation of Saho's parents' grief made them amenable to the authorities' suggestions, and they came to believe that their son and his girlfriend, after sharing the beer, had rashly decided to go for a swim and been carried off by a riptide. But Saho refused to reconcile herself to this scenario. "Takashi was a lizard," she said now. "He hated the cold, he always hogged our space heater—even in the hottest weeks of summer he preferred to just lie on the sand and get tan. He would *never* go swimming in May." Like Yumi's parents, Saho stubbornly believed, without evidence or anyone else's support, that some person or persons had forcibly taken her brother and his girlfriend, though she had no conception who would do this or why. She only knew the catastrophe might not have happened if she'd told the truth sooner.

"But how?" asked Tobias. "How could your telling your brother's secret in the morning, instead of at night, have made any difference?"

"Perhaps the people who took them were still near our town in the morning! Perhaps they could have been caught if I'd spoken up sooner!" Saho pressed her palms onto her face.

Yumi's Mom shuffled next to Saho and put her arm around Saho's shoulders. Saho took one of her hands from her face, and laid it over Yumi's Mom's that was holding her shoulder, and then Yumi's Mom laid her free hand on her own streaming face. The two women mirrored each other like links of a chain. After a time they each took a deep shuddering breath, in tandem. Surprised, they looked at each other and laughed, that they'd taken their breaths simultaneously. They turned to wipe each other's tears. "I have actual tissues," Saho remembered. "These napkins were just for the cookies."

"I'm sorry to use them all up."

"No, Yumi's Mom! I just meant they're too scratchy to rub on your cheeks. Now your cheeks are all red."

"That's okay, I don't need a soft tissue."

"You're a tough one," Saho agreed.

Tobias pursued, "Is it still your belief that a person or people took your brother and his girlfriend?"

"I no longer believe it: I *know* it."


Far from blaming Saho, as she herself did, for her brother's disappearance, Saho's parents clung to her. They aged abruptly. Now the only child, Saho had to act the parent, cajoling her parents to eat, reminding them to bathe and change their clothes, persuading friends of theirs to take them out for meals or join them for card games. At the same time, every teenage freedom she had been on the brink of receiving was revoked. Saho's family knew nothing of Yumi's disappearance almost two years before—their towns, though both on the coast, were a day's drive apart, and for all the horror of the three disappearances, the media stories about them were local. Yet, despite their ignorance of Yumi's disappearance, Saho's parents forbade Saho to walk home from school alone. They forbade her to join her peers at the town playing fields or browsing the shops, and even forbade her from taking class trips. Above all, she was forbidden to go to the beach.

With difficulty Saho persuaded her parents to allow her to attend university, and then they both died, of natural causes, just six months apart. They had only been in their mid-sixties. Saho's pain was leavened with relief that her parents were no longer suffering, but that bit of relief only made her feel even more pain. Though she'd initially done well at her studies, she soon almost failed out. She requested a semester's leave and packed her dorm room, doubting she'd ever be back. The idea of suicide, which had been so ludicrous when applied to her brother, seemed inevitable for her.

Under the weight of these thoughts Saho carried the boxes of her things from her dorm to her car, trudging back and forth through the small, busy quad on which students stood in clusters smoking and talking, or sat at tables calling out for support for this or that cause, or for customers for this or that event. After several of these tedious trips, while again shouldering open the doors of the dorm with a box pressed to her chest, Saho noticed an anomalous locus of stillness amid all the student activity. It was a table covered by what looked like an old quilt and toys. Behind it sat two older people. They appeared as disregarded by the students around them as a pair of midstream boulders by the river in which they're marooned. Their seeming isolation reminded Saho of her parents, in the least welcome way. She averted her eyes and hurried the box to her car.

"Can you imagine?" Yumi's Dad interrupted, beaming with pleasure at Saho's unvarnished remembrance. "She almost did not speak to us!"

But finally, she did, with reluctance and even annoyance. All the while that she'd trudged back and forth, box after box after box, she'd felt their presence at the edge of her vision like a growing reproach. It was as if they were watching her—"And we were!" Yumi's Mom interrupted. "We felt bad, that she was carrying all of that stuff." Despite the indifferent crowd, and the many meters of distance, and the several decades of age, and even the aversion, at least on Saho's end, that separated them, by the time Saho was finally done with her boxes it seemed to both parties as though some sort of conversation had already begun, regardless of how little Saho desired it. Shoving the last box inside, instead of climbing in her car and driving off as she'd been eager to do for hours, Saho slammed shut the door, locked it, and strode across to the table as if to a confrontation.

"So what are you selling, anyway?" she demanded.

"I felt delighted just looking at her," Yumi's Mom remembered. "She was almost exactly the same age as Yumi."

"And I said, 'We're not selling anything—we're giving these away. These paper cranes. Can I make one for you?'" Yumi's Dad continued.

"And I said," said Saho, "'I don't need a paper crane, thank you'—but then I saw the flyer with Yumi's face on it and somehow I knew. Before they even explained, I knew what had happened to them."

"And that was how," Yumi's Dad added, "we started learning what had happened to us all."


In the early 1990s, a well-dressed man traveling on a Japanese passport had entered the Seoul Central Government Complex and informed a security guard he was seeking asylum from North Korea. In his subsequent debriefing, the defector claimed to have spent his childhood as a member of the relatively privileged North Korean Communist Party elite, after which he had entered the spy services. There he received training in Japanese language, culture, and norms of social behavior from a group of Japanese nationals who had been forcibly brought to the DPRK for the purpose of training agents to pass. Some of these kidnap-victims-turned-instructors had been fishermen, snatched off their vessels in abductions of opportunity by North Korean agents who plied the waters separating the Korean peninsula from the Japanese archipelago, but the far greater number were relatively urbane and educated Japanese people seized from the dry land of their own streets and beaches, for these were the sorts of people the agents most hoped to resemble.

The defector's account of receiving language and culture instruction from kidnapped Japanese citizens corroborated the 1988 account of the KAL Flight 858 bomber after she was taken into South Korean custody, but neither story escaped the files of the South Korean National Intelligence Service into the Japanese media until the mid-1990s, after a Japanese journalist heard both stories from a South Korean intelligence source. When the journalist published his story, it was mostly dismissed as implausible or even a joke, except by a small number of widely scattered people. These were the bereaved of the vanished, the lonely champions of cases made cold by unlikely surmises of accidental drowning or well-planned suicide unsupported by physical evidence. These were the people called stubborn holdouts at best, or mentally ill at worst, by even the most sympathetic observers. They had begun slowly finding each other. In some cases, as with Yumi's parents and Saho, the connection was made serendipitously. In many more, it was made by the amateur sleuthing of those whose particular grief would not let them believe that their loved one had vanished either by their own volition or by accident. For years they had been told by the authorities, by their friends, and even by other loved ones that their grief blinded them to the facts. Their assertion was the opposite: their grief showed them facts to which others were blind.

The more that families found each other and shared their stories, the more certain patterns emerged. All the disappearances had taken place in coastal towns if not on the actual beach. Most had occurred during the off-season but not at the height of winter: March through May, September through November. Most of the disappeared had last been seen at or near dusk. All—except for Yumi—had been adults in the prime of life. No old people, no little children, again except for Yumi, but she had been, as Tobias had experienced himself, so unusually tall for her age as to resemble an older teenager or even a young

woman. The stronger-stomached among the amateur sleuths recognized in these patterns a serial killer. Their enemy exhibited clear
preferences in hunting grounds, time of day, time of year, age and
condition of prey. What none of them could have imagined, until the
defector's story was reported, was that their predator wasn't one person, "but a nation," as Yumi's Dad said.

For all her own stubborn belief that someone or something had
taken her brother, Saho initially balked at the spy explanation. It had
been years since she'd met Yumi's parents and begun making appear-
ances with them. In that time, while she'd received much compassion
from strangers, she'd also fended off her share of people she thought
of as crazies, who regarded her as their comrade and insisted, for example, that her brother and his girlfriend now lived on board a UFO.
When Yumi's parents showed her the story about the North Korean
defector—not in a paper of record like *Asahi Shimbun*, but one of those
attention-seeking general-interest magazines—she'd cautioned them
not to have hope. "I mean, how could we believe such a thing?" But
Saho also doubted both her instinct of doubt and her instinct of belief, after years of over-exercise of both these fragile capacities, due
to how deprived her life had been of certainty. "When you're forced
to go without an explanation for so many years, you'll believe anything—we go mad if we don't believe something. But, knowing this,
I disbelieve my own beliefs—I distrust all of them." According to this
logic, the very unbelievability of the defector's story, to Saho, might
mean it was true. After all, if the mad hunger of her believing was
inclined to embrace anything, it must be inclined to reject anything—
perhaps even the truth. "So—I believed it, because I couldn't, just as I
disbelieved things—because I did." Outside the sky had grown dark,
and in the light of her overhead lamp Saho looked tired and diminished. It was a good thing Saho had met them, said Yumi's Dad as Saho
trailed off. For Yumi's Dad and Mom, belief wasn't a thought but a
reflex. You just *did* it—the same way you just never used the past tense,
the same way you changed your name to reflect the one bond fate
has tried to rupture, which rupture you just won't allow. The resemblance of the Families of the Disappeared Group to a church wasn't

simply in the eye of the beholder, Tobias. For all their brutally rational sleuthing, the group was, at heart, a faith exercise. Yes, they traveled, raised funds, printed flyers, lobbied politicians, wooed members of the media. But mostly they kept up each other's belief. It was hard to believe all alone.

For more than half his life, and despite his keen awareness of the role and the many who had played it before him, Tobias had allowed his ardor for Japan to be his sole occupation. He was an expatriate, an exoticist, a typical gone-native white man. He knew he deserved these disparaging labels, however inevitable—fated, even—his life in Japan felt to him. Unable to climb out of his skin, he had dressed himself up in Japan—no better than that spy-turned-defector. But here, with the families, Tobias found a crucial limit, his father's deathbed scorn fresh in his mind. *Here's the would-be savior.* In the months that followed his first meeting with Yumi's parents and Saho, Tobias chalked out his place in their movement: dedicated, subservient, above all marginal. He would save their footsteps by putting up their posters and flyers, he would save their saliva by licking their envelopes, he would save their strength by bringing them coffee and snacks—but never could he sit at the table tempting children with the offer of a crane. Never could he stand at the microphone pleading for the ears of rushed, suspicious passersby. He couldn't put his white foreigner's face on their catastrophe. "It's wrong," he tried to explain to Yumi's parents and Saho, who did not share his scruples about this. "If I spoke for you, it would bring *me* attention, and that's an insult to you."

"But we *need* the attention," Saho argued. "Who cares how we get it! Why not just say what you mean: that our loved ones aren't yours."

"But that's *not* what I mean!" cried Tobias.

Tobias and Saho had developed a propensity for bickering when together and brooding when apart that Yumi's parents eagerly exacerbated with all the intrusiveness they'd never had the chance to inflict on an actual daughter. Fall had come, and soon would be the anniversary of Yumi's disappearance, for the first time since Tobias had met them. All three wanted him to participate in the commemoration; he wouldn't dream of not being with them, but did not want a role for himself; they found his distinctions incomprehensible and another cause of grief at a difficult time; and so the argument had gone in circles until Tobias was finally worn down to agreeing to sit at the table on this exceptional occasion, when Yumi's parents as well as Saho would obviously need to be doing every other thing including speaking at the podium, taking photos with local officials, and organizing the crane-folding children from Yumi's old school. In the end Tobias was less defeated than ashamed, that his desire to avoid self-aggrandizement had done the opposite and made him such a problem to his friends.

The day of the commemoration was overcast and cold, with a bite of incipient snow in the air, although the bright red flags of the star-leaf maple were more striking against this backdrop. But they were also more anomalous and pitiful. Sitting nearby at the table, where the strings of cranes were swinging hard in the unpleasant wind and the flyers were almost entirely obscured beneath the various rocks Tobias had found to weigh them down, Tobias felt the same way. Turnout was small. Even the phalanx of schoolchildren who sang the "Yumi Song" while each held an illustrative crane—schoolchildren who had been born so long after Yumi's disappearance that Tobias imagined her story must be their version of the bogeyman, a spooky, even silly story told by adults—appeared dutiful only, as well as cold and eager for their bit to be over. Their bundled audience consisted almost entirely of their parents and the handful of local officials who proceeded and followed them in the program. The BRING YUMI HOME! banner snapping in the wind gave a desolate maritime feeling and was all that Tobias could hear, given how unnecessarily far from the little speakers' platform the table had been placed. Tobias knew the table was placed this far away so that its educational activities would not disrupt the performance, but this consideration hadn't been necessary. No one came to the table. Tobias was surprised—heartbroken—by the greater loneliness of this annual rite in Yumi's actual hometown, compared with the other travels of the table he had seen. And then he understood that where the story had grown too familiar, it had been leached of all hope. Yumi's parents and Saho hadn't begged him to come here because they'd wanted him in their spotlight; they had begged him to come because they'd known that the spotlight was gone.

Blinded by these thoughts, he did not notice the approach of the woman until she was right there in front of him, gazing at him in dismay as he grimaced and wept through his interior monologue.

"Are you okay?" she asked him in careful English.

Tobias leaped to his feet. "Please forgive my rudeness!" he begged her in his always-surprising Japanese—he saw the relief it immediately brought her, that the strange foreign man who'd been crying alone at the table at least spoke her language.

"Please don't apologize. This is always a sad day."

"Thank you so much for coming. Do you know Yumi's story?" He was trying to extract a single flyer without letting the rest be snatched up by the wind, but the woman helpfully restored all the rocks he had moved.

"I know the story," she said. "I remember these flyers being all over the place, thicker than snow." The woman fingered the edge of the flyer she had stopped Tobias from giving her, while peering down at it as if she could read it through the stone paperweight obscuring most of its text.

Tobias had never been very good at guessing the ages of women, whatever their appearance or culture, and had recently blundered very badly with Saho by saying that, when they first met, he had assumed she was still in her twenties. This had been because her skin was so luminous—like the petals of a magnolia blossom, he had thought but not said. "Of course you assumed I must be in my twenties, because I'm not married!" Saho had said, her luminous skin turning red. "Apparently it's inconceivable that a woman who is practically forty would not have a husband!" Such thoughts had been so far from Tobias's mind that this outburst left him dumbstruck, which Saho took as vindication. The woman before him now, unlike Saho, did not glow; her cheek was weathered like the leaves scudding over the ground. But she was very striking, with high cheekbones, a long elegant nose, and a fierce brow that made it difficult for Tobias to determine if she was scowling at the flyer or if this was her face's usual expression. She was older than he was, but by how much he couldn't have guessed, even if he had not feared accidentally insulting her.

The woman turned her gaze from the flyers to the stage, where Yumi's parents now stood together at the microphone, telling the story they had told so many days of each week, so many weeks of each year, for so many years that this was perhaps the five-thousandth time they had told it. The wind distorted each familiar phrase—*Yumi had just come from tennis practice . . . Yumi's first thoughts were always of others . . .* —into a single, tremulous vibration. "Those poor people," the woman said. "I'm a mother, too, of grown men. But you might not guess it from how cruel my thoughts were when she first disappeared. Just like our useless police, I thought she'd run away. I thought those parents were hysterical ninnies. All these years I've felt so bad for ever having those thoughts that I've wanted to apologize to them in person. Year after year I've lacked the courage to do it. Year after year my lack of courage has made me feel even worse and even more like I need to apologize and even less able to do it. At this point I don't deserve the chance to offer my apology. I only gained the courage to walk up to this table today because instead of them sitting here it's you, and you're not one of their family, forgive me for assuming."

"Of course your observation is right," Tobias said. "I'm just a helper, keeping an eye on the table for them."

"Well, I'm glad, because if it was those two sitting here, I could never have faced them. I actually have come in previous years. Sometimes I've gotten as far as the park entrance." She indicated this place with her chin. "But then I'd see them sitting here like a pair of winter ducks in the one tiny patch of free water, with ice circling them on all sides."

"And you never spoke to them?"

"No, never."

"Can I persuade you to speak to them this time? They're such kind people—they would never want you to feel this way."

"I don't want to but I have to—I don't know who else to talk to!" The woman clapped a gloved hand over her mouth at the same time as a sudden percussion of drops sounded on the table's surface—not from the dark clouds, Tobias realized, but from the woman having surprisingly started to cry. "I'm so sorry," she said, rooting into her handbag as Tobias frantically patted himself for a handkerchief. But then, dragging a sleeve over her face, the woman found what she was seeking, not a tissue but a photograph, and with a sudden movement as if she'd also found resolve, laid it on the table amid the paperweight rocks. Tobias's first thought was it must be a joke, elaborate and perverse. His first emotion, even before astonishment, was anger. *Who do you think you are?* he wanted to say, though his lips and tongue couldn't comply. *How do you dare show this picture to me?* "You see, I need to talk to them because anyone else will say I'm crazy," the woman was saying. "Or worse. And even I think I'm crazy. But it doesn't matter. Crazy as I feel, I'm still convinced. But I have no proof. Only the proof of my crazy conviction," she concluded in an onrush that still was too slow, because before she'd even finished her speech, Tobias in his outrage stood up from the table and fainted, his body's favorite response to an overwhelmed mind.

When his awareness returned, he was lying on the cold and lumpy ground with several overcoats heaped on his torso and legs. His head was propped on Saho's kneeling thighs. Her face, uncharacteristically pinched and pale as she glared into his, was upside down in his vision.

"I'm beginning to understand what you meant about self-aggrandizement," Saho said.

"Where is it?" he cried. "Where is she?" Tobias struggled to sit up, but Saho's exquisitely slender, small hands held down his shoulders like a vise.

"Would you just lie there, please? Yumi's Dad called a medic."

"But I must—I have to speak to that woman—she can't leave without my speaking to her!"

"Please lie still, or I really might slap you. She's not going anywhere, Yumi's parents are talking to her. They all went to get coffee. She thinks she might be one of us. Her brother disappeared from the beach a few towns north of here, the summer after it happened to Yumi."

"Her *brother,*" Tobias repeated. Then he sat up with such force he overpowered Saho and almost slammed his head into her jaw—

"—which was hanging wide open because of how he was acting," Saho later shared with the others, when they had all told each other the story again and again, still not understanding, as Tobias could not in that moment, if it was better to cry or to laugh. "It's a wonder I didn't bite off my own tongue," Saho added.

"Her *brother*," Tobias had kept crazily saying, and then, as he saw the woman coming back over the dead matted grass of the park, Yumi's parents at each of her elbows, five steam-billowing Styrofoam cups of take-out coffee distributed among their six hands, "so she's our *aunt*."

"I thought he meant," Saho also said later, "that she could be our auntie in this funny second family we have, where you're kind of my parents, and I'm kind of your daughter, and Tobias is—whatever he is."

"I think he *did* also mean that," Yumi's Dad said, and Yumi's Mom and Soonja and Tobias agreed.

# Louisa

**When Louisa remarried** she and George went to City Hall, inviting no one; they both came from small, strange families and avoidance of group celebrations was an instinct they shared. Soon after, Leo was born—and if Louisa's life had been made temporarily easier by the help of another adult, the addition of an infant erased that advantage. Two years passed. Then Leo started preschool, and George surprised Louisa with a trip to Hawaii. "When I said I didn't want a wedding, I didn't say I didn't want a honeymoon," he deadpanned as she gaped at the itinerary he'd printed out and hidden in a giant box otherwise full of cheesy plastic leis that he'd wrapped and put under the tree. He'd hired Julian and Teddy and Leo's miraculous sitter Nthabe to move in for the week and even made an itinerary for *them*, and it was this Louisa pored over in the weeks leading up to the trip, sometimes bolting out of bed in the middle of the night to make sure, for example, that Julian's allergist's after-hours number appeared correctly on the printout despite Nthabe's having that number, and every other emergency number Louisa could think of, saved into her phone. So it was that Louisa hardly looked at her own Hawaii itinerary even up to the point of getting onto the plane, but this was life with George: the inexhaustible thrill of his reliability. Whatever they did would be risk-free, enjoyable, and meticulously planned.

From Honolulu they would hop to the southernmost Big Island to

spend two days and see the active volcanoes; then they'd make their
way back up the chain for two days in Maui, concluding with two days
in Kauai. Even before their flight from New York had landed Louisa
was electrified, as if a stimulant had been shot in her veins. The landing gear had just extended, the wheels hadn't yet touched the ground,
and Louisa seized George's forearm. "I've been here," she said.

"You have? I thought you'd never been here. You said you always
wanted to come."

"I did say that. I thought I hadn't. But I have. I don't know when. I
just know—I recognize how it *smells*."

When they came down the jetway stairs onto the tarmac, into
impossible amber light, the plane having landed—they must time it
this way—right at sunset, a line of Hawaiian women in traditional
skirts stood waiting with their arms full of leis, the real kind, their
flowers luminous as stars in the fading light. It was corny stagecraft
of the sort Louisa normally hated, yet as she bowed her head to receive her lei her vision blurred, so suddenly her unexpected tears
rained down onto the flowers. Her greeter was delighted. "Aloha!"
the greeter repeated as she deftly turned Louisa toward George so he
could steer her away. As Louisa stumbled toward the terminal building she cradled the lei in her hands and raised the flowers to her face.
They were still cool from whatever nearby fridge in which they had
been waiting. That cool touch on her cheeks, that aroma that made
"paradise" a concrete location, not some abstract cliché . . . "I *know*
this smell," Louisa kept repeating as they waited for their luggage,
as they waited for the small plane that would take them to the Big
Island, where they'd spend their first days. The shock of that smell, so
ravishing yet somehow reassuring, as if to prove an Eden persisted and
could yet be regained—none of which Christian nonsense Louisa believed in—had unleashed passionate recognition. But as the Hawaiian
evening breeze coursed around her, bathing her in that aroma from
her lei, and from all the other leis decorating all the other clumsy ar-
rivals, and even from the actual trees she soon spotted on which the actual, bewitching flowers grew, the sense of recognition paradoxically
faded, because the scent grew familiar. On first contact it had told her

it came from somewhere distant, long forgotten, and specific to her. Now it came from everywhere. She had a feeling of losing her chance, though what sort of chance she couldn't have said. George noticed the change once they'd boarded the short flight to Kona. "Are you okay?" he asked.

"I'm just tired."

"Have you figured out when you were here? Maybe you were Hawaiian royalty in a previous life?"

She laughed and put her head on his shoulder, which she found uncomfortable but knew that he liked.

The trip was beautiful, pleasurable, and required no thought, George having booked everything. They saw actual lava—the slow-moving kind—ooze its way to the ocean and plop in with a roar and great billows of steam. There was nothing familiar about this. There was nothing familiar about anything. Soon it was the newness—of the flowers and fishes, of the absence of her sons and every care that came with them, of George in his element—that enveloped Louisa, and she forgot about that déjà vu moment that had so unsettled her when they'd arrived. She had never tasted anything so delicious as this wedge of papaya with a wedge of lime squeezed over it. She had never laughed so hard as when George asked a waiter for "another cocktail for my wife" and then widened his eyes at her as if to say, *Wife? When did that happen?* She had never felt such peace as when they snorkeled in the resort cove and a prehistoric creature glided out of the depths, almost touching her hand, and she realized that it was a turtle—and the turtle seemed to realize she was *her*, she told George later, as excited as her kids would have been when the turtle gave her a sly, sleepy look—truly met her gaze—before drifting away.

They arrived in Kauai for their last two days and were picked up at the airport by a shuttle van from the hotel. "There's a whole lot of beautiful places I'll be showing you right from the road," the driver told them as the van climbed and climbed. Then the view opened out and the driver pulled over. The driver slid the van's passenger door aside like a curtain and Louisa walked toward the view of the Pacific spread like the skirts of the island to the faraway edge of the earth.

They were very high up; a metal railing that had once been painted red kept sightseers from plunging from the roadside parking area into the abyss below. Louisa closed her hand around the rail, which was warm from the sun. To either side, the island's plush emerald drapery-folds fell it seemed almost vertically into the sea. "It was here," Louisa said, though George didn't hear her, but she didn't need him to. She'd said it to herself. They got back in the van and drove to another overlook, where twin pillars of seething white water stood connecting the lip of a cliff to a turquoise-blue bowl far below. "Turn around," George said, and took her picture. She had been there; she had posed for that picture.

"It was here," she said to him. "I've always thought that I wanted to come here. But what I really wanted was to come *back*."

That night after dinner she called her mother, forgetting that their time difference was momentarily in reverse, that in LA it was three hours later and not three hours earlier as when she called from New York. For years they had talked so infrequently almost a year could go by between calls, but since the boys, and even more so since George, Louisa tried to call monthly, without always succeeding. Anne was still awake, or pretended she'd been. Louisa said, "Sorry it's so late, I got mixed up about the time difference. George surprised me with a trip to Hawaii."

"Wasn't that nice of George," Anne said, sounding crabby, but she sounded crabby more often than not, especially late in the day. She was always behind on her mandated eight glasses of water, and earlier that year had had a serious dehydration episode and been hospitalized.

"Are you drinking your water? Your throat sounds really dry."

"Did you call me at midnight to bug me to drink water? Geez, Hawaii must not be as nice as I remember."

"When were you here? Were *we* here?"

"Well, yeah. We stopped off there a couple of days on our way to Japan. I don't think there was any direct flight, or something like that. And your father was nervous about you being cooped up too long on the plane."

"Why don't I remember this?"

"Heck, *I* don't know."

"Why haven't we talked about it?"

"We haven't *not* talked about it."

"How long were we here? Did we stay on Kauai?"

"For Pete's sake, I have no idea! It was a long time ago!" She really
was crabby and Louisa, who since becoming a mother herself had
learned a little about which battles to fight, said good night. George
was outside on the lanai in one of the recliners. She took the one next
to him. The sky was shockingly clear; the starscape plunged right into
the sea. There was almost no wind and the darkened Pacific was sighing and sloshing as if no larger than a small backwoods pond. She felt
sure she remembered being lifted and gently set down by that water.
She told herself this was likely not a true memory of Hawaii but borrowed from later in life. She'd spent plenty of time in the ocean, she'd
even lived on a boat, she was an excellent swimmer; despite what had
happened she felt she had no fear of water, beyond the wise person's
healthy respect for its power.

Once she and George returned home from their trip the oceanic
tumult of daily life overtook them again. What had felt so compelling
to her in Kauai that she'd imagined doing it the instant they got back
did not just cease to be compelling, but was completely forgotten, until a day she went down to the basement as it turned out too soon to
shift the wash to the dryer, and looked for some task to fill up the time.
Then she remembered. After she and Roman divorced, an enormous
box had arrived to her building in New York that the super had to help
her get upstairs and that, once empty, was so enthralling to then-five-
year-old Julian and three-year-old Teddy they had actually managed
to share the box as fort, vehicle, soccer goal, thing-to-be-punctured,
and, finally, thing-to-be-crushed for what remained, even several years
later, their single achievement in cooperative play. How ironic, she
had thought at the time, that their father had in this way accidentally
and uncharacteristically met the needs of his sons. Inside the huge box
had been Louisa's college duffel, which she'd abandoned at his family
flat. His shipping it to her was equal parts inside joke and fuck-you,
equal proof of surviving affection and absolute rupture. The visita-

tion that slid out of the box, when unzipped, revealed a storm-tossed garbage salad of the personal effects of a very young person with little money and vastly less taste. As if afraid of infection Louisa quickly zipped it closed again and heaved it in the basement.

She found it dusted all over with whatever the grayish-brown substance was that precipitated steadily onto objects in the basement, and with the zipper starting to corrode; when the bag had returned to her not so many years ago the zipper had still worked perfectly. There was the difference between Roman's origins and her own: for all his "generosity," as his lawyers had described her modest settlement, Roman would always be the person whose family owned a rarely used London flat where a duffel-bag zipper would never corrode, while Louisa would always be the person who could barely afford a New York City co-op that swiftly destroyed everything that it sheltered with mildew and rust. She finally worked the zipper open and groped inside with the feeling of violating a carcass, until she had found it. Upstairs, the laundry changed to the dryer, the duffel with its newly broken zipper bundled back into storage, Louisa sat down at her desk and took the pages from the envelope. They were so small. Earnest labored not-quite-chicken-scratch it took getting used to, but once you did the cursive was remarkably legible. She'd been the same age when she wrote this as was Julian now. It was impossible to imagine Julian writing a paragraph of any kind, let alone in cursive. Who had taught her to write cursive letters? She no longer remembered either the skill or how she had acquired it—she knew childhood amnesia was normal, but how deep should it normally go? She remembered coarse-textured beige composition-book paper with dotted blue lines, or did she just imagine she remembered, had she seen such paper recently and patchworked it into the past? Rereading the little handful of pages each the size of her hand, she easily recognized them as describing a dream of Hawaii. She remembered, when Tobias had given them to her, thinking they related a nightmare about her father's actual and her almost drowning, but now she was sure that was wrong. Her college-self had thought her childhood-self had mistaken the year, but it was her college-self who was mistaken, her childhood-self who had been right. Now that she'd been to Hawaii again, she could remember or at least could intuit—could plausibly guess—how as a child of the Midwest, who had never before seen a mountain or even a hill, never seen a waterfall let alone one that fell free of any obstruction for hundreds of feet like a pillar of foam, she'd been awestruck, and had dreamed of that awe, her dreams reinforcing her memories, her memories perhaps ceding place to her dreams.

That night after the boys were in bed she called her mother for the first time since Kauai—she'd missed her monthly goal again. But Anne didn't seem resentful the call hadn't come sooner, or relieved at receiving it now; in fact, she seemed slightly beleaguered, saying "Yeah" when she picked up, instead of hello. Louisa wondered if this way of answering was new, as it seemed to her, or if her mother always answered this way. All Louisa's memories, even the most mundane, felt uncertain.

"That school shrink I saw, Dr. Brickner—did he ever make me write things down?"

"If he did I wouldn't have known. You had *confidentiality*. You loved bragging about it. But you sure did write things down all the time, whether he was making you do it or not."

"Why did you say that so snidely? Why did you say I '*sure did*' write things down?"

"I'm not saying it some special way, for Pete's sake! If you want to know something, just ask me about it."

"I just did."

"So explain why you did! Maybe if I knew what you're talking about I might be more helpful. You're always coming around asking things and you get so annoyed when I don't have the answer."

"I do?"

"Yeah! Why didn't I know that we went to Hawaii, which island was it, blah blah blah."

It occurred to Louisa for the first time that her mother seemed to take questions as a form of criticism. "You know," she said, trying to strike an altered tone, "lately I don't trust my memory. Stuff I was sure of, suddenly I'm not sure of. That's why I asked you about Hawaii. I was sure I'd never been there before. I told George I was dying to go because I'd never been there. But I *had* been there. And I still really don't remember, although I have a feeling it made an impression on me."

The altered tone had worked; Anne seemed mollified. "Well, it wasn't very long. It couldn't have been more than a couple of days. And a whole lot of stuff happened later."

"Yeah. Very true. But that's the other thing. Some of the things that came later—I feel like I've got them mixed up. I have this memory, or it's not even a memory, more like a feeling, that I used to tell Dr. Brickner about being with my dad somewhere high up, and then being down in the water, and the water is—*roaring*. I can't remember saying any of this to that doctor, it's more like there are details that stick in my mind that I feel like belong in one place and not some other place, and that detail of being high up with my dad, and of water that's roaring—I've always thought that those details belong with what happened to us, when he drowned. But now I feel like they belong somewhere else. I feel like they belong to Hawaii. Does that make any sense?"

"No," Anne said finally, but Louisa could tell she'd been thinking about it. "I can't say that it does. But I'll tell you one thing, your dad hated the water. I don't think he could swim. Now that we're talking, I do remember one thing from Hawaii. I remember the ocean being so calm the waves weren't even breaking, they were just sort of rising and sinking. You were dying to go in the water but your dad was too nervous to let you. Then this other nice family who were swimming invited you in, and you ran off with them, and your dad stood on the sand sweating bullets, he was so nervous—but the sea was so gentle we could see you the whole time with those other kids, all of you bobbing like corks."

"I think I remember that. I really think I do."

"I hadn't thought of it in I don't know how long. Maybe not since it happened."

"A lot of stuff happened later," she said, just as her mother had just said to her.

"Yeah. Listen, the CNA just brought my dinner, so I ought to go eat it."

"Why aren't you eating in the dining room?"

"I'm sick of it. I'm sick of sitting with those people."

"They're your friends!"

"They're *not* my friends. My friends are dead. Yeah," Anne confirmed into Louisa's shocked silence, "I'm in a bad mood."

"Okay. I'll let you go."

"How're those boys?"

"Terrible. As always."

"How's that nice husband?"

"He's great."

"*That's* great. Okay, kid. I'm going to go now." After they hung up, Louisa put down the pages; she'd had them clutched in her hand the whole time. She'd wanted to read them out loud, but then her mother's strange mood had made her forget. She couldn't remember any previous time Anne had ended a call; it was usually Louisa who had to go first.

Only a few days later, the head nurse at Anne's assisted living called Louisa to report that her mother had been hospitalized for dehydration again. "She doesn't drink her eight glasses," the nurse said. "She'll be all right this time, but it brings other problems. You'll talk to her, I'm sure. Sometimes they listen to the family more than to us."

Louisa would have guessed the opposite. "I'll do my best," she said, and even, in the coming weeks and months, felt she did, judging from how much they argued about it, and how often and bitterly Anne complained of Louisa's "nagging" and "nannying" her.

It was the afternoon before Thanksgiving when Louisa received an email from Tobias, the address a string of letters and numbers, the email domain some equally cryptic entity she assumed was connected to his dedication to siphoning all forms of communication—email and texting and phone calls—without having to pay for them. He was in Harlem at some sort of hostel. He had slept, she imagined, on a cold floor without pillow or blanket and with great satisfaction. He had arrived there that morning on the subway from JFK, had arrived at

JFK even earlier that morning from, she assumed, Japan, though she was only assuming, as she hadn't heard from him in months; for all she knew, he had despite evidence to the contrary read her several emails about Their Mother and her multiplying physical problems and, instead of simply answering Louisa, bankrupted himself flying directly to LA, and instead of simply calling Louisa from LA, had further bankrupted himself and flown here; the major obstacle to Louisa's not finding Tobias enraging was what a terrible communicator he remained, even as the world offered ever-more and ever-cheaper means and even as they both continued to accrue years with which should have come wisdom. The difficulty with Tobias was that the only communication form that really suited him was the long, pensive, poetical physical letter, which suited neither Louisa nor the efficient handling of the one concern they shared. Tobias knew this, and was forever repentant, and forever writing from this or that brand-new bewildering email address, which would be as short-lived as his various telephone numbers; there remained no way to reach him quickly, yet here he'd given Louisa less than one hour's warning he was about to appear at her door. He would be proud of himself, she realized, for managing to give her any warning at all.

In the kitchen Nthabe was cutting up carrots for Leo. "Carrots for Leo!" cried Leo when Louisa came in.

"Yay! Thank you, Nthabe!" Louisa responded with commensurate exultation, as every transaction with toddlers must be Outsize and Happy. In the same children's theater spirit Louisa shared with Nthabe the remarkable news that her free-spirit-brother-who-lives-overseas had surprised her by coming to visit.

"Oh my!" marveled Nthabe, whose Outsize and Happy reactions were never a put-on. "This is so wonderful for you!"

"Yes. But I want to go buy something special to serve him for dinner, is there any way you could stay later? For time-and-a-half?" Nthabe could not imagine any bigger treat than to get to be there when Julian and Teddy came home, the most disruptive event of Louisa's day and one that Nthabe regularly mourned fell outside of her hours now that both boys could walk home from school on their own. How sad it was, not to be able to greet those Big Boys who no longer needed her, but today, she would make them their snacks, like old times! Thank you so very much, Louisa!

Escaping from the apartment while still pulling her coat on, Louisa wondered why she'd cut back Nthabe's hours this year just because Teddy and Julian were too old for a sitter. It still made them so happy to spend time with her, so much happier than they seemed spending time with Louisa. The rare times she'd recently kept Nthabe late for whatever "me time" she'd concocted, she only ever returned to scenes of utter paradisal tranquility, the big boys not only talking and laughing with the radiant and musical Nthabe but actually paying attention to their much-resented and mostly ignored baby brother. Since September Louisa had only employed Nthabe from 10:30 a.m. to 2:30 p.m., putting herself back on duty as soon as the big boys got home—why? Was Louisa's mothering so precious that she should spend every chaotic afternoon with them, doing an equally bad job of managing homework and instrument practice and arguments and playing with Leo and making dinner because she refused to cede more than the bare minimum to her sitter? It wasn't the boys' gratification or George's she sought but her own; *do it right* was the mantra that thrummed in her mind, but what was the right way to do it?

Downstairs in her building's lobby she put on her scarf and hat, buttoned her coat, and checked her watch: forty minutes since the email was sent from a neighborhood about forty minutes away. It was relatively mild for November; she'd be all right standing outside. It felt imperative to not let Tobias set foot in the lobby; this was unkind, irrational, but a necessary condition to inviting him to join them tomorrow for Thanksgiving dinner; she had to feel uninvaded today. And here again she wondered what fueled all these calculations. Tobias almost certainly didn't remember that it was Thanksgiving; if he had, why had he left Their Mother all alone in LA (if that was where he had been, and if it wasn't, then why was he here?). No sooner had she stepped outside onto the stoop of her building, which was reached by a brief flight of steps so that it gave a view all the way to the corner, than she saw him loping toward her down the sidewalk like a scarecrow come to life. As always, she was startled anew by his resemblance to Anne. Then, as always, resentful. Sick as Anne was, ill-kempt as Tobias was, they would still make a head-turning pair with their flawlessly WASPy bone structure, their matching triangular jaws and high cheekbones and strong-but-not-too-strong noses and their deep wide-set eyes. The ways in which both looked hard-used burnished them in the eyes of the world, Louisa imagined, while the non-white person of middling bone structure had it held against her if she wasn't turned out to a tee. Such were her habitual and ignoble thoughts as pale, haggard, angular, beautiful Tobias drew near in a wool overcoat too large for him, no hat or scarf, bare pale ankles visible between the tattered cuffs of his slacks and a pair of battered loafers with seams so extensively split as to flash out at Louisa like some kind of podiatric Morse code bone-white glimpses of his unprotected feet. His gaze was bent to the sidewalk and he hadn't seen her yet; she had a moment to further study the seeming haste of his forward-slanted gait, which seemed unlike him.

He surprised her again when the gap between them narrowed enough that she could voice her excuses about the older boys needing to concentrate on their homework and Leo needing to nap. He cut her off with a gesture. "That's better—I wanted to talk to you alone."

So it was true, then. He had been to LA, things were worse—so much worse they must have a private emergency conference. She felt hot all over and yanked off her scarf and hat and tried to undo her coat buttons. In the corner café where she led him with the hammered-tin ceiling and mismatched cups and broody acoustic music, the insufferably mannered Tobias made a brief return ("O, you have green tea? My God, wonderful. I would not have expected to find—yes, thank you, madam, yes, please," to a blank-eyed college student extending a tea-sampler box) before, settling at one of the tiny unsteady tables, this familiar yet newly dubious Tobias disappeared again, leaving in his place a Tobias whose expression, as he gazed at Louisa, reminded her less of Anne than of George at a moment of crisis: searching her face for some clue as to how not to harm her. Despite how frequently Louisa now spoke to Anne, despite all her "nannying" efforts, with Anne's ramshackle health having reached a point that it couldn't be patched up anymore, it was apparently Tobias in whom Anne had confided, Tobias who after all had never made demands like a normal child let alone an abandoned one. "What's happened?" Louisa said sharply. "Just tell me."

"It's hard to know where to start." Tobias was rotating and rotating the saucer beneath his teacup. He startled at the slightest other movement in the cluttered and crowded and noisy café. "Might we walk?" he said anxiously. "Perhaps they'll give us—what do you call them?—to-go cups—"

"If she's that much worse, just tell me," Louisa burst out, "for fuck's sake!"

"If who's that much worse—*Anne*?"

"Weren't you just there? Are you not coming here from LA?"

"No—oh God!"—gaping at her, all agog at his own clumsiness. "Oh, good heavens. Forgive me. Our Mother—I imagine you've spoken to her more recently than I have. I've come to talk about your father."

This was unexpected and even eccentric, but only in its timing, in his sudden arrival, his insistence on a private conversation. Ever since Louisa could remember, Tobias with well-meaning and unwelcome ham-fistedness sought to supply her with her missing Asian heritage. When she was younger this was pursued via Japanese-language workbooks and calligraphy kits. In her college years and since, a steady stream of English-language histories, from Hirohito to Hiroshige. However inapt at this moment, the sounding of this familiar theme dissolved her sense of imminent danger. Of course he hadn't been to LA; as usual he was moved by his incomprehensible whims, not by outside imperatives. Her tea was also untouched; she pushed it to the center of the table and stood, saying, "I guess we can talk about that tomorrow—you'll come to us for dinner? It's Thanksgiving Day—you knew that, right? George wants to have The Meal at three."

"I think he's alive," Tobias said.

"He died decades ago," Louisa reminded him calmly, thinking of her mother's theory, shared with her recently and in strict confidence, that Tobias's brain tumor had left him permanently damaged, if in a manner that was hard to define.

"Please give me twenty minutes—walk with me. Hear me out. I'm not comfortable here—there are too many people."

This turn to paranoia also didn't surprise her. And once they were outside and walking, his long-winded nonsensical exegeses about some old couple and young woman and his own inadequate efforts to assist whatever their activism didn't surprise her, though they did tax the last of her patience, so that she was on the point of finally putting her foot down and telling him that he needed to go back to his hostel and sleep, that he was clearly jet-lagged and exhausted, and she had children to feed and a Thanksgiving dinner to make, when in illustration of something she had not fully heard he took out of his pocket a photo, recent and bright, of a handsome, stern Asian woman with some gray in her hair. Although Louisa knew she did not know this woman she felt an impact in her sternum, a blow, as if someone had just struck her there with the edge of their hand. "Who is that?" she demanded.

"Please," said Tobias. "I have so much to tell you."

# Part V

# Serk

**Never walk there**, *it's too close to the fence. If they can make it look like you were trying to escape, the guards will shoot you, and collect a reward. Sometimes they'll try to chase you toward a fence, so they can shoot you and collect a reward.* But he was too tired to climb up those escarpments toward where the fence zigzagged into the far distance, metal stitched to the teeth of bare rock. *Sometimes, the guards have a detail of prisoners work on fence maintenance, and they shoot a few dead, and claim they were escaping.* But he was not chosen for fence maintenance. *Never walk there, the prison camp is an hour's walk that way where they have the coal mines. I once met a man who was discharged from there into our camp, in all my years here he's the only one I ever heard of who left there alive. In there, all the men sleep in a pile in a shed with a dirt floor that doesn't have heat, and their rations are even less than ours are, just a handful of corn, and they can't even go in the woods to pick grasses. They dig out the mines with their hands and a few broken shovels and they push the coal carts uphill through the underground tunnels and sometimes they'll slip and the coal cart goes backward and runs over them and they bleed to death there on the track. When parts of the mine collapse, that's their grave. Their work shift is from five in the morning to ten in the evening and then they do self-criticism for two more hours and if they fall asleep during the session or can't come up with something to say then their rations are cut. I heard of all this from the man who got out and he thought our camp here was a paradise.* It was possible to think this. *Don't take that shortcut that runs up and over that hill. The far side of the hill is where the guards and their families live and if the guards' children see you they'll throw rocks at you and they're strong little shits, they have very good aim.* The guards' children, though, preferred to stone prisoner children, for which they were praised. It was possible to stop feeling surprised at the number of children who lived in the camp, some of whom had been born there to prisoner parents, others of whom had been sent there with their condemned parents to expiate ideological sins. It was possible to see such children with their hunger-shrunk noses and not feel pity but hostile wariness, because the children were the camp's most skillful thieves. *Don't go down in the gorge toward the river. If the guards catch you, they'll think that you're trying to supplement your rations with a fish, and they'll shoot you.* It was possible to be totally blind to the wild beauty of this harsh wilderness where spires of granite rose straight from the rain-blackened pines, where foaming white water, demonstrating its freedom, rarely showed a fish to starving eyes, let alone put one in numb, bony hands. The wet winter cold too incessantly forked through one's bones or the wet summer hot too incessantly smothered one's lungs and the hunger, through every season, too incessantly burned to take notice of beauty. The vast size of the camp, a nation-within-the-nation, was less seen than felt as the body struggled to meet the day's quota of work, struggled to avoid a mistake that would double the quota or cut the day's ration in half. It was possible, heating the head of a shovel in order to cook the dead rat you had managed to catch, to feel such impatience for eating the rat as to only bother singeing off the fur. The meat you devoured raw, finding it headily sweet. If a fellow prisoner, fellow skeleton, came upon you in this moment you would beat them to death with your shovel head without hesitation. You would not share your rat.

Time is not a river moving ceaselessly into the future but a stagnated pool. Breathing at its surface, drowning in its depths, are the same.

Here, thankfully, we do not have to work in the mines. That's the worse place. There is always a worse place.

Here, thankfully, we only have to watch the executions, when the guards tie those who can't be redeemed to a post, and stuff their mouth with rocks, and cut their body in three with gunfire. In the other place, the prisoners execute each other by stoning, and if you don't throw your stone hard enough, or if it takes the group too long to get the job done, then everyone's ration is cut. That's much worse. There is always a worse thing.

Here, thankfully, we can roam around gathering wild grass to eat in the morning before our work shift or at night after self-criticism. Imagine if we couldn't do that.

If you're appointed a rabbit-hutch-keeper, sometimes when you deliver the rabbit, the guard who ordered it won't want the entrails and then you can eat them. It's a feast for a king.

If you're appointed boiler steward for the Education Building, where the Leader's publications are stored and his portraits displayed, you get to sleep on the floor by the boiler, lest the boiler go out over-night and the Leader's publications and portraits experience a fluctua-tion in temperature. Nowhere else in the camp is there a boiler, only in this room that is essentially an uninhabited shrine, even the guards heat their homes with cook stoves. But you, boiler steward, will keep cozy all winter long. Your luck has changed, your modest mechanical know-how has turned out to be rare, no one in this country seems able to fix anything. Once you live in the boiler room you'll discover the rats like it, too, canny beasts that they are. This is how you'll become skilled at secretly trapping and killing them. Nights of sound sleep through the brutal winter cold on the floor of the boiler room, and a secret ration supplement of rats: this is how you'll survive.

In early spring of every year all prisoners enjoy a morning off to cel-ebrate the Leader's birthday. The celebration takes place in the Ed-ucation Building, where the prisoners assemble on the hundreds of benches lined up to face the Leader's portrait. As always on the oc-casion of the Leader's birthday it is still very cold outside, but unlike anywhere else in the camp it is very warm inside the Education Build-ing, so this is a gift for which the prisoners are grateful. In the unusual warmth the prisoners struggle to stay awake, but falling asleep would be a grave error, because the second gift is a program of declamations of some of the Leader's most beloved speeches, which will last several hours. While the workings of the camp, despite the camp's stated mission, seem almost to have been designed to sever all bonds of mutual care, and instead foster savage individualism, the penalty for nodding off during declamation of the Leader's speeches is so severe that even when a prisoner is seated next to his sworn enemy, if the enemy starts to nod off, he will rescue him with a sharp elbow.

The third gift is clemency for a selection of prisoners, usually a few dozen. No one ever understands why certain prisoners are chosen. Families who arrived at the prison together are sometimes chosen for clemency and also leave as a group, but just as often family members are separated from each other, one or some leaving while one or some stay. Prisoners who have been in camp decades as opposed to just years, or who are very elderly and clearly on the verge of death, or who are unusually productive workers, or who are very young and still might salvage something of their lives, are not more likely than anyone else to receive clemency. The only system seems to be a lack of system. Prisoners who hear their name called never expect this to happen. If it does happen, care must be taken to show no emotion. The reeducation camp in its very existence, and in each of its details, is an expression of our Leader's loving care and his belief in our potential to redeem ourselves and be of service to our nation, and so it would be more appropriate to express sorrow than joy at being removed from this place, but sorrow might imply that we doubt the decision that has led to our discharge. The best course, if we happen to hear our name called, is to remain very neutral in our expression. This is not difficult, because we never expected to hear our name called and are usually stunned. No one ever expects to be called, because every sentence is of undisclosed length and will most likely last for the rest of your life, but even more potently, because expecting to hear one's name called is a form of self-torture, like all forms of hope.

One year, sitting at the end of a bench near the exit to the stairs that lead down to the boiler room, as he always does during this annual assembly, in the highly unlikely event that the boiler will choose this most important moment of the year to go out, he hears his name called. Initially he thinks there must be a mistake. When names are called, the prisoner number follows, as some prisoners have similar names. He hears his number. No one seated near him looks at him, as few people know who he is. Since becoming the boiler room steward, he has withdrawn as completely as possible from camp life. He has always been taller than almost anyone else in the camp, even most of the guards, and he also is now better fed, and these are dangerous distinctions. The prisoners whose names and numbers were called are told to report to the main gate guard post. When the mass of prisoners begins moving in its many directions, each prisoner to their work detail and the scattering of children to their "school," he goes out the side exit, down the stairs to the boiler room. He feels dread like a fist in his gut. Goodbye to his warm den, where he had been safely forgotten. In a tin box is a ration of matches, a tool of his trade. He empties the matches into a pocket. He wants to bring the shovel head with him. His thin, filthy, bug-crawling bedroll yields a few strips of cloth and he binds the shovel head to his chest, under his shirt. Then he reports to the main gate guard post. Around a dozen other scarecrows are waiting expressionlessly, whether they are women whose breasts have been eaten away by systematic starvation, or men, or whether they are adults whose height has been stunted by systematic starvation, or children, he does not bother to discern. A truck arrives and they climb in the covered bed and seat themselves on the facing benches, by habit avoiding eye contact. It occurs to him they might be about to be executed, not freed, but executions are usually public. The truck begins to move and they must pass through the gates of the camp from which no one has ever escaped, at least so they've been told, though many have died in the effort. There was a time, unretrievable eons ago, when he thought of nothing else but escaping, a time when he made the effort to befriend other prisoners, the effort to learn where the guard towers were, the effort to determine if the fence's electrification could be sabotaged, when he hiked to far reaches of camp and risked being spotted and shot by the guards who loved finding such renegade prisoners because they received bonuses for each would-be-escapee they caught. And there were other times, also eons ago, when he had schemed to steal a guard's gun, and thought he could foment a prisoners' uprising, a laughable dream in a place where many prisoners could barely stand up unassisted, and then there were times he had looked for a means to commit suicide, but the guards were no less vigilant in preventing this form of escape, and would-be suicides were sent to the prison camp hidden within their own camp, into the mines to be worked to death, rather than shot, because shooting them would have granted their wish.

He passed out the gates in the back of the truck.

All along the unpaved mountain road they were jounced violently, their bodies tossed against each other like unsecured freight. Because the bed was covered it wasn't possible to see where they were, but it was obvious when the truck left the mountains and its tires found a level dirt road. In the bed, despite the utter unknown into which they were traveling, the roar of the truck, and the clouds of sooty diesel exhaust rising up through the truck bed's rust holes, everyone fell asleep. He had scarcely noticed everyone was asleep before he was asleep.

The truck left them at a small collective farm like a ghost town beneath a thin crust of snow. This was where they would work, repairing collapsing structures for their own shelter and then planting rice when the weather grew warm. He used his shovel head for countless small tasks and searched for wood straight and strong enough to make a replacement handle, but wood was burned for warmth or charcoal almost as soon as it was wrested from the tree. The farm manager arrived with their reissued citizens' cards, which identified them as former political prisoners. As many did, he noticed Serk's height. "You look like you ate meat every day of your life," he remarked. "Were you some kind of party official, were you born to some kind of elite family? How'd you screw up?"

"The less you know, the safer for you."

"We'll get along, in that case."

Later, when the farm manager noticed that Serk could repair things, he took him aside and explained he ran an off-the-books business. "You don't need to know details," he said. "You load and unload what I tell you and you fix the truck when it breaks down. I'll make it worth your while." But in time, as Serk began to accompany him on long "business trip" drives, the manager grew more expansive. The farm had stopped receiving rations the previous year. "The rations we have came from the security services, because you're former prisoners. When those run out, you can be sure that they won't be replaced. Why do you think this farm's a ghost town? Where do you think the workers went who used to be assigned here?"

"I don't know," he said. "Where did they go?"

"The ones who couldn't get a reassignment, some of them are in trade like me, but they know better than to step on my network. They've gone far away. Some of them are up in the woods burning charcoal to sell and living off whatever they can find. In the spring they'll eat tree shoots like bears. The rest are vagabonding. You'll see. I've registered this truck as a bus. If we meet vagabonds on our trips and they're able to pay, then we'll give them a ride."

"How could this truck be a bus? It has no seats but the two that we sit in."

"When it's empty in back, it's a bus."

Soon he saw them, the vagabonds plying the sides of the road, the rags they wore even more tattered than his own prison-issue that he'd been wearing for years. They rarely had money to pay for a ride. "Don't they get picked up for traveling without a permit?" he asked after they'd passed by the wandering scarecrows, who shrank into illegible scratch marks and then disappeared past a curve in the road.

"The police can't be bothered with people like that anymore. There's too many of them."

Despite being well fed by his off-the-books business, the manager enjoyed talking about foods that he couldn't obtain. "What do you think your old cronies are eating in the capital?" he would ask as they drove. "It must be roast pork and steamed egg. Do you miss your old cronies?"

"You must meet plenty of people who come from the capital."

"Never. They don't even know we exist."

When the weather warmed, Serk and his fellow former prisoners planted the rice, wearing socks of mud day and night, by day gooey and slick and a weight sucking every footstep, by night brittle and itchy but less so than the bites of the plagues of insects. His gaze was irresistibly drawn from his work to the movements of insects, and followed them as the tiniest knitted their clouds, as the droning biplane dragonflies made their daredevil runs, and his gaze also followed the lightning-fast paths that the smaller birds cut through the sky, and the slow-motion progress a heron made stalking the farthest-off part of the field. The heron's patience was so prolonged Serk's tired eye sometimes faltered and misplaced the minuscule form, or he concluded he'd been watching a stick, and then, as if to emphatically state how wrong was Serk's discernment and how inferior his bodily discipline, in a motion so compact it ended before it began the heron stabbed at the water and swallowed its catch. The insects, the birds, even the invisible fish Serk himself never saw underfoot inhabited a substance of freedom. This water and air formed a continuous substance with all the earth's water and air. Somewhere, it touched his daughter, his long-ago wife, his long-lost family.

"Plant them closer together, much closer together!" the farm manager cried as he strode in dry shoes up and down the bund paths. "'It is imperative we faithfully follow the Leader's revolutionary new method in order to attain this year's rice harvest goal! The imperialists are striving to inflict a food shortage on us, to break our faith in socialism, and subdue us to their dominance. We must deal them a crippling blow!' Okay, you all know what the new method is," he said, returning the *Workers' Newspaper* to his back pocket. "Six seedlings where you used to plant one. 'Maximize planting, maximize harvest'!"

"That many seedlings crowd each other to death," many on the work crew had already objected.

"Party's orders! This is the *revolutionary new method*, do I need to read the orders again?" Later, when the planting was finished, Serk and the manager resumed their business travels. "The crop will fail," the manager told him, "because the seedlings are too close together. But what can I do? I can't defy party orders. They send around spot inspectors, to make sure the seedlings are all jammed together to 'maximize planting.' When the crop fails, the local committee will blame some other factor, and then we'll all fake our books to show we met quota. Whatever rice does grow just goes to your cronies, so what does it matter? I'd like to see the banquet those old cronies of yours are stuffing themselves with today."

In the high summer heat, as the rice plants were killing each other for space, Serk and the manager arrived at a small factory where as usual Serk unloaded the truck of its undiscernible contents to a supply shed while the farm manager and the factory manager had a discussion behind a closed door. Serk sat in the shade of the loading dock waiting. It was the factory's lunch break, and workers milled around smoking. A loudspeaker shrilled to life suddenly. "Prepare yourselves for a special broadcast." A portentous march followed at deafening volume. He saw the farm manager and his colleague emerge from the office with uncertain faces.

"With much bitterness, we must inform the people of our nation that our Great Leader has died of a sudden disease." A scream pierced the air. Serk startled and his cigarette fell from his hand. A woman worker in a smock, her hair tied out of sight by a bandanna, had collapsed to the ground in a ball, so only her bandanna taut over her head and her smock across her thin back could be seen, yet her screams were so loud her words were easily heard along with those continuing to thunder from the loudspeaker.

"How will we live now?" she was screaming. "How will we live?"

"Our Great Leader turned our country from age-old backwardness to a paragon of powerful and self-reliant socialism," the loudspeaker continued. "He was the sun of our nation."

Pandemonium erupted. The factory workers screamed and sobbed. They fell to their knees and pounded their fists on the ground. Serk's teeth were chattering with a sound like gunfire in his ears, although moments before he'd been streaming with sweat. The farm manager was at his elbow. "Let's get out of here," he murmured urgently into Serk's ear.

The cab of the truck was a furnace from having been left in the sun.

There were never trees anywhere within sight of a settlement, they had all been reduced to firewood. The sun seemed affixed to the up-permost point on its arc, as if it hadn't risen and never would set. Serk's eyes stung from the salty grit carried into them by his freely flowing perspiration, which could never be mistaken for tears. The farm man-ager's face also streamed with liquid. After they had driven in silence far enough that there was nothing but their dust plume behind them, the farm manager pulled over onto the verge of dead grass, crossed his arms on the steering wheel, dropped his face on them, and sobbed. To give the man privacy for his grief, Serk let himself out of the cab and waited unsheltered from the sun against the side of the truck. In the coming days, he witnessed cataclysms of mourning it was impossible to believe were contrived. In his work for the farm manager, he had traveled the length and breadth of the hinterland. He had seen that his camp was just one of many in which untold thousands were arbi-trarily imprisoned, that the farm manager's cooperative was just one of many that no longer received a food ration. That the vagabonds tramping the roads were just the scattered detachments of ever more numerous flocks centered on the train stations, where they pecked at the ground for any edible crumbs, and that many of these were small children.

Like children, they all wailed beyond consolation. Strangers seized hold of each other, freely soaking each other in tears. The people of this land had seemed to him thoroughly atomized and hopelessly beneath trust because each had to battle so hard for survival. In fact, they were a being that was larger than their sum. They were a nation after all.

After the rice crop failed and the cold weather returned, the farm man-ager disappeared. With him went Serk's only source of food, his pay-ment for their off-the-books activities. He joined the charcoal burners on the mountain, who accepted him because he brought his shovel head. With it he could pull the charcoal from the kiln, but to get all the charcoal from the kiln's farthest side he had to crawl in head and shoulders, the ash filling his lungs and sparks singeing his face despite the rags he tied around his head, and the poisonous gases sometimes overpowered him to the point that the other men dragged him out by his ankles, before he was turned into charcoal himself. He had been poisoned in so many ways already, this new way must have had to search hard to find parts of him not yet corrupted. He imagined the tendrils of poisonous gas, their silent, sinuous efficiency. Starvation was also efficient, it subtracted equally from his mind and his body. He did not think, as he once had, about anything but his own survival. He and the charcoal burners traded charcoal for food, but there was little food to trade for. The flour of powdered acorns, his colleagues' staple, felt like a bear trap had clamped on his guts. He left the charcoal burners eventually and joined the vagabonds, and eventually made his way to a train station where at least there were rats, though also fierce competition for them. The trains obeyed no schedule and some days there were no trains at all, but he saw that when a train did arrive, whether passenger or freight, and particularly if it came at night, dozens of vagabonds moved toward it across the rail yard, a disturbance of shadows. No security force slashed the darkness with flashlights or tore open the secretive hush with a whistle. The stationmaster and the handful of outnumbered police seemed to have pulled down the visors of their uniform caps so these covered their eyes. A quality of darkness persisted even when the sun shone. What trees could be found and cut down for firewood had already been stripped of their bark. When no bark remained to be eaten, they filled their mouths with snow, but even the snowfall that winter was stingy.

Serk joined the disturbance of shadows in the rail yard one night and climbed onto a passenger train. The electricity in the compartments was no longer working, and the security agent, making his way car to car with a flashlight, could be easily spotted a car in advance. When Serk saw the light's beam playing over the car before his, he went out the back of the car, climbed the ladder, and clung to the roof. Later in his journey, when he saw other riders slipping out of the compartments and jumping off the couplers into the darkness, he understood there must be a document check coming up, and he also jumped off the train and then, with other shadows, walked for miles along the tracks until he reached the next station and a new chance to board a new train. Once, he rode a freight train that seemed entirely empty except for its unpaying passengers, and stretched out in a boxcar sheltered from wind and slept an unbroken fearless sleep for the first time since his days with the farm manager. When he woke up he understood he had already made a decision, and his slow northward stowaway progress by train was the decision's enactment. He stowed away on a passenger train that exhausted its fuel miles short of its destination, and the passengers uprooted the seats, removed them from the train cars, and made bonfires of them. When he had been warmed by the bonfire, he continued to follow the tracks, and at least for a full day while walking this way, no refueled train ever passed by him.

The end of the line was Musan, but he'd already been warned not to ride the train into this station. Again when he saw other passengers jump off the train he jumped also, and walked along the tracks the rest of the way to the town. In working societies, roads are physical marks on the land, visible even when not being used. In collapsing societies, the movements of people mark out the new roads, changeable and unseen except while they are traveled. He had learned how to see these new roads. Outside the Musan train station he squatted next to a wizened old man. "Do many people cross the river?" he asked.

"Back and forth all the time. And it's frozen over, and so shallow that even if you fall through, though you're wet to the neck, your feet still touch the bottom."

"And you die from the cold."

"Then don't fall through. In the daylight it's easy to spot the thin ice."

"But also easy for guards to spot you."

"They can do that at nighttime as well. Up and down with their flashlights: one carries the flashlight, the other carries the gun, so if they spot someone crossing, they're ready to fire in the blink of an eye!" The old man showed Serk his few teeth in a grin of delight, as if they were discussing a sporting event.

"Yet you say people cross all the time."

"They give the guards something to not notice them. Cigarettes or a snack or some money. Especially money. It's simple!"

"Unless you have nothing to give."

"In that case don't cross. Or do cross, and get shot. Death is inevitable anyway."

"Do many people get shot?"

"Of course!"

"Do many people get captured, and sent to a prison?"

"Why go to such trouble when you can just shoot them?"

He walked out of Musan again, this time following the river and not the train tracks. He was surprised by the river's insignificance. It meandered in its bed, a pathway of ice tracing broad, lazy curves. If it was really frozen solid it would take only minutes to cross. From the riverside road he could see the guard posts, far more guard posts than visible guards. The days were longer, the cold had been relinquishing its grip, what snow remained on the ground was in shadowed niches and nibbled at its edges by melt. The ice looked intact but might be a mere skin in some places, there was not enough light to determine, but if he waited for daylight he himself would be much too exposed. It was the in-between hour, the sun having set but the landscape not yet fully shrouded by night. He saw two guards meet at a point between guard posts, then turn and walk together downriver. He had not meant to do more than study the movements of the guards, try to understand when they did a shift change, indecision still pinioned his mind, but his body broke into a run. He ran down the incline and then he was out on the ice, not looking back to see if he was seen. His ragged intakes of breath barely opened his lungs. What little light remained in the sky was thrown back by the ice. Against it he must stand out distinctly enough to be shot. As if the ice had read his thoughts, with his next step it vanished and he was plunged into heart-shocking cold, and only the river's lazy movement and its shallowness let him fight for his life. He thrashed desperately for the opposite bank, breaking ice as he went. If he had been shot he would not have felt it. Where he reached the other side the river slightly undercut its bank, it was only a matter of inches but he couldn't crawl out. This was where he would

finally die, his upper body in China, his lower half an interruption in
the re-forming ice. He'd survived a living death for so long, for so long
his body had expended without replenishment yet still remained on
this side of the line; he could not believe, had numerous times been
driven to despair by, and even when not actively despairing refused to
ever read a false message of hope in the number of times he had failed
to die. But the moment had come. He would die with his waist ringed
in ice. His feet felt nothing, but it must have been their flailing contact
with the riverbed silt that sent shock waves of pain through his bones
as his hands met and closed around something, exactly the thickness to
allow a strong grip. Perhaps it was the handle he'd so long been seeking
to wed to his decapitated shovel head. Perhaps someone in China had
casually lowered a ladder. But there was no one here, even the shovel
head was gone to the bed of the river. He had pulled his legs and feet
out of the water and continued his death throes in a juddering ball at
the base of the riverside tree whose roots, in warm weather, had been
half excavated by slow-moving water so that now, as hypothermia ate
its way up his body, the roots had come to his hand.

The air temperature was even colder than that of the water and it
froze the small twigs and decomposed leaves and soil to his ill-fitting,
ill-preserved clothes that he'd been wearing since his prison camp release. After some unmeasurable amount of time, during which his
scant body heat contended like a guttering flame against the overwhelming cold and yet somehow wasn't extinguished, he was able to
half rise again. He crawled up the bank through more trees that, by
their mere existence, heralded an enormous change of circumstance,
because they hadn't all been cut down for fuel. He looked like a tree
himself, plastered by dead twigs and leaves. When at last he saw a hut
he approached without fear, because fate held the rudder. Whoever
found him crumpled on their threshold had long ago made up their
mind what to do with such migrants. They would either shelter him,
ignore him, or call the authorities on him.

His fate took the form of a withered little woman, quick eyes in
an indistinct face. "Go in the woodshed," she said in Korean, with the
accent of an ethnic-Korean Chinese. After some time she appeared

with a change of clothes, a bedroll, and a bowl of porridge, which he struggled not to drop while devouring.

"Change clothes first. And don't eat it so fast. You'll puke." Then she left him again.

Sickened from eating too quickly and sick to the marrow from cold, he had as hard a time removing his stiff-frozen clothes and putting on the dry ones as if he'd been two wrestlers, one of whom was refusing engagement by folding in half like a shrimp. His fingers were too numb to work the drawstring for the pants. The pant legs were far too short. He got his hand in one end of a sleeve and saw both hand and a hand's-length of his wrist and forearm emerge from the other. But the too-small shirt was dry and immediately warmed his skin with a phantom smooth warmth, as if of the sleeve of a shirt his wife plucked carefully by its collar and handed to him from her ironing board.

His snatching the shirt, roughly shrugging it on as he walked away from her, shoving the tails in his pants, reaching for his briefcase.

This memory housed in his body had no possible place in the world. There couldn't exist such a world of smooth-handed, ironing wives and the smooth shirts they made.

"My son's," the woman said of the too-small clothes when she returned. "He's a grown man, but you're the tallest man I've ever seen."

When he thanked her for the food and the clothes and the bedroll, which he had pulled around his shoulders, he saw the oddness of his accent register on her face. But she wouldn't ask questions. The less she knew about him, the better it was for them both.

"You'll have to go to the city. There's people there who help people like you."

"But more authorities there."

"More authorities but also more people. Here you'll only stand out. The authorities don't come that often, but when they do, they round up anyone like you and send them right back, to get credit for doing it."

He had a few days on sufferance from her; sizing him up she had asked if he did carpentry. "I do anything," he said. After sleeping long enough to be able to stand without falling, he didn't just repair the many perforations in her roof but made square all the angles of the tiny house that up to then had apparently, like its owner, approached the world at a steep lean. It was a new house when he finished with it, of a workmanship the woman could never have dreamed of in her threadbare widow's life. Under other circumstances he might have paid for comfortable accommodations of his own with the money such work merited. Under these circumstances he received temporary use of the woodshed and bedroll, scant food, and when nothing remained to be fixed, a few coins. Before dawn one morning the woman reclaimed the bedroll and told him to be on his way.

He walked to the village down footpaths he barely discerned by the light of the stars. A food vendor's small fire burned by the side of the road. A few silent forms had drawn to it for warmth, their twitching firelight shadows made bulbous and strange from the parcels that burdened their shoulders and backs. He held nothing but his own upper arms, gripping warmth to his chest. He squatted down where he still felt some warmth from the fire but was barely revealed by its light, studying faces while hiding his own. When the bus came he fell to the back of the line, watched what the other new passengers did, and saw that the pay he'd received from the woman was exactly enough for his fare. He dropped the coins in the box and was destitute, in too-small peasant clothes, and with too little flesh on his bones. He must be glaringly obvious to the other passengers, as dawn light filled the bus, while they remained illegible to him. Of course there were Chinese on the bus, but which passengers they were, let alone how sympathetic or hostile or opportunistic they felt toward escapees from the DPRK, China's troubled and troublesome neighbor, there was no way to tell just by looking. And there were China-born ethnic Koreans, but again he could not pick them out just by looking or even by listening, as they might speak Korean only in their homes, or have never learned to speak it at all; and even if he knew who they were, this didn't tell him whether they had ties of family or black-market trade or mere altruistic compassion to the river's far side that might disincline them to turn in an escapee, or whether for opposite reasons they might do the opposite thing. And finally, there might be other North Koreans on the bus, but whether escapees like him—though having come by better clothes—or spies, or escapees-turned-spies, or spies posing as escapees, he could not even guess. There were too many signals, any of which might be noise. Surrounded by stone-faced or sound-asleep people all of whom shared with him enough in physical character as to make their affiliations invisible, he felt himself in even greater danger, having escaped from the DPRK, than he had almost two decades earlier when he'd arrived.

He forced his eyes closed to appear to be sleeping. The city outskirts, then the city itself, took its shape in his mind from the noises he heard. The first time the bus stopped, he fluttered his eyes as if roused, but didn't otherwise move. Only a few passengers had extricated themselves and their luggage. The next stop was heralded long before the bus arrived by a generalized rousing and struggle to retrieve packages and get into the aisle. He joined in the tumult and hoped it concealed him.

Here again was the late twentieth century—though not the American one Serk could hardly believe he once knew. It had more in common with the late twentieth century of Serk's return to Japan when, having grown used to American suburbs, he cringed from the noise and disorder of bodies and wheeled vehicles and unwrapped food-stuffs all teeming together in deafening streets while receiving a black mist of soot. He forced himself to walk: brisk and stone-faced. His self-consciousness redoubled in this urban place where his malnourished skin and hair and vagabond clothes were even more noticeable; he had to find his way quickly, if not into the shelter of an actual building, then into that of a self-assured attitude. He was a survivor of a most extraordinary ordeal whose luck would expire if he could not impersonate some version of the unremarkable. China's policy was to treat North Koreans found on China's side of the border as trespassing migrants, not refugees meriting aid. They were unceremoniously yanked into vans by Chinese border guards, driven over the river, and placed in the custody of the same DPRK border guards who had accepted the migrant's bribe to look the other way when the migrant had passed in the other direction. If he was thusly "repatriated," Serk would go further backward from freedom than the reeducation camp where he'd survived on a diet of rats. He'd be sent to the prison-camp mine from which no one emerged. Even the dead were disposed of inside.

Suddenly a woman took his arm. She was hectoring him in the bossy older-female's Korean unchanged from his boyhood: "You passed by here a half hour ago! You need to be much more careful. I know who you're seeking—I'll take you to him. He's my husband, you know." The age of her skin was concealed beneath powder, rouge, and a thick application of lipstick. Her Western-style slacks, blouse, raincoat, and shiny leather shoes were conspicuously new. Her hair was the lurid artificial color of an eggplant, without a telltale salt-grain of white. Her frame was narrow and upright and broadcast prosperity, whether in the new Chinese style or that of some other country, he was too disconcerted to guess. A well-dressed woman on his arm was its own camouflage, and fate still held the rudder. He didn't resist.

The woman led him down a deserted side street and up a narrow staircase at the top of which she unlocked a heavily fortified door. From the twilight behind it, a quintet of ghostly faces stared at Serk a moment before returning to the task his entrance had interrupted. This was a monotonous staring at something and droning that Serk realized was praying.

"Nothing fancy," his guide said, "that's why it is safe, thanks to my husband and Jesus our Lord."

In a kitchen stocked with ramen packets and a hot plate, the woman measured him for pants that would reach to his ankles and a shirt that would cover his wrists. She had him stand on paper and traced his footprint. "For your journey to freedom, everything will be South Korean: you will have shirt, pants, jacket, socks, shoes, a backpack, a nice watch, even your underclothing will be South Korean–made. I don't blush talking about underclothing because my husband and I are fighting a war. You will look like any South Korean tourist. Your back is straight, your mouth is still full of teeth—please don't compromise us with your personal story, but clearly, you're one of the lucky ones. That's lucky for us. You will be convincing." When she opened a cupboard he hoped she was bringing out food. Instead she seized his hand in one of hers. What she pressed into his palm was a Bible. "Here at last is the truth," she whispered. "I know it will be difficult for you to accept. Your whole life they have fed you the lie that God doesn't exist. But please: Study hard. Let God save you. And then *we* will save you."

The room she showed him to was just behind the kitchen, barely large enough to hold two bedrolls side by side. "Isn't God great? Until just a short time ago, we had a family of four in this room. Husband and wife, the wife's sister, a child. We found them barely clinging to life. The preparation was long, but just a few days ago they set out on their journey to freedom. And then you appeared! God always shows us the way. Now I'll go find my husband and bring him to you." She closed the door and he heard a bolt thrown.

Immediately he went and tried the handle. Then he banged and called out, but neither the woman nor the other inhabitants of the apartment responded. Another cell, and not even a window.

He scarcely remembered the self who would have misspent his scant energy banging and raging. He lay on the bedroll and slept. Later he woke up to the ravishing smell of roast pork. His stomach roared. The door opened to a portly man in a suit, a tie, and brightly polished shoes. "My friend. Please join me in the kitchen. The toilet is down this hallway if you need it."

A table was set out with enough food for numerous people but there were only two cushions, and when Serk and the man had sat down only Serk attacked the food, unashamed to devour the largesse of a stranger who had just freed him from a locked room. The man asked Serk to call him Reverend, and his wife Mrs. Reverend. "I don't need to explain why it's better we don't share our names. As for the locked door, please forgive my wife, but I'm the one who insists that she take this precaution. My wife is all-trusting, and when she sees someone in need, she can never believe that her eyes might be lying. I take a bit longer to make up my mind. In this way my all-trusting wife and I have not yet been murdered or thrown into prison. So many of your countrymen have now made their ways here that there are also agents of your secret police, disguised as escapees, seeking to destroy the operations of people like me. As my wife said, you're tall and you have decent teeth. You don't look like the typical person we help. But for these same reasons, your NSA wouldn't likely choose you to play the part of a starved refugee. And my wife observed you for a while and concluded you really were lost." Knowing this might be the last meal this man ever gave him, Serk continued to shovel food into his mouth while the Reverend paused, smiling benignly. His seemed to be the pleasure of one who, in having provided roast pork, was in receipt of the abasement the roast pork provoked. "And there is one more reason I still have to make up my mind. You haven't enjoyed meat like this in a while, but I can see that for most of your life, you were eating your fill. I can only assume you were a highly placed party official, and so in my view, you have blood on your hands. However your downfall took place, it could not have been enough to expiate your past sins against your countrymen, suffering by the millions."

Serk was finally able to pause in his ravenous eating. "If you think such a thing, then why help me?"

"Because I'm not God, I'm His servant. His son Jesus Christ is my Lord. Whoever you are, whatever you've done, if you accept Jesus Christ as your savior, then I'll save you as Christ wants me to."

"What if I told you I'm not North Korean at all?"

"In that case, I would gladly hand you over to the Chinese authorities. I have no interest in helping imposters."

"For all you know I might be Japanese. I might be American."

"With rags on your feet, and nothing in your pocket but a card from the DPRK that identifies you as a former political prisoner. But don't let me stop you. I'll unlock the door. The nearest embassies are in Shenyang, just an eight-hour drive or a seven-days' walk, with Chinese authorities every step of the way. As I've said, I have no interest in helping imposters."

"Or nonbelievers."

The Reverend had actually stood from the table to unlock the door. He relocked it and resettled himself on his cushion. "Of course you are all nonbelievers." He watched Serk with what seemed a heightened curiosity. Serk wondered what he saw, and what Serk should want him to see. "No, I don't think you're a spy," he said after a moment. "Not just in appearance, but even in how you speak, you're too strange. A purged party official, with blood on your hands, seems most likely." The Reverend reached into his jacket and removed a black snub-nosed object and Serk startled with such violence his spoon flew in the air and he almost knocked over the table. "Sweet Jesus!" the Reverend exclaimed. Like a hammer, Serk's heart had nailed him to the opposite wall. The Reverend was back on his feet, and he stood with his soft, plump hands raised in surrender, the snub-nosed black thing having crashed to the floor. They breathed heavily, watching each other. At length the Reverend tilted his head at the object. "Pick it up. I assure you, it's harmless."

Serk could hardly get the thing in his hands, they were trembling so ridiculously. It finally lay on his palm, a tapered sort of walkie-talkie with "Samsung" in English letters above a small window, and numbered buttons beneath.

"Do you know what it is?" When Serk answered with silence the Reverend went on, "It's a mobile telephone. And no, that's not just the half that you hold, missing the half that plugs into the wall. There is no other half. There is no plug. That's the whole thing. Anywhere that I am, I can get a phone call. Even while I am sitting here talking with you."

The phone blurred in his vision. Of course it existed. It would be simple, a matter of radio waves. It wasn't the phone's presence but his own absence, the world having so heartlessly gone on without him, that he couldn't endure.

"I believe I can trust you," the Reverend said after he took the phone back. "I hope you will trust me, and, more important, trust God. Read His word. Accept Christ as your savior. When you are ready and the time is right, I will get you out of China. Until then, never leave this apartment. Since your Great Leader's death and the transfer of power, the Chinese authorities have been increasingly aggressive in hunting down escapees from your country and sending them back. China doesn't want this region flooded with impoverished North Koreans any more than it already is. More to the point, China doesn't want your country's regime to collapse, because they very

much do not want a unified Korean peninsula, run by the South Koreans and their allies the Americans, right next door. This is the last
thing China wants. And so they're eager to keep their North Korean
friends reasonably content and in power. If they ever looked the other
way while North Koreans crossed into their country, they do so no
longer. The cross-border black-market trade they ignore; in fact, they
foster it through their inaction because it props up the North Korean
economy. But the escapees they seize, and those who help the escapees, like me, they harass and arrest. If you want my protection, you'll
stay out of sight." When the Reverend left later that night, he didn't
lock Serk's bedroom door, but he didn't need to. Serk closed the door
himself, to shut out the robotic sound of prayer from the apartment's
farther side. He put the Bible under his head for a pillow and slept.

Over the coming days, he let the apartment assimilate him. A
man and three women shared the room on the kitchen's far side. The
names they gave him he knew must be fake, as the name that he gave
them was fake. They spent the greater part of their time trying to
memorize Bible verses and the much lesser part studying Mandarin.
When Serk asked to borrow their phrasebook they told him to keep
it, as they'd soon be leaving for Mongolia and freedom. Twice a day
Mrs. Reverend brought food, led prayers before letting them eat, and
afterward administered memory tests on the verses and delivered herself of lengthy remarks on the goodness of God. When the Reverend
returned, he came into Serk's cell of a room and closed the door so
they wouldn't be heard. "Mrs. Reverend says you don't read your Bible
and haven't learned any verses by heart."

The diminishment of Serk's being had proceeded so far over such a
long time he was slow to recognize in himself the symptoms of resistance. "Mrs. Reverend is a dedicated woman," Serk said.

"We don't only rescue the bodies. We salvage the souls," the Reverend reminded.

"The harder the work, the greater the reward," Serk returned.

The Reverend barely perceptibly frowned. "I can tell that you're an
educated man, but learning Mandarin can wait. Learning God's word
is the task I've entrusted to you."

The day on which the quartet was scheduled to depart came and went several times. The Reverend had intended to send the quartet with a guide, but either the guide would become unavailable, or the use of a particular guide was concluded to be more a risk than a help; more than one "farewell dinner" took place. Serk had learned that the Reverend maintained many scattered apartments. There were many small flocks, all their members equally dependent on the Reverend's protection not only from the Chinese authorities but from gangsters who entrapped female North Korean escapees into sex slavery, and male ones into a modern indentured servitude, in which they took on enormous debt in exchange for being smuggled out of China. The debt would then be collected by force, and with ballooning interest, by the gangsters' South Korean counterparts, if the escapee succeeded in reaching that country. The Reverend, by contrast, funded his mission with donations from his South Korean flock and other mysterious overseas forces he called only "our friends." The Reverend housed, fed, and clothed in South Korean–made garments, down to the underwear, his escapees, and asked in return only that they convert to Christianity. Serk came to see the Reverend's terms as not just authentically charitable, but even sadly self-defeating. It seemed to Serk it was the Reverend and his tireless wife who were the most exploited. The quartet with whom Serk shared his meals cared no more about God and His Son than they had cared to win glory in the Arduous March, as the famine was called in their homeland, by valiantly drying and pounding a wild-growing root into a toxic inedible flour. They memorized and regurgitated the Bible because that was what this Dear Leader asked them to do, in exchange for bus fare to the China-Mongolia border, where they would hike through the Gobi to an unguarded stretch of the border, climb through the barbed-wire fence, claim to be South Korean tourists who'd lost their way, and beg whatever Mongolian authorities they encountered to hand them over to the South Korean consulate in Ulaanbaatar. The material support for this literal arduous march that the Reverend gave them was at considerable risk to himself. Another Christian missionary working in the region with escaped North Koreans recently had been murdered—yanked into a van by masked men, shot, and dumped back on the street as a warning. Of this the Reverend had said, without visible apprehension, "The Chinese authorities look the other way as the DPRK's spies attack our networks. The Chinese don't want us here any more than they want you here. And the more of us come here, the more of you come here. The more of a headache for them." In time Serk not only stopped resenting the Reverend but came to admire him. Yet, because Serk was also regaining his strength and some sense of himself, the Reverend's reasonable price of demonstrated Christian faith was one he found he couldn't pay.

One night not long after the quartet finally embarked, he was awakened by the sound of argument from their former, now unoccupied room. He went into the kitchen to listen. He heard the Reverend say, "He escaped with his life and you sent him back *in*? Who do you think you are, waving money around like a gangster?"

"They're the gangsters you treat like such delicate flowers. Among other things, they come here for freedom of choice, and his free choice was money."

"You take advantage of their victimization."

"Come down off your cloud, holy man. These people don't even have souls to save. Why can't you care for the souls of your countrymen?"

"These *are* our countrymen."

"I will never be able to stomach how our South Korean countrymen are ignored by all you do-gooders and even our own government, while instead you help the Communists who abduct them."

"My people are victims, not perpetrators. With the exception of your honored father, and you know you have my heartfelt sympathy, most South Koreans *you* claim were abducted joined the Communists of their own free will. They defected—no! Don't interrupt! Why else do you have such a hard time getting them to come out? I've heard the stories. I've heard about your so-called victims calling the authorities on their own rescuers!"

"That's because they live under totalitarianism and can't trust anyone! Such as your so-called escapees who are actually DPRK intelligence agents with the blood of South Koreans on their hands!"

"You think these people without enough teeth to eat rice are *spies*?"

But by now, although the two men sounded close to trading blows, they suddenly burst into the kitchen together saying, "Where the hell is that bottle?" On seeing him, both showed immediate affront at his presence, as if they weren't enemies but intimates on whom he'd intruded. And this wasn't far from the truth, he would learn. The two men—one soft and rounded in a suit, tie, and loafers, the other muscled and grimed in a worn leather jacket and jeans; one consistently godly and the other insistently profane; one passionately loyal to the Good Book and the other to a good punch in the face—for all their seeming differences shared a single obsession, destroying the North Korean regime by depriving it of victims, one at a time for as long as it took.

"Who the fuck is this?" the visitor demanded. "I thought you said your group had left."

At the same time the Reverend admonished, "You should have made your presence known to us, but I'm sorry for our noise. We're just going."

The next morning when Serk emerged from his room, the man was sitting in the kitchen, clearly not having slept. "I hear you still haven't found Jesus," he said.

"I don't think Jesus needs me."

"I agree, but you're causing our mutual friend great anxiety. He's a fool, but he's also a good man. Turning Christian is all he asks in exchange for the ticket."

"I don't want the ticket."

"What, you want to go back?"

"No, I want to get someone else out."

"Then we're in the same business," the man said.


The Reverend's friend told Serk to call him the Fisherman. Like the Reverend he was South Korean, though not from Seoul but a small coastal village on Korea's East Sea that Serk in his earliest boyhood had been taught was the Sea of Japan. The Fisherman's father had been a literal fisherman, a profession the son would have followed.

But one evening in the Fisherman's childhood, in the late 1960s, his father's fishing boat didn't return.

Weeks later, a handful of the crew came ashore in a dinghy. They'd been captured by a North Korean gunboat, brought to North Korea, and split up. The group who would eventually return were first detained in a jail where they saw no one else. When they were taken back out to sea and dropped into the dinghy, they were told that the rest of their crew had begged to stay in the socialist paradise. "Lies!" the Fisherman cried when he told Serk this story, as if these events had transpired just hours and not almost thirty years previously.

The anti-Communist dictatorship that had ruled the South at the time had been glad to write off the missing fishermen as defectors. Even the crew members who returned were regarded by authorities, and subsequently their own friends and family members, as tainted by possible Communist leanings. The son whose father had been kidnapped by Communists from the North was tormented by anti-Communist bullies at home—children who beat him up and taunted his sister, adults who ostracized his mother. On her deathbed his mother had told him, "Do your duty and rescue your father, because no one else will."

He had tried letter-writing, petitions, and a protest encampment in Seoul, but the only result of these efforts had been meeting people like himself—not tens of them but hundreds—with a family member who had disappeared, presumably to the DPRK, usually off a boat. Like him they found their own government uninterested if not hostile to their pleas for assistance. Unlike him, a few had letters from their disappeared family member, smuggled to China and then mailed. The points of origin of these illicit letters abruptly constituted a map, where before there was only blankness. The map constituted a plan of attack. In the early 1990s, as the DPRK's centralized system for food distribution was failing, the fatherless son abandoned his Seoul protest shelter and relocated to northeasternmost China, where the border with the DPRK grew more porous the less there was on the far side to eat.

Like the Reverend, who had come to the area around the same time, the Fisherman assumed his fake name, learned which local officials to bribe, accumulated paid informants who were crossing the border as part of the burgeoning black market trade, developed legitimate and illegitimate sources of income, and made extensive use of the new mobile phones. Radio waves originating from towers in China for use by China-based service subscribers worked no less well where they spilled over into North Korea. If someone from China crossed the border with a phone, they could easily communicate back. The Fisherman paid North Korean escapees to reverse their journey, locate abducted South Koreans, and smuggle them out, all the while reporting their progress by phone and risking a death sentence to the gulag if caught. They did not, like the Fisherman, do the work out of love, nor out of principle, nor for any reason other than cash, because they were desperate people living as fugitives on both sides of the border, whose other options for income were drug smuggling and prostitution. It was this total lack of ethics in his method that brought the Fisherman into conflict with the Reverend. Many of the escapees the Fisherman sent back into their country did not escape a second time.

"That man is little better than a criminal who cares about no one apart from himself," the Reverend warned Serk in what would not be their last meal—once Serk deserted the Reverend, they would in fact develop a grudging collegiality that would have been impossible had Serk remained a black sheep of the Reverend's flock. "He doesn't help the North Koreans, he treats them as disposable—like a tissue you'd fill with your snot and throw out."

"I understand his single-mindedness, and I don't understand your godliness. I admire it, but I'll never share it. I can't keep taking food and shelter from you."

"What will he ask from you, in return for his protection? If the Chinese authorities pick you up, he'll wash his hands of you. And you give up any chance of future help from the South Koreans. The South Koreans despise him. He dedicates more energy to embarrassing them than to his so-called rescues."

"I understand and appreciate everything you're telling me."

"Perhaps you really are a spy, as I first thought. In that case, I send you to him with my blessing." The Reverend was smiling, if sadly.

"I intend to repay you for feeding and clothing me."

"Repay me by not going back to that hellhole, neither by your own two feet nor by letting the Chinese arrest you. You have the advantage of not looking like most North Koreans. You never did, even when you first came to us half-starved and in rags."

Serk forced himself to imagine Louisa as she must be today. A woman. Like him, unusually tall in the context of North Korea. She'd already been tall for her age the last time he had seen her. A strikingly Eurasian face, perhaps even more so as her features matured. He wondered if her hair was still straight or if it had a slight wave like her mother's, if its color was still a paler brown than his own. But his hair had turned white.

The Fisherman's detective work ran in two directions. From his informants inside North Korea, he gathered any scraps of information on persons brought against their will from South Korea to the North. From South Korean records and press, he gathered instances of missing persons, especially those who had vanished at sea. Then he tracked down their family members, and tried to persuade them he wasn't a madman or, worse, an intelligence agent of their own government, investigating their missing loved one as a possible defector or spy. If the family was convinced of his trustworthiness, he asked for some intimate detail of family life, to test any possible match. This might be children's birth dates, or a pet name. The detail was conveyed through the chain of messengers, each link so vulnerable, that stretched from wherever in the Chinese border region the Fisherman sat talking on his cell phone, across the river Serk had forded that sub-freezing day.

How often did these efforts succeed? The Fisherman refused to give exact numbers, and it was clear that his claim of "dozens" was exaggerated. But indisputably there had been two, because two such men had given interviews to the press. Their interviews had been reluctant and brief. The taint of possible communism had not been dispelled but intensified by their return to South Korea. Their welcomes had not been those accorded to heroes, and their government had regarded as a headache rather than a joy their reappearances, courtesy of the extrajudicial activities of a person whose earlier propensities for letter-writing, petition-circulating, and street-protesting had not been forgotten. All of this inadequate appreciation for his efforts aggrieved the Fisherman and moved him to tearful complaint when he overindulged, but nevertheless the two men existed: proof that the Fisherman did what he claimed.

And while he did it—spread his net—the Fisherman also trawled for any scrap of information about an unusually tall woman with a mixed-race appearance. The test of a possible match: this woman would recognize the strange Western name of Louisa. The Fisherman never asked Serk why the woman he was seeking would have such an appearance or recognize such a strange name. But if the woman was ever encountered, the name would serve as both confirmation and message.

In exchange, Serk did any task the Fisherman gave him. He met skinny, cheaply dressed, cold-eyed younger men in crowded public markets and handed them envelopes he knew pertained to other of the tireless Fisherman's shadow activities of which by mutual agreement with the Fisherman he otherwise knew nothing. He monitored the Fisherman's multiple mobile phones, recording and conveying messages in a code to which, by mutual agreement with the Fisherman, he did not hold the key. More than any other activity, he read through the papers and listened to hours of radio news, on alert for anything relating to the Fisherman's work. In this way he relearned the world.

Just as living in the American suburbs had required learning which of Louisa's playmates had parents who smoked cigarettes, or did not supervise the use of their TVs, or provided soda as a refreshment, or harbored undisciplined dogs and incorrectly assembled swing sets, living by the seashore that summer had required learning the currents and tides. This would not have been needed had Louisa not swum, but Louisa had a passion for swimming. It was a passion Serk found deeply foreign and threatening. Swimming had been no part of Serk's boyhood. He did not view his inability to swim as a deprivation, although sometimes, watching Louisa caper and shriek in the water, a pastime that caused him shooting pains in his jaw hinges from how hard he was grinding his teeth, he could grasp the possibility of finding joy in the water, had his earliest experience included this idea. He never admitted this to Anne. To Anne he made clear that he blamed her for inculcating in their child a perverse, self-destructive desire. In Louisa's babyhood, Anne enrolled in a swim class for mothers and children who had not even started to walk, and in this class, the mothers stood in the shallow end repeatedly dunking their babies while the babies spluttered and, if they could draw the breath, screamed. Only the inhibition that overcame Serk in those settings in which he was unusually anomalous, as he was at the YMCA pool—not just the only foreigner but the only person in a suit, his shirt sticking to his sides in the chemically pungent humidity, his dress shoes slipping on the pool deck as though he were trespassing in some stranger's giant bathroom, the incessant thundering echo of screaming and splashing almost, but not quite, emboldening him to give vent to his rage on the spot—had prevented him from giving vent to his rage on the spot. He'd managed to wait until they were in the Y parking lot, chlorine-pickled Louisa unconscious in her buggy from the exhaustion of almost being drowned, before he unleashed on Anne—but Anne had planted herself on the asphalt and unleashed right back, with her razoring first-language tongue. Once home, Serk reinforced his offensive with plates, but he'd known he had already lost. There had turned out to be a few things for the sake of which Anne matched Serk's fury, and then overtopped him. Louisa's learning to swim the so-called modern way, starting in her babyhood, was one. Louisa's riding the yellow school bus with all the other neighborhood children, despite the bus being driven by an old white man it was obvious, just from looking at him, was an alcoholic and perhaps even a child-molesting former felon, was another. By the time Louisa was riding the yellow school bus, she was a "dolphin" in the YMCA swim-school hierarchy, the uppermost tier for her age.

Serk concealed his delight in this achievement of Louisa's—one of so many, each as much miracle as inevitability, given that she was such an exceptional child—as he always did, beneath whatever stern warning was apt. There was always some danger that only Serk was not such a fool as to blithely disregard. At the shore in Japan, it was

currents and tides. But Serk noticed the small local paper published a
daily tide table, pertaining to the port of Niigata an hour away; came
to understand, studying it, that it required some math to be accurate
to their location; double-checked his calculations by observing the behaviors of the town's small fishing fleet; and then was ready to teach
Louisa, as if he'd been born with his knowledge of tides. It was the
same with the currents, with anything else that made up the marine
conditions. Love, for Serk, always flowed first through authority's
channel. As he loved no one more than Louisa, there was no limit to
the topics on which he meant to be the authority for her.

On days of wind, then, there was no swimming because this was
when rip currents formed. Even when the tide was receding and the
wind was not strong, Serk would roll his pant legs to the knee and stand
guard in the water while constantly admonishing Louisa to stay close
to him. What would he have done if she'd strayed, if something—he
could not name it—had happened? Let the sand drop from under his
feet, and he was as helpless as an infant, but this was a catastrophe to
be strictly avoided rather than contemplated. His jaw-hinges throbbed
painfully. There was a breakwater of massive jagged chunks of rock
stretching out from the shore that Louisa begged to walk on, but this
was only permitted when the tide was very low and would still be
receding for several more hours—the least appealing time, Louisa argued, because no thrilling whitecaps were smashing the breakwater
then, sending handfuls of foam in one's face. Which of course was
exactly the point, Serk inflexibly lectured. He was a fiercely besotted
father. To give his child what she wanted he would gladly trample
anything or anyone—except her safety. Only in the year before they'd
come to Japan had she finally been permitted to play with arts-and-
crafts glitter, so certain was Serk she'd inhale it and end her days with
tiny motes of metal in her lungs.

And there was not merely high and low tide, like some sort of machine! The height of the tide also changed, which had to do with the
heavenly bodies. Serk was teaching Louisa astronomy, the joy of which
sometimes came in conflict with safety's imperatives, as darkness was
required to see planets and stars. Carefully, then, Serk consulted the

tides even when they would only be walking, during sunset and dusk, waiting for sufficient darkness to use the constellation wheel, flashlight ready at hand to guide them safely back to the house.

*Tonight is a spring tide*, he told her, which had nothing to do with the season. The spring tide came twice every month, with new moon and full moon, because moon, earth, and sun were all strung on a line like three beads. That extra gravity tugging the water was what made the high tide extra-high, the low tide extra-low. Tonight's spring tide was from the new moon and would not reach its peak until late, which meant conditions were perfect for stargazing, unthinkable for walking the breakwater—but this never happened once the sun had left the sky, notwithstanding the tide. Louisa knew better than to even suggest it. Armed with constellation wheel and flashlight, hand in hand, they crossed the coast road, descended the stairs, and left their rubber sandals side by side at the bottom.

A stirring that's less than a breeze moving over Serk's arms pleasantly. Louisa's left hand in his right, the sand cool on the soles of his feet. High tide, absent moon. Somewhere offshore, concealed in the featureless darkness, the sound of a motor.

The page from the *Asahi Shimbun* was still in his hand, the Fisherman was still standing there, waiting. "You okay?" the Fisherman finally said.

Lately there were times Serk suspected he'd had a small stroke. Time blinked; he startled as if from an unscheduled nap.

" '*It was an unusually high tide that night,*'" he resumed.

"You read that part already."

"Stop interrupting if you want me to translate. '*It was an unusually high tide that night, but the lovers would not have noticed even if waves splashed their feet.*'" Serk got no farther before the Fisherman let out a groan of disgust and a string of profanity.

"Don't make me puke!" the Fisherman said. "These people think we should care that a couple of horny kids disappeared from the beach just because they have '*all the joys of life ahead, not yet tasted*'? Ugh! They probably did some stupid lovers' suicide. Who cares? But they're eating it up over there—I bet it's even international news."

Serk doubted this; it was not even news in China. But the Fisherman was right that the story was becoming a minor sensation in Japan. The lovers had disappeared in the late spring of 1979, a period of numerous other disappearances that at the time had been variously attributed to drowning, suicide, voluntary flight, or the work of one or many serial killers. The vanished were some two dozen Japanese men and women with nothing in common except for having last been seen on or close to the beach. Their disappearances had been so many small local catastrophes, and there had been no reason to view them in relation to each other.

Eight years later, Korean Airlines flight 858 exploded over the Andaman Sea, killing all 115 people on board. The captured bomber, a North Korean intelligence agent, told South Korean investigators that she and her fellow agents had received language training from kidnapped Japanese civilians, including a girl who was still in her teens. Since then a few more North Korean spies had defected, and told similar stories. A lesser Japanese publication than *Asahi Shimbun* had published an exposé that was largely ignored. But with time, a growing number of the family members of missing persons had embraced the explanation that their loved ones had been abducted by North Korea. A growing percentage of the Japanese public agreed, perhaps motivated in part by resentment at Japan's emasculation since the end of the war. Having one's citizens snatched off one's beaches by spies from a neighboring dictatorship was just the kind of thing, many Japanese felt, that happened to a country that had allowed the West to disarm its military. It was those same Western nations, namely the US, of which the believers in the abductions were demanding action: if not military strikes on North Korea, then at the very least a suspension of the UN food aid.

Serk agreed with the Fisherman that it was typical of the Japanese national character to demand global mobilization on behalf of a few dozen shore residents when it was a known fact, not disputed and yet somehow just shrugged at, that the North had abducted literally thousands of South Koreans—at least this was the Fisherman's estimate, and Serk didn't dare argue with him—hundreds of times even the highest estimate of Japanese abductees, which number was generally considered absurd even by those who took the abduction stories seri-ously. But that was Japan all over, Serk continued to placate the Fisherman, whose vulgar outbursts were the outward sign of a concealed sensitivity.

"Japan: the only nation crappy enough to make North Korea look good." The Fisherman winked at Serk, referencing their particular joke. As with many jokes this one stood for far more than the hollow laugh from Serk it could reliably provoke. The joke was a form of acknowledgment, between two men whose policy was not to talk about themselves, that each had shared a painful secret with the other.

The Fisherman's secret was not the story of the loss of his father, which Serk had known since the first time they met, but his feelings about it. Very late one drunk night the Fisherman told Serk, "I know he will never come back, and that feels very lonely for me." Then, hiding his face, he had sobbed like a child.

Serk had known he must share something too. "My family chose to go there," he said after a moment.

This was sufficiently astonishing. "You!" the Fisherman cried. And then, converting his surprise to vindication, "I knew you couldn't have come from that shithole. You're too tall! You left the *South* and went *North*? You're a piece-of-shit Communist!"

Serk ignored this. "Not the South. Japan."

"You're *Japanese*?" The Fisherman must have felt that for once he'd had too much to drink. Serk's being Japanese was even worse than Serk's being a Communist.

"I'm Korean. My parents were from Jeju. They went to Japan in the war years, for work. I was born there, and my siblings. The war ended and that's where we were—the South didn't offer us citizenship. Then my parents were fed lies about North Korea. And they were poor—we were poor. We were Koreans in Japan. Think about it."

"Do you speak Japanese?"

"Why do you think my Korean's so shitty?"

"That could be very useful to me," said the Fisherman, dry-eyed now and once again scheming. Hence their project of tracking the abduction obsession, as it took hold and was reported in Japan.

Back on that night Serk continued, "I told my parents they were fools. But those fools wouldn't listen to me."

"So you went? You left Japan for the only worse place you could go?"

"We did," Serk lied, his confession having accomplished its aim. It wasn't necessary, and it was certainly not safe, to be more accurate.

Though Serk did not want to admit it, his best protection from an encounter with the local authorities was likely not the fierceness of his brow, which had distinguished his face since childhood; or the Mandarin he'd taught himself; or the equal effort he'd spent learning the city's side streets and back alleys; or even the money the Fisherman paid him, which, here as anywhere, was the key to belonging. His coat of armor was his age. Though his hair still grew over the crown of his head, it was white. Strangers sometimes addressed him as "Grandpa." He was as tall as ever—unlike in the past he would thrust out his chest to appear even taller—yet people still saw him as old.

And he felt old, not despite but because of his efforts. Memorizing his grab bag of Mandarin, learning the alleys and streets, had been unnervingly difficult for him after a lifetime spent taking the powers of his intellect for granted. Lately, when the Fisherman gave him an errand, Serk had to write down the directions in case he forgot. Most disturbing were the moments when he felt himself return from some unplanned hiatus, as if, as often happened in this city of exploding electrical use and inadequate grid, the lights in his brain had gone out.

Not long after Serk translated the "high tide" article for the Fisherman, they sat in their usual lunch restaurant watching the news. The cook, as he worked, watched as well, although the story had been playing for days. Everyone in this region as well as the world—in America, even—had seen it already. A woman tried to scale a white stucco wall while a second woman jumped up and down anxiously with a toddler-age girl in her arms. Men in dark suits descended on them, followed by Chinese police. Two police yanked the first woman down off the wall, two others tackled the second woman so the toddler flew out of her arms. One of the police lost his hat in the scrum, one of the dark-suited men plucked the hat off the ground. With a discordant fastidiousness that afterward caused almost as much of an uproar as the acts of assault on the women and child, the dark-suited man restored the cap to the policeman. At that point the recording camera had been toppled by forces unseen.

The news anchors reappeared to reiterate all the same information as if it were new, at machine-gun velocity: after being prevented from scaling the wall of the Japanese Embassy in Shenyang, the two women and toddler girl, all illegal North Korean migrants to China, remained in Chinese police custody. The two North Korean men who had successfully scaled the wall, leaving the women and child behind, had been removed by Chinese police from the embassy grounds and were also in custody. The government of Japan vigorously objected to this violation of its sovereignty by China, which vigorously objected to this anti-China rhetoric from Japan. According to China the Japanese consular officials had requested Chinese police protection from the invading North Koreans—had no one noticed the Japanese official's grateful gesture in restoring to the jostled Chinese policeman his hat? Judging from the global news coverage, the world community had noticed this, just as it had noticed the toddler being hurled through the air. The cook made a sound of disgust with his tongue as he flipped Serk's and the Fisherman's lunch specials onto their plates. "Scum," the Fisherman said around a mouthful of food. He meant all the governments involved—Japanese, Chinese, and South Korean, the North Korean government's ultimate responsibility being so obvious as to be beneath mention. South Korea had offered asylum to the five North Koreans, but only after the footage of the desperate women and child had been broadcast around the world, and only if China released them, which South Korea knew that China would not do, as it didn't want to antagonize North Korea. Japan had called the Chinese police rather than accept the North Koreans, because it didn't want to antagonize China. South Korea didn't want to antagonize its neighbors, either, but found the assets in this case greater than the liabilities. "They don't give a damn about their own citizens being kidnapped—

they call them Communists who ran away!—but now they're playing savior because the whole world is watching. And because of the kid."

Serk steadily emptied his plate. He hoped never to see the footage again, but it was sure to replay in a couple of minutes.

"Sons of bitches," the Fisherman continued. By this he meant the two North Korean men who had flung themselves into the embassy ahead of the women and child. They'd gotten what they deserved. "You know, they chose the Japanese Embassy because the wall is so low. They thought the women had more chance to get over. And they would have, if those shit-brained men had stayed behind and given them a boost." After another few moments of Serk's silence, the Fisherman added, to lighten the mood, "The wall's so low at the Japanese consulate even an old man like you could get over."

"They'd throw me right back out again." If Serk had ever doubted this was true, he didn't doubt it any longer. Being thrown right back out, like the innocent child, might even be too much to hope for. He was hopelessly tainted, by his family's long association, while in Japan, with the pro–North Korean Organization; by their voluntary repatriation; and even by his abduction itself, which would never be believed for what it had been, but called the cover story of a North Korean spy. Even the Reverend had never fully put to rest his suspicions of Serk, although he'd sought him out not long ago to say goodbye. The Reverend had lost another colleague in the rescue-mission business to murder, likely by North Korean agents, and had finally decided to put self-interest first. He and Mrs. Reverend had gone back to Seoul.

At Serk's comment the Fisherman hooted with glee. "They would! Filthy Communist swine that you are: they'd dump you in a sack, tie it closed, and kick your commie ass back where it came from."

Somehow, Serk had spent five years in this place. All his worlds were gone. The America he had called home—how had he failed to realize his good luck? The absence of welcome he'd been deluded enough to resent he retrospectively saw for the prosperity it had offered and would never renew. That place was gone also—vanished behind the luxuriant black billows of smoke he and the Fisherman had watched together on this very same grease-darkened TV in September of the previous year.

Despite Serk's resentment, America had in fact welcomed strangers,
however coldly, like those women on the block where they'd moved
when Louisa was five, who used to invite Anne for something called
Tupperware parties, and then not address a word to her as she sat sip-
ping coffee and feeling obliged to buy some piece of plastic before she
could leave. And yet, that had been invitation, however unfriendly. Unwelcome though Serk had felt, he'd been granted a visa. That grudging
American trust in outsiders was now officially retracted, and little as he
liked Americans, Serk sympathized. He couldn't trust anyone, either.
Even the Fisherman still didn't know who he was, nor who "Louisa"
might be—although year after year, true to his nickname, the Fisherman baited the nets of his far-flung network with "Louisa." Year after
year, Serk concealed his despair as the nets came back empty.

That September, one year after the attack on America, came an
equal shock, at least in his part of the world. The North Korean leader
not only received an official visit from the Japanese Prime Minister
but also acknowledged the abduction, more than twenty years earlier,
by North Korean intelligence agents, of exactly thirteen Japanese civilians. Eight sadly had died, but five were looking forward to visiting
their surviving family in Japan, to share with them details of their lives
in the socialist paradise. The five would be accompanied on their visit
to Japan by North Korean government escorts, would be unaccompa-
nied by their North Korea–born children, and would return promptly
to North Korea, after which the matter of their so-called abduction—
and anyone else's—would be considered officially closed. No further
so-called abductions of citizens of Japan or of any other nation would
receive Japanese advocacy or North Korean acknowledgment. Also,
Japan would apologize to North Korea for its many imperial crimes,
as well as give North Korea a generous package of low-interest loans
and humanitarian aid. The two leaders smiled and shook hands for the
cameras.

The Fisherman had his head in his arms, so that Serk could not
make out his exact imprecations, which was not necessary. His curses
were all directed at the Japanese Prime Minister. The North Korean
leader's villainy went without saying. "It's over," the Fisherman said

when he finally uncovered his face. Serk was not surprised to see the other man crying, but he was surprised to be crying, himself. "The story is over—that's what they've decided. The whole world can shrug and say, *This was resolved. Ji-hoon got his dad back*. But I didn't!"

Serk was glad his own tears were unnoticed. He was not good at offering comfort, but suspected he would be even worse at receiving it, if it were ever to come. He clapped a hand on the other man's shoulder.

"You'll keep going," he said.

# Ji-hoon

**Ji-hoon set the meeting** to take place in one of the several lunch restaurants he felt secure enough to use as an office, knowing the staff was watching out for him, and of course he'd only given the American his "Fisherman" sobriquet. But these security measures were more gestural than actual. If it turned out the man couldn't be trusted, the damage would already be done. It had been over a year since Ji-hoon had first begun trying to establish a safe contact within the US diplomatic community.

The man he was meeting today had actually contacted Ji-hoon first, through an American reporter who'd done a human-interest story about Ji-hoon's lifelong quest to recover South Korean abductees and embarrass the South Korean government for its inaction. The story had been so flattering Ji-hoon had even permitted a photographer from the paper to take his picture, in his closet-size "office," backgrounded by the dozens of photos of lost loved ones in the center of which was his appa. Later he'd scolded himself for this vanity, because the last thing he needed was for the Chinese authorities to have an up-to-date photo that showed them how fat he'd become. But in truth he had sat for that photo because he wanted his appa's face in the paper. A photo of a photo, in which his appa is so young that at this point he could be Ji-hoon's son. When the article ran, he cut out the photo of the two of them to add it to the wall, but first he showed it to its subject. "Check us out, Appa!" he said, holding the newspaper photo up to his appa's portrait's eye level. "You and me, in a photo together!" Was he losing his mind, like his friend?

The reporter had called knowing that Ji-hoon was pleased with the article's slant and likely willing to do a favor in return. But he couldn't have known that the person on whose behalf he was calling was exactly the kind of person Ji-hoon had been looking for. Of course, Ji-hoon didn't betray this. "It's really sticking my neck out to meet with some American government guy," he told the reporter. "They're always fucking me over with the South Koreans. And depending on their angle they'll even fuck me over with the Chinese. Did you notice I answered my phone? That's only possible if I stay out of prison."

"He's not actively in government, although he's well connected there. But he's not working on their behalf."

"How well connected is 'well connected'?" Ji-hoon persisted in a complaining tone, as if he didn't in fact hope the guy was well connected enough for his own purposes.

"You have it on my word he won't compromise you."

"What good is your word? You're a fucking reporter!"

"Thanks a lot!" The reporter was laughing because he and Ji-hoon had good rapport. "Why not say what you *actually* think?" And so the meeting was set, and now Ji-hoon was waiting and as usual worrying—not about the meeting, but about the friend for whose sake he was having the meeting, whom in Fisherman-ese he had nicknamed the Crab. Crabs have hard shells, as his friend did, and snap threateningly, as his friend did, but mostly, in Ji-hoon's opinion, crabs despite their armor and weaponry are excessively wary and easily startled. At the least sound or movement, they scuttle away, and so he'd been watching his friend do for years—until recently.

When the change in his friend first began, Ji-hoon told himself it was more of his friend's touchiness—he had always been quite the crustacean. But then the Crab was thrown out by his landlord for not paying rent, though the wage he earned was more than adequate, a fact Ji-hoon knew because he paid it himself. When he asked the Crab—dodging scissor-like claws—why he hadn't paid rent, his friend replied that he'd lost all his money. He hadn't meant due to gambling or some stupid investment. He had literally lost every coin—hidden it all for safekeeping and then, less like a crab than a squirrel in winter, forgotten where the hiding place was.

After Ji-hoon moved the Crab in with him—less out of kindness than self-preservation, because along with forgetfulness the Crab had gained a previously highly uncharacteristic tendency to say whatever came into his head—had come the many nights on which Ji-hoon's sleep, fitful at best, was destroyed by the Crab flinging open the door separating their bedrooms, usually around three in the morning.

"Who's in here?" he would yell, never less terrifying for how familiar the scene would become.

"It's me, Ji-hoon, you maniac!" Ji-hoon would yell, while struggling to turn on a lamp. It could take fifteen minutes or more of shouting and confusion and inchoate accusation before the Crab's eyes clouded over, not with recognition but with irritation.

"Why all this yelling?" he would demand then. "I'm going to bed."

And more and more often, he spoke English—a language Ji-hoon had not even known he possessed. "You're a class-A motherfucker," he told Ji-hoon one day. Ji-hoon's English was more than adequate to this universal insult, but not to the long diatribe that followed.

"Where did you learn such good English?" he asked in Korean when the speech had wound down.

Apparently misunderstanding Ji-hoon's question as specific to "class-A motherfucker," the Crab, returning to Korean, answered, "My American wife called me that when she got really angry."

"Your American wife who you fuck in your dreams?" had been Ji-hoon's reply. He was not proud of this; he had been very tired, as it seemed that he always was tired, now that he lived with a madman who disrupted his sleep on most nights. But Ji-hoon still was not prepared for what the Crab had said next, after gazing down on him at length and unapologetically from his superior height.

"Fucking Koreans. I went to the States to get away from you people."

This quelled Ji-hoon's remorse for his crude comment about the dream-wife. "Oh yeah? Let's see your passport, American big shot. Let's get you back on a plane to, what, Hollywood? Back to your mansion?"

"I never had a passport, I had a US green card. I was a permanent resident," the Crab surprisingly parried.

"Of course, a US green card—that's why you're stuck here in China, working under the table for me. Hand it over, let's see what it looks like. Is it green like their money?"

"How the fuck could I have it?" the Crab yelled. "When I have nothing? When even my child is gone!" And then, most shocking of all to Ji-hoon—despite that his life's vocation might be poetically described as an ocean of tears, in tribute to the ocean that had taken his appa, and from which his nickname of the Fisherman came—the Crab folded into a heap, and sobbed for so long and so loudly that Ji-hoon feared his limbs would rust in that position, and fall into pieces, and each of the pieces to dust.

Ji-hoon would never know if it was the loosening of mental bonds that had clearly begun, or if it was Ji-hoon's subsequent efforts—the tiptoeing questions he started to ask, always in the mornings, when the Crab was most lucid and calm—or if, as was most likely, it was both of these processes working together, but however it happened, Ji-hoon eventually learned a new story of who the Crab was. It was a story he could hardly believe.

It was also a story it would be difficult to make anyone else believe. Because the Crab had been born in Japan to Korean parents left stateless after the end of the Japanese empire, he had never had Japanese citizenship; and he'd vanished from his life in the US while only holding a green card that would have expired years ago, even if he hadn't been declared dead. How to corroborate his tale without exposing his existence to authorities in China, who would sooner throw him back to the DPRK, and from there to a prison-camp grave, was a forbidding challenge even for a professional fixer, as the Fisherman considered himself. Still, Ji-hoon wept that the Crab hadn't trusted him sooner, so that they could sooner have tried. "Why didn't you tell me?" he asked, although he knew the answer. Why, apart from the onset of senility, did the Crab trust Ji-hoon even now, in this place where trust was almost always a mistake? Ji-hoon himself had never trusted the Crab; he'd used him, as he used everyone from whom he extracted a service in exchange for the least payment they would accept. And the Crab had been using him, also. "My daughter," the Crab began, and at last Ji-hoon knew who the mysterious "Louisa" had been. Unable to finish his sentence, the Crab put his face in his hands.

"Wherever she is," Ji-hoon said, "it's time to save yourself while you still can."

After this, the floodgates opened. Perhaps it would have happened in any case, as the Crab's brain continued to change. But Ji-hoon couldn't help feeling that after years of a battle Ji-hoon couldn't imagine except to know it was lonely, the Crab had surrendered. The lost life drifted in more and more, obscuring the present like fog. Two words recurred: *school* and *home*. Both words provoked great agitation, as if to reprimand the Crab with duties undone. "I need to get to school," he would tell Ji-hoon, pacing here and there in the tiny apartment as if he could no longer locate the door. At first Ji-hoon would say to this, reasonably, "You don't go to school—you're old! You're all done! It's okay!," imagining that perhaps the Crab suffered from that universal nightmare, of some final exam in some class he hadn't known he was taking. Even Ji-hoon still dreamed this sometimes. But one day, instead of greeting Ji-hoon's nice reassurance with disregard, the Crab wheeled on him and shouted, "You think you're funny, dumbshit? You won't be laughing when you fail!"

Oh, so the Crab taught the class? The Crab had never told Ji-hoon what he'd done for work in his previous life, but now that he said this, many of the past episodes emerged as a pattern. "What class do you teach?" Ji-hoon tried.

"Same damn one as always, introductory shit with these assholes who don't know anything!"

"Oh, that one?" Ji-hoon performed recognition. "I just heard: that one is canceled today."

"What, it's snowing?"

"Snowed all night. All the classes are canceled."

Sometimes Ji-hoon almost felt he could watch the idea pattering down, sinking in, fog transformed into rain slowly melting away. The pacing would slow, stop. The Crab would hover a moment, immobile.

"Are we having lunch, or what?" he would finally say.

More often, it was the women: the wife Anne and the daughter Louisa. "I must go home," the Crab might beg urgently when he burst through the door in the night, it seemed always the instant after Ji-hoon had finally gotten to sleep. "We have to go, come on!" The Crab would snatch up any item of clothing of Ji-hoon's, even pants, and yank it over his arms in the role of a coat. "Anne is angry when dinner gets cold! Louisa has school tomorrow!"

Ji-hoon had learned that at moments like this there was no reminding the Crab of his real situation. Instead, Ji-hoon would say something like, "I told Anne you'd be late and it's fine! She's not angry. She'll warm up the dinner."

"She'll *warm* it?" That had perhaps been a detail too many. But then it seemed that in fact, this was the detail that pinned down the rest. The Crab stopped tugging on his "coat." "She hates cooking because she isn't good at it, and this makes her get offended easily," he observed.

"Women," Ji-hoon commiserated cautiously.

"But Louisa is going to bed—"

"That's right! And we can't disturb her! That's why we're going first thing in the morning."

"The first thing in the morning?"

"What time is it—three twenty-five? We're going at seven. So you should go get your rest."

"You know how to get there?" The Crab's eyes were narrow, suspicious.

"The number of times that I've taken you there, and you still think I can't remember?" Ji-hoon yelled, with no need to fake his exasperation. If he was lucky, the Crab would turn on his heel and go back to bed without so much as closing the door he'd thrown open. Ji-hoon would close it and pray for peace until morning.

Because the periods of slipping away to the past alternated with periods in which the Crab was perfectly lucid—and seemed to have no memory of his time travel—at first this playacting made Ji-hoon feel cruel and even afraid. He feared the Crab might also be playacting and would at any moment reveal his true self and castigate Ji-hoon for treating him like a fool. But the more often they repeated these scenes, the more Ji-hoon could see that the Crab was his true self at these times. The playacting came to seem necessary, perhaps even a sign of respect.

Recently, the fog moved with ever greater speed and stealth, and then the weather would change mid-conversation and even mid-sentence. Ji-hoon would watch the Crab switching his selves as easily as he switched from Japanese to Korean to English. "Don't be such a pig," he said to Ji-hoon one day as they were grabbing a lunch at their usual place. "How many times has Mother told you to slow down? You're not at a trough."

"Sorry, Dad," Ji-hoon tried, watching the Crab's face to see what would happen. But his friend didn't even glance at him, only cocked an eyebrow with scorn, eyes still on the TV.

"Even when Louisa was a baby she wasn't as messy as you," was his verdict.

So it wasn't Louisa's mother who would not like the way Ji-hoon ate. Ji-hoon realized that, as adept as he'd become in changing masks for the Crab's shifting stories, at the same time he'd grown more aware of the depth of his ignorance. He sometimes wondered if the identity the Crab had revealed to him was even real, or just another cover story. And if it was a cover story, was the Crab lying to Ji-hoon on purpose, or had the Crab, in his fogs, permanently lost track of himself? Ji-hoon felt himself being enveloped by a fog of his own, in which anxiety, paranoia, sleep deprivation, and a keen sense of time running out were equally mixed. It was into this miasma that the call from the reporter had come.

The reporter's acquaintance looked exactly the way Ji-hoon, who considered himself an experienced realist, expected a CIA agent to look: not the movie version in a dark suit and mirrored sunglasses but the version who actually believes he won't be made for an agent because he has a slight paunch and is dressed like a tourist, complete with fanny pack and pricey hiking shoes. After thanking Ji-hoon for his time and going on too long about the restaurant's noodles, which weren't anything special, the CIA guy told Ji-hoon that he was investigating the disappearance of an American student who'd last been seen hiking in the mountains of southwestern China, a mere three thousand miles from where they were sitting. The CIA guy laid a photograph on the table and Ji-hoon saw an unlined Western male face, porridge-cheeked and generic. Ji-hoon could have stared at the picture for decades and not remembered what the kid looked like. "He will have aged since this was taken," CIA added, ridiculously. If Ji-hoon couldn't remember the face while staring at it, it wasn't likely he could envision its future. But, playing along, he asked:

"By how much?"

"Six years. This photo was taken shortly before the last time he was seen."

"This kid disappeared six years ago and you're still looking for him? Maybe it's time to give up."

"You haven't given up on your father."

"Wow," Ji-hoon said after a moment. "That felt unkind."

"I meant no disrespect. Quite the opposite: You're tenacious. That's why I wanted to speak."

"I can tell that you read your friend's article. I think he used the same word."

"It was a good article. How's it played out for you, pro and con?"

"It's nice to be a sad story that someone might read while they're drinking a coffee and then never think of again."

"It had to be helpful publicity."

"Sure. Now the Chinese know I've gained fifty pounds and I'm losing my hair."

"And the world knows that the South Koreans would rather protect their relationship with a rogue nation in the interests of reunification than protect their own citizens."

"Your friend the reporter would fall over laughing if he heard what you said. His paper's circulation is a pretty minuscule fraction of 'the world.' And the South Koreans don't want reunification. They just don't want a nuclear missile in the middle of Seoul."

"The South Koreans want to project to certain audiences the image that they're pursuing reunification."

"Okay, I'll accept that analysis. It's just like how you guys want to project the image that every American life is sacred and worth sending out some CIA guy to show a kid's picture to an unaffiliated South Korean good Samaritan most people think is either crazy or a self-promoting jerk. Why aren't you talking to the Chinese authorities? Shouldn't they help you out?"

"I'm not CIA," said the CIA guy, as of course he would. "And I agree with you, but obviously their help hasn't been helpful enough, because he's still missing."

"So you guys can't pressure them to give more helpful help? An American kid who disappears teaching English in China? I figure you government guys would have, like, the Navy SEALs on that one."

"Like our mutual friend already told you, I'm not a government official. I'm retired—"

"So you were CIA!"

"I wasn't, but I know my way around the US government, which is why I'm trying to help the family."

"You know your Mandarin, which is how I know you're a spy—I hear you guys get great language training. Your Mandarin's better than mine."

"I learned my Mandarin as an undergraduate. And my former government service isn't really the point."

"I'm disappointed," Ji-hoon admitted. "I always wanted to meet an American CIA agent."

"The reason I wanted to meet you is that there are circumstances with this disappearance that have made the US government be less helpful than they could have been. Just like their Chinese counterparts. Both sides have closed their investigations. They say he fell into a gorge, on his hike. But the family don't think this conclusion is supported by evidence, and neither do I. The body has never been found."

"Doesn't that happen, though? Gorges are deep."

"And he was last seen on the far side of the gorge from where he started. By multiple eyewitnesses."

"So he must have gone back in the gorge."

"But that wasn't the direction he was traveling. He had plane tickets home from the city where he was last seen, but he never showed up at the airport. Also"—and here the man paused and Ji-hoon knew he was going to lay down his cards—"the place where he was last seen in that city was a Korean restaurant with known ties to North Korea."

"Wow, the Case of the Korean Restaurant. This restaurant we're sitting in has ties to North Korea. Those guys who cooked your lunch are North Koreans, just doing their best to survive."

"I mean the restaurant has ties to the regime. It's state-owned. Its employees are North Koreans under strict government supervision. Its profits are all remitted back to North Korea. That's the place this young man was last seen."

"So what? There's loads of North Korea–owned businesses here. Those Pyongyang elites love to vacuum up the foreign currency. Those restaurants want tourist dollars—they're not going to kill some tourist kid and put him in the soup."

"You've spent practically your whole life trying to bring attention to these kinds of disappearances. You know I don't think this young man got put in the soup." The bland-faced vanished young man who was not thought to be in the soup gazed up at Ji-hoon from between two plates of half-eaten noodles. After a pause the man added, "Within a month of his disappearance, the eyewitnesses all changed their stories."

"What did they change them to?"

"That they weren't sure if this was really the young man they'd seen. That maybe it was some other young white male American tourist. Clearly someone had gotten to them."

Ji-hoon didn't want to say that uncertainty on the part of the eyewitnesses about whether a generic white man they had seen was the generic white man in the photo seemed perfectly plausible to him and not necessarily the result of a threat or a payoff. Ever since the DPRK's acknowledgment back in 2002 of the thirteen abductees from Japan, the whole story had changed, as Ji-hoon had feared, but not quite in the way he'd predicted. Ji-hoon's deepest fear had been that the remaining abductees would be as good as forgotten, at least by the powers that might have helped them, and this had indeed come to pass. But at the same time, a different subset of people had taken up the idea with fervor. These were ordinary people, without power, who had loved ones who had disappeared without explanation. These bereaved people might be as far-flung as Zagreb or London or even America, but they'd come to share the same bleak conviction, that their vanished loved one had been abducted by North Korea. Certain as Ji-hoon was that his father, and hundreds of other South Koreans, and a large number of Japanese, and maybe even the Crab, had been abducted to North Korea, Ji-hoon very much doubted that so many other unexplained disappearances in other parts of the world could be explained in this way. But nor did he like to cast doubt on such claims, for the obvious reasons, and especially now, as he was waiting for the right moment to ask this man's help in the case of the Crab.

"Are you this kid's uncle or grandpa or something?" Ji-hoon asked tactfully.

The man sighed and palmed his pale pink scalp through its mesh of gray hair. "My identity should not be the mystery here. My name is Roger, I'm from a place called New Hampshire, my career was in the Asia bureau of the State Department until I retired and got involved in human rights. I'm trying to help this man's family because they haven't gotten the support that they should have—from the Chinese government or our own."

"Like you said to me before, I mean no disrespect, but my dad's abduction by the North Koreans isn't an idea that I had to come up with to make myself feel better about losing him. They sent us the proof—they staged it as propaganda. Nothing's telling me that's what happened to your guy—some kid on a hike more than three thousand miles from the DPRK. His being abducted by North Koreans is literally the least plausible explanation. What about, thugs murdered him and did a great job of hiding his body? Or tigers ate him? Or he met some gorgeous girl and ran away?"

"It's always hard to imagine," Roger said, "when it isn't your own situation."

Here was the transition Ji-hoon needed. "That's well put and true. I'm really not sure I can help, but I'll try. And maybe you can also help me, or actually a friend that I'm trying to help. His situation is also hard to imagine."

"I hope we can both help each other. I'd appreciate if you put the word out through your contacts, and see if something comes back. Any mention of a person like this in the DPRK."

"Just don't get your hopes up. If your guy's in the DPRK, he would never come into contact with the kinds of people in contact with me. My people are poor and they're criminals, to put it bluntly. Your American white guy? He'll be in a VIP cage in Pyongyang. If the state-run media haven't released a video of him praising the socialist paradise, I think you have to conclude they don't have him."

"Maybe there are rumors. Maybe that video is reserved for the party elite but the word has leaked out. We'll be grateful for any effort you make. This kid is a son, with a dad and a mom." He didn't need to say, *Just like you.*

They'd finished eating and their plates had been taken off the table and thrown in the restaurant's sink. Roger picked up the kid's photograph and put it back in the envelope it had come out of—the kid's face disappearing instantly from Ji-hoon's mind as he'd known that it would. As if reading these thoughts, Roger then removed a smaller copy of the photo from the same envelope and gave it to Ji-hoon—wallet-size, like Ji-hoon might carry if his life were ever normal, if he ever gave up and went back to Korea, and met some woman who didn't mind that he was middle-aged and fat and drank and swore too much, but loved him despite this, and married him and gave birth to his children, a responsible older girl and an irresponsible but irresistible younger boy, of whom people said, rolling their eyes but with affection, *He's just like his father,* and the two children, who adored each other, posed for a photo,

the boy chipmunk-cheeked and crazily grinning and the girl smirking
at him in knowing bemusement with her hands on his shoulders, and
Ji-hoon put the picture in his wallet to carry with him everywhere and
to show anyone who stood still even after the children were grown.

Ji-hoon took the picture of the porridge-faced young American
man and put that into his wallet instead.

"Now tell me about this other situation that's hard to imagine."

Even after Roger gave him his cue, and even though this moment was the reason he'd agreed to meet Roger at all, Ji-hoon suddenly couldn't find words. They had to be enough and could not be
too much. And they had to succeed. He had to have this man's help.
He was suddenly as afraid as if it was his own life he was asking this
stranger to save.

"I know a man here," he finally said. "He walked out of North
Korea with only the clothes on his back. He didn't even have shoes.
He says he's an ethnic Korean who was born in Japan. And he says he
had a US green card and a wife and a daughter. And he says the North
Koreans kidnapped him and his daughter, I'm not even sure how long
ago but my guess is the late seventies."

"How were their disappearances reported?"

"I have no idea."

"If he's here, what about the daughter?"

"I also don't know. He says she was taken there with him, but after
that he never saw her again. Just like you asked me to put out the word
about your guy, I've been putting the word out for years about her. I've
never heard anything back."

"Do you have any other details?"

"Even what I've told you, I'm not sure I have right. Because he's
going senile. But I'm certain he isn't just dreaming."

"Do you have a photo?"

Just a few days before, he had gotten himself a new phone and was
trying its camera. The Crab had been sitting across from him at this
same restaurant, staring up at the TV as if staring not outward, but
inward, and into an infinite distance—as if something like the void of
outer space lay behind his mind's eye, and he was traveling that vastness

and finding it teeming with interest, not empty at all. Glancing up from his phone, Ji-hoon had seen the old Crab in this state and been shocked by a sob taking shape in his throat, which he forcefully swallowed and later suffered as indigestion. That was the moment he had taken the photo, the Crab staring half into and half through the camera, never noticing he had been captured.

Roger studied the photo far longer, Ji-hoon felt guiltily, than he had studied the porridge-faced kid. Then they exchanged their numbers and shook hands. Each man's errand for the other was so impossible, Ji-hoon doubted if they'd ever meet again. But one never knew what chance meeting might change everything.

# Part VI

# Louisa

**The beach quickly grows** wider and wilder. It does not take long for the little town to be left behind them, kept back by the rocky black headland that also forces the coastal road inland, so that there are no lights at all but the stars. An end-of-the-earth sensation, but easily obtained. Easily cast off, if you're feeling afraid. Simply turning around shows the lights of the little town right at one's back, sparsely curving away in the shape of a hook. Ten minutes of brisk, cheerful walking, or fifteen minutes of crabby foot-dragging, will return them to the small rented house across the small coastal road, where her mother may still be sitting, looking out toward the restless dark sea from the faint pool of light that is cast by the bulb screwed in over the door. That very bulb recedes, blurs, joins its light with the other small lights of the town as one walks away from it, but it's never entirely gone, even after you can't pick it out anymore. The light of weak bulbs, no less than the light of the stars, just keeps going forever, a fact one accepts. Some of the stars they can see, once they've entered the zone of darkness, may be dead, this light of theirs a transmission made eons ago. Similarly, the porch light being battered by moths, under which possibly sits her mother—unless her mother, too tired, has gotten in bed—may become visible in the future to extraterrestrials, those queasy fetusy beings of light from *Close Encounters of the Third Kind*. But with no thought of such creepy intrusions she capers on the cold, clammy sand in the near-perfect darkness. Her father points out constellations. As usual, they're alone on the beach. Their habit of walking at sunset, of staying out on the beach to view stars, is probably viewed by the people in town as American, pointless but harmless.

Her father was born in Japan, but he left here a long time ago to become an American. There wasn't enough opportunity here for somebody like him. Even in America, he had to compromise. He would have liked to have been an astronomer. Perhaps she will do this, and discover unknown galaxies. This is one of his many quashed dreams he would like to bestow.

Since they've come to Japan, particularly since they've come to this town, he bestows more and more. He tells things as they walk. If she can even remember how things were before, they weren't like this at all. But nothing was like this at all. Their past selves aren't better or worse, just completely discredited.

The figures materialize from the dark, a confusing nebula of heads and limbs obscurely visible against the stars. She hears their shoes grinding into the coarse sand—like her and her father, they're walking close to the surf, below the recent high-tide line, so that the sand on which they tread is firm and wet. She is barefoot, dressed in a skirt her mother sewed her last fall that's already too short, a rather ugly pink plaid frilly blouse they bought here in Japan because she's already outgrown most of the clothes they'd expected to last her the year. Her father, as always, is wearing a white Hanes T-shirt and loose khakis he's rolled to mid-shin. They've left their rubber sandals fifteen minutes behind them, on the stairs that lead down from the top of the seawall. They've no more hesitated to do this than to leave the front door of their house standing open all day for the breeze, than to walk on the beach at night looking at stars. The figures materialize so abruptly there's no time to comment on them, no time even to count them, before they pass by. She feels her father grab her hand as she turns to look over her shoulder. The town's lights are behind them, they are not at all far from the town. Outlined against that relative brightness are four figures, bulky as if overdressed for the warm summer night. Her father has pulled her around in an arc as if he means to strike out back toward town farther up from the surf. Then one of the figures says something, calls it out in a high tone that might be of warning, or offense, or just confusion. Her father stops short, though still gripping her hand. Her father asks a question in return, his voice gone strange to her, alone and disembodied in the dark. He's speaking some language she's never heard him use before and doesn't recognize.

As if in answer, the figures close the gap, and she feels her father's hand torn from hers, a damp pad clapped over her mouth. She is just ten years old: screams come easily to her, screams of joy or indignation or pain; her parents are sometimes annoyed that she screams for no reason. She screams now, unthinking and possessed. The pad, which smells and feels like a bandage clapped over her mouth, keeps the screams in, keeps the air out, she struggles raggedly for breath and gets a taste that makes her gag. The bellowing noise of her smothered screams or perhaps they are her father's smothered screams goes on without her, as do the rapid, dull sounds, like a rain of rocks into the sand, the gasping and urgent exchanges, disagreements, exhortations, her own arms and legs melting away, warm helplessness consuming her fingers and toes like a stain. She's stuffed in a sack, hears the swift ripping noise of a zipper. Now she finds her voice again and she screams for her father and even her mother, or perhaps she's not screaming at all but just dreaming of it, while her outraged throat and tongue and lips struggle to be understood.

* * *

These are not events Louisa recalls as she lies on the futon sofa in the midday twilight of the Seochon apartment, as close as she can get to the laboring air-conditioning unit, which hums and groans and clicks as it exhales its barely cool air into the room, reminding her of a dragon with its rumbling sentience and its vents that ripple constantly like gills. These are not the events Louisa recalls because she has never recalled them, they live nowhere in memory. If she was somehow aware of these events that she isn't aware of, she might wonder if the events, housed nowhere in her memory, buried in some unremembering stratum of her body or perhaps expelled like noxious vapors into the impersonal air, can even be said to have happened. Are events that are forgotten by all the participants, or that weren't admitted to cognition in the first place, something other than events, or are they nothing? Do the witnesses make the event? Louisa didn't stay in school long enough to discover philosophy. She did not possess any events to fill the space between stepping with her father onto the damp sand and waking up in a hospital bed. From somewhere outside her had come a continuous story of falling and drowning or falling and somehow not drowning. Even when she tries to pursue memories that seem certain, they morph. Even the stepping onto damp sand with her father may not be an admissible point on the timeline. That tactile memory of coolness on the soles of her feet may have been lifted from any of the other summer nights of her childhood when they did this, or any beach walks of her whole lifetime since. The brain excels at storing such tactile sensations and recapitulating them on request. She has been told, in one of her many therapies, to conjure the sensation of damp sand on her foot soles, and has found she can do it with ease. The story of her father's death by drowning is one she somehow both authored and received passively. It emerged in response to a logic and it equally dictated logic. Now the rupture of its invalidation has left a void she can't fill. She lived and he lived, and their shared history is a blank. It's not even a rewritten timeline or even a line. Louisa wonders what shapes lives might take when a change takes away all the points representing events and all the lines forming stories. All this change is unthinkable, is as far as her thinking on this has progressed.

What she's instead thinking about, as she lies on the sofa of the Seochon apartment, is the challenge of forming the sounds of Korean with lips and tongue—even throat, jaw, and cheek—that have so long enjoyed the imprecision of English. During the months-long diplomatic logjam, as Seoul began to emerge as the most likely place for reunion, she found a Korean tutor and began taking twice-a-week classes. The tutor is young enough to be the daughter she never had, but she's found herself falling for the girl's ardent praise of her efforts, found herself blushing with pride as Heejin crows over her ability to pronounce the different *ooo*s and *uh*s and *oh*s with consistent accuracy, has even caught herself indulging in completely uncharacteristic flashes of race-pride, of amenability to the idea that a facility for Korean vowels is in her blood. This is the language her father apparently discarded to the back of his linguistic closet before she was ever his child, a language he possessed in its totality and never bothered to use. In two months of lessons she's learned the alphabet and a handful of greetings she knows she'll never utter. Compared to her prior knowledge of Korean it's enough to make her feel like a virtuoso, this dinky bit of recent learning, as insignificant a fraction of Korean as the fraction representing her knowledge of her father to whatever the whole. The sum of the things she knows about her father could fit inside the sum of the things she'll never know about him an infinite number of times. The things she knows about him are as meager as a pair of backgammon dice rattling in their cup.

The Seochon apartment belongs to a man named Charse Kim, whom Louisa is unlikely to meet. Charse Kim is a colleague of some kind of Roger's in the world of not-quite-extragovernmental diplomatic fixing. Charse Kim resides in the US but owns this apartment, which he has loaned Roger, and Roger has loaned Louisa, so that Louisa need not stay at a hotel. Charse Kim interests Louisa because of his name spelling; according to Heejin, this name spelling is not uncommon due to the popularity of the name Charles among a certain generation of Koreans, whose rendering of the name in the Korean alphabet often results in this alternate spelling when translated back into English. Louisa is fascinated by this detail and has taught herself to write Charse Kim's name in Hangul, which has led her to feel that the standard English spelling of the name is in fact unjustifiably bizarre. Louisa is aware, remotely, that she is in shock; that perhaps she has been in shock for four-fifths of her life. Louisa's favorite of her therapies doesn't believe in talking about past events at all, but rather in performing mundane acts of self-distraction and self-soothing, for example imagining the sensation of damp sand on the soles of one's feet, or handwriting the name "Charse Kim" in Korean alphabet letters, or

lying beneath an air conditioner on a very hot and humid day in a foreign city to which one has traveled on an unimaginable errand, and so
these are the things Louisa is doing, ten hours after her flight landed
at Incheon at 5:00 a.m. local time. In another half hour Charse Kim's
colleague Roger—whom Louisa has come to know interestingly if
not well through years of incredibly permutating bureaucratic processes and intergovernmental standoffs—will arrive at the Seochon
apartment in a taxi, and he and Louisa will ride in the taxi to the National Medical Center hospital. Louisa's husband, her grown sons, her
brother and his wife, even her aunt Soonja, all have assented to her
request that she do this alone; for some reason, her greatest fear is not
seeing her father, but being seen while seeing him. *No press*, she had
told Roger—an easy enough thing for Roger to arrange, given the host
government's eagerness for their role in the reunion to remain unknown lest this antagonize their most volatile neighbor, North Korea,
their most powerful neighbor, China, and their own citizenry. Even
the nurses on the ward are not aware of anything unusual in their
new patient's background, and once Roger has seen Louisa through
the hospital's various burcaucracies as he has seen her through every
other kind of bureaucracy, he will vanish to some nearby bar; he will
leave her alone.

Then she is sitting in the taxi next to Roger, gazing out at the Seochon streets transformed from the inert predawn twilight in which she
saw them on arrival. The narrow, nonsensically bending and sloping
streets and sidewalks teem with activity, pedestrians of all ages bound
or stride or shuffle along with bags of all kinds hung from their shoulders or dangling from their hands; it's the post-school, post-work, pre-
dinner hour, she realizes. She has no idea what time or day it is where
she lives, or how long it's been since she last slept or ate. The busy
streetscape enthralls her, she stares out her window with her nose
near the glass like a child. With a start she realizes she can read a few
letters, on street signs and above the shop windows, but she has no
idea what they mean. She whispers the sounds to herself like Julian
used to do when he was two and three years old and had learned a
new word but wouldn't say it until after a long period of private re-

hearsal. Then the taxi turns onto a broad boulevard like any big street anywhere in the world.

Roger's interpreter is waiting for them when they step through the sliding glass doors into the garishly lit, disinfectant-smelling lobby, a pair of young men at either end of an empty gurney having entered at the same time and already moved out of sight into the hospital's depths, obeying the exigencies of some other reality. Roger's interpreter is a young woman, funereal in her black skirt and blazer and low-heeled flats. Louisa fails to pick up her name or perhaps isn't told it as they all pause and bow, Louisa catching a glimpse of her own hoodie and sweats—she's still in the same clothes she wore on the plane. She had meant to change clothes, though she now can't remember what clothes she brought with her, if she even arrived with a suitcase. Roger's interpreter has a laminated visitor pass, about the size of a passport. Its upper corners are hole-punched for the knotted ends of a loop of yarn. "Please," Roger's interpreter says, indicating, and Louisa understands to bow her head again so that Roger's interpreter can hang the pass around Louisa's neck as if bestowing a medal. Another memory of her young children, field trips when they were so small their knees seemed not to bend when they walked and their regulation backpacks hung down past their bottoms and they were made to walk in a duckling-file, holding a rope, and each wearing a laminated sign hung from a yarn necklace telling the name and address of the school: IF FOUND PLEASE RETURN TO. No need for such a sign with her children, Louisa had gone on every single field trip they ever took, what a wonderfully involved and helping class parent the teachers praised her for being, but she was only there for her own children, to keep her hawkeye on them, God forbid they stray into the path of a car, she never trusted the teachers to pay close attention.

Her father's daughter, she realizes, somehow for the first time. He was exactly like that.

"The pass identifies you as the Responsible Party for your patient," Roger's interpreter is explaining, "and so the nurses may try to ask you questions, but just say 'American' and they'll understand that you don't speak Korean and leave you alone. Are you ready? I'll take you up to the nurses' station on his floor so you know how to find it, but your pass lets you come and go whenever you like, you won't need us to sign you in or out."

Louisa feels a tactful fingertip on her elbow. Roger. She blinks and turns to him, her toddler's IF FOUND sign almost weightless on her chest. Some objection wants expression but she can't find the words, perhaps it's *How can you leave me alone here?* Or *Why can't you leave me alone here?*

"I'm sorry?" she says brightly to Roger. "I didn't hear you."

"I said, are you ready?"

Then they're standing somewhere else, they've left the elevator and are standing disregarded at a counter behind which mostly Korean women in pastel scrubs and sneakers move about, talking to each other, sometimes picking up telephones and talking into them and putting them down. "His room is down this hall, number seventy-four," Roger's interpreter says. "The nurses say he's awake. He's had dinner."

"Louisa," Louisa now hears Roger saying. "Why don't you let me come with you? Or, if you prefer, Miss Yi can come with you?"

Louisa feels sure they've discussed this before. "No, thank you," she says. "Thank you so much, Roger. I feel like I haven't said thank you enough."

"Louisa, you don't owe me any thanks at all."

"But I do."

"I think maybe," Miss Yi says, "we should stand over here, out of the way of the nurses. This is a busy time. They're starting evening rounds."

"I'm ready," Louisa says again, or possibly she hasn't said it until now. Roger and Miss Yi make to walk her down the busy hallway, and she forestalls them. "It's okay," Louisa says, though actually she is saying this to herself, because studies have shown that self-talk is remarkably effective in focusing and calming the brain, though most effective if the self-talker addresses themselves by name (*Louisa: it's okay*), which she hasn't. "But I don't remember the room number."

"Seventy-four. Straight down here, on the right. Are you sure you're all right?"

"Yes," Louisa says, "yes, yes," and she's already moving quickly away from them like those appointed young men with their gurney. Seventy, seventy-two, seventy-four. The door is standing slightly open, but she can't see in the room. The number plate next to the doorframe has a small whiteboard mounted below it on which someone using a green dry-erase marker has formed the three shapes—half square, half cross, and circle—that thus combined form an unfamiliar sound that is apparently her surname. Louisa pauses with her hand on the door, feeling astonishment that she has just recognized her own surname, without forethought or effort. Many times in recent months she has wished she could say to her mother, *Did you know that you've said our name wrong all these years? Did you know you've never once said it right?*— and each time this wish crosses her mind, she has more felt annoyance at the impossibility of smarty-pantsing her mother than grief at her mother's absence. It's true! She experiences her bereavement for her mother as *annoyance*, that her mother isn't there for her to scold with the things her mother couldn't do right or gobsmack with the things her mother couldn't have imagined. *Guess where I'm calling from*, she will never be able to say, nor, *And you'll NEVER guess what he looks like now: YOU*. All these years later, and Louisa still cannot see a wheelchair without feeling revulsion, not at the chair or the person bound to it but at herself. In those years after coming back home she never pushed her mother's chair, wouldn't even touch the handles. Their hard plastic grips made her nauseous. Everything about the chair's structure and materials horrified her: its flabby slinglike seat, its dingy gray rubber rims, its very spokes, which were the worse not for differing from, but so strongly resembling, the spokes of her own bicycle. Here, the wheelchair is the only thing she's brave enough to look at. She isn't even fully in the room, her hand is still holding the door open. She's been startled to find the wheelchair angled toward the door expectantly, though it seems not to hold a person but an armload of laundry.

But no, the laundry holds a person. The chair's paddle-shape metal footrests support thick-soled vinyl orthopedic shoes out of which a pair of dusty smoothnesses—his shins?—briefly rise before disappearing into tartan flannel cuffs that disappear beneath layers and layers of various blankets, a vaguely person-shaped heaping of blankets such as teen-delinquent Louisa used to fabricate to fool her mother into seeing the sleeping presence of her in fact absent self. At the summit of this fabric terrain is something brown, spotted, sparsely tufted, and precariously balanced. An ancient mummy cranium barely protected by delicate skin. Dried-apple-doll head. Louisa has to have closed the door behind herself, the ceaseless inattentive hospital-hum fading away, has to have stepped closer, groped sightlessly for a visitor's chair and pulled it under herself, but these causative moments have fallen, are still falling, silently down and away. Louisa sits on the edge of a chair thunderstruck by life-lag, herself moving too swiftly or not swiftly enough. Now she sees, where she had missed them before, a pair of liver-spotted hands collapsed in the blankets, clearly unconscious of each other, unpaired. She knows that if she dares to look at it again, the face will be as unconscious of the hands, and of the shins, as the shins are unconscious of the face, and of each other, and of the likely feet, hidden inside the shoes. Yet another unwanted recollection of her mother: a comment her mother made about Julian, the first time they met, when Julian had just started walking and would no longer wear socks and shoes. Her mother said, "I've seen those feet before." *I've seen those feet before on your father,* is what Louisa now understands Anne to have meant on that day years ago. Louisa gazes with new eyes at the thick-soled orthopedic black vinyl shoes within which feet like her sons' might be hiding. She might kneel on the floor and pry the feet out of those casings and see if they really are the source of one of the very few traits her incompatible sons have in common. She only entertains this thought to further defer looking into the face.

At last she does, and finds it looking back at her with a sentience as remote as a turtle's, eyeing her from his opposite branch of the tangled tree-crown of their unlikely shared ancestry. Then his reptile's mouth hinges open just slightly.

She hadn't been aware of retaining his voice, but here it is: The boxed energy scaling the back of his throat, the note of complaint— she remembers! A voice that was constantly shaping these moods— impatience, prideful arrogance, grievance. He utters his rising complaint, peering at her and jutting his turtle's head slightly for emphasis or to see her more clearly. There's too much irate music in the sound and not enough distinct syllables. Louisa edges forward on her chair, intently maintaining eye contact as if with an animal that might be terrified to flight by her presence, but his gaze pinpoints her without fear. His irises do not look as they do in the photos. Historically his irises were brown—the doubles of hers—but now they are an opaque, lusterless blue rimmed with white. It suddenly seems possible he is blind, that the fixity of his gaze does not in fact hold her as its object. Is it possible he's blind and she hasn't been told, or is it possible he's blind and she has been told and forgot? Then she hears them: a pileup of familiar interrogatives all clamoring for utterance at once. *How . . . ? Where . . . ? When . . . ?* They are demands without astonishment, complaints without grief, but they are clearly aimed at her and no one else. Her heart gallops; though the air-conditioning in the room is working well—witness his swaddling as if for the Arctic—she breaks out in a sweat.

"I don't speak Korean," she tells the turtle as calmly as she can. "Can you speak English with me?"

He glares at her, launches a barrage of unfamiliar syllables, but this time she needn't have taken any lessons at all to understand what he's saying: What the hell is *she* saying? With strange exultation she dives into her bag for a notebook and pen, fumbling the rest of the bag's contents onto the floor, feeling him peering at her with increasing annoyance; he is not blind, she understands now: he's going deaf. With effort to control her trembling hands Louisa prints in block letters, "CAN WE SPEAK ENGLISH," and reverses the notebook, offers it to his view. His brow bunches—there is still enough flesh on the shelf of his brow to bunch up.

"*I* speak goddamn English. Since when do *you*?"

The meager features of his face have transformed: his turtle-mouth is so turned-down its corners meet his skinny jaw; a vertical seam like an exclamation point of scorn divides his eyebrows. Laughter bursts in her chest. She conceals it to not offend him, but she remembers this, too!—and what to do, how to step daintily through his field of land mines, even when he wasn't blind, or a turtle, or three decades dead, even when he was only her father. She had been good at this, fearless and deft; she had marveled at her mother's obtuse clumsiness, her inability to handle this block-letters-legible man. "I ALWAYS SPEAK ENGLISH," she writes in the notebook, then, having reversed it to show him, adds audibly. He looks up from the page to her face.

"I taught you. But you were no good."

Now she does laugh out loud, as he glowers, a cantankerous tortoise. Later she will wonder if it was stubborn child's pride, and not adult intuition, that confirmed he wasn't speaking of her. Of course she had been good at speaking English; she had been good at everything. This had been the creed of their shared faith, and the foundation of her fearlessness of him. My God, she remembers this, too: his utter faith in her. No one, least of all her, ever held such faith in her again.

Thinking a moment of how to put it, she hovers her pen over the notebook, which says, "CAN WE SPEAK ENGLISH," and "I ALWAYS SPEAK ENGLISH." Then she turns to a fresh page and writes, "WHAT IS MY NAME?" He reads, looks at her as if unsurprised by her stupidity.

"Which one?"

"Which *name*?" she says, forgetting to write this. But her confusion is obvious. One of his lifeless hands suddenly elevates out of his lap—as surprising as if he'd leaped out of the chair and sent his blanket-pile flying. With a rough flick of his wrist, he seems to send not his blankets, but an invisible irritant—her inaudible question—hurtling across the room to be splattered lifeless on the opposite wall. More compressed energy of impatience is released in that flick than would seem owed to the rest of his body for the rest of however much longer he'll live. This is recognition, Louisa thinks: a matter of clouds moving over the sun. In grasping this way that she sees him, she intuits the way that he might see her. Through moving clouds, changing each moment from brightness to dimness without a fixed pattern.

After thinking a moment Louisa draws a line through "WHAT IS MY NAME?" and writes, a good space beneath it, "CAN YOU WRITE MY NAME?" When she reverses the pad and holds it up for him to see, after peering at the letters a long moment he exhales a weak puff of derision. From tortoise to tiring dragon. The same hand that a moment before flicked with such energy gropes uncertainly toward Louisa as if expecting to find a doorknob in midair. Louisa realizes he's seeking the pen. As she extends it to him, it seems impossible that he will, as he immediately does, without visible struggle, take the pen between his fingers as if reclaiming a part of himself. He was very particular about his pens, she remembers. When she was a little girl he had a desk, or perhaps it was only a table, she sees it vaguely in a corner, perhaps with a window behind it. This desk is unreliable, it is a memory of convenience, its only purpose is to uphold a bright thing to her gaze, a glowing yellow pad of legal paper on which lie, fastidiously lined up end to end with each other along the legal pad's vertical axis, three gleaming black pens.

The legal pad flashing into her vision is exactly the same as the one she's now offering him, so that perhaps the whole vision, plausible as it is, is just another invention, a lie she tells herself about a life she once shared with this man.

So he'll have something to write on, Louisa scoots her chair nearer his and holds the legal pad facing him braced on her knees. Slow as a heron homing in on a fish, he bends over the pad until the pen makes contact. After a few movements as sure as incisions he leaves behind a stack of tiny characters so perfectly made Louisa recognizes them easily even looking at them upside down.

"'Seung,'" she reads, taking care with the vowel as Heejin has taught her. "Is that *my* name?" She tries to strike a bright, curious note. She goes to write this question but it doesn't seem necessary.

"You don't remember your own name, I guess you don't remember why they chose it. Because it means 'victory.' So if a Japanese criticized them for your Korean name, they could say they meant 'Victory for Japan.' Goddamn stupid shit." He still curses with relish, the *shhhhh* protracted like a blade slicing paper. Louisa's heart is rioting dangerously, she's afraid she'll dispel her own transfiguration into this Seung—a brother? And "they" who named Seung: his parents. Delicate as a soap bubble, this memory chamber quivering in his mind, to make sense of her presence. What can she say to expand it, and not make it pop?

Together they gaze down at the syllable block, its characters so tiny and tidy and pleasing, each letter fitted perfectly to its companions. Learning to form these letters in her lessons with Heejin, Louisa had found her hand contained the memory of other, different yet similarly alien letters, the katakana and kanji her long-ago sensei had taught her to form. Ink poured over the block, twirled tip of the brush. The tacky sensation of inked fingertips, hanging sheets on the line with two clothespins, the black strokes flashing wet. Down across slant slant: movements loose but controlled. Working with Heejin a lifetime later, she immediately felt it again in the root of her thumb, in the tension formed between her thumb and index finger pads, in the pleasure of forming the straight marks, the angles, the slight curves, in how the rightly executed order of the marks guaranteed somehow the letter's authenticity, even if the marks themselves were tentative and sloppy. Set them down in the right order, connect the right points, the letter somehow turns out right, as it doesn't when the marks are steadier and sharper but their order of creation done wrong. Downstroke, down-stroke, sidestroke, sidestroke; sidestroke-down, downstroke-side—and bit by bit they formed up and spoke their sounds into your ear. Now, after what feels like a doctoral degree's worth of reading and googling and expert-consulting and exhausting late-night calls to Soonja with Tobias or Saho interpreting, Louisa understands that her father was born to Korean migrants to Japan; that he spoke Korean at home and Japanese at school; that in 1952 because of being an ethnic Korean he was made an alien registrant in the nation of his birth; that his US green card expired after he was declared dead; that he is now, as he has been for decades, stateless, in a hospital in a Korea that is not even the Korea where he was held captive nor the Korean island where his parents were born. Nothing aligns. Her father is alive instead of dead, ethnic Korean instead of native Japanese, alien-Japanese instead of na-tive Korean, she herself has turned into some heretofore-unknown-to-her and apparently rather stupid other blood relative. But this language that she never to her knowledge heard her father speak still apparently lives in his hands. Its sounds and meanings still presumably live in his mind. And the lost siblings and parents who spoke those same sounds and were named with them, and even the events that befell them—they must also be in his mind somewhere, if many twisting corridors away from wherever in that mind her father's version of her is preserved.

If she can just get there, she thinks. If she can just find those chambers and scoop up whatever they hold. It would— She doesn't want to let herself think, make up for some of their loss. Nothing can. But it would still be some small gain she hadn't expected.

Thinking all this, still gazing at the letters and thinking he's gazing with her, she doesn't immediately realize his head is inching nearer and nearer the legal pad's surface because he's asleep. For a long time she continues to sit with him, studying his slumped form and the sparse whorl of white hair on the crown of his head, and listening to the sigh of his breath. She very likely goes to sleep herself. When a nurse opens the door Louisa is aware that the room has grown dim. The nurse smiles and bows and with great economy of wordless expression makes clear to Louisa that it is bedtime for the patient, the visiting hours have ended. As the nurse readies the bed Louisa gathers her things and stands out of her chair almost in a panic—she's afraid he'll wake up, she realizes. She doesn't know how to say goodbye to him. The casual goodbye of an everyday visiting daughter? The lingering goodbye of a daughter who is suddenly convinced that she'll never see this person again and perhaps isn't seeing him now?

But he doesn't wake up, in fact appears so profoundly asleep Louisa wonders how the petite nurse will get him into his bed, wonders if she should stay and offer help. Instead she attempts the polite-formal versions of "thank you" and "goodbye" that are perhaps her most-rehearsed phrases and that tumble nonsensically from her mouth as with equal confusion she hurries out of the room. Downstairs in the lobby she finds Miss Yi, tapping away with her thumbs as if she has no other office. Miss Yi says, rising, "I will call you a taxi," and precedes Louisa out the front doors.

When Louisa hurries into the room the next day with the same notepad opened to the same page, so that the thread of their communication stays as much as possible uncut, a wordless turtle peers from the mountain of blankets. His gaze is vigilant but detached, as if en-

gaged by something very far away. When she shows him the notepad,
his gaze remains on a distant horizon; she can't seem to enter his field
of vision. Louisa is afraid she will cry, although she knows she's not being ignored; she's simply not there. But it had been so much better—
wonderful, even—to be mistaken for somebody else. That day, and the
days that follow, finding herself as disregarded as the discreet, efficient,
interchangeable nurses, she passes the time talking to him. She talks
about how well or poorly she has slept in Charse Kim's apartment,
what she's eaten, how she enjoyed it, and whether she remembers its
name. She talks about legal intricacies of citizenship that, though they
concern him and his immediate fate, seem absurdly irrelevant, as if she
were burdening a young child with the finer points of estate law. She
talks about her grown sons and her husbands and finds there is something very distracting, from the uncertain grief of her situation, about
abstracting the people she knows best, and describing them as if they
were the subjects of an elaborate psychological experiment. She comes
to conclusions about all four men that never occurred to her before and
which now seem glaringly obvious.

Much of the time, her father sleeps while she's talking. Sometimes
he grows restless and dissatisfied and then extreme expressions distort
his face, or unexpected movements twitch his hands or feet; he will
glare angrily at his foot, and the same foot, as if in reply to admonition,
will shove weakly at the wheelchair footrest until it has fallen off the
footrest entirely and its heel grazes the floor. The first time this happened, Louisa knelt down to try to put the foot back, having to fold the
footrest out of the way before attempting to bend his knee, and then
was nearly scared out of her skin when he barked, "Neh, neh!" of the
folded-up footrest: *Yeah, yeah!* He *wanted* the footrest folded out of the
way; with one foot on the floor, he began pushing himself. Very slowly
but steadily, first he went backward, until the handles of the wheelchair
bumped the wall. Then he inched forward again—all by means of the
foot, never touching the wheelchair rims with his hands—re-crossing
the room until he'd almost bumped knees with Louisa. "Mom would
have been impressed with your technique," Louisa said, and unexpect-

edly, because he hadn't seemed to notice her in days, his gaze met hers keenly.

"Mother?" he demanded. "How is she?"

Louisa's heart floundered around for the answer that would inflate the memory-bubble but not make it burst. "She's well."

"Did you take care of her?"

"I tried to."

"I saw her after her bath. She didn't know I was there. She was so thin, I could see all her ribs. And *you*—you just give her more babies. You should have yourself fixed." Once again he'd reached the backward limit of his movement, against the far wall from Louisa and adjacent to the door. As Louisa sat stunned and wordless the nurse on duty opened the door, performed gestures of great surprise at seeing her father located where he was, knelt down to disconnect his rogue foot from the floor and reconnect it to the wheelchair footrest, bowed with great charm to Louisa, and rolled her father, suddenly unseeing as a statue, out the door to the dining and activity room.

Louisa frequently miscalculates the time of her arrival; she has learned the bus route to the National Medical Center to be more independent from Roger and Miss Yi, but she cannot seem to learn the hospital's schedule so as to avoid the hours of rounds, meals, or activities, during all of which her father is either outside his room with other people or in his room with other people. Louisa wants him in his room with no people, the only conditions under which he has ever seemed able to hear and see her, if not recognize her. *No,* she's told Tobias and Saho, or she's told Leo and George, or she's told Teddy (despite this extraordinary situation in their family life, or because of it, she and Julian are not currently speaking), repeatedly over the phone, *he doesn't recognize me, but I don't care, I just want to see him and hear him without other people around.* For one thing, any kind of ambient noise seems to shroud him in deafness; outside his room, where some level of hospital clamor continues whatever the hour, he's as inert in his chair as the pile of laundry she first took him for; not being able to hear seems to turn off his vision. For another thing, the presence of other people increasingly annoys Louisa, because increasingly she feels a simplicity of emotion toward her father that might be called possessiveness. She wants him to herself. Other people—even the indispensable nurses who actually tend her father's alien body, who manage its voidings of waste and who clean it and dress it and swathe it in its quantities of blankets and otherwise preserve it, preserve *him*—antagonize Louisa with their very existence, they set her teeth on edge so her false smile must look like a grimace. And so she keeps trying to determine the hour of the day when she can find her father alone waiting for her, as he was the first time that she came, but today once again she's misremembered the schedule or the schedule has changed, and her father is in the community area with the ruins of some snack on a plate before him. *Oh,* the beautiful nurse with the heart-shaped face indicates of Louisa's unexpected arrival, or her father's unexpected location, and once they've finished their greetings and bows, *Do you want to go ahead with him?* the nurse conveys in the international language of spreading an arm in the direction of her father's room seventy-four. At first Louisa isn't sure she understands; questioningly she indicates the wheelchair handles, then points to herself. The nurse nods and smiles and again spreads her arm toward room seventy-four.

Louisa's hands are clumsy as she goes to seize the chair's handles as if faced with a wheelbarrow of dirt, something requiring brute force and momentum, before she notices that rogue foot in its shapeless black shoe, dangling onto the floor—she was about to catch that shoe in the undercarriage of the wheelchair and drag her father's body under like mowing him down with a bus. Her hands are actually shaking from what feels like the barely evaded disaster as she kneels before him to lower the footrest and lift the rogue foot back in place. Squaring herself behind the chair again, she throws all her weight against it, but it is so heavy she cannot budge it at all. She realizes the brakes are engaged, bars of metal levered onto the wheel rims, struggles at length to understand how to release them; the secret turns out to be, lift each bar by the obvious handle.

Did she really never once push Anne's wheelchair? They're moving now, Louisa driving carefully, generic smile on her face for any
passing nurse, but her real attention is on her father's head, whether
it's upright, alert for signs he's slumping forward to the point he'd fall
out of the chair. His hair, she notices, appears to emanate from a central source, extending tendrils like galaxy arms. And like a galaxy—an
apparently actual thing that is also just an image made somehow by
telescope—his head contains a boundless world she'll never know
apart from a few motes of dust. At the closed door to room seventy-
four she's stopped by the problem of how to hold the door open while
pushing the wheelchair inside, and then is visited by the muscle memory of pushing a child in a stroller. Rotating him in a half circle, she
uses her ass to push open the door, even remembering to tilt him back
slightly, to soften the bump of the threshold. She rotates him forward
again and they face the room that has grown familiar, with its adjust-
able bed and its visitor's chair. For the first time on this day her father
stirs, lifting an arm from the nest of blankets. As her children did when
they were babies, in a gesture she'd found so eloquent in them, her father points at his bed. "Are you tired?" she asks. In answer he raises the
other arm to join the first, as if he wants the bed to embrace him. She
pushes him as close to the bed as the wheelchair will go, then reaches
to engage the brakes, but almost before she is finished he shockingly
launches himself from the chair, grabs the bedrail with one hand, and,
flailing with the other, hurls himself in, landing short of the pillow,
while Louisa gasps and gapes in helpless shock. Marooned on his side
now, his head twisted toward the ceiling, he appears to have fallen on
the bed from a great height. His legs have not made it in—his shoes are
tangled in the footrests. If she doesn't do something he'll slide out and
onto the floor. "Wait!" she cries. "Let me help you." Moving the wheelchair out of her way, she kneels before him again, pries off the shoes
and uncovers the frail, thin feet, sheathed in socks, unimaginable as the
base for a vertical body. Looking up, she finds him gazing wonderingly
in her face. *How did I get here?* his face asks her. *Who are you? Why?* "Let
me help you," she says again. "I'm going to get you on your pillow."
Standing and bracing herself, she takes him under the armpits, feeling

his meagerness, the worn upholstery barely clothing his bones, and, closing her mind to this, hauls him up the length of the bed while his upside-down face stares at her in surprise. He seems possessed by surprise; even once she lets him go his surprise continues. It isn't angry or frightened, but it keeps dawning on him, renewing, as might some less sudden emotion. Then at last it is ebbing away.

"Thank you," he pipes in a strange, small, docile voice.

"Are you comfortable?"

"Thank you," he repeats.

Louisa sits down in the visitor's chair. It's too far from the bed for her to see her father's face, she only sees his feet in their socks and the empty wheelchair, discarded at an angle to the bed. The empty wheelchair seems sinister to her, as do her father's toes-up feet. She should get up and pull the blanket over him.

His voice breaks the silence. "Louisa?"

She is so startled to hear him speak her name that for a moment she can't summon her own voice, can't move lips and tongue, as if paralyzed in a dream.

"Yes?" she says, stumbling to her feet and approaching the bed. His eyes wide open, he stares at the ceiling as if something has appeared there; when she bends into the line of that gaze, interrupting its path, he startles, his eyes hard and bright now with recognition. A shudder passes through Louisa, literal and sequential, asking her to name parts of her body of which she is ignorant. She can only vaguely follow the avalanche path from her chest to her stomach to her bowels. All the intervening years of her life, from her childhood in which he'd last seen her to this moment, now seem understood by him and calmly set aside. There is no question he knows who she is, his crying her name is no arbitrary short circuit in the tangle of broken connections that make up his brain. Beneath that tangle is a zone of understanding, a well-built cellar fireplace for the very last embers to send up their smoke. "Yes," she says again, as he stares at her.

"I wanted to make sure you're still here."

"I'm still here."

"Where were you?"

"I was sitting in that chair."

His forehead forms itself into those ridges and furrows with which the scant flesh, to denote his exasperation, imitate the permanent glower of that shelf overhanging his eye sockets, which age has only made more prominent. The glower tells her to stop being facetious. And then Louisa understands what she perhaps has never understood before.

"They threw me out of the boat, and I swam."

His gaze leaves her a moment, to see this. "All the way?" he asks with a new falter in his voice, as if imagining her effort. "All the way?"

She understands this also. "All the way to the shore," she confirms, although she remembers, now, collapsing in the frill of the surf as she crawled up the incline of shore, unable to go any farther. But the tide must have recently turned and was ebbing, and she'd been found before it turned around again. She hadn't drowned.

When he closes his eyes again, she feels the presence of that outer limit—death—as she felt it that night. It had not been a thought, or a fear. Only a presence, empty and total as the air she'd lived in all her life, and enclosing and filling her as the air did. She had understood it was there for her without having the words, then, to explain it to herself. And her struggle against it had been purely instinctive, it had carried no ideas or emotions, and the fact that her energy outlasted that presence was not a matter of will but more a matter of mathematics or physics, of near-balanced forces in steady contention until one slightly outweighed the other. It was only later that fear came, after understanding departed, which had been the worst thing, that fear with no conception of its source. If only she had known, all the decades between then and now, that death had enveloped her in the water, not the same as the water or limited by it, simply borrowing it, and that its nearness had been unremarkable, an invisible transfiguration of the molecules around her that had left her untouched. If what is happening now is a belated understanding it doesn't occur in ideas or words. Her body is leaden as if she has swum all that distance again, through the muscling, relentless, gelatinous cold force of waves, and she is barely able to reach behind her for the wheelchair and drag it under

herself before she sinks into it and lets her head sink to the edge of his
mattress. Her eyes are closed, but she registers the cotton of the bed-
sheets and the flowery smell of their detergent. The simplest physical
act feels impossible.

After a moment he says, "Your mother taught you to swim."

Louisa tries to make a sound of assent but is not sure she does, and
regardless, it isn't required.

"How is she?" he creaks out another beat later, as if his voice has
gotten going now, like an old porch swing, and will keep uttering, at
longer intervals, and a bit less robustly each time, until its energy is
spent.

"How is *my* mother?"

"Anne," he says, with something almost querulous in his voice, as
if Anne herself has appeared. "How is Anne."

Louisa feels the warmth of tears bathing her eyes and seeping into
the bedsheet. It is so quiet she can hear the faint buzz like a distant
cicada which must be coming from the fluorescent light bulb in his
bathroom. "She's fine."

"She is?" he cries. "She's alive?"

So it's true, they really did know each other: she and he, and she
and Anne, and he and Anne. "Yes," she lies.

"Oh thank God," he says hoarsely, as if the effort of saving Anne's
life has been completed by him just that moment.

Then he must travel somewhere in memory, because when she
leans into his sight line again, it passes through her. She touches his
shoulder, and he makes an answering sound in his throat: *Why are you
bothering me?*

"Daddy, I'm going to go now. But I'll see you tomorrow."

"You've gone to the land of the dead," Tobias says that night when
she calls him. "Like Odysseus."

For once his conversational flamboyance doesn't annoy her; she
accepts the simile. Another small strangeness: for the first time in their
lives, they are speaking on the phone from within the same time zone.
In Tokyo the sun has already set, and in Seoul it won't set for another
half hour, but these variations of a region, such as Louisa shares with

all her loved ones who live in the northeastern US, are something she has never shared with him. Being relatively this close to him makes her actually wish he were here, she's surprised to realize, though he's staying away only at her insistence. But her insistence has also made things easier for Tobias with Saho. Saho is devastated by Louisa's reunion with her father. It's a devastation that much worse for how guilty it makes Saho feel not to be glad. "He asked about Our Mother," Louisa says at length. "Without any prompting. He asked, *How is Anne.*"

"That's remarkable. In fact, it's miraculous."

"Is it? Why? I told him she was alive."

"Of course you did."

"But I lied!"

"I don't think it counts as a lie. She thought he was dead all those years and it gave her peace. Thinking she's alive will give him peace."

"But what if he finds out I lied?"

"He won't, Louisa."

"How can I be sure he recognized me? How can I be sure that he wasn't pretending? Sometimes he's—docile. He'll say, 'Thank you!' Like a wind-up toy. 'Thank you!' Don't say how wonderful that is. Don't be predictable, Tobias."

"How was he when he recognized you? Surprised?"

"He was not even slightly surprised. The first time I saw him he thought I was someone named Seung and he wasn't surprised. Today he thought I was me and he wasn't surprised."

"Because he's had you in his mind all this time."

It was true that he continued to call her by name from time to time, but all those subsequent times, the interaction was generic, as if he'd assigned her the role of a child, with its usual themes. "How is school," he most often demanded, a vigilance she couldn't remember him maintaining in her actual school days. Or perhaps he'd asked the question then also, not out of concern but for the pleasure of her usual answer. He'd always assumed she was doing brilliantly, and perhaps in part from that assumption she always had been.

Periodically, Louisa saw Roger, when his salvational, extragovernmental, perhaps borderline-extralegal diplomacy brought him through

Seoul. Then they met to discuss the glacial progress of her father's case, or they attended meetings with Miss Yi at various government offices, or they attended meetings without Miss Yi at the US Embassy building, which interested Louisa for how ostentatiously, unignorably, almost aggressively it sore-thumbed the rest of sleek and tasteful Gwang-hwamun Plaza, as if to say that not even bothering to put one's scores of soot-covered air-conditioning compressors out of sight was the prerogative of true power. The rainy season was nearing its end. Louisa had been away from home almost twelve weeks. "I think he's going to decide the question himself," she said one day as she and Roger ate lunch at the Buddhist restaurant they often chose because every table had its own room. "The question" was, to what nation would her father immigrate? It contained a great tangle of sub-questions, of which the most technically complex—those touching on things like legal-resident status and health-care-benefit qualification—were in some ways the least difficult.

Roger asked what she meant, though Louisa had a feeling he already knew what she meant. "I mean, I think he's going to solve this problem—of where and how he should move—by not moving." He was done moving. Or, he was already moving. Louisa hadn't known this until she said it. The Buddhist restaurant was on the seventh, top floor of what appeared from the outside to be a generic office building and which did in fact, on the first through sixth floors, contain the administrative offices of the Buddhist temple, the complex of which sat across the street. Louisa looked out the window of her and Roger's private dining room at the various roofs of the temple complex, all of them lifting their edges like wings. It was raining, as usual. Broken lines of water formed and re-formed on the glass. The temple complex contained an enormous pagoda tree that corkscrewed upward as if it would shortly levitate and fly away, bearing the many strings of candy-colored lanterns that had been hung from its limbs. Louisa had read in her guidebook that the tree was more than four hundred years old, which made it one of a very few things in the entire megacity that predated the mid–twentieth century. From the perspective of the tree almost everything else here was alien and new, which perhaps meant alien and new things were all equally at home.

In early September, her father contracted pneumonia; the nurses fetched an attending who spoke beautiful English, who asked Louisa what her father's directive was. Louisa asked for the forms of resuscitation to be listed for her. Her father was asleep, a carved face slightly denting the pillow. When she laid her palm on the cotton blanket covering his chest, the body beneath felt like a delicate box made of wood. The slightest pressure could splinter it into kindling. She said, "No," one by one to each form of resuscitation. She said, "Yes," to morphine when she noticed that his hand, which she now held for hours at a time, had begun to twitch, a movement that made her think of a guttering flame. She didn't interpret this movement as an effort to communicate with her, but as a possible signal of discomfort, or a signal of nothing at all. His hand was an impossibly vulnerable framework of twigs and stretched skin, and it felt as she imagined a bat would, if a bat went to sleep on her palm. The skin of his throat also now seemed exquisitely fine; it rippled like water with each inaudible breath. She kept her gaze on his throat and she saw when the rippling ceased.

# Acknowledgments

The idea for this book would never have become a reality without the many people who helped me either directly or indirectly through their own books. Andy Beasley was a phenomenal research assistant who both helped me locate information and helped me overhaul my whole approach to information; and he was an invaluable sounding board. I'm indebted to Adam Haslett for connecting me to Andy. Mickey Bergman generously shared his unique perspective on North Korea, as did Robert S. Boynton, who also shared with me his original research materials. Jin Auh championed this book from the beginning and Jenna Johnson improved it a thousandfold with incisive observations and questions that kept me energized to the very end. The Bogliasco Foundation gave me the time and support I needed to finally finish. The short story from which this novel began was made immeasurably better by the editing of Deborah Treisman, the copyediting of Ken Marks, and the fact-checking of Danyoung Kim, all of *The New Yorker*. Finally, I am grateful beyond words for the following extraordinary works of fiction and nonfiction:

Robert S. Boynton, *The Invitation-Only Zone: The True Story of North Korea's Abduction Project*

Barbara Demick, *Nothing to Envy: Ordinary Lives in North Korea*

Blaine Harden, *Escape from Camp 14: One Man's Remarkable Odyssey from North Korea to Freedom in the West*

Masaji Ishikawa, *A River in Darkness: One Man's Escape from North Korea*

Charles Robert Jenkins, *The Reluctant Communist: My Desertion, Court-Martial, and Forty-Year Imprisonment in North Korea*

Adam Johnson, *The Orphan Master's Son*

Kang Chol-hwan and Pierre Rigoulet, *The Aquariums of Pyongyang: Ten Years in the North Korean Gulag*

Melanie Kirkpatrick, *Escape from North Korea: The Untold Story of Asia's Underground Railroad*

Krys Lee, *How I Became a North Korean*

Tessa Morris-Suzuki, *Borderline Japan: Foreigners and Frontier Controls in the Postwar Era*

Tessa Morris-Suzuki, *Exodus to North Korea: Shadows from Japan's Cold War*

Sonia Ryang, *North Koreans in Japan: Language, Ideology, and Identity*

Edward W. Wagner, *The Korean Minority in Japan, 1904–1950*

Sakie Yokota, *North Korea Kidnapped My Daughter*

Kim Yong, *Long Road Home: Testimony of a North Korean Camp Survivor*